FROM *THE WALL STREET JOURNAL* BESTSELLING AUTHOR

RHIANNON BEAUBIEN

A RUMOR OF SPIES

A Rumor of Spies
Rhiannon Beaubien

ISBNs
Paperback: 978-1-9992989-6-8
Hardcover: 978-1-9992989-7-5
eBook: 978-1-9992989-8-2

PREVIOUS WORKS BY THE AUTHOR:

Fiction

Alone Among Spies
The Wrong Kind of Spy

Nonfiction

The Great Mental Models series (Co-author)
Volume One: General Thinking Concepts
Volume Two: Physics, Chemistry, and Biology
Volume Three: Systems and Mathematics
Volume Four: Economics and Art

Berlin 1976
EAST GERMANY
Spandau
West Berlin
East Berlin
EAST GERMANY

CHAPTER ONE

It wasn't working. Jillian had been over the connections a dozen times. Run diagnostics. She'd even crawled around the campus communications lab after hours, checking wires and plugs. The conclusion was inescapable. The satellite feed she'd been collecting for the last two years as an undercover signals intelligence officer was broken.

Fixing it was going to be like walking through a haunted house—potential danger lurking around every corner.

It was possible the connection was fractured somewhere upstream, where the satellite data was routed through Telekom Berlin. But to investigate would take her off campus, and with a cover as a Canadian exchange student, she didn't have an obvious reason to go poking around West Berlin's communications infrastructure.

There was also the possibility that the copy she made had been discovered and severed deliberately. And her cover gave her even less reason to knock on BND's door and demand to fix it. The West German intelligence agency would detain her on the spot.

Jillian rested her head in her hands and closed her eyes. She just had to think. There was an answer to this problem. She didn't need to solve for world peace. She just needed to fix a broken comms link. It might be difficult, but it wasn't going to be impossible. It was a matter of proper diagnosis and resourcing.

Of course, because she had to be cautious and not blow her cover, this problem was also not going to get solved in a day.

She typed up a note explaining the situation and the actions she'd taken thus far. Picking up her bag, she put the note in her pocket for easy access at the dead drop. Instead of the usual tapes of compressed satellite data, all she'd send home this week was her update. But it needed to get done. It was the first time the feed had gone down, and Jillian wasn't going to be able to fix it before someone at the newly named Communications Security Establishment, or CSE, noticed it was out.

She hoped they'd give her time to diagnose the problem. As an electrical engineer employed by Canada's signals intelligence agency, she had a good chance of being able to find a solution.

Before she could get to the door of her small office, someone knocked on the other side.

"Jillian," Gerhard Fens said, stepping in and closing the door behind him. "I think I have a next step to your problem."

Gerhard was a professor at the West German Science Institute. On paper he was her PhD advisor. In reality, he was the man who had approached CSE about making a copy of the

BND satellite feed. Consequently, he was the one person in West Berlin who knew the full scope of Jillian's mission.

"Really?" she asked. Because that would be amazing.

"When we originally set up the data flow, there was one part that needed to be installed at the main cable relay that comes into West Berlin, yes?"

It sounded right, but Jillian didn't actually know. She hadn't done the initial setup. That had been her old boss Frank, who had then trained her on maintenance of the feed.

"There was a tap, or something like that it was called, to divert the traffic long enough to make a copy. My nephew, he works at the cable company and was able to help us set it up. But I remember, the tap needs to be reset every so often. The exact timing, I'm not sure. My nephew takes care of this. But he has been promoted. And I forgot about the tap reset. I'm sure that is the problem."

It made sense. The tap in question would allow the traffic to be buffered for a couple of seconds so the CSE copy could be made, and buffers sometimes got full. Often the data never fully purged, so little bits stayed in the buffer, over time reducing its capacity. Hence the device required a periodic reset. It was the kind of thing that in Ottawa she would have been able to diagnose quickly. But covert operations did not come with easy access to the infrastructure.

"Your nephew, can he introduce you to his replacement?"

Gerhard nodded. "Yes, I'm sure he can. But when we set this up, Frank, he said that anyone new who needed to be included in the operation had to be vetted by your office."

Of course they did. And wasn't that going to be difficult. "Yeah. Okay, if you could get the replacement's name, plus date and place of birth without raising any suspicions, I can put him through the vetting process. If he passes—and let's hope he does—you can approach him and figure out if he's interested in helping us."

It was work that, at home, Jillian would never have handled. But here in the field, she was it. She hoped that this new guy, whoever he was, would be sympathetic to helping West Germany's allies in their efforts against Soviet Russia and its followers—without breathing a word to anyone actually in the West German system.

Jillian could only sigh. It might happen. But she supposed she should come up with a plan B, because the chances of this problem having an easy fix were becoming less and less likely.

The only part of her job that Jillian didn't like was her isolation. She had no one to problem solve with. The few people in this city she could talk to honestly knew nothing about the engineering behind signals intelligence operations. Even her handler out of the embassy in Bonn, Jean-Marc Belanger, was more a traditional spy. Running agents and the like, he didn't know anything about how to collect signals intelligence. There wasn't anyone in West Berlin to help her when she hit a technical roadblock.

Sitting in her apartment in front of a fan and eating mint chocolate chip ice cream, Jillian sorted through her options.

If the new guy didn't want to help, should she try to recruit someone else? Was there anywhere else that tap could be placed to create a buffer? The person who would have the best insight was Frank. But he wasn't even at CSE anymore, having been sent on assignment to the human intelligence section of Canada's policing and security organization, the RCMP.

Jillian tapped her spoon on her lips, thinking. Frank still had his clearance. And this setup in West Berlin had been his baby, the access he was most proud of. The chances were high that he had all the details in his head. He was anal that way. If she could get to a secure phone somewhere, talking to him would probably be enough.

There were secure telephone units, called STUs, all over this city. The question was, which one was the most legitimate for her cover?

Her friend James was a captain in the British army stationed here in West Berlin. No doubt he had access to a few STUs, but they would all be buried in high-security rooms on the base. Even if he could get her in, to reveal her clearance would be to reveal her cover. Safe enough maybe, with British intelligence, but she'd have to get authorization ahead of time.

Her best bet was probably the Canadian consulate. Although mostly focused on issues involving trade and commerce, they still had a means of secure communication.

The only problem was, she tried never to go to the consulate. Like the embassy in Bonn, it was heavily monitored by adversary agents, and to go more than reasonable for the average expat would raise suspicions. But foreign students did need to interact with official government services, so her cover would be appropriate for a rare visit.

Jillian knew her current situation was exceptional. The entire collection program was disabled. It either had to be fixed or shut down.

She rummaged around in her kitchen for a pen and paper. Another note for her next dead drop, this time to Jean-Marc. He was in the best position to set up the consulate access. She figured the easiest way was to go in saying she'd lost her passport, but Jillian would leave that up to him.

"Frank, it's Jillian. It's, um, been awhile."

"Jillian, we're on secure phones. What is going on? And please tell me that feed in West Berlin hasn't been compromised."

Jillian smiled, relieved. She wasn't good at idle chit chat either. "No. But it's broken, and I'm pretty sure the problem is the tap on the source cable."

Frank sighed. "The weakest link. I knew that tap was going to cause us problems. It's the reset, isn't it?"

Even though it was Frank, and he was usually irritated with her about something, it was great to be able to talk to someone who understood the engineering. "Yes," she replied. "I mean, I'm not one hundred percent sure, and I won't be until I can verify the flow somehow, but at this point the reset is the most obvious technical issue."

"Why has it stopped?" Frank asked.

"Gerhard's nephew has moved on to a new position."

"And what? He can't get down to the cable room every few months and press a button?"

"How would I know, Frank? It's not like I ever met the guy. Until Gerhard showed up in my office last week, I didn't even know about the reset."

"It was part of our commitment to him," Frank said. "He was nervous. He agreed to help if only his uncle and I knew about his involvement."

Jillian thought for a moment. "And someone in personnel security, right? Did you clear him?"

"Are you telling me how to do my job?"

Jillian rolled her eyes, but only because he couldn't see her. "No. I'm just trying to figure out what to do now."

"Yes, I had him cleared. Your best bet is getting him to keep on doing what he was doing."

"What if he can't?"

Frank was silent for a moment. "It's going to be a pain in the ass."

"I've already asked Gerhard to get the new guy's name, address, and date of birth. Then, I figure, Gerhard can do the approach if I give the thumbs up."

"Listen, Jillian, personnel security is going to take weeks, if not months, to clear someone new for that op. Unfortunately for you, it got on their radar last year, which is why I've been exiled to the RCMP. Once you put the request in, Bob Cranton is going to use it as an excuse to snoop around. I can't guarantee that he won't try to shut the whole thing down."

Jillian started, unprepared for that news. "What? Why?"

"Because he's pissed off at the world. When I connected you with James, Cranton came in waving the Official Secrets Act at me, saying I broke the law and was one step away from treason. He wanted me fired. He didn't get it, and now he's looking for an excuse to dismantle what I built over there. This is not a man who puts the mission first."

Jillian thought about that. "So my best option really is to get Gerhard's nephew to agree to keep on doing the resets."

"That is far and away the best choice."

"I need a plan B though, Frank. The nephew might not have the access we need anymore."

There was silence on the line.

"Frank?" Jillian asked.

"Shut up, I'm thinking."

Jillian let the silence churn on awhile longer. Whatever Frank could come up with would be better than getting into a fight with someone back at CSE and sacrificing the collection to a territorial pissing match.

"Okay. The first thing you need to do is confirm it's a reset issue. Gerhard's nephew surely can do that. If the light is green, then the buffer is working. If the light is flashing red, then the buffer needs to be reset."

"Seems clear."

"Idiotproof. No reflection on the nephew, but human error is almost always the thing that fucks these operations up."

"And if it's not a reset issue?"

"I'll have to think on that. It would have to be somewhere between the buffer and the copy you get."

"Right," Jillian said. "Like BND has figured out what we're doing and is rerouting the traffic."

"If that's what's going on, get ready to come home, because there's nothing you're going to be able to do about it. Of course, in that case you need to get that tap and send it back via the consulate. We don't want BND to find it and connect it to us."

"Noted. So our best-case scenario is that it is a reset issue. Can I evaluate the new guy by myself?" Jillian had gone way outside her official SIGINT duties over the last year. Not that she was now an expert in human intelligence, but here in the field it wasn't as easy to stick to one's official area of expertise.

"No. And before you get all defensive, it's not because you couldn't. It's because it's so far outside protocol that you'd come home and find out you don't have a job anymore."

"So, are you going to come over to Berlin and check out the replacement yourself?"

Frank barked out a laugh. "It's not in my area of expertise either. But that feed gives us really good intel—a lot of which we share with the RCMP, which means they have a vested interest in it continuing. And vetting people for loyalty and discretion is what they do."

"Aren't you working with the RCMP now?" Jillian asked.

"Yep. On anything that's of interest to both our agencies."

Jillian's brain whirled as she tried to keep up. "You seem to be making an argument that this feed qualifies."

"I think it does," said Frank. "I also think I can make the argument that I'm in the best position to direct how it gets fixed."

"Which means?"

"Let me figure it out, but I'm going to try to send you someone."

"Someone who can properly vet the new contact?"

"Yeah, and who can confirm this operation is staying off BND's radar."

Jillian's stomach muscles relaxed. "Thanks, Frank. Are you going to send me the contact?"

"No. Just let me know when you verify if it's a reset issue. I'll start the paperwork in the meantime. And when she gets to Berlin, she'll have instructions on how to find you."

"She?" Jillian asked, intrigued. There weren't a lot of women who did overseas intelligence assignments. In CSE Jillian was the only one. The RCMP might have a few more, but it wouldn't be many. The old boys' club was hard to break into.

"Yeah. You're going to love her. You can spend all your time commiserating on what a pain in the ass I am to work with."

Jillian smiled. "I would never say that about you, Frank."

"Sure," he said. "When you confirm, just leave me a message. Unsecure phone is fine. 'Yes' if it's a reset issue, 'no' if it isn't. This is the better way to go, because neither of us has a friend in the head of Personnel Security at CSE. This way allows us to bypass him entirely, while still somewhat following protocol."

Great. "Does this stuff ever get uncomplicated?"

"Yeah, when you get home. But trust me, you're going to miss it when you do."

CHAPTER TWO

Anya pushed her hair back from her face and secured it with a bobby pin. She'd put blush on and carefully applied a light-colored eyeshadow, but there was no masking the fact that she was tired. She dabbed more concealer under her eyes, hoping to reduce the dark circles. As unfair as it might be, her job was much easier if she looked attractive. There was something about a pretty woman that distracted men, as if they got too focused on wanting her to pay attention to who she was.

If she'd been looking to find a marriage partner, she might be frustrated. But in her line of work, distracted men were the ideal.

She finished with her lipstick and put it in her purse. Refusing to let her hands shake, she added some coins for the U-Bahn. Part of her tiredness was on account of her poor sleep the night before. But much more was an exhaustion that she felt down to her soul these days. A weariness that came from trying to differentiate each role she was playing and the struggle to remember who she was underneath it all.

Anya left her apartment and locked it more out of habit than anything. The people she worked with, and the people she worked for, would not stop at a locked door. Affixing the thin thread at the bottom, she sighed, wondering if this time it would really be over. If she could finally stop this life and move on to the one she dreamed of relentlessly.

She got on the U-Bahn and emerged three stops later at Friedrichstrasse station. She felt like she spent half her life coming and going from this underground place. She didn't raise any flags with the Stasi because she was on their payroll, and so coming to the bahnhof was how she filled her commitment. Her handler always met her here. After she cleared the border security—the checks perfunctory, or maybe they weren't, but that's how it seemed to her—she would be approached as she emerged into East Berlin.

Part of her, the part that threatened to take over, felt the whole charade ridiculous. These men, always men, took the job of the state so seriously that they no longer knew how to trust, not even those they loved.

But Anya knew she must not give in to that part. Because then she would slip up. Make mistakes. Get her roles confused and speak the wrong words and lose the only thing in this world she cared about. She held on tight to that caring, for she knew it was what kept her human.

"A fine day for a walk," said the man as he fell into step beside her. "Perhaps today we can walk through the park."

She nodded, not minding the suggestion. No doubt he was headed to the park beside the Marienkirche, a lovely, quiet green space amidst the grayness that was East Berlin. The park was a window to another world, where one could imagine one's experiences being guided by dreams instead of fears.

His name was Emil, and he was too close to her as always. Anya hated him. Hated the way he smelled of last night's dinner and shoe leather, hated the sight of the hairs that grew on his neck, hated the way he contrived to touch her all the time, on her back or her arm, as if hell would ever get cold enough for her to turn into any embrace that he offered.

Those were thoughts, however, that she kept to herself. Kept out of her eyes and lips. She didn't flinch at his touch, didn't pull away, didn't let it affect the smiles she occasionally offered him. Anya knew it was important to keep playing along. This role, Stasi courier, was the most important one she played.

"And how is the work with your American friend proceeding?" Emil asked, taking her elbow to steer her into the park, as if she couldn't get through the gates herself.

"Very well. The CIA, they think they are the best in the world. It is not so hard to get information if you play to their ego."

"You think he accepted the documents you gave him?"

Anya shrugged. "He will do his due diligence, but since you assured me you also have in place the corroborating source, I am expecting that he will head in the direction you wish him to go."

Emil suddenly grabbed her arm. "I wish for more than your expectation."

Anya did not react to the pain as his fingers squeezed her flesh. "I can offer you no further assurances, except to say that nothing in his demeanor or action has changed. He is CIA and so naturally suspicious, but nothing in our pattern has altered to suggest that he no longer trusts me. Americans are like that. You only have to prove yourself to them once." *Unlike East Germans, who demand constant evidence of fidelity.* But she knew she shouldn't be so hard on her fellow countrymen. When one has one's trust shattered repeatedly, it grows back a very fragile thing.

The grip on her arm loosened, but the fingers stayed in place. "This is good to hear. It is important, for both of us, that this CIA man takes the bait."

On that point, Anya thought, she and Emil were perfectly aligned.

"Is there anything else?" Anya asked.

Emil finally dropped his hand and continued their slow stroll through the park. "On that front, no. We now only have to wait and see. But there is something else that has come up. Something else you can do."

Anya held in her sigh, letting it roll down into her stomach. There always was something else. The East German government, and by extension the Stasi, always had another plot to execute, always some intrigue to perform. She supposed it kept them from facing the slowly crumbling structure of their grand social project.

"Yes?" she asked, injecting just the right amount of eagerness into her voice.

"There is a friend of our socialist cause who has landed in West Berlin. He is in a position to pass us much valuable information. We would like you to be the courier for him?"

It was phrased as a question to keep up the pretense of a benevolent state just trying to do right by its citizens. But the tone would not fool anyone who had grown up in East Germany.

"Of course," said Anya. "It would be an honor, as always."

"Yes," Emil said. "To be entrusted with such a mission is a sign of the value of our work."

"Who is the man?" Anya asked.

"I do not know yet. I will have the needed details for our next meeting."

Anya was surprised. It was unlike Emil to admit to not knowing something. From what she knew of his character, he would have been more likely to avoid the subject completely until he had the facts he needed to manipulate her.

"I look forward to next week then. When I'm sure you will know more."

"Yes, yes," Emil said. "I just got notice this morning that I was being asked to put this new operation in place. And, of course, you are one of my most trusted couriers."

"Thank you," Anya said.

Emil leaned in. "The German Democratic Republic values your service."

Anya backed away slightly, needing always to do this dance, forestalling Emil from confusing service to her country with service to him. "I am happy that I can do my part. Now, I do not want to keep you from doing yours, given the importance of the work you are entrusted with. I have promised to visit a friend this afternoon."

"Of course. Enjoy your day. Until next week."

She returned his nod and immediately turned and walked away. This role was one she would not be sad to give up.

CHAPTER THREE

Jillian closed the door behind Quentin. Her small office space off the lab at the institute was a rare place they could meet with minimal risk. There were always students and faculty coming and going, and it was easy for him to blend in here, just another person connected to the school.

The shadows under his eyes had deepened since the last time she saw him, but she felt the pull of attraction regardless. She leaned up to kiss him, smelling the familiar scent of his detergent. He took a moment to deepen the kiss like he always did, and Jillian relaxed into the connection.

She loved kissing him. Loved it in a way that was both spectacular and terrifying. Jillian felt like hours could pass and she wouldn't notice, focused instead on the texture of his lips and the feel of his body under her hands. She felt her heart rate increase, her breath come more rapidly, her knees go soft, forcing her to lean into him. As she held on tighter, she peripherally noticed that all the same effects seemed to be occurring to him.

Jillian didn't have to ask. She knew that they shared the escape. Moments like these were a break from the reality of their almost impossible relationship, from the turmoil and tension of their everyday lives. The momentary peace couldn't be extended further, not even into their words that filled the rest of their time together. The jobs that brought them to this city meant that there were few times in every day that could be carved out of the ongoing demands of secrecy, of staying under the radar.

It was hard to break the contact, to step back and away from the distraction.

"Jillian," Quentin murmured, resting his cheek against her hair.

"Rough week?" she whispered, content to be held for a little longer.

"Yeah," he said.

He stepped back and looked at her. "You?"

"Better."

"You're the only person that I have that effect on."

Jillian laughed. "Oh no. Now it's awkward to tell you that it's not on account of you. There's a solution to my feed issue, and Frank's sending me some help."

Quentin leaned back against the counter. "I should have known."

"Not that seeing you doesn't make me happy too."

"Not like your signals."

"Totally different kinds of happy," Jillian said.

"Yeah," Quentin said, "I'm okay with that. So, what kind of help is Frank sending you?"

"Well, the problem was the tap, the main copying point, on the cable where the feed gets transmitted. It's the only part I don't have direct control of over here. Sometimes the buffer fills up, and the collection basically overflows. So the mechanism then needs to be reset. The original guy doing that for us was promoted, so we have to determine if the replacement is approachable."

Quentin's eyes narrowed. "And?"

"Relax. I'm not going to vet the new guy myself. That's the help. Frank is sending someone to me."

He looked thoughtful. "You could have asked me. I do have some experience finding out who people really are. I can get information that would make you less vulnerable."

"I know," Jillian sighed. "I do, really. But I'm okay with this one. I can't just put the CIA on a private citizen of West Berlin because I'm nervous."

"I'd be doing it as a friend, Jillian."

"And if you found out something that was useful or relevant to you? You're telling me that you'd just put it aside?"

"Fine," said Quentin. "I don't want to fight with you either. And you're right, it's better that it's someone from your own country."

"Exactly. You're not even supposed to know about what I do here," Jillian said.

"And I don't, really," Quentin smiled. "SIGINT's not that easy to figure out, even for those of us in a similar business."

"Part of the mystery," Jillian said, returning the smile.

"So, this help Frank is sending you, it's likely someone in my line of work."

"Probably," Jillian shrugged. "All I know is that it's a woman."

"Well, I can tell you her name is Veronica, and she's a good person to have watching your back."

Jillian stared at him. "How on earth do you know that?"

"I met her when I was in Nicaragua. She's smart. And no pushover."

Jillian took in the information. "She's not exactly like you though? Because we don't have a foreign intelligence service."

"No, not exactly like me. She'll be here on an embassy cover or something. An attaché of some sort is the most likely. My guess is that she won't be expected to develop agents or anything, not if she's here to help you."

Jillian was looking forward to getting Frank's help. There weren't a lot of women in the intelligence industry outside HR and the secretarial pools. It would be nice to meet one, to have that kind of contact. And to be around someone she didn't have to continually hide things from.

"Do you think I'll like her?"

Quentin shrugged. "I have no idea. But I do. Not that I know her that well. But in Nicaragua, she ended up saving my life after I'd made a very bad decision."

"Well then, I have to at least give her a chance."

"What I'm telling you, and what's way more important than liking her, is that you can trust her. She seems to be guided by what she thinks is right, not necessarily what anyone else tells her to do. So I guess, in that sense, you two have something in common."

Jillian smiled. "I hope that doesn't scare you."

Quentin regarded her for a moment. "Almost everything about you scares me."

Silence descended for a while. Jillian appreciated being able to discuss her job with Quentin, but part of her wanted to talk about life and memories and normal things people starting to date might talk about, if only to pretend for five minutes that they were average. However, she thought the abrupt topic change would seem artificial now.

"You look a little worn out," she said.

Quentin rubbed his eyes. "Yeah. I haven't been getting much sleep lately."

"Anything you want to talk about?"

He was quiet for a moment. "I've got this agent here. Her usefulness is coming to an end. I had promised her that when that time came, I'd help her get her daughter out of East Berlin. Which, as I'm sure you can imagine, is not an easy thing to do. Some days it seems like the Stasi have got the whole country acting as informants."

Jillian's heart kicked up at the story. Getting someone out of East Berlin definitely wasn't a regular workday for Quentin.

"Do you know how you're going to do it?"

"There aren't really a ton of options," he shrugged. "And the kid's only eight. She's small enough to fit in a special compartment under a car. The trouble is finding someone to drive the car."

"How do you solve that?"

Quentin shook his head. "Normally, luck and intuition. My network fluctuates, but since it's a kid, I'm not taking any chances. Adults can accept risk. An eight-year-old can't. So I need to be sure about the driver. But these days it's hard to be sure about anyone."

What a situation. Jillian understood how heavily the responsibility would be weighing on him. She reached over and rested her hand on his cheek. "You can ask for help too, you know."

"This isn't something you can become involved in, Jillian."

"I know," she said. "I'll admit that it frustrates me, how I can never really do anything for you while you've risked your career, if not your life, for me multiple times."

He turned his lips into her palm. "Listening helps. More than you probably realize."

Her heart suddenly ached. Leaning up, she kissed him. He began returning the kiss with an urgency that made her shiver. So much was bottled up inside him, she was worried it was going to eat him alive one day.

Eventually she pulled back from him, needing the space before she drowned in the confusion that he caused. She rested her hand in his and let her blood pressure return to normal. Best to refocus on the problems. It seemed safer for her heart.

"I wasn't talking about me. Helping you. James would do it. For someone's kid. He would do that."

Quentin was quiet for a long while. "I don't think I should involve him either. If he gets caught, it would be the end of his career. He's in uniform. The Soviets would be all over that."

"It was just a suggestion," Jillian said, "because you know you can trust him. I'm no expert in your line of work, but is there anyone who wouldn't be taking that kind of risk? Getting caught, for anyone, means a Stasi prison sentence, a prisoner exchange, or an international incident. If it wasn't risky, it wouldn't be so difficult to find someone."

"I wonder what James would think of you volunteering him like this?" Quentin smiled slightly.

"If you do ask him, I'd appreciate you not mentioning that part," she said.

"Coward."

"Maybe," Jillian smiled. "But he's already done so much for me. I don't need anything else on my side of the ledger."

"Don't worry," Quentin said. "I'll be sure to reassure him the fate of the free world rests in his hands."

"Right," Jillian laughed. "I can just see him being swayed by that particular argument."

"Seriously though, Jillian, me sharing my life means sharing some of my problems. I like that part. But not if you feel like you have to help all the time. Being able to talk about some of this stuff is all the help I need from you. A lot of it, there aren't any solutions anyway."

She was thoughtful for a moment. "You know, I read this book once, about this detective. He was midcareer, and he was at the point where nothing surprised him and he knew it wasn't going to get any better, yet he showed up to work every day anyway. The author described it as 'it takes a special kind of courage to go on fighting the battles when you know you cannot win the war.'"

Quentin stared at her.

"Anyway," she said, almost whispering, "that's how I think of you. I think you're a better person than you give yourself credit for."

He rested his forehead against hers. "You're wrong, Jillian. Everything I'm doing now, it's just trying to balance out the scales."

It revealed more than he probably intended. Jillian wondered how much it would take for him to atone for the death of his asset Isabella in Nicaragua all those years ago. She hoped, whatever it was, he'd one day be able to make amends with himself for his past.

Anya picked up the broom and swept around the chair after her last customer left. Thousands of shards of salt-and-pepper strands caught up in the bristles as she angled them into the dustpan.

She didn't mind cutting hair. It was the one part of her job that she enjoyed. It was uncomplicated, and the gratitude she received was satisfying. It was amazing how clients came and left as different people, the only real difference being the length of their hair. For some reason a haircut often made people feel renewed, like they'd just been given a chance to lead a new life by taking on a new identity.

The salon was an ideal place to work. Each stylist was independent, so although they all knew each other, they rented their chairs and their schedule was their own. Some started their days earlier, others worked well into the evening. There were split shifts, days off, and working an important or loyal client into the schedule.

Anya had lots of clients. She was good at her work, pleasant, not too intrusive, and available at odd hours for a last-minute updo. Her only inflexibility was the Sundays she spent with her daughter. She wouldn't sacrifice that time for any client.

Her cover was easily maintained. No one questioned the coming and going of clients. Some came for just one haircut, others came regularly for years. Those who worked in the industry were used to all types. Some men came every week to get a buzz cut. Some women came twice a year to chop off inches. In hairdressing, there was no such thing as a suspicious pattern.

The work allowed her to meet with all types of contacts while hiding in plain sight. It was an ideal position in which to courier messages back and forth between people who needed to communicate but who could never meet. As far as Anya knew, she was the only one in the salon who participated in these extra duties, which prevented the salon from raising suspicions by becoming a hub.

She had a one-hour break until her next customer. She'd turned to go to the back room for her purse, thinking to sit outside and have a cigarette and enjoy the sunshine, when the bells on the front door tinkled.

It was early in the morning, with only one other stylist set up for the day, so Anya went to the reception desk. "Can I help you?" she asked the man who had just entered.

"Yes, please," the man replied in accented German. Anya wasn't sure, but she thought he sounded English. "I'm looking for a haircut. I only have twenty minutes, and I'd like a little extra taken off the sides."

Not a flicker of surprise or expectation touched her face. "Yes, of course. The sides grow out much faster. I can help you now if you'd like."

"That would be great, thank you," the man said.

Anya led him over to her chair. She had long ago taken the chair farthest away from the door, tucked in the back beside the washing sinks. After wrapping a cloth around the man's neck, she pulled out the electric razor to do the back and around the ears. He had medium-brown hair, but some strands were tipped with gold at the ends, as if he spent a lot of time in the sun.

The sound of the razor stifled any conversation, but there wouldn't be much anyway. Not on this initial visit. The purpose today was to make contact. To memorize the face. For her to communicate her optimal availability so as to not raise suspicion. For him to be able to visualize how the handoffs would go.

Of course she would verify with Emil next time she saw him, but she was certain this was the man he had spoken of at their last meeting. No further biographical details had been forthcoming, just that he was an important contact. And that he was British.

Anya didn't much care. Years in, and she'd couriered for people from all over. Berlin was a hub for exchange, and information pushed against the Wall from all directions.

It was not her job, however, to wonder about his motivations. Why an Englishman should want to help the Stasi was not her concern. There were enough of them—English, French, Argentinian, Australian. It was easy to romanticize helping the East German socialist cause when you'd never lived there. Neither was she supposed to vet the accuracy of his information. Someone else far inside the Stasi machine did that. Emil would ask for her impressions, as he was always worried about double agents. And this man, however valuable his information, would always be under suspicion. Anyone who would betray their country would always be handled carefully, as if they could betray anyone. It was not Anya's direct responsibility to do anything other than courier information.

She finished with the razor and picked up her scissors. "Just a half inch off the top?" she asked.

"Right. About that. Not the current look, I know, but I've never been able to pull off anything too shaggy."

"It will look good, I promise."

"I'm sure I'm in good hands," he said.

Just the usual banter between stylist and client. Developing a rapport so he'd continue to come back. Of course, in their case, him coming back was inevitable, but the more real the situation looked, the less likely the charade would be revealed.

She answered his easy questions about how long she'd been a stylist and if she'd always lived in West Berlin. They chatted about the weather, how important it was to get out and enjoy it, because it wouldn't last too long. She finished up, dusting off his neck and shaking out the cloth before using her fingers to get that last little finish.

"Looks great, thank you," he said.

She led him over to the reception desk. "Would you like to book your next appointment? I recommend every two weeks to keep it from becoming too sloppy looking."

"Sounds perfect. Need to avoid looking like I'm in a rock band."

After taking his money for today's haircut, she noted the appointment time on a little card and handed it to him. "I look forward to seeing you then. If you need to reschedule your appointment, you can leave a message for me at that number. I work every day from Tuesday to Saturday and can come in whatever time suits your needs. Just include a new date and time in your message, and I will fit you in."

"What wonderful service. I'm happy I was walking by today."

Anya gave him a slight nod and watched as he walked to the door. The chimes above tinkled as he swung it open and disappeared into the sunshine.

When she had her daughter, they were going to have to, at the very least, leave West Berlin. There were too many loose ends in this city for her to ever relax.

CHAPTER FOUR

Jillian sat on a bench off a quiet side path in the Tiergarten. It really was a beautiful city park, full of lime trees in the full bloom of late summer. It seemed like half of West Berlin was out enjoying the day, with blankets and picnics spread all over, and soccer balls being kicked around.

She'd received a note when she did her last dead drop. It had instructed her to meet her new contact at the third bench along the path to Rosengarten coming from the south. Whoever had set it up, the location was a good choice. The path had less foot traffic, and the bench itself was under a willow, which offered an ethereal kind of privacy.

Jillian sat hugging her knees, reading *Goodbye to Berlin* by Christopher Isherwood, part of her ongoing effort to better understand the history of this city where she lived and worked. She had arrived early because it was a beautiful day to read in the park, and because she had a lot of extra time on her hands these days. With her feed still down, the most she could do was tinker around with possible upgrades for when it was back up and running.

Despite the brilliance of the story, Jillian's senses were aware of her environment, so she knew immediately when someone sat on the bench beside her.

"The weather is great for swimming," said the woman who'd just sat down.

Remembering her line, Jillian responded with, "I plan to go to the lake this weekend."

"Jillian," the woman said. There was no smile, just a small raising of one brow and a slight inclination of the head.

"Nice to meet you," Jillian responded. "You're here to help me fix a small problem, I understand."

Now there was a flicker of a smile. "Yes. I hope so. Frank briefed me with as much as he knew about the situation."

"You're the one he was in Nicaragua with. Veronica. I'm assuming I can call you that, because no one gave me a different contact name."

"Veronica is just fine, seeing as it's the name I'm using over here. And yes, I was in Nicaragua. Frank also filled me in on how our information from there helped you over here."

"Yeah, it did. A lot. More than I've even really been able to tell him, seeing as how it's hard for me to communicate certain details. Are you still working with him?"

"Yes," Veronica said, "on joint missions where there isn't something happening already. Ostensibly. But there's a lot of paperwork and a lot of people to convince to get a whole unit up and running. In the meantime, he thought I could help you."

"I hope you can. Are you working out of the consulate?"

"No," Veronica shook her head. "Training with military SIGINT in Teufelsberg, which is how we sold it to the RCMP. But officially, in terms of West German passport control and all that, I've come over as a civilian doing administrative support at NATO HQ for the Berlin Infantry Brigade."

Jillian smiled. "It's a full-time job for someone, isn't it? Figuring out how to move all of us around the world."

"Yeah, no wonder the government generates so much paperwork."

Veronica seemed genuine, and both Frank and Quentin thought she was smart and trustworthy. Two qualities Jillian was happy to have in her life at the moment. For the first time in weeks, Jillian had hope for her problem being solved soon.

"So," Veronica said, "what can you tell me about how I can help you?"

"Did Frank explain how the main tap works? With the reset on the buffer?"

Veronica nodded.

"Okay, so my advisor's nephew, who used to do the reset job for us, gave us the name of the new guy we need to vet. He's Sebastian Holt. Born here in West Berlin. Not sure when, but the guess is that he's in his late twenties. He works at Telekom Berlin, in the systems maintenance department. Depending on what you find out about him, we might have a couple of options. I've been thinking about it, and, well, he doesn't need to know anything about the origin of the feed, where the information goes, or even who he's really helping. If we think it's safe enough, we could just tell him that he's helping the science institute."

"Why would that not be transparent? As in, an official assignment from his boss?"

"We'd need to work on it, no question," Jillian said. "I'm just saying, it's literally pressing one button every three months. He needs to know nothing in order to do that. So it gives us options on the story we could tell."

"Understood," said Veronica. "I'll keep it in mind. But the first step is to learn more about him. The Stasi have been building their informant network for over thirty years. Everything I read about this place suggests that they have an incredible amount of people on their payroll, especially in West Berlin."

Jillian sighed. "I know. And the Soviets have their fair share running around. Both countries would be over-the-top excited to penetrate our collection program."

"Or get a hold of you." The way Veronica said it made Jillian think it was more than just a simple observation.

"Did Frank tell you about Carlos? About what happened here before he went to Nicaragua?" Jillian asked.

"You mean when Carlos kidnapped you?"

Jillian shivered despite the warmth of the day. It was a long time ago, if not in years, then maturity. She'd been so much more naive then, not understanding that because her lover was working for the Soviets, whatever they shared in bed was inconsequential to his pursuit of power. "Yes. It was…awful."

"I'm sure that word doesn't really cover it."

Jillian smiled slightly. She sensed that, for whatever reason, Veronica understood in a way that the others who knew—James, Quentin, and Frank—did not. "Not at all. But I brought it up so you know that I'm not unaware of what would likely happen should any of our adversaries get close to the program. And you being connected with it, however peripherally, makes you vulnerable too."

Veronica was silent for a moment. "Thank you. I know, maybe more than you do, about the risks of being in the field and how those risks are more precarious for women in many ways. But this job, if you could do it without ever being vulnerable, it wouldn't exist. Meaning that, it goes together."

Wasn't that the truth. One never needed to covertly collect intelligence from a friendly environment. If you needed to be covert, you were automatically in enemy territory of some sort.

"So, what are your next steps?" Jillian asked.

"I'll find this Sebastian. I'll follow him. I'll also run him through the system back home, see if he's ever popped up in reporting."

"If nothing flags and he's just a regular Berliner going about his regular life?"

"Then we'll craft the approach together. I can't stay in West Berlin indefinitely, but long enough to see this through. We'll figure it out."

Jillian nodded. Who knew where it was all going to land. Could the relationship with Sebastian stay with her advisor, Gerhard? Would Jillian, or even Veronica, have to get involved? Were there even options?

"Here," Veronica held out a piece of paper. "I've planned out a meeting schedule for the next week. Committing it to memory would be best. If I don't make it to the next one, don't panic. Just show up at the one after that. I'll update it as things progress."

Jillian was a little startled but tried not to let it show. For all her interactions with Quentin over the last year and a half, for all the time she had brushed up against HUMINT activities here in Berlin, she'd never actually been part of a formal human intelligence operation. It wasn't her area of expertise, and she didn't really know much about how they worked.

One of her struggles with Quentin, especially at the beginning, when he was helping her while helping himself, was that she had no way to contact him. She had to rely on him showing up whenever suited him and on hoping the timing matched her needs.

Working with Veronica was going to be different. First, it was official. That alone brought with it a host of responsibilities and complications. But they had a commitment to each other too. So it made sense to establish a more reliable connection.

Jillian took the paper and slipped into her back pocket. She'd memorize it when she got back to her apartment then burn it.

"Is there anything I can do right now?" she asked.

"More of what you're probably already doing: thinking of cover story options if we think it's safe to make contact with this Sebastian."

"Who gets to make that call?"

Veronica smiled slightly. "I do. I mean, technically, it's Frank. I think. The chains of command aren't exactly sorted for me and him, and I think he's working this situation somewhat on the DL. I get the impression there are people he wants to avoid."

"Par for the course when it comes to Frank. But he's got a lot of friends too. I have to tell you, though," Jillian continued, "the Frank you're describing isn't a perfect match to the one I know. He was never keen on me making my own decisions in theater."

Veronica looked thoughtful. "I think he changed a little in Nicaragua. Something about being away from the SIGINT bureaucracy. I think he realized that he'd be better finding people to trust than trying to control all the compromises himself."

"I'd like to know more about what went on there. I know you can't tell me everything, and I've heard a lot from Quentin, but about Frank and what the two of you did."

"Do you see Quentin?" Veronica asked.

"Sometimes. He's here in West Berlin."

Veronica looked a little startled. Jillian didn't know if it was unwanted or just unexpected.

"Tell him that I say hi."

"For sure. He's grateful you know. For what you did for him in Nicaragua. He said you saved his life."

"I don't know if he's someone I want to work with again. He made a few—from my perspective—bad decisions. But I understand, too, a little of what drove him. When we talked with his asset's family, Isabella, I don't know what I'd be like if I was responsible for someone's death like that."

Jillian willed herself to keep her breathing steady. This was a part of Quentin's past that he never talked about, except to say that he screwed up in so many ways that he'd lost part of himself in the process. She was curious about it because she felt that it was at the core of every decision he made, every action he took.

"You were there, weren't you, when he shot Carlos?"

Veronica regarded Jillian with something like sadness, whether for what happened or what had led up to it, Jillian wasn't sure.

"It was terrible. Frank and I had lit the house on fire, and by the time we got in, the flames were raging. It was hot and terrifying, and Isabella's husband was losing control. Frank knocked Carlos unconscious. I was injured and Quentin was bleeding, and we were trying to get out of there before the whole thing fell down around us. Then Quentin pulled the trigger, and that was the end of Carlos."

"Do you think Quentin did the right thing?"

Veronica was silent for a long while. "It was murder. But was it also justice? All I know is that I hope I never have to make that call."

Jillian sat there, letting the images settle in. More than anything, Quentin had taught her that the right side was often far from obvious. But self-justification was often a thin band-aid when the memories of choices came rushing back in the depths of sleepless nights.

Veronica stood up. "I'll see you as soon as I can. If I can find Sebastian soon, and if he's boring, that'll be progress."

"But not too boring," said Jillian.

"Right," Veronica said. "Too boring is always suspicious. We're all quirky in some way." She paused for a moment. "I don't know how much I have to tell you, and I don't want to patronize you, as you've been here a lot longer than I have. It's just, well, with Frank, he didn't know much about protocol. How these kinds of intelligence operations work."

Jillian smiled. She could just imagine how much fun it had been for Veronica to tell Frank he didn't know what he was doing. "I'm like Frank, I'm an engineer. Don't assume my expertise on anything except how signals work. Tell me what you need. You won't offend me."

"Okay. Stay here for at least five minutes after I go. Read your book. And when you leave, head in a different direction."

"Absolutely. Good luck."

"Thanks," Veronica replied before walking off in the direction of the Brandenburg Gate.

Being in no rush on account of having nothing she needed to do, Jillian enjoyed her book in the park for another hour before heading back to her apartment. As she passed the soccer players and picnickers, lovers and friends, she wondered how many of them were keeping their eyes and ears open for anything that might be of interest to their Stasi masters. It would be nice, one day, to be in this city without having to worry about that.

Anya slowly walked among the gravestones, pretending she was reading the inscriptions on each one, as if she were looking for a long-lost relative. In reality her ears were attuned to the sound of feet on the gravel path, knowing that her contact should be here shortly.

She wasn't nervous. Too many times she had walked around cemeteries and parks, left folded notes under coffee cups and slipped into the back rooms of stores. It wasn't routine, not exactly, but the nerves were long gone. In their place was a resolve so deep that no amount of clandestine meetings and playing both sides could shake it. She lived only to get her daughter out of East Berlin and go somewhere, anywhere, they could make a home. It was the thought of her daughter that kept her strong and focused. That removed all sympathies and let her give everyone what they wanted so she could one day get out.

She heard the crunch of stones and dust, the cadence familiar. She stopped and turned toward a gravestone, noting briefly the bright-red flowers that had been placed against the old, degrading rock.

"Valentina," said a voice.

She looked up. It was the American. "Rob," she said. He was not a Rob. It was too friendly a name. Laid back. Meant for a man who spent his life relaxed, having fun. He should have gone with Robert. More serious. But it didn't matter, no one else would notice. *Who knows, maybe sometime, in some other part of his life, he has reason to smile.*

"Did your contact accept your story about handing me the documents?"

There were many things she liked about him. Rob. He got to the point. He didn't waste time. He didn't flirt. And he didn't try to convince her she was doing the right thing.

"Yes," Anya replied. "Because I did. It's easier to lie when it's based in truth."

One corner of his mouth ticked up briefly before the intensity fell back into place. "Yeah, I get that."

"And you," she asked, "when will your response be ready?"

"A month," he replied. "Sooner if I can manage it."

"What will be in that response?"

"Enough misinformation to keep them confused about microchips for years."

She didn't say anything else. She cared little for the details. Microchips or bombs, at this point it was irrelevant to her. The conflict between East versus West was so large it had a momentum of its own. "I will see you in one month then," she said, turning to go.

He touched her elbow lightly. "Two weeks, Valentina. Because after you take those documents back, it's time to get your daughter out."

She stopped. Her lungs seemed to compress, a pressure building until she wasn't sure she could breathe.

Anya turned around and looked at his face, her American contact, the man she had gone double agent for because he promised he could get her daughter out. Part of her hadn't believed him, but he was the only one who was offering. So she'd agreed. Always looking for someone else who could help her if this man proved to be manipulating her. She rarely made eye contact with him. Theirs was a relationship of brief exchanges passed quickly so as to not attract attention.

But she had to look at him now. Had to see, as best she could, if he was telling her the truth. It was so hard not to hope, but she shoved it aside and met his eyes.

"It is?" she asked.

"Yes," he said. "I told you. I only needed to action the microchips. That's it. That was my mandate, and a month from now, you'll have completed it. So now we move on to what I owe you in exchange."

"I know it would be better for you to keep me here. There is always another mandate. So why are you doing this now?" *Why not string me along for another few years until my desperation implodes and I've got nothing left to offer?*

"For exactly that reason: this business never ends. The war is never going to be won. So I figure it's important to know when to stand down. You hating me because I'm not fulfilling my commitment does me no good. And hey, another defector in the West who's critical of East Germany doesn't hurt."

At his words, the hope sprang free, and the fear along with it. She wanted so badly for him to be telling the truth. Now that he was offering to make the dream tangible, she could feel the need rising within her. She couldn't afford to place her trust in the wrong person, but in order to get her daughter out, she had to place her trust in someone. In all the years she had been doing this, Rob had emerged as her best bet.

"Okay. I will believe you. What do I need to do?"

"How tall is she? And how much does she weigh?"

Anya started a bit at the specifics. "About a hundred and fifty centimeters. And maybe about twenty-five kilos."

"Good. The smaller she is, the easier on her. We have to plan for you to be in East Berlin to take your daughter to the meeting point. You need to figure out how to prepare her. She's going to go over in a specially made compartment under a car. It's going to be dark and cramped, but it will only be for fifteen minutes. You need to make sure she's going to be okay with that. Because if she starts panicking, it will all fall apart."

He didn't need to tell her that. She knew all too well what happened when people got caught trying to escape. It was considered a crime against the state. People went to jail for interminable lengths of time, disappearance often turning into death.

If something happened, Anya knew she would never see her daughter again.

"Can you do this?" Anya asked him. The reality of the trust she was placing in this stranger had become scorchingly real.

Anya had risked her own life many times. She had siphoned off all emotions until what was left was more machine that executed without qualm in order to one day be able to live freely with her daughter. But now, at the thought of it happening, at turning the risks into concrete problems, she felt her trust in herself slip. Had she gone about it the right way? Could she trust her daughter's life to this man?

She realized she hadn't paid enough attention to her own vulnerability.

"Yes."

Anya heard his reply. Saw the honesty in his face. But saw the sadness as well.

"Look, Valentina, I'm not going to sell this to you. You have to want me to do this. I'll tell you that I've done it before. That I'm going to do my best, and I'm going to do it myself. And that I'm not taking any chances with an eight-year-old. Nor do I plan to end up in a Stasi prison. But you know, like I do, there are no guarantees. I can't give you that. So if you don't want to take the risk, I accept that. I'm not sure what I would do, or could do, in your situation. If you want to walk away from working with me too, that's okay. Once you hand those documents back, we can never see each other again. You don't owe me anything. You just have to tell me what you want."

"Do it." The words came out as barely a whisper. She swallowed and repeated, "Do it."

"Are you sure?"

"Yes," she nodded. "I know, I've always known, that getting my daughter out was not going to be easy. Easy is for people who live in different countries with other lives. But you, I think you are our best chance. So yes, I will take it. Because how my daughter is living now, how I am living now, this is no life."

"Okay," he said. "Meet me back here in two weeks. I'll have the details for you. And then we can plan the rest."

Anya watched him walk away. She could do this. For her daughter, she would.

CHAPTER FIVE

James stood at the polished wood bar and flagged the bartender for a Tennent's. One of the most remarkable things about the British military was their ability to recreate an English pub everywhere they went around the globe. Outside the doors could be an arid desert, a hostile jungle, or an ultra-modern urban environment, and still there would be a room with a fireplace, a full selection of British alcohol, and an indifferent civilian behind the counter.

He didn't often drink on base. Usually the end of his shift saw him head out into the city, like anyone leaving their office job at the end of the day. He spent enough time in uniform, and had spent enough time in English pubs, that he didn't want to extend his day in the mess.

Today, however, he was meeting an old school chum who was here on some diplomatic assignment.

He took a sip of the Tennent's when it arrived, never tiring of the barley flavor hitting his taste buds. Made with the water of a Scottish loch, it was a bit of continuity in a life that had seen him posted all over the world.

"Jamie Murphy," a voice said over the din of pub chatter. "Never thought the next time we met would be in West Berlin. We almost had your team that last go on the pitch."

James smiled at the man who came up to stand beside him. "Not a chance, Fenwick. You English boys don't know a damn thing about a proper rugby match. Like I always say, you'd be better off sticking to football."

Edward Ashton, future Earl of Fenwick, returned the smile while clapping James on the shoulder. "Good to see you, Murphy. I was happy to find out you were here when I got pulled into the latest diplomatic row. Should keep me from perishing from boredom while I help them sort out whatever the Soviets are moaning about now."

"Right then, order your beer and you can entertain me with how it's really diplomats who are saving the world."

Edward grinned. "You've not changed. Still think rock and roll is more effective than careful treaty negotiations."

"Your treaties put people to sleep. Jimi Hendrix, on the other hand, spurs people to action."

"Absolutely. I suppose I should get 'All Along the Watchtower' piped in over the speakers at my next meeting."

James grinned. "It couldn't hurt, mate."

They moved to a table, and the next hour passed at the easy pace of an old friendship. James had known Edward Ashton almost twenty years; their respective rugby teams had played in the same league. Edward's team was made up of mostly posh English boys represented perfectly by Edward himself, the oldest son of an earl. Originally James hadn't paid much attention to the details of his opponents, lumping them all together as posh twats who were easily beaten by his army team. James himself didn't think much of the English nobility, the lot of whom had proven themselves both useless and greedy throughout history. But Edward had come up to him after the first match and told him that he admired his play. And then he asked James to teach him.

James was skeptical at first, thought he was being played by some entitled public school boy. But Edward had persisted, even offering to take him out for a drink. He commented on the match with enough detail that James could tell he took his rugby seriously.

So a somewhat unlikely friendship had started. James had invited Edward out to the army practices and watched as Edward improved. After a while, James, the son of a Scottish laborer and Canadian nurse, became friends with a man whose blue blood went back a dozen generations.

They had stayed in touch over the years, meeting up in friendly matches when their jobs put them in the same city. Anywhere the British went, there was a recreational rugby game to be had.

"You like it here, don't you?" Edward asked after James had filled him in on his latest radio contest.

"Aye, I do. There's something both surreal and spectacular about having a wall through the middle of a city. I figure, this is as close to history as I'm ever going to get. And I damn well plan to be here when the bloody thing finally comes down."

Edward lifted a brow. "You see that happening in your lifetime, then? The end of Communism?"

James shrugged. "I don't do the politics. I'm just after a reunification of the people. It's blokes like you who can sort out the isms after that."

Edward was silent for a few moments. "That's always the problem, isn't it? What goes rushing into the void. I was speaking to a man the other day who survived the war in Krakow. He said the years after the war were worse than the war itself. Granted, he wasn't a Jew. But he said the turmoil in trying to get the dust to settle, plus people arrested or displaced, and the reasons and rules changing daily, made the idea of peace seem like a unicorn."

James wasn't insensitive to the sentiment. He might want the Wall to come down, but he was aware that he was doing his part while in a uniform. Thus, he couldn't claim to be neutral about which side he wanted to come out ahead.

"Makes me bloody happy to have been born in Inverness. A sleepy backwater it might seem, but sometimes off the radar is better. Of course, Inverness in the 1930s was fine. Three hundred years ago, and I might have felt like that Polish bloke."

"And isn't that the right sentiment? It's like a birth lottery. Why am I a lord? We like to pretend it's about birthright, but it's really only an accident of fate. Born to people who have the means and circumstances to hold on to power. Did I ever tell you how the first Earl of Fenwick came into being?"

"Ye might have, but we do often get up to a lot of drinking. Especially when we were younger."

Edward smiled. "That we did. Anyway, he was a favorite of the mistress of George I. Old Georgie spent most of his time in Germany, him being the first of the German kings of England, but he did like to have a woman on hand when he stopped in London. Meredith was her name, and after years of devoted service to the king, she requested a title and her choice of husband. And that was the birth of the Fenwick line."

"You know, it's nothing to be ashamed of. I suspect, if you look close enough, most of the nobility started the same way. Backing the right horse at the right time."

"I suppose I ought to be grateful for it," Edward said, raising his pint glass. "To the first Earl of Fenwick then, who we at least know was good in bed."

"I'll drink to that."

James finished off his pint and went up to the bar for another round. "So, how long do you reckon you'll be here in Berlin?" he asked, sitting back down.

Edward shrugged. "No guess really. There's a meeting to attend in two days. Depending on how that goes, they might thank me and send me on my way, or they might find another use for me. Being the son of the Secretary of Defence often means someone gets to thinking I'm useful to bring out at parties. Direct line and all that."

"Any thought of chucking it all in?" James asked.

"To do what? Putter around the estates? Unfortunately, one can't retire from being a lord."

"Aye, I suppose one can't," agreed James.

After another pint and promises to see each other again while Edward was in town, James said goodnight and began to make his way home. He decided to walk. It was a bit of a hike to his flat in Wilmersdorf, but it was a grand night for what the Germans called a spaziergang. Early September in Berlin was lovely, but he knew that didn't mean much, considering he enjoyed every season here. The air was still warm from the heat of the day, and the breeze rustled through the many linden trees that filled the city. In consideration of how much of the day he usually spent behind a microphone, and to fit in with the locals, James tried to walk as often as possible.

It also helped him process his thoughts.

Seeing Edward tonight had been nice. Nice in that someone familiar with shared history, but not sure how much more we have to chat about, kind of way.

Even though they'd forged a friendship during their rugby days, the weight of time had taken them in very different directions. James had spent almost twenty years in the army, seen tours in heartbreaking places, been shot at, and had to construct a very nuanced worldview to keep on with what he did.

Edward had graduated Oxbridge but before going into the foreign office had spent some years playing polo or fox hunting or whatever other useless pursuits the nobility got up to. They'd reconnected when Edward had become a diplomat, but James was never sure how serious the career was for him. James knew there was enough family money for Edward to spend his life attending parties and calling it networking.

Ach, maybe I'm being too hard on the old boy.

James could imagine what it might have been like being the offspring of the Earl of Fenwick. The man had a reputation as impatient, elitist, and a general arsehole. Growing up trying to please him couldn't have been any fun.

Ah well, having a pint with Edward again wouldn't be a big deal. Soon enough it was likely Edward would be called back to London, back under the earl's thumb.

49

CHAPTER SIX

"Well, did he pass the test?"

Jillian was meeting with Veronica in the Tiergarten again. A different path, a different bench, but it was still a great location for a private chat. The park was so full of people going about their day, enjoying the early autumn sun, that it was like being invisible in a crowd.

Veronica carefully unfolded the wrapper of a Ritter chocolate bar, its bright colors standing out against the black of her shirt. "I'm not sure," she answered, breaking off a square and offering some to Jillian.

"Because, you know," Jillian said, taking a piece of the chocolate, "I can't collect anything until the reset button gets pressed."

Veronica chewed on her chocolate. "Better than going home because your whole operation gets compromised to the East Germans."

"I know," Jillian sighed. "Fine, I'm not going to tell you how to do your job. But how's it looking at least? Does he seem suspicious? Any red flags?"

"I'm not sure," Veronica said again as she broke off another piece. "Nothing stands out in terms of his contacts or his daily routine. I've started looking at the people he seems to talk to regularly. This kind of work, it takes a while because he really only needs one contact. If he's good, most of his connections are going to be with regular West Germans to maintain his cover. That's how he's going to get his info. I've sent a couple of information requests back home to see if we can flesh out some biographical details."

"So I have time for a vacation in Italy is what you're saying."

"Yeah. Probably." She offered Jillian the Ritter again.

"No thanks," Jillian said. "I'm one of those people who lets it melt in my mouth."

"In the long run, a cheaper way to eat chocolate."

Jillian sat back on the bench, letting her thoughts wander. She hadn't felt this useless in forever. Not since she'd come to West Berlin at any rate. She was pretty patient. Understood the need to take the time to do something right. But it was easier to be patient when you could at least participate in achieving the outcome.

"There is one thing," Veronica said, "that stands out as unusual."

"Unusual in a problematic way?"

"Not necessarily. More unusual in a genuinely unique way. Most evenings he goes to this house at the very edge of Spandau. Later, after work and maybe dinner, he comes out of his apartment in dirty pants and a T-shirt. Not filthy, but more like how a certain set of clothes look after you've used them to paint the walls a few times. Like working clothes. He goes to this house in Spandau and stays for a few hours, then goes home. From what I can tell, other than being right up against the border Wall, there's nothing special about it."

Jillian thought for a moment. "It's not his house? Maybe he's housesitting?"

"Possibly, and I'm trying to find that out. But why the work clothes? It doesn't quite add up. I'm going back tonight to do some poking around. It's a quiet, residential neighborhood, the kind where irregular activity stands out. I haven't been able to just park myself at a café and watch. I'll wait for Sebastian to leave and then see if I can find out any more."

Jillian sighed. "I really want him to be normal. Just a regular guy who plays soccer and drinks beer and has never talked to an East German."

Veronica smiled. "It's never that easy. Besides, if he hit all those markers, that would be suspicious in itself. Everyone has a story of some sort."

"I guess you're right. I just don't want to have to shut the program down. But I also don't want to get picked up by the Stasi and be followed everywhere I go."

"I get that. Just so you know, this unusual activity, it's actually a point in his favor, because he's not exactly trying to hide it. It feels to me like he'd be quite surprised to know anyone was paying attention to him."

That, at least, was some hope.

"Until next time then," Jillian said, preparing to leave first this time.

"Yes," Veronica nodded. "Until next time."

"The timing of this, it's okay for you? You're not leaving anything unfinished that's going to cause a problem?"

Anya was resting her hand on a gravestone, ostensibly looking at the inscription. "There is always something unfinished." She shrugged. "Just a couple of weeks ago there was a new Englishman. It never stops."

Rob was beside her, pale in the overcast gray morning. The weather had changed. It had rained all night, and the dampness still coated the city. The cooler temperatures promised more precipitation.

"You've been asked to courier for a British guy?" Rob asked. "Has that ever happened to you before?"

"Yes. Meaning that, they come from all over. English is no different than anyone else. I get them because I speak the language."

"Was it the same setup as mine?" Rob asked. "Is he in our line of work? For MI6? Or is he just a sympathetic Englishman who works at a computer company or something?"

"I do not know exactly. I do not get told those details to do my job."

"Do you have a guess?"

Anya thought for a moment. "I think he is someone important. When Emil first found out this man was being assigned to our section, he could not wait to tell me. I do not know about MI6, but someone who is very important to the GDR."

"Have you been given anything to pass back?"

"No. This man has been working for the Stasi for some time. I don't know why they've changed his setup, but I suspect it's part of their ongoing loyalty test. I do not think he is a permanent resident here."

"What has he passed so far?" Rob asked.

"Nothing. He is slow to connect, and Emil has said nothing other than to maintain my usual level of availability."

He was silent for a moment. "So you'll be gone before you find out what he sells?"

Anya held her breath for a moment. "Will I?"

"Are you leaving with your daughter?"

"Yes." Anya tried to keep the criticism from her tone. "I cannot stay here."

"I know. I'd never ask you to. So yes, you'll be gone soon."

She looked at him then, not even trying to calm the pounding of her heart. "I hope so."

Rob took a cigarette out of his pocket and rolled it between his fingers. The silence lasted longer this time. "You know as well as I do. You plan as much as you can, plan for as many contingencies as you can handle, and then proceed as if it's all going to fall into place. There's no sense in thinking about your daughter in prison. Or yourself either."

Anya briefly closed her eyes. Yes, she would plan and prepare and not allow any emotions to clutter her thinking until she was holding her daughter safe and well in West Berlin.

"Have you worked out all the details?" she asked him.

He pulled an envelope out of his coat pocket and handed it to her. "It's all in there. I'm not sure how much you want to know about what's going to happen after you drop her off."

Anya clutched the envelope. "This is about my daughter. There is no plausible deniability here. Everything. I want to know everything."

"And so I've told you everything. The make of the car. The names of the guards who are supposed to be at the crossing. Even the names of the Americans who will be stationed at Checkpoint Charlie."

"Good."

"There's the address of where I want you to wait. Don't come to the checkpoint. I'll bring her to you. You both can stay at the apartment. In the kitchen are all the documents you'll both need to fly out of Tempelhof the next day."

Anya didn't know if she could control the emotions roiling around inside her. She wanted to. Knew it would be better. Would keep her head clear. Would better allow her to react and respond if she needed to. But it was hard. So hard, when it was so close. Her dream was taking shape into a concrete thing that she could almost touch. A concrete thing filled with so much danger and risk she wondered if she was a terrible mother. Was it right what she was doing? Putting her daughter in that kind of danger, risking her life—was it worth it? Because that was the calculation Anya had made, that risking death was better than growing up in East Germany. But as a mother, could she do it? Could she put her daughter in the compartment under a car and trust her to this man who spent his life manipulating people for information? It was breaking her apart.

"Okay. I will give her to you and come right back."

Rob put his hand on her arm. "That's really important, Valentina. You leave us and you cross right away. Before anyone notices that you two aren't coming back from your Sunday afternoon outing. Don't make any mistakes. Don't try to bring anything with you. You have to behave as if this was any other Sunday."

Anya knew he was right. She had prepared herself for many months. She had money hidden in West Berlin. The two mementos from her mother, the only things of sentimental value, she had long ago brought over and stored in the hair salon. Everything else she was prepared to leave. Everything else she had, on both sides of the Wall, could be replaced.

"I need to ask you—and nothing we have planned is going to change—but this British guy, do you meet him at the salon? Is the contact like your others?"

Anya nodded. "Yes. We have only met twice. He is booked to come in every two or three weeks. He will be back on Saturday. The day before…my daughter leaves." She held up the envelope. "The day before this happens."

"So you will be meeting him one more time." Rob looked thoughtful.

"Yes. As you say, nothing changes. Until the minute you have my daughter, I will not make a single alteration. If he shares anything, would you like to know?"

Anya noted the pained expression that came over his features.

"I suppose I should," he sighed. "After all, information is the currency of our business. And him being British, it doesn't seem like something I should ignore. If he works for their government, he could definitely be in a position to compromise American interests."

Anya didn't quite understand. She had always thought the Americans were in charge of the West, like the Soviets in the Eastern Bloc. To reveal a mole was no big deal. The Soviets often erred on the side of caution, imprisoning and killing whole swaths of people on the faintest of suspicions. In the Soviet Union, as in East Germany, everyone was always a suspect. To denounce a neighbor or colleague was a daily occurrence. "Would you not just report him?" She was curious.

"No. Accusing an ally of treason is not something you can do without some compelling evidence. He'd deny it, and I'd become an embarrassment. I'd end up in a desk job stateside, shuffling paper around. So, I'm going to have to determine, as best I can, who he is, what he has access to, and where his loyalties lie. And then get some kind of proof. And figure out how to do it all in a way that doesn't cause an incident. In short, it'll require hard work, and not what I planned on doing right now."

"But you cannot ignore it?"

Rob shook his head. "No one can afford treason, but there are a lot of people who just bury their heads in the sand because they don't want to admit they trusted and supported a traitor."

Anya was thoughtful. "Very different from the GDR then."

Rob's face broke into one of his rare smiles. "Yes, very different from the GDR. And one of our vulnerabilities that the Soviets take advantage of all the time."

It was the most he'd ever spoken to her at once. Something that wasn't transactional. Something that revealed who he was.

"His appointment is at nine a.m.," she said, "if you want to make a delivery to the shop. He will be in my usual chair."

"Yeah, I'll do that. In the meantime, go over the contents of that envelope and prepare your daughter. You haven't said anything, so I'm assuming she's not afraid of small spaces?"

"No," Anya confirmed. "She plays hide and seek with her friends in the building she lives in with my aunt. She is very good. Almost never gets caught because she can stay in her spot quietly for hours. Yours is an ideal plan for her."

"Will you tell her she's leaving Berlin?"

Anya bit her lip. "This I have struggled with. She doesn't know how terrible it is in the East, because it is not safe to tell her. The GDR indoctrination starts young, and when they question your loyalty, they punish everyone around you. So I cannot give her the chance to say good-bye. We have both always dreamed of going to Paris together. I will tell her I've arranged this special trip, but we must keep it a secret. It is only when we are on the plane that I will tell her we are not going back."

CHAPTER SEVEN

Jillian was worried she was becoming soft. She hadn't worked in weeks. Didn't need to be anywhere or do anything. She hated being idle. It made her fidgety and unsettled. Too much time contemplating life.

She wondered if she should take up a hobby. Poetry? Painting? She wasn't an artist of any sort. She'd much rather join a sports team, but given her covert mission, that wasn't in the cards. She'd been jogging a lot lately, just to stop the boredom from making her do something stupid.

Since it was raining, she was meeting Veronica in a café. Jillian pulled up her hood and hustled to get out of the weather. It looked like mist. It felt like mist. But it was drenching her. Her coat was soaked, and she was sure the water was going to start seeping through any minute.

Jillian opened the door to the café Veronica had pre-selected. It was warm and humid, the various wet clothes releasing a gross mix of smells. Jillian spotted Veronica immediately, so she walked over and sat in the chair opposite, shrugging out of her coat and adding to the puddles on the floor. Veronica had thoughtfully bought Jillian a coffee, which was still letting off steam. She took a tentative sip so she didn't burn her mouth.

"Have you been doing your homework?" Veronica asked.

Jillian had a moment of panic. Was she meant to have done something?

"I mean, have you sorted out your story yet?"

Oh, that. As if she'd been thinking about anything else. "No. It's not my forte. I've got a few different ones planned out, but without the details, I'm not sure how to frame it."

These public place conversations always felt a little bizarre. They had to sound innocuous to anyone who might overhear them but still get across the needed information in the most unambiguous way possible. Wouldn't want someone going after the wrong target or getting the wrong logistics for an op.

"I think we can begin to sort that out. There's nothing that's got me worried. If we can keep it fairly simple, like you think, then I'm comfortable."

"That's great news. I mean, really great."

"Yeah. I talked it out with Frank. Not that he knows much about my kind of work. But we looked over the reports that came back, and I've got a to-the-minute schedule on Sebastian for the past two weeks, and there's nothing concerning."

"So, he seems pretty average?"

"Except for that house. I still want to know what he's doing there. There's another guy who goes too, and I've done all the same leg work on him. Again, nothing flags. They're up to something, but at this point I think it's a point in our favor. You keep our secret, we'll keep yours."

"Except you don't know what that secret is," Jillian said.

"Yeah, well, I'm going to find out. Once you make contact, that's going to be our leverage."

Veronica was keeping her voice down, pitched low so it was drowned out by the clinking of cups and chatter of the other people who had packed into the café. But there was no mistaking her expression. She was clearly determined to figure out the mystery.

"Is it going to be my advisor, Gerhard, who does the ask?"

"No," Veronica said. "I don't think that's the right approach. We're aiming to limit curiosity, not encourage it. If Sebastian thinks something's up at the science institute, he'd have no reason to sit on it. There's no point in pretending this is normal scientific research. I think it needs to be you, and it needs to be simple. And you need to convince him that we're all working together."

Jillian felt the little tingle of nerves spring to life in her stomach. She preferred engineering. There was no ambiguity. Things either worked or they didn't. And, of course, a machine couldn't turn around and sell her out to the Soviets. Jillian's default was always to trust people. Strange, she knew, considering that she worked in intelligence. But in the kind of intelligence she did, trusting was pretty easy. SIGINT had a giant moat around it. If you had the clearance to pass the moat, you were trustworthy. In signals, it was that simple.

For human intelligence officers though, trust calculations were always dicier. Background checks and surveillance could only tell you so much. At some point, you just had to make the leap.

It had never appealed to her, HUMINT. Not once had she ever been envious of what Quentin did. She didn't want to live in the shadows, all human interaction being a series of calculations about the likelihood of any given person betraying you. SIGINT was like an alternate universe with a door where you could come and go at will. You spent all day with people you could trust then left that world to go home to your family and friends, who embodied a different kind of trust. The people issues in either world were the ones that everyone faced: annoying colleagues, whiny siblings, self-absorbed friends. But in neither sphere did she have to worry about getting compromised to the adversary by the people around her.

"I'll need your help," Jillian said. "I don't have much experience with approaches or figuring out what to tell people. In my work, I tell people whatever they need to know to get the job done or I say nothing at all."

Veronica studied her for a moment. "It's similar. Don't overthink it. You probably have a much higher intuition on the right thing to say than you know. Essentially, you're just going to tell him what he needs to know to get the job done. His job has two parts: flipping the switch and not telling anyone about it."

Yeah, it made sense now, in this café. But would it make sense when she was face to face with the guy?

"When I start talking to him, what are some red flags I should watch out for?" Jillian asked.

"It's a problem if he seems too eager. I'd say it's also an issue if he doesn't ask any questions. No one in this situation is going to say 'I'm happy to help' unless they're walking across the border right after. He should push back a little. He should have concerns. No one here is apolitical. He's going to want to make sure you're both roughly on the same side."

"Trust, but verify," Jillian said.

"Exactly. Then at some point, you just have to make the call. It's not a science. It's an art. If the outcome were entirely knowable, there wouldn't be any risk. Yet here we are."

Veronica pushed her coffee cup to the middle of the table and stood up. "Let's go. There's something I want to show you, and we can do a little role playing for your upcoming moment."

Jillian followed Veronica out of the café. The rain had let up somewhat. It was still misting but didn't seem to be as thick as before.

They walked to the S-Bahn station, Jillian deep in thought about how in the hell she was going to do this upcoming approach. She knew she needed to be herself. She'd learned that lesson already in the almost two years she'd been in West Berlin. She didn't want to flirt, because keeping up that pretense was something she wasn't prepared to do. Threatening was a nonstarter, as she didn't have anything to back it up, and it was out of character anyway. She wondered if this Sebastian guy was the type who got excited about how telephones worked. He did, after all, work for a national phone carrier. Maybe he was as fascinated by the wires and currents as she was. It would be an easy in if that was the case. Jillian could build the connection on shared geekiness.

"Do you have any idea why he's working at the telecom company?" Jillian asked Veronica as they rode the train west.

"No. Why?"

"I was just thinking," Jillian shrugged. "If he likes technology, then I might have an easier time building a rapport."

"If he likes technology, isn't he more likely to ask a lot of questions?"

"Yeah, but if we could focus him on the engineering, he might not wonder as much about the stuff going on behind it."

"I don't know," Veronica said. "I think it would be better if he wasn't interested at all."

"What are the chances of that?"

"Higher than you'd think. Most people aren't that curious. Offer to pay him fifty bucks a month and that might be enough."

"Is that an option?"

"Of course it is," said Veronica. "That's what we're trying to figure out. The minimum amount you can do to get what you need."

It was probably not a good sign that paying the guy off had never occurred to Jillian. It seemed obvious once Veronica said it. Hell, the history of espionage was littered with people who looked the other way for money.

"How will I know if he wants payment?"

Veronica smiled. "In my experience, those kinds of people will let you know."

"Should I show up with cash, just in case?"

"Yep. I'd say there's a good chance it's going to head in that direction. This guy, he's not rich. I don't think he's struggling, but some extra cash isn't something he's going to reject outright. Unless he's idealistic, but I haven't seen any sign of that."

Jillian was silent for the rest of the ride. She should've taken a drama elective in university. Improv or something.

Maybe she'd take a class when she got back on the off chance she was ever in a situation like this again.

They got off at the last stop in Spandau. Veronica led the way further west, winding through the streets until they could see the border Wall.

Jillian had only been here once before, and then only out of curiosity. The Berlin Wall was the name for the divider between East and West Berlin. Out here it was technically called the Outer Ring Wall, separating West Berlin from East Germany. But it was all connected. One continuous stretch of madness that encircled West Berlin. The original barbed wire had gone up on August 13, 1961, and the East Germans had been busy adding to it ever since. When you have to build a wall to keep people in, it's a prison, regardless of how much land it covers.

It was quiet out here. Although they were still in West Berlin, it was far from the city center. It was almost like being in the country. Small, detached single-family homes that had yard space lined the street. There was no car traffic, though the occasional bike whizzed past. The rain didn't seem as smothering here.

They turned onto a street, the end of which was cut off by the Wall.

"It's amazing," Veronica said. "Hearing about the Wall and seeing the Wall. Totally different. Like, this street probably used to continue out into the countryside. Now, you look out your window and see that massive concrete block instead of a field."

"I know. You really have to wonder what the East Germans are thinking."

They kept walking slowly. Jillian supposed the Wall was enough of an attraction that they didn't seem too out of place.

"It's that house there, the yellow one, on the right. That's the house that Sebastian goes to every evening."

Jillian looked at it as she turned back, as if taking in the whole street. There was nothing remarkable about the house. It was a one-story bungalow with wooden window frames. It looked like any other house on the street. They weren't carbon copies, but it fit in seamlessly.

"Do you notice anything?" Veronica said.

Jillian looked carefully at the house. It didn't look like anyone was home. The shutters were closed, no lights on behind them.

"Am I supposed to?"

"Do you see the sign on the front door?"

Jillian squinted. There was a small gray sign at about eye height affixed to the door, but she couldn't make out the details. "What does it say? No junk mail?"

"No," Veronica said. "It says 'Danger—No Entry.'"

"What?" asked Jillian, surprised.

"This is a hydro house."

Jillian took a good look at the house again. The fence that came around the sides, the lock on the gate. The fact that it was well maintained but didn't have any personal touches in the front yard. "Cool."

Veronica turned to look at her. "You know what that is?"

"Of course," said Jillian. "We have them in Canada too. They're like mini substations that are the final step in residential power delivery. In order not to piss off the neighbors, they're given the appearance of a regular house. They aren't supposed to stand out. But a warning on the door makes sense. A thief would probably kill himself and cause a local blackout."

"I didn't know that. Now that you explain it, I get it. But when I was first poking around and saw the sign, I thought it was something more sinister. Then I went to the city records office, and it was clearly marked on the city specs."

"For sure. It's part of the public infrastructure. Anyone in utilities, or road works—all sorts of people have to know the location of these houses."

"What goes on inside them?"

"Not much," Jillian said, "in terms of people. They'd be inspected and maintained, but no one works inside one of these on a daily basis."

"I thought as much. So, I've still got no idea what Sebastian does out here. Whatever it is, it happens inside the house. Which is crazy, as you tell me it's full of live electrical equipment."

Jillian looked around again. "Do you think it has something to do with the Wall?"

Veronica looked at her. "What do you mean?"

"Well, maybe it's a combination of being attached to the electrical grid and being close to the border Wall. There would be some underground connections to this place. Maybe he's trying to dig underneath the Wall."

Veronica's eyes widened. She turned back to the concrete façade looming over them, looking thoughtful. "Holy shit."

Jillian took out her camera, getting some shots of the Wall with the house on the side. They might come in useful, but also, she and Veronica needed to play tourist to avoid raising any suspicions.

"I didn't even think of that," Veronica continued.

"You just got here," Jillian said.

"Is it like a thing? Digging under the Wall?"

"Not anymore," Jillian replied. "But my friend James, he's always trying to educate me about the city and its history. When the Wall first went up, it was just a barbed wire fence. For the first year or so, there was a lot of tunneling, but mostly downtown, where there are buildings close to both sides. The Stasi got on it pretty quick, though, and either dismantled the buildings or put them under heavy surveillance. Then the Wall got wider and wider, with the watchtowers and no man's land, and tunneling became impossible."

"Impossible?"

"Okay, really really hard," Jillian said. "So hard it was impossible to do it while staying under the radar. The risk calculation became lopsided. Someone would figure out what you were doing long before you reached your destination."

"Because of the tools you'd need?"

"That, and the dirt that would pile up. It's pretty hard to hide metric cubes of soil. The Stasi make a point of looking into West Berlin at the border. A large mound of dirt piled up against the Wall wouldn't go unnoticed."

Veronica looked thoughtful. "There's no extra dirt in the backyard. And I've not seen him carry any away. He leaves as he shows up."

"And the house isn't big enough to have a basement that could handle everything you'd dig up to get underneath that," Jillian said, motioning to the looming Wall behind them.

Veronica gestured for them to walk, moving away from the house and the Wall, as if they'd got their pictures and were on to something else. "Still, I think you're right. The proximity to the Wall is interesting. It's worth considering how that plays into it."

"It could be surveillance. From inside the house."

"What could they be watching? Change of shift at the nearest tower?"

"Not your kind of surveillance," Jillian said. "My kind. If there are signals passing by, they could be collecting them. It's also possible we're overthinking it. Maybe his high school sweetheart is on the other side, and they're talking on a radio all evening."

"That would be sad."

"It happens. I was on one of those platforms once, you know, along the Wall where the West Berliners can climb up and look across. This man was there, eating peanuts, and having his weekly visit with his sister who lives in an apartment on the other side. A lot of people, families, lovers, got separated when that thing went up."

"Well," said Veronica, "if he's interested in the Wall, that's good for us. It makes him more likely to be on our side and against the GDR. From what I understand, if he wanted to go over, he could. The fact that whatever he's doing, he needs to hide it from them, is a good sign."

"It's not definite, but I get what you're saying. Playing the probabilities, it's unlikely that he's a Stasi plant working the Wall from the other side."

"So let's talk about what you're going to tell him."

Jilian's heart rate kicked up in immediate reaction. "Does it ever get less nerve-racking?"

"Not to my knowledge, but I haven't been doing this for very long."

"Where do you propose I start?"

"Let's role play it," Veronica said, "and see where we land."

CHAPTER EIGHT

Jillian smoothed down her skirt and fidgeted with her hair. She didn't really care how she looked, but the nerves translated to a desire to keep her hands busy.

You'd think, after almost two years doing various espionage-related activities that she wasn't trained for, she'd be more nonchalant about it all by now. But no luck. Machines were easy to figure out, people much less so. If she screwed up this meeting, she might be heading back to Ottawa sooner than planned.

Gerhard, her advisor at the science institute, had set up a coffee chat with his nephew Ernst and Sebastian, the man who'd replaced him at the Telekom. Ernst, the nephew, was understandably anxious about getting into trouble for what he'd already done. But out of loyalty to his uncle, and possibly because he sensed ignoring them wouldn't make this go away, he'd agreed to help. Sebastian, the new guy, was like the bottom of the ocean: a complete unknown. Sure, Veronica's intelligence had provided some contours, but speculation wasn't fact. Jillian had best guesses, not knowledge.

They were all meeting at a café close to campus. Jillian had talked with Gerhard about the story she'd planned with Veronica—leaving out the Veronica part, of course.

She and Veronica had debated whether to involve Gerhard at all. Would it help or hinder their success to have him there? In the end, they'd agreed that his presence legitimized the situation. In truth, he was deeply involved. He made it possible for Jillian to do the collection without raising any suspicions. Gerhard was the single most important ally in terms of maintaining her cover. Since he was West German and clearly trusted her, they'd hoped that trust would convince Sebastian to take a chance on her too.

So in the end she'd sat down with Gerhard and fine-tuned the story with him. It was starting to become a little confusing, but Jillian had a lot of practice compartmentalizing the details of her life. Gerhard and Veronica were in different buckets, that was all.

Arriving at the meet, Gerhard and Jillian took a seat inside, away from the open windows and the patrons crowding the patio. The interior was pleasantly cool and smelled of roasted coffee. Gerhard went to get them each a cup while Jillian sat and tried to still her fingers.

Two men arrived at the table at the same time Gerhard came back with the coffee. Introductions were made before Ernst went to order more coffee.

Gerhard began to exchange pleasantries with Sebastian, asking about where he lived, how long he'd been at the telecommunications company. It gave Jillian a chance to study him. He was around her age, maybe a little older, but no more than late twenties. Dark hair. Scruffy two-day beard. But what struck her most was the energy he radiated. He wasn't nervous or apprehensive. It felt more like he was completely in tune with his surroundings. And he smiled a lot.

Ernst returned, setting a cup down in front of Sebastian before taking a seat. He looked at his uncle expectantly, as if Gerhard had the magic needed to normalize this situation.

Gerhard began to tell Sebastian the story of the satellite feed. Using the details that he and Jillian had discussed, he tried to walk that fine line between generating understanding and minimizing suspicion.

Watching Sebastian, Jillian wasn't sure which way he was leaning. There was no outraged stomp out of the restaurant. No expression of distaste that floated across his features. Except for the occasional raised eyebrow, he listened without expression. It could go either way. He might be sympathetic. Or he might be waiting until he could get out of there to turn them all in to the authorities.

After Gerhard was finished speaking, Sebastian turned to Jillian. "You are the Canadian?"

"Yes," Jillian nodded, remembering to smile.

"And you need these satellite images?"

"Yes. Well, need might be a strong word. The institute is very interested in oceans. So, the fact that they're getting satellite pictures of them, that's the real need. Understanding the oceans could open up a lot of valuable scientific research possibilities. It's just that, when they collect those images, they collect a lot of other interesting pictures. When Gerhard saw their value, he knew we could help see that the information didn't go to waste."

Jillian felt her heart pounding. It was true-ish. True enough to be plausible. But if one factored in lies of omission, the story wasn't the truth at all.

"And who does it help, these images you collect?"

"It helps West Germany. It helps Canada. And anyone we're friends with."

Sebastian was silent for moment, sipping at his coffee and studying each of them in turn. "Because we are here, it means that the telecommunications company does not know about the box in their basement."

"That's right," Jillian replied. "To get permission would take forever. And it would expose what we are doing. I know it seems suspicious, but I can show you some images if you like." And she could—topographical images taken from outside the earth's atmosphere. They were beautiful in their way, but certainly not controversial. If it would help him feel better and not think to ask what else the satellite was sending, she'd show him all the images he wanted.

Sebastian smiled at her, holding her gaze with his. "Well, who am I to stand in the way of such important research?"

Her next argument died in her throat. It was too easy. He was agreeing too quickly. Jillian looked at Sebastian, at his smile and his eyes. He didn't believe them. She could tell. He somehow knew they were lying.

Sebastian turned back to Gerhard, "So, all I have to do is press this reset button when the red light begins to blink?"

"Yes," Gerhard nodded. "Ernst can show you. It happens only about every three months, depending on the amount of data it's had to buffer."

Sebastian threw another smile at Jillian. "I think I can handle that."

Oh no. Something's wrong. There's something else going on.

Jillian forced herself to project control, but inside her thoughts were racing. In her mind, the possible outcome had been a binary. Either Sebastian would buy their story and feel no qualms about helping, or he'd be suspicious and Jillian would be forced to pack up everything and go home. It had not occurred to her that he could be well aware they were lying and not care. For her, lying was a dealbreaker. This guy was obviously built differently.

She knew then that she needed to try to get to know him better. This wasn't a one-and-done. Click the reset button and forget until the red light started to flash again. She had to invest in this relationship, build a rapport or establish trust or whatever it was that people like Quentin and Veronica did.

She didn't know how to proceed. Didn't know which buttons to push. The guy was technically onside. He'd agreed to help them. He didn't need convincing. But something in his expression said he needed monitoring. Veronica had warned her. Too easy was a red flag. Too easy could mean he saw an opportunity to get in good with one of their adversaries.

Think, Jillian, think.

This was just another problem to take apart and examine. If he wasn't going to go running to the Stasi, and he wasn't going to congratulate them on saving the world, and he wasn't wanting a part of the action, then what could it be? What else could be going on?

She thought back to that house in Spandau, right up against the Wall. The house where he went every evening and spent a few hours, coming out again with nothing to show for it. A house full of electrical equipment, out at the edge of West Berlin civilization.

Was it possible that Sebastian just wanted to be rid of them? That he didn't want to draw their attention in any way?

"If you'd like to come by the institute this week, I can show you those images and the lab. It's pretty cool stuff."

Sebastian looked hesitant for a moment, then the smile came back. "That would be nice."

Jillian suddenly felt the urge to laugh. Nice it wasn't. Not for either of them.

"Okay, well, here's my number. Call me and I'll set up a tour."

What am I getting myself into?

CHAPTER NINE

Jillian waited at the door to her building. It was six o'clock, so the campus was quiet, with most students finished class for the day.

Small flutters of anxiety rocketed around her stomach at the idea of seeing Sebastian again. It was another role, another compartment. She knew that giving him a tour of the data lab so he could see where the researchers worked and learn about the different scientific goals they were pursuing was the right move. It gave the situation a deeper context to justify the subterfuge.

Jillian glanced at her watch. He was late. Six minutes. Not so much time, but she was already nervous enough. Adding impatience was causing her stomach to cramp.

Maybe he got stuck at work. Maybe his bus was late. Maybe he wasn't as anal about punctuality as she was.

Three minutes later, while she was trying to remember the twentieth digit of pi, Sebastian pulled up on his bike.

"Jillian," he said, her name coming out like a question, "you have been waiting long?"

"Yes, it's Jillian. And not too long. Maybe ten minutes or so."

He pushed his bike into the bike stand by the base of the stairs. "I am sorry to make you wait. But the evening is nice."

That was true. "Do you bike every day?" she asked.

"No. I am not one of those who will persevere through rain and wind. A fair-weather biker only." He grabbed his backpack and came to stand beside her. "I am very much looking forward to this tour. I have never been in the science institute."

"Where did you go to school?" Jillian asked, curious because it likely meant he didn't have a technical background.

"The Free University. For art history."

Before she could ask how that connected to telecommunications, he put his hand lightly on her forearm. "I should tell you first, I have pushed your reset button."

"Yeah," Jillian said, breaking into a grin. "I noticed almost right away. The machines hadn't been doing anything for weeks, so I was pretty excited when they started up again."

Excited wasn't strong enough a word. She'd felt the most crushing wave of relief to see the traffic start to come in. It meant that she could start copying again. Start sending information back home to .be decrypted and analyzed. Reports could start flowing. She could stay in West Berlin.

Sebastian smiled. "That is good. It's not such a hard job, and if it makes someone so happy."

Jillian studied him for a moment. Oh Lord, did she want it to be that simple, that he was just a nice guy who wasn't bothered about helping out. But given her experiences in this city so far, she knew she had to be skeptical.

"It does. It's so wonderful to be working again. But part of the reason I wanted to get together with you is to ask if you have any concerns. I mean, I know it's your job that might be at risk, and I wouldn't want you to feel like we were being dismissive of that. So, come in and I'll give you the tour. Then you can ask any questions you want."

She led him up the steps and into her building.

Given that she wasn't actually a student herself and that she purposefully avoided developing a relationship with anyone in the building lest it blow her cover, she had chosen a time for the tour when the lab would be almost empty. Sometimes a researcher or two worked late, but they usually at least left to get some dinner. Being the data lab for the school, it was shared by researchers from multiple departments. She wouldn't be expected to know everyone anyway, but Jillian hoped Sebastian wouldn't notice the lack of introductions.

She opened the data lab door. It was an impressive space, rows of machines whirring away, lights flickering here and there. Desks were arranged wherever they would fit, with computer monitors fighting for space with reams of printed sheets.

After walking around for a bit, with Jillian pointing out some of the latest technical acquisitions and explaining the use of a few of the machines, she turned to Sebastian. "What do you think?"

"I feel like I'm in a science fiction movie," he said.

"True," Jillian nodded.

Sebastian ran his fingers lightly over a printer. "I would like to understand how you do the research."

"What do you mean?" Jillian asked.

"Well, you said the satellite takes pictures of the oceans. And those pictures are what? How do they go on the cables? I would like to understand the mechanics."

"Oh," Jillian said, "it's pretty simple. The satellite changes the pictures into a digital code, which it then sends to a receiving box here on earth. The box separates the code by type and transmits it to the government department that owns the satellite. Because they tag the different kinds of images, we were able to code that box you reset to only pick up the ones we want. We then transfer them to a box in this room so they can be analyzed by the researchers."

"What is your role? Do you analyze the pictures?" Sebastian asked.

"That's Gerhard's department, Ernst's uncle. He's the topography expert. I'm one step before, focused on the production of the digital image."

"Are you a scientist?"

"No, an engineer. I build the systems that the scientists use."

"Ah." Sebastian was contemplative. "So the problem is not with the mechanics, it's with the politics."

Jillian's heart started to beat a little faster, but she focused on keeping the thread of her story. "Isn't it always? Earthquake science—seismology—is an exploding field. Ever since plate tectonics was proven almost ten years ago, everyone wants to make a name for themselves outlining the next impact of the theory."

"And is that what you want to do?" Sebastian asked.

"Make a name for myself? No, not really. The engineers rarely get their names on the papers anyway. Mostly I just want to work, so I go where the need is. And I'm a really good engineer," she smiled at him.

"Science is so interesting," Sebastian said. "So many studies, so many things I didn't even know about the world."

"How did you go from art history to telecommunications? Did you study it after?"

"No," he laughed. "After finishing art history and wandering the world for a while, I needed a job. A friend of the family runs the department. My father is a lawyer, and my mother is a doctor. Both have helped many people, and both have a lot of friends. I don't do anything technical. Most days I inspect the cables under the city to make sure a rat hasn't chewed on them."

Jillian liked his laugh. It was like warm caramel and made his eyes crinkle at the corners.

"So, it's not your dream?"

"Not at all. I have work, so my parents focus on something else for a while. But," he sighed, "it will just be a short while. Once they get used to me having a job, it will be pressure to get a better job. A manager. Run the division. Something they can be proud of."

"I'm sorry for you," Jillian said. "That doesn't sound like a good way to live."

"But there is reason for optimism," he grinned. "I have two older brothers who like to compete for my parents' attention. One has just now trained to become a surgeon. The other one will probably go for another accomplishment. My dream is that they compete with each other forever so my parents don't think to turn their eyes back to me. I take it this is a problem you don't have."

"No," Jillian returned his smile. "I'm an only child, and my father's an engineer as well. It all fits pretty nicely."

"Well, Jillian, how would you like to go find some strudel and talk of ideas that are more interesting? More on my family will only cause me indigestion."

Jillian laughed. "Sure."

They left the lab, Jillian making sure the door was locked behind her, and made their way to the exit. "Are you from Berlin?"

"Yes, I was born here. My parents moved here right after the war. It was a place where there was a need for people with their skills. Right through the fifties my mother worked at a hospital in the East as well, but they only ever lived on this side. They have no time for the Soviets or what they're trying to do in Eastern Europe."

"And you?" Jillian asked. "What do you think of the Soviets?"

"I think the American pursuit of money is equally tragic. But I cannot abide by any government that tries to ban books and music and art and anything else they don't want to hear. It is impossible for me to imagine following a system that doesn't see the beauty of 'Bohemian Rhapsody.' So, I suppose I throw my lot in with the rest of the West Germans, hoping someone figures out a better way to live than any of the choices we have now."

"You're a poet," Jillian said as the emerged into the early twilight of the West Berlin evening.

Sebastian picked up his bike and walked it beside her as the made their way off the campus. "More a dreamer. Life is a beautiful mystery to be experienced and appreciated before the inevitable end. I do not understand so much the constant desire for power that seems to grip so many in the world."

"No plans for world domination, I take it?" Jillian asked.

"I have only a mission to bring beauty to the world," Sebastian said. "But it is one I take very seriously."

Jillian thought that sounded like a fine goal. It wasn't something she'd ever thought of before. In her world it was ideology and morals. People needed to be free and safe. They needed to be able to make choices and not worry about getting shot because they didn't agree with their boss. But, she supposed, freedom also meant the freedom to create without censorship. Even though she'd never thought of art as a right, Jillian reflected that maybe her and Sebastian's goals weren't so far apart.

"My friend James is on the British army radio," she said. "His show is all rock and roll. But when I talk to him about it, like why he doesn't broadcast talk shows full of serious analysis, he says rock and roll is as serious as it gets. Music can inspire people and change their minds in a way that all the words in the world never can. He says that music speaks to us on an elemental level, that its rhythm reminds us that we're alive. He claims there is no force in the world as powerful."

"You are friends with Jamie Murphy?" Sebastian asked, eyes widening in surprise and pleasure. "I listen to his show every day."

"Oh," Jillian smiled, "I didn't even think. But of course you might. A lot of people in the city listen to him."

"Yes, he is very good. What he says to the East Germans, how he pulls from song lyrics. It is smart. I do not have quite the same goals, but I can appreciate someone else who recognizes the value of art."

Jillian liked Sebastian. She hoped she wasn't being naive, but he didn't seem suspicious, like he was spying for the Stasi. Jillian didn't get the feeling that he was cataloging everything she said, like he was trying to build a profile or was going to report it somewhere. She would still be cautious, but no more than she was every day in West Berlin.

"What's your plan? For bringing beauty into the world."

Sebastian's eyes lit up. "I have many plans, but my latest one, I would be honored if you would come. It is an art show."

"Like at a gallery?" Jillian asked. She wasn't sure of the last time she went to something like that.

"No. There is no beauty in a gallery where there is a price tag beside everything. The beauty of art is the experience of art. It is at a warehouse. In Spandau. I will give you the address and you will come on Saturday? It is one night only."

"Well then, I'd love to."

"It is a date," Sebastian said, stopping to write on a piece of paper he'd pulled from his backpack. "If you want to bring your friend Jamie Murphy, he is welcome too."

Jillian wondered. No question James was in a bit of a rut, what with his girlfriend Jasminka away in Leningrad researching a story and him irritated with himself for that making a difference in his life. Plus, he was always on about experiencing the real Berlin and how important it was to get out and be with the locals, to remember this was a real place full of real people trying to make the best lives they could. It wasn't all spies and cover stories and clandestine activities. But it would mean mixing compartments, and she wasn't so sure about that.

"I'll ask him, for sure," Jillian said. "He may have to work, but it does sound like something he'd be interested in."

"Wonderful," Sebastian replied. "Here they have great strudel. Can I buy you one before we part?"

Jillian could never say no to strudel. "Absolutely."

Jillian chose blaubeeren, and they came out of the shop munching on the delicious, flaky pastry.

"I am happy we got together today, Jillian. I think it is the beginning of a good friendship. I look forward to showing you my art next weekend."

Jillian smiled at him. "And I look forward to seeing beauty in the world."

Jillian returned to her apartment. After the strudel with Sebastian, she'd wandered for a bit, as usual amazed at how big West Berlin was. There were no shortages of interesting streets, nooks and crannies filled with both memories and dreams of the future.

Perhaps the conversation with Sebastian was coloring her mood. It had been unique. Jillian didn't often talk about art or the ephemeral. She didn't think she'd ever met someone before who felt it a duty to bring more beauty into the world. There was a magic to the sentiment that was almost contagious.

As if, in that moment, experiencing beauty was the only thing that mattered.

Veronica fell into step beside her as she neared her apartment. It reminded Jillian of the early days with Quentin, when he would appear unexpectedly, finding opportunities to talk that wouldn't compromise his cover or hers.

"How long have you been waiting for me to show up?" Jillian asked.

"Longer than I'd planned. Something happen?"

"No. It was just an interesting conversation, so I decided to walk a bit longer to think."

"Now I'm curious," Veronica said.

"Right. You were curious anyway; otherwise, you wouldn't be here."

"True," Veronica smiled. "Extra curious then."

"Sebastian. He's…interesting."

"That's not a great word," Veronica said. "Interesting good or interesting bad?"

"Let's say interesting good," Jillian replied. "But really, not the kind of guy you probably meet on a regular basis. He seems grounded enough. Normal, if high-achieving, family. Comfortable with himself. But he says it's his mission to bring beauty into the world."

Veronica raised a brow. "What does that mean?"

Jillian shook her head. "I don't know. He's an artist, he says, but not like in galleries. It's something different, art as life or something. Like the experience is the only thing that matters. Not money or recognition. Giving people beauty is the goal of art, according to him."

"What kind of art does he do?"

"I'm not sure. He invited me to a show on Saturday. At a warehouse in Spandau."

"Where the house is," said Veronica.

"Well, Spandau is big. The show isn't at the house, but it's in the same general region, yeah."

"You're going."

"I think so," Jillian said, "unless I'm reading the situation wrong. It'll be a great opportunity to get to know him better. Isn't there something about art being a window into the soul?"

"I think it's true that people reveal themselves in their art. Their hopes and fears. Often artists use their art to make sense of the world."

"Something you know from experience?" Jillian asked.

"No. I majored in psychology and have never picked up a paint brush. But my grandmother, she believes that to understand a culture you pay attention to their art. People who create reveal more than they realize in their creations."

"I imagine she's right. Our ancestors started painting and storytelling before we were technically homo sapiens."

"We could be getting off track. He could plan to throw paint at the Wall or play some screechy instrument. Something that will tell us nothing concrete."

"Well, at least I'll get a sense of who he is. If it's a room filled with pig blood and roadkill, I'll stick to daytime meets in public places."

Veronica smiled, "Hey, all those pig guts could represent East German socialism. You never know."

"Yeah, I'll make sure I ask for the interpretive pamphlet when I get there," Jillian said.

"I'd like to go with you."

"Really? Wouldn't that be breaking protocol or something?"

"Well, my job is to keep your operation safe, so protocol is blurry. You said it's a one-night-only thing, and it's a significant opportunity to gather information that I haven't been able to get anywhere else. So yeah, I want to go."

"Sebastian wanted me to invite my friend James. I don't know if Frank told you about him."

"His nephew, right? The Scottish guy?"

"Yeah. He's on the radio here, and Sebastian's heard his show. It's music, and popular, so not surprising. It came across as being about a fellow lover of art."

"Do you want him to go?" Veronica asked.

"Normally yes, because I don't get to surprise him often in our relationship. He's been posted here a few times and loves it, and he spends his time making sure he's discovered every detail. This one-off art event would surprise him. But it's not a real thing. It's my job, and I work hard to keep James away from as much of it as I can."

"At this point it's an op, and realistically, it's got to stay that way. It's safer for everyone if they stay in their boxes."

"Just so you know," Jillian said, "these ops have a way of leaking out of their constraints over here. If I get into trouble, James is one of two people I can ask for help."

"Well then, I'll come on Saturday, and we'll do our best to make sure this isn't one of those that end up going sideways."

Jillian hoped Veronica could manage that, but she wasn't holding her breath. Berlin had taught her that there were no guarantees.

91

CHAPTER TEN

It was time for Lena to get into the compartment. Anya's throat was so tight she could hardly breathe. Tears she hadn't shed in years were piling up behind her eyes. She desperately hoped this would not be the last time she saw her daughter.

She pulled Lena onto her lap and lifted the backseat in the car—Rob's car, which was idling on an East Berlin side street. Trying not to attract attention. Underneath the seat was the back of the trunk. Wedged between the end of the trunk and who knows what machinery was the small compartment that would take her daughter to freedom.

"Remember to not be scared," Anya said, knowing time was short. They would not stay unnoticed for long. "It is just like those tiny spaces you crawl into playing hide and seek. It will only be for a short drive. When the car stops the second time, you can come out. Just tell yourself the story of *The Nutcracker*, and before you get to the end, this will be all over."

Anya thought her heart might break as she helped her daughter into the compartment. She took in every detail of Lena's face: her long eyelashes, the two small freckles on one cheek, her beautiful eyes, and her serious expression. Anya fought down the desire to pull her daughter close, hugging her and running back to the apartment where Lena would be safe, if not free.

"I can do this, Mama. I can do anything to go to Paris."

Anya kissed her daughter's soft skin before closing the lid. Anya didn't let her fear show in her expression, but she thought that it might stop her heart.

Anya had prepared Lena as best she could. The next twenty minutes would determine if she'd done the job well enough.

They had spent their Sunday as always. Anya had come over on the first train. A quick exchange with Emil, and then she had gone to her aunt's. They'd all had breakfast together, eating toast spread thick with strawberry jam. Lena had put on her favorite blue dress, and Anya had braided a ribbon in her hair. She and Lena went for a long walk around the city, stopping in parks and making up stories about the people they saw. They had lunch at their favorite restaurant, not because the food was good, but because of the happy memories. Then it was off to their friend Heidi's for cake and tea and play. Anya had to summon up all the concentration she possessed to carry on a normal conversation. Humming through her mind was the apprehension and excitement. Within hours she might finally be free with her daughter.

After Heidi's they usually went for a walk along the Spree. It was their day, their only day together. As best she could, Anya always tried to keep her job out of this day. She wanted Lena to have one day to breathe freely, away from the propaganda of the education system or the suffocating youth clubs that pressured kids from birth to buy into the myth of the GDR. Anya had always kept these days free of politics, free of even talking about the country. She and her daughter talked about fairy tales and cities they'd like to visit and what they should bake next.

Today Anya turned off the Spree earlier than usual, not that they retraced the same steps every week. The path varied a little. They still had that freedom.

No one would notice they were gone until much later. Frau Lanin would likely come by her aunt's after dinner with her usual complaints about her foot and her neighbor's cats. The two older women would commiserate. It would be unusual that Anya and Lena weren't there, as Anya tried always to spend Sunday evening snuggling with her daughter before taking the last train out of Friedrichstrasse. It was the only time of the week she got to hold her.

The good Frau might start asking around, asking people to keep an eye out.

It was possible the flag wouldn't be raised until the morning when her aunt got up and realized they hadn't come home. Or when Lena did not go to school, someone would come around to question why. Her aunt might try to cover for them, but if more neighbors were looking for them this evening, then the watch would come poking around earlier.

Her aunt would be worried at first that something had happened to her and Lena, but that wouldn't last long. Nothing bad happened in the GDR, so if they were in trouble, it was their own fault.

Anya hoped it wouldn't matter. By the time anyone became suspicious, she would be safe with Lena in West Berlin.

She'd kept her pace normal, talking with her daughter about the penguins she wanted to see in Antarctica one day. Anya knew it was important not to rush. She had to give the impression that this walk on this day was like any other. As they neared the rendezvous with Rob, Anya started the final preparations.

Turning to her daughter, she said, "My darling, I have a wonderful surprise for you. We are going to Paris for a vacation."

Lena's eyes grew wide. "Really, Mama? To see the Eiffel Tower and Hall of Mirrors?"

"And to have pain au chocolat for breakfast every day."

Lena giggled.

"But, sweetheart, we have to play a little trick to get to Paris. The only way we can get there is to cross to the other side of Berlin."

Lena's face froze. Just eight years old, and the idea of crossing the Wall scared her. "But Mama, we are not supposed to cross. It is a bad place on the other side."

"We can. I have to live over there, and I cross every week to visit you. We have special permission. But we must hide a little, because we don't want to make Heidi and your friends envious. Not everyone can go to Paris. We are allowed because I have done such good work for our leaders that they gave me a reward."

"You are very good, Mama. You help catch a lot of bad people."

"Exactly, sweetheart. So we get to spend three days in Paris. My boss has provided us a special car. There is a compartment under the seat. It is the perfect size for you. It will be like the hide and go seek you play with Fritz and Wally. You will hide in there so one sees you. The car will take you to an apartment where I will be waiting. Tomorrow we get on the plane and go on our adventure to Paris."

Anya saw the hesitancy in her daughter's eyes. She was suspicious.

A surge of anger welled up. This is what the great program of the GDR did—made children distrust their own parents. Made them afraid to leave. The Wall was as much psychological as physical for those who had never known anything else.

Anya realized that it had to be now. Any longer in the GDR and her daughter might refuse to go with her.

"I know you are worried. But I promise it will all be okay. We will spend our three days in Paris, and then you can come back and tell your friends all about the baguettes and the dancing show I am taking you to."

A wave of relief hit her as her daughter's expression turned dreamy. "At the Lido, Mama?"

"Yes, sweetheart, at the Lido. We will have sparkling juice and macarons and watch the beautiful dancers."

Anya had been building the dream of Paris for a long time. She and Lena had pored over books from the golden age of the City of Lights. They had watched whatever movies they could get their hands on that featured the city. Anya had given Lena a beret on her last birthday. She felt a little guilty about manipulating her daughter in this way, but they would get to Paris eventually. Anya would make all these dreams come true, so in this way it wasn't a lie.

"But to get to Paris, we must cross the Wall. Remember, we do not want to make anyone envious. The government cannot send everyone on a vacation as a special treat. So when we get to the car, you must climb into the box under the seat. I will close it behind you. Then I want you to tell yourself the story of *The Nutcracker*, just like we read in the winter. About Clara in the land of snow and the Mouse King. Work hard to remember every detail so when we go to see the ballet in Paris too, you will know the story."

"Oh, Mama," Lena squealed, "*The Nutcracker* too?"

"Of course, my sweet. It is not every day that we get to spend time in Paris. These special trips are very rare, and we must make the most of it. But you must stay very quiet. And remember, the car will stop twice. On the second stop the box will open, and you will climb out and get ready for Paris."

Now the moment was here. Lena was in the compartment, and Anya's path would be decided by the actions in the next short while. She hoped that the dream of Paris, of the shows and the dresses and the magic, would be enough to see Lena through the next twenty minutes.

Anya didn't say anything to Rob. Didn't introduce him to Lena. He was just the driver provided to start their adventure. She closed the box, her dreams of the future along with it, stepped from the car, and closed the door behind her. She didn't watch it drive off, just started walking to the crossing. She would not think about what could go wrong. About Rob getting stopped. About Lena panicking and being discovered. The lives that would be ruined should everything not go perfectly. Instead, she fixed her jacket as she walked, willing herself to get back into character.

She had made this crossing on Sunday evening many times. Emil often sent her back with an urgent message, something that could not wait. As much as Anya was protective of her Sundays and tried to wait until the last train, her position with the Stasi meant she was always available.

She had never been grateful for that unpredictability until this moment. Her aunt would assume she was still out with her daughter, but the border guards wouldn't question her actions. No one would think anything was out of the ordinary until it was much too late.

Anya pulled out her papers, getting ready to cross out of East Berlin for the last time.

Eighteen minutes into the longest twenty minutes of her life, Anya's heart exploded in her chest as the apartment door opened and her daughter raced in. She embraced her in a hug that dissipated eight years of desperation and worry and despair that she would ever get out from under the psychological pressure that was living in East Germany. Anya knew the strain would never fully go away, that she had been marked by those years in a way that no amount of freedom would ever erase. But she hoped that her daughter would uproot her beginnings and replace them with all they imagined life in the West had to offer. All those fuzzy ideas would become solid now that they were both free to explore the world and say what they thought and not be afraid.

Rob had closed the door but hung back. He looked relieved, like a burden had been lifted from his heart. Anya wondered why he had done it. Smuggling out a child was more reward than the typical double agent received. Perhaps now they were all together in the West, she might learn this about him. Whatever his reasons, her trust in him had not been misplaced. He had given her the greatest gift, the most monumental present that she would ever receive.

She was sorry that she had one more favor to ask of him.

"Lena, my darling," Anya said, "there are books in the bedroom and a new doll. Why don't you go look while I speak to this man for a moment?"

Lena ran off happily, no doubt invigorated by her adventure. Anya was almost sad for the day when her daughter would realize what she'd done. Anya hoped that Lena would be able to forgive her. That the life they would build in the West would compensate for the risk they took to live it.

"The tickets are in the top drawer over there," Rob said, pointing to the right of the stove. "You're both booked on the two p.m. flight to Frankfurt out of Tempelhof tomorrow, then you'll connect on to Paris. I hope you and your daughter are happy, Valentina."

Anya sighed. It was, unfortunately, not going to be that easy. "We will not be able to use those tickets," she said.

Confusion settled on Rob's face. "Why not?"

"Because of the names."

"You have a passport for Valentina, don't you?"

So, he knew Valentina wasn't her real name, yet he had never pressed her to reveal any more. She wondered, not for the first time, how he chose his boundaries.

"It is not me that is the problem. It is Lena. The West Germans, well, even they will not let her fly out of the city."

The confusion on his face was hardening into trepidation. "Why would the West German border security care about a little girl with an East German passport? Your passport is West German, isn't it? You're her mother. They're not going to care about debriefing an eight-year-old."

"They might."

Rob just waited. Anya took a deep breath and pursed her lips. "They might when they figure out who her father is. Which they will, because he will pull on every connection he has to make sure we're found."

"Who is her father?" Rob asked in a voice that said he didn't really want to know.

"Michael Polenz."

"Jesus Christ, Valentina. You didn't think to tell me this before now?"

"You wouldn't have helped me."

No denial intruded on the silence.

"So, you see, I need more time here to procure us new identities."

Rob exploded, throwing up his hands. "What does that have to do with me? I've already smuggled the daughter of the chief Stasi interrogator out of East Berlin. I think that's enough."

"It is. If that's all you can do, it is enough."

Rob looked at her, panic in his eyes, then started pacing around the apartment.

Anya watched him take a few steps. "I know that you have just done something for me that almost no one else would risk. And your reasons, they are not of the usual kind, like love or family, which makes me even more grateful."

He stopped and looked at her, one brow raised. "What do you want, Valentina?"

"I need your help."

He shook his head. Dismay, frustration—to Anya's eyes it was both. "You're like one of those Russian nesting dolls," he said, "eight different identities layered in one package."

Anya crossed to him and put her hand on his arm. "What you have done, I do not have the words to tell you how much it means to me. One day, when Lena is grown and doesn't remember what it's like to be locked up, I will tell her that any life she has is because of a smart, brave, generous American. I do need your help, but I understand. I do not expect you to do this for free. I have information that I can give you about the Stasi networks here in this city. Their targets. Their agents. And the others on their payroll."

He was quiet for a long time. "You aren't just a courier, are you, Valentina?"

"It's Anya. And no, I'm not just a courier."

"What do you want?"

"Time. A safe space for my daughter. And to break my ex-husband until he throws himself into the Spree. I want to leave here free in every sense of the word."

"Not asking for much, are you?"

"It will be good for you too, I promise. But just you. I will not go into your station or be subject to American debriefs. I have much that is valuable that I can share, but I do not become one of your assets. When I have achieved my goals, I will leave here with my daughter, and it will be no one's business where we go."

"Right," he sighed. "I guess this is a new phase of our relationship. You can call me Quentin. It's a better name for you to use now. And you'll have to deliver something spectacular in exchange for all the help you're going to need. In the meantime, let's start with something specific."

"Anything," Anya said. "You have given me my daughter. I will give you anything in return."

"That British guy you pointed out to me. I want more info about what his game is, and I want to know who his connections are."

"I can do that. I know who his new courier will be. I will try to find out what he shares."

Quentin stared at her. "Why do I get the impression you're a dangerous woman, Anya?"

"Everyone is dangerous when they are cornered, and I've been cornered for a long time. But you have nothing to fear from me. You have earned my loyalty."

"Okay. You'll be safe here tonight. I'll be back in the morning after I figure out somewhere we can put you two."

Anya let her mouth tick into a small smile. "Wir sehen uns."

"Yes. We will see each other." He gave her a nod and left, closing the door softly behind him.

Anya took a deep breath. That could have gone worse. But she was confident she'd chosen her ally well. He knew how to play the game. Almost as well as she did.

CHAPTER ELEVEN

"Here for my company or free beer?" James said, closing the door behind Quentin.

"Both."

"Want a Radegast or a Tennent's?"

"Both," said Quentin, crossing into the living room. "A beer or ten is what I need right now."

"Ah, rough day at the office?"

"Yeah, one of those," Quentin scowled.

James thought Quentin looked a mite angry over a regular day in the life of a spy, but he didn't press. Instead he opened a couple bottles of Tennent's, gave one to the spook, and sat in the chair opposite.

They drank their beers for a while. James appreciated how Quentin was comfortable in silence. He never felt the need to fill it with mindless chatter. James supposed it came with the job. Keeping your own counsel and all of that. Still, it was nice to drink with someone once in a while without having to talk.

"I need a favor from you," Quentin said, halfway into his beer.

"Why do I get the impression you aren't after a restaurant recommendation for an evening out with Jillian?"

"Because I don't live that kind of life."

"Nae, you don't. Well, what is it then?"

"I need you to let someone stay in your apartment for a while."

"You what?" James couldn't be hearing right.

"I don't have anywhere else to put her right now. And, well, I need some time to think."

"Who?" James asked.

"A woman who left GDR today," Quentin said. "She and her eight-year-old daughter."

Ah, Christ. It had been on the tip of his tongue to tell Quentin to sod off and spend some CIA money on a hotel. But now there was a kid involved. "So that's it then. You just drop 'eight-year-old' and I'm supposed to go all soft and not ask any questions?"

"What do you want to know?"

Right. The thing was, James wasn't sure what he did want to know. Anything related to Quentin's job, it was dangerous to be too informed. "Who is she? The mum."

"A Stasi courier who agreed to go double agent for me in exchange for getting her daughter out. Which I did, earlier today. Now they need somewhere to stay for a while, which I didn't expect, and so I'm asking you."

James was silent for a long stretch.

"I don't buy it. You're always so careful to not say any damn thing about your job. Which, by the way, I'm quite appreciative of. Now, you're asking me to host a former resident of the GDR whose daughter you busted out today. We've gone from zero to one hundred, and it doesn't feel right."

"It isn't right," Quentin sighed. "Nothing about this fucking day has been right."

"Except getting the daughter out?"

"Yeah, except that."

"Why me? You always seem to have enough resources for whatever you need to do. All those times you helped Jillian. Don't you have a safe house or whatever you lot call them?"

"Anya—that's her name, by the way—she's refusing to become a CIA asset. She's not defecting in exchange for a new life," Quentin said. "Our continued relationship is conditional on it being off books."

"And you're agreeing to her demands?"

"She's not who I thought she was. She might have access to information that could give us huge insight into the whole Stasi system. I have to check it out."

"Maybe I'm not understanding. Why is she different?" James asked.

"Most people who defect, they want to be set up in a new life in the US. They want a chance at the American dream and hopefully to be well hidden from the assassins the Soviets will send after them. Yes, they hate their Soviet masters and have a crisis of conscience, but since they often come with nothing except what they know, they exchange that knowledge for a new life stateside. The CIA is well set up to deal with that scenario.

"Anya, however, has no interest in becoming an American citizen. Her goals lie elsewhere, and I don't have any real idea what they are. But she doesn't want what the CIA can give her. She just wants my help for a brief amount of time. That predominantly means keeping her daughter safe in West Berlin while her mom goes about her business. In exchange for this help, she has promised information gold.

"So you see my dilemma. I go official, she disappears. I get the feeling that she's got options. I, on the other hand, have very few. If it was just Anya, it would be different. But there is exactly no one else in this city I'd trust with the daughter. Except Jillian, and I think you agree with me that she's an even worse idea than you."

James could think of a dozen reasons about why this was a bad idea all around, but the truth was, they all stemmed from the fact that he didn't want to do it. He didn't want to be involved at all. This cloak-and-dagger stuff was completely foreign to him. He thought most of MI6 was useless, an estimation that applied to their counterparts as well, and he'd not experienced anything since meeting Quentin that had changed his mind.

However, he liked Quentin. Underneath it all he was a good guy, someone trying to make up for past mistakes by doing the right thing. James had seen Quentin take risks for Jillian, and knew that if he were in trouble, Quentin would probably do the same for him.

He'd never asked anything of James before, except a quiet place to have a beer once in a while. James thought that maybe it would be the right thing to do, helping Quentin out.

"It's not dangerous, is it? She's not going to kill me in my sleep?"

"I'm not vouching for this woman. She did an amazing job convincing me she was just a courier. I checked her out, and nothing came up. No indicators that she might have the keys to the whole Stasi bureaucracy. So, yeah, she might kill you while you're snoring away. But I got her daughter out today, and I have a feeling that's the most valuable gift anyone could give her. So she won't want to upset me, and you're my friend. That's all the protection I can offer you."

Not exactly reassuring, but at least it was honest. "Right, then, what do I have to do?"

"Nothing, except let them stay here. Honestly, Anya is an enigma. Her only vulnerability is her daughter, Lena. Does the idea of a kid make you nervous?"

"Not at all. I've got loads of nieces and nephews. No one is a bigger draw at family get-togethers than Uncle Jamie."

"Seriously?"

"Can't picture it, can you? But aye, I'm the number one request for a Christmas guest. Among the younger set, I'm a proper celebrity when I go back to Inverness."

Quentin let out one of his rare smiles. "This is still going to be a nightmare, but maybe less than I thought."

"Happy I could make your day better, then."

"Marginally. But I'll take what I can get."

"Good. So, when can I expect these houseguests to show up?" James asked.

"Tomorrow morning. Early. What time do you leave for work?"

"Half nine."

"Okay," Quentin said. "It'll be before then."

"And I'm just supposed to be fine with leaving two strangers in my flat all day?"

"On the bad side, Anya's definitely going to go through all your stuff. Anything you don't want her to see, take it to work with you."

"I'll not be bringing my entire boxer drawer to the base tomorrow," James said.

"If that's all you have to worry about, you'll be fine. She'll probably find you charming."

"Just what I need," James replied. "Is there a good side, then?

"Yeah," said Quentin, "when she leaves here, you're never going to see her again."

CHAPTER TWELVE

"We're not walking, are we?"

"God, no. It'd take forever. It's not at the Wall where we were the other day, but close enough."

"What's the address?"

Jillian looked down, consulting her quickly scribbled note from Sebastian. "In an old building by the Zitadelle. We're meant to take the S-Bahn line right to the end then walk. He said something about following the blue hands. We'll see when we get there."

"This sounds a bit mysterious for an art show."

"I don't think it's going to be anything typical. Like I said, Sebastian said it's his mission in life to bring beautiful things into the world. I have a feeling this is going to be an idea of beauty that we've never seen before."

Veronica and Jillian got on the S3 toward Spandau. They settled into their seats on the train, each caught up in their own thoughts. Jillian didn't know what to expect from today.

She hoped it was something fun. What she did in West Berlin, fun didn't often enter into it. It would be nice to experience something different, frivolous, entertaining. An evening where she didn't have to worry about blowing her cover or being too on her guard.

Getting off at the end of the line, they crossed through Old Spandau as they made their way to the Zitadelle. They walked down Judenstrasse, the window boxes still spilling flowers. They were well into autumn now, and Jillian knew those balkonpflanzen couldn't last much longer. It was cute here. The mostly three-story buildings were painted different colors, and the cinema on the corner was advertising a Marlene Deitrich film festival on the coming weekend.

Soon they found themselves approaching the Zitadelle. It was basically on an island, its old red-brick buildings glowing in the evening light.

"See any blue hands yet?" Veronica asked.

Jillian looked around, not seeing anything that might fit the description. "No, but Sebastian said I couldn't miss them. And we can't be the only people coming from the S-Bahn."

Veronica looked around for a moment. "I can't imagine this show will be right in the Zitadelle, seeing as it's a historical monument. But those buildings there," she said, pointing to a line of buildings that were attached to the fortress but distinct, "they might be a place for an art show."

It sounded reasonable to Jillian. "It's worth a try, I guess," she said.

They began to walk along the outbuildings. The early October evening was warm, and the walk was pleasant. Jillian had never been here before and was enjoying the new scenery. It never ceased to amaze her how much was packed within the Walls that surrounded West Berlin. Before she came over, she had assumed the city would start to feel oppressive after a while. But after almost two years, she knew it would take a lot longer to feel confined. West Berlin was actually quite a large area with lots to explore. Plus, its lack of a grid system and its twisty roads made it extra interesting to walk around. It was easy to get confused about how streets connected and even what direction you were going in.

"Oh look," she said, pointing at a rock at the base of one of the buildings. "A blue hand."

Jillian stepped closer to the rock. The blue handprint was clear against the gray stone, and there was a helpful little arrow, also in blue, under the palm. "This arrow is pointing down that alley."

Veronica craned her neck. "Looks like your average alley in the middle of old historical nowhere."

Jillian smiled. "Yeah, sounds normal. Shall we follow the arrow?"

"We've come this far."

"You have to admit, it's pretty complicated for a setup."

"My ESP isn't kicking it," Veronica said, "so I guess we're fine."

Jillian didn't know whether to take Veronica seriously. "Is your ESP usually reliable in empty alleys? So you'll know if you might get thrown into a van and interrogated for ten years?"

"Hell yeah. All part of the training of Canada's finest."

Now Jillian laughed. "Wow. You got such different training than I did. Okay, let's go."

They made their way down the alley. Every so often there was a blue handprint reassuring them they were headed in the right direction. After a couple of turns, the hands directed them into a doorway covered with strings of shimmery gold beads.

"Definitely not part of the original infrastructure," Veronica said.

They found themselves in a dark space, maybe a hallway. Jillian could see the space continuing, but it was hard to make out exactly. The beads blocked most of the light and reflected and refracted the beams that did make it through.

"I feel like I'm in a disco," Veronica said.

"Wrong music."

It was soulful. Strong sounds backed by a strong voice. Jillian guessed it would be described as abstract. There were no words. Not exactly. Maybe in a different language? She wasn't sure, but it was captivating as it boomed around the darkness. As they walked further into the building, even the little bit of light from the doorway disappeared, and it was only the music that gave them a sense of the space they were entering.

Not knowing if there was anything else to do, Jillian kept walking. It was slow going, because she didn't want to trip, but she supposed that was part of the experience. The building of expectation.

The space was cold. It clearly wasn't heated. With the pervasive darkness, her other senses stepped up. Beyond the music, there was a sweet smell. It couldn't be natural to the building. An old empty brick building like this wouldn't have the scent of flowers. Or candy? Jillian wasn't great with smells. She could only notice the smell itself and felt herself being drawn in. She was so used to thinking art was something experienced with just the eyes. This experience was proving to be unique.

The volume of the music began to decrease, fading out slowly. Jillian could now hear other people around her. They'd made it through to a central room. Pitch black, but there was no mistaking the feeling of a larger space. The air seemed to swirl above them.

She bumped into someone and decided to stop. There was nothing guiding them further. No blue hands or helpful arrows. So maybe she was where she was supposed to be.

Faintly at first, then with growing intensity, a glow started on the ceiling. Jillian could only describe the color as icy purple. As the light grew, she could make out what looked like giant balls. There were at least ten, pushing right up to the edges of the light. They looked like balloons, but large enough that someone could curl up comfortably inside them.

Music started up again. Violins. Piano. Nothing classical. It was modern. Mysterious. Jillian had a sudden sense of listening to the Pied Piper as he led all the children away from the village. The audience was being taken somewhere, but it wasn't entirely comfortable. They were being drawn into an unknown, the risk obscured by the dressing.

Looking up, transfixed, Jillian registered the shards of glass or ice that appeared. Before she could react, they cascaded down. She lifted her hands instinctively, but it was water. Shiny droplets raining down, caught up in the lights, fitting somehow with the music.

She was getting soaked, but it didn't feel uncomfortable. The iciness of the light faded, leaving a deep, dark purple. The music seemed to be reaching a crescendo, and she was still staring up, water dripping down her nose. As the tempo of the violins increased, the balloons started to shake.

Without warning, lights began to flash. As each color lit up, a balloon popped, the color cascading down.

Blue. Green. Red. Yellow. Pink. Orange. Purple.

Jillian could feel the colors coating her skin. What the substance was, she had no idea.

The popping stopped. The music stopped. The rain stopped.

A door opened at the far end of the space, seemingly opposite to where they'd come in. There was an outbreak of applause before people made their way to the light. Like everyone else, Jillian was coated in whatever substance had exploded from the balloons. She could hear it squelching under her shoes as she tried not to slip on her way to the exit.

Emerging from the doorway into what appeared to be a large tent, she spotted Veronica a couple steps in front of her.

"What is this stuff?" Veronica asked, picking a splotch of green off her jacket.

Whatever it was, it didn't appear to be sticking or staining. Jillian wiped at some red on her sleeve. "It's like slime."

"Slime?"

"Yeah. You know. That stuff you play with when you're a kid. It's mostly borax. You can color it, and it feels gross dripping through your hands and you pretend that it's snot."

"I think you had a different childhood than I did."

"What, you never made slime?" Jillian asked, incredulous. Slime had been a staple of her childhood.

Veronica shook her head. "I was encouraged to read."

"I was encouraged to play science. Our countertops were always covered with my experiments."

"That explains a few things."

"Yeah," Jillian smiled, "I'm sure it does."

They continued picking off the goo, helping each other get it out of their hair. Jillian wondered how they were going to get dry. It wouldn't be fun riding the train back downtown with cold, wet clothes clinging to her body.

As if to answer her question, the walls of the tent started to shake. One by one they dropped to the ground revealing walls of fans blowing warm air.

"Ah," said Veronica, as the wind made her hair fly around. "How thoughtful."

Jillian raised her arms and moved closer to a set of fans. The jet of air was warm and smelled like more of that candy from the beginning of the show. As her clothes began to dry, she could truthfully say that she'd never experienced an art show like this.

Veronica, whose jacket was more waterproof than Jillian's, was waiting at the tent entrance. Jillian gave herself one final spin in front of the fans before going to join her.

"So," she said as they made their way out, "how does that fit your profile?"

"I'm not even going to write it up. Can you imagine Frank's face, reading something like that? He'll think I'm on LSD or something."

They had emerged into a different courtyard in the Zitadelle, but enough people seemed to know where they were going that Jillian felt they could just follow.

"Jillian," a voice said, "I'm so happy that you made it."

Jillian turned to see Sebastian, conspicuously dry and goo free. "Sebastian. Thanks for inviting me. It was the most amazing art show I've ever been to."

"This is a compliment that means so much," he smiled.

Jillian gestured to Veronica. "James couldn't make it, but this is a friend of mine, visiting from home. Veronica. She's over here for a few weeks, and so I thought she might enjoy coming with me."

"An international audience. More than I expected. Welcome."

Jillian watched as the two shook hands. It was a testament to Veronica's skill that Sebastian didn't seem to recognize her at all. She had been following him for weeks, but there was no glimmer of suspicion on his face.

"How long did it take you to put all this together?" Veronica asked.

"This group, we do one show every three months. So we work on the design of one and the execution of another at the same time."

"Those balloons, or whatever they were, were impressive. Did you build them yourselves?"

"Yes. Part of the art is the construction. We have a warehouse space not far from here. Sometimes we perform there. But the space is also the art. To appreciate the piece, sometimes the location must change."

"Fascinating," Veronica said.

Jillian saw where Veronica was going with her questions. Whatever Sebastian was doing in the house by the Wall, it didn't seem to be related to the art shows. Which wasn't surprising. With its role in the power grid, it would be far too dangerous to do much there.

So it seemed that Sebastian was a man of multiple identities. Communications worker, artist, and whatever he was doing in that house.

"It was really amazing how you coordinated the light colors with the goo. It was like a rainbow waterfall."

"It worked out. But I confess, at first I wanted to have lights inside the balloons as well, to make them glow from within. But we could not get the electronics to work."

It was an opening Jillian wondered if she should take. She felt the panic of a quick decision: keep her distance or try to build a more solid connection. "Well, if you're using electronics in your next one, I'd love to help. My work at the university doesn't include a lot of artistic challenges."

"You can do this kind of work?" Sebastian asked.

"I mean, I can't make any promises, but I am an electrical engineer. Electricity only works in so many ways. If there's a solution, I can probably find it."

Sebastian broke out into a huge grin. "I am so lucky we have met. I must go now," he said. "There is much to clean up. We only have the permit for one day. But I will call you."

They watched him walk off, back into the building where the show had been.

"He looked like you gave him an early Christmas present," said Veronica. "The one at the top of the list that he'd been praying Santa would give him."

"No one has ever been that excited that I'm an electrical engineer."

"Maybe he's got an even bigger challenge for the next show than light-up balloons."

"Or maybe it relates to something else altogether," Jillian said.

"I'm not leaving Berlin until we find out."

CHAPTER THIRTEEN

James felt awkward. There was no getting around it. He wasn't used to having houseguests and didn't have the temperament for them as a rule. But these two weren't of the regular type.

The daughter was cute: light-brown hair tied up in two blue ribbons, gray eyes looking around with curiosity. She was holding a doll and walking around the living room in stocking feet examining everything.

The mother, on the other hand, was like a diamond—hard, beautiful, and multifaceted. In the three minutes she'd been in the flat, James was certain she'd taken in every detail.

"Thank you for letting us stay here," Anya said.

"I, uh, figured on you and your daughter taking the bedroom. I don't mind the sofa."

"That is very kind of you. But we can sleep on the cushions. My daughter has gone camping in the summers."

James shook his head. "Nae, it's better if you're in the bedroom. I sometimes watch the telly at night or come in late, and I wouldn't want to be waking up your daughter."

"Mama," Lena said, coming up to them, "where can I open my suitcase?"

"In the bedroom," Anya said, giving James a nod. "Come, let's go find a good spot together."

James watched them go, wondering what to do now. Turning, he went into the kitchen and put on the kettle. When in doubt, brew tea.

He was pouring three cups when they came back out. He'd found a small mug for Lena and put extra milk in it. He carried it to the table where she was setting up with pencil crayons and paper. "Here's a cup of tea for you."

Lena looked up at him. "I don't have tea very often. Sometimes my neighbor Frau Lanin makes it because she says it helps her digestion, but my other friend Heidi says tea makes your teeth go soft."

"Rubbish. The Chinese discovered the beauty of tea over a thousand years ago. Did you know that all tea comes from the same plant, and it only grew in China for most of that time, and that the Chinese think the rest of us are heathens for drinking it black?"

Lena looked at him, eyes wide. "Have you been to China?"

"Aye, once. There's one port where they don't mind us British coming in for a gander. I was spending some time in Hong Kong and thought to cross the water just to say I did."

"My father has been to China too. He says China is a good friend to our country."

"Lena," Anya came up to her daughter from where she'd been by the window, "can you draw me a picture of some flowers? Bright and colorful. We can tape them to the inside of my suitcase."

"I'm very good at flowers," Lena said to James before picking up a red pencil.

James went back to the kitchen to get the other two mugs of tea. Anya followed him in, stopping a couple feet away.

"Do you have children?"

James offered her a mug. "No. But I've got a passel of nieces and nephews back in Scotland."

"You are Scottish." It came out as a statement, and James wasn't sure what the sentiment was behind it.

He took a drink of his tea, feeling inexplicably tongue tied. All of his usual questions, innocuous in the life he lived, seemed ridiculously out of place given who she was, or at least the small part he knew. What was he supposed to ask? Have you ever been to Scotland? Given that she was from the GDR, she'd have only been to Scotland on premises that she wouldn't share with him. He sure as hell wasn't asking her what she did, or what her plans were after she left. Hell, he wasn't even sure he should ask her about where she liked to spend time in Berlin, East or West.

"I've left some extra towels on the dresser, along with a key. I'm out most days from ten in the morning. I work on the base during the day, but evenings are a bit all over, so I figured it was best for you to have your own key. You can help yourself to anything in the fridge, and I'm not bothered about you using my shampoo and whatnot."

"Does anyone else have a key?"

James was surprised at the question. "Just one friend of mine. More for emergencies."

"Sometimes I might have to leave Lena here on her own. I would like to make sure no one will come in but you and me."

"She will be safe here. My friend doesn't come over very often, and it's to see me. I'll make sure that when we get together, I meet her somewhere else."

Anya's features softened slightly. "I thank you. I will only leave her if I have to. She is very good though. She has had to be on her own more than I wanted. So she will not cause any trouble."

James looked at the little head bent in concentration over her paper. He knew from experience that no children were angels. They were inquisitive and loved to explore, and they were endlessly curious, which could cause all sorts of problems. But he believed that Lena would respect the boundaries. She'd grown up in East Berlin and had been indoctrinated to obey the rules since birth.

"Did Quentin tell you anything about me?"

"Only that he trusted you," Anya said.

"Well, sometimes that's more of a curse than a blessing. But I reckon you should know a bit about me, if you're staying here." *Because I wouldn't want you to waste your time checking me out.* "I'm a captain in the British military. I do the afternoon music broadcast on Radio Free Berlin."

"You work on the radio?"

"Aye, playing mostly rock and roll. But I do let some pop songs creep in now and then."

"Your military does this?" Anya asked, evidently confused. "It plays the music?"

"Well, it comes under the official heading of psychological operations. That's just a fancy way of saying we want East Germans to appreciate our culture so they stop fighting with us."

Anya looked skeptical. James got the feeling she couldn't imagine a more useless pursuit for a government than playing rock music. It didn't bother him. The East German inability to understand fun was, he reckoned, a large part of the problem between the two.

"And can I hear you, on this radio show?"

"Today, starting at noon. And tomorrow. And every day. I pre-record the weekend shows, but they go on at the same time."

"Does it work? Playing the rock music?"

James started to laugh. "Well, they keep paying me to do it, so I guess that's something."

"I will listen to your show today. Maybe I will learn something," Anya said.

He doubted it. She didn't look like she'd appreciate his type of propaganda at all. But then again, she wasn't his target audience. He wondered what had brought her here, why she had taken such great risk getting Quentin to smuggle her daughter out. It wasn't something done on a lark; it had to be grounded in deep personal conviction. That, or abject fear. And his first impression of her was a woman who did not scare easily.

"Well, even if you don't, I play some really good music. It'll be better than sitting here in silence." James thought he saw the smallest flash of a smile. "Right then, I'll just be getting ready for work."

He went into the bedroom to change into his uniform, leaving Anya sitting with her daughter at the dining room table. She was a tough nut, that one. Not giving a thing away. James knew this was for the best. They weren't set to become friends, and given that she would be leaving as soon as she could, he didn't see much point in trying to build a relationship.

He had to admit, however, that he was curious. Despite trying to convince East Germans every day that the West was a better place to live and being able to use his uniform to cross into East Berlin any time he wanted for research purposes, he didn't actually spend much time with people from there. He tried not to let his understanding of East Germany devolve into clichés based on assumptions and bias, but it was hard to update his thinking when he didn't have much access to primary sources as it were.

Having Anya and her daughter here was an opportunity to understand more about life in the Soviet Bloc. He could get a sense of the day to day, the challenges and constraints, but also of the joys. Because even in East Berlin, there had to be joys.

Perhaps he would spend his commute thinking of ways to get Anya to open up without making her suspicious that he was in the spooking business. He got the feeling she hadn't had an honest conversation in years.

Anya sat on the sofa braiding her daughter's hair while Lena watched television. It was a cartoon that was more entertaining than educational. Watching her daughter's smile, Anya thought it was perfectly frivolous. She'd had enough of official GDR programming to last a lifetime.

She let her thoughts wander, having decided to take one day to rest. Yesterday had been the most emotional day of her life, and there were more taxing days to come. So she was taking just one day to be with Lena, to do their hair and look at pictures of Paris and giggle about all the plans they were making. A ruhetag. One day to just be.

She thought about the man whose apartment they were in. She did not think he was in intelligence, nor did she think he was working for Quentin. First, the uniform had looked authentic. Second, she had listened to him on the radio. He did broadcast rock music, and the accent was the same. The music wasn't to her taste, but she had smiled a little when he'd dedicated a song called "Jailbreak" to a woman he'd just met.

It would be a little awkward, as the apartment wasn't very large. But she felt safe. And that was more important than anything.

Perhaps she would do something nice for this new friend. Quentin called him James, but he called himself Jamie on his show. Anya preferred Jamie; it sounded friendlier.

"Sweetheart, I'm going out for some groceries," she said to Lena. "I won't be long."

"Okay, Mama," Lena said, not taking her eyes from the television.

"I will get something for dinner, and maybe to bake cookies. Would you like that?"

"Yes. Do they have the same chocolate chips here that Great-Aunt Frida uses?"

Anya had been living in West Berlin for three years but had never been able to bring anything over for Lena. She knew the chocolate chips here were better. Suddenly she was excited to buy things for Lena that she'd never been able to share without being accused of betraying the GDR. "Oh, they have much better ones. And caramels too."

Lena turned to her and smiled. "Maybe we should make extra, and we can all have them for dessert."

Anya smiled at her daughter, her heart breaking a little with happiness. "That's a wonderful idea."

A half hour later, she returned carrying bags of groceries. Too many, but she couldn't resist spoiling her daughter. Anya had told her that Paris had to wait, that her mother had one more job to do. But they would stay here and have fun, and Paris would be very soon.

She would do everything she could to make that dream come true for her daughter.

As she was putting everything away, Anya jumped a little at a knock on the door. She wasn't expecting anyone, but this wasn't her place. Perhaps it was just a neighbor. But surely they would know that Jamie was at work?

Another knock. She let out a sigh of frustration. Couldn't they just go away? Maybe they could hear the television. But still, if no one answered, it meant that a visitor was unwelcome.

At the third set of knocks, Anya pressed her eye to the peephole. Relief swept through her seeing Quentin on the other side.

"Hello," she said, letting him in.

He came in, looking both weary and wary. She deserved the suspicion, she supposed. It must have been quite a shock when she told him who her ex-husband was.

"Jamie is not here," she said.

"Yeah, I know. He's just getting off shift now. That's why I came, because I need to talk to you alone before he gets home."

Anya gestured to the living area. "Shall we sit?"

Quentin nodded.

"Lena, honey," Anya said, going up to her daughter and placing her hand on Lena's back, "could you please go do some reading in the bedroom? Mama needs to have an adult talk right now."

Lena nodded and scampered into the bedroom after giving Quentin a curious glance.

Anya turned down the television but left it on.

"I want to say thank you," she said, "for finding us this place. Your friend, he is very nice. Very good with Lena. I think we are safe here."

"You are," Quentin said. "At least, if anything goes wrong, it's not going to be on account of James. He's a good guy."

"Yes. I hear him on the radio. He talks about the West but is still very kind to those listening in East Berlin. As if he wants to be their friend."

"He does. He loves this city. Both sides. It's one of the things I wanted to talk to you about. It's really important to me that you don't mess with him, Anya. He doesn't live the same kind of life that you and I do. So, whatever happens, you do your best to keep him out of it."

"What have you told him about me?"

"The bare minimum," Quentin said. "You're East German, you were one of my assets, and I got Lena out for you. I told him that you're just trying to procure new identities, and then you'll be off. I have not mentioned your ex-husband, just that you'll be giving me some useful information in exchange for a little help."

"And he doesn't ask questions?" Anya asked.

Quentin shook his head. "No. He's good about that. Mostly because I think he doesn't want to know. That's fine by me."

"It is better to be around people who know not to be curious."

"There aren't enough of those."

"Perhaps that is why you are his friend," Anya said.

Quentin raised a brow. "Perhaps."

"I went out today. I have asked someone—not someone I trust very much, but who I know needs money—to make contact with the new courier for that British man you are curious about. I will connect with him in a couple of days to see if he has anything to report. It may not be a lot, but you understand I cannot make the contact myself."

"You have to hide," said Quentin. It wasn't a question.

"Yes. For now. Until it becomes useful to be visible. But Lena I must hide always. He will take her, and not because he loves her."

"To have control over you."

"Yes," Anya said.

Quentin looked at her for a moment before heading to the door. "I hope you know what you're doing, Anya. There's only so much help I can give you, and you can't stay here indefinitely."

She gestured to the apartment. "This is all the help I need. I will give your friend his life back soon."

Quentin nodded and left, closing the door behind him.

Anya stared after him, forcing herself to take deep breaths. What she had planned, it was never going to be easy. But it was necessary. For Lena to live a life free of fear and manipulation, Anya would do anything.

CHAPTER FOURTEEN

As he was leaving the broadcasting station, James was surprised to see Edward coming into the radio building.

"Ah, Jamie Murphy. Just the man I was looking for."

"Edward. I didn't realize you were still here. Usually you diplomats hang with the uniforms for a few days at most."

"Well, we're on some joint assignment, keeping Berlin open for everyone and all that. But listen, do you have time for dinner? There's something I want to ask you about."

"Sure, but not in the mess. Too many years of that food. Do you mind taking a taxi downtown? I know a place that serves great pierogies close to my flat."

"Thank goodness for immigration," Edward said. "Lead on."

James didn't broach the point of the dinner until they had been seated at the restaurant and the pierogies were on their way.

"So, what was that favor you're needing?"

"A small one really. How often do you go into East Berlin?"

"Not as much as I'd like to," James said. "Firsthand research is important, and I should be going over more. Why are you asking?"

"I've got an old friend, decades old, in the East." Suddenly Edward looked uncomfortable. "I know I'm not supposed to. Son of Lord Ashton, sworn enemy of all things Communist. But my friend came over to study in the fifties, and I was at Cambridge at the same time. I've done a miserable job of staying in touch, but was cleaning out the old family flat in London and I found a book that has some special memories. I thought, well, I'd like to send it on."

"And you feel you can't do this yourself?"

"Not with the father I have. The Stasi would be all over me from the second I crossed the border. I'm sure even associating with me would get my friend in trouble. Plus, if my father heard of it, well, let's just say that I wouldn't be welcome back in Blighty anytime soon. Besmirching the family name and all of that."

Not for the first time James felt sorry for the weight of the title that was on Edward. It certainly made growing up middle class attractive.

"I reckon I might be able to help. We have to clear visits ahead of time, but I could look to set something up next week."

"Wonderful," Edward said. "Let me figure out where to send the book, and then I'll let you know."

Like he'd told Edward, James was overdue for a research trip east. It was pretty easy going over in uniform. Berlin was still an occupied city, and the militaries of the four occupying countries had agreements that allowed for ease of movement. The East Germans didn't like it, but they didn't have much of a say.

Dropping off a book seemed innocuous enough. Lord knew he'd done far worse in East Berlin.

James woke up to the pounding on his door. At least, he hoped that's what it was. After a night of whisky, pierogies, and reminiscing with Edward, there was the possibility that the pounding was in his head.

The sound continued, and James rolled himself out of bed. Might as well check the door and see if that would at least shut it up. He reckoned it was about fifty-fifty either way.

He swung the door open and found Quentin pacing the landing outside his flat.

James didn't even have time to bellow about the lateness, or earliness, of the hour before Quentin pushed past him.

"I suppose I shouldn't bother asking if you want to come in," James said.

He shut the door and turned around to look at his guest. Quentin looked as emotional as James had ever seen him. He was still pale, but slightly flushed, as if the agitation was bursting to get out. James felt a profound certainty that he didn't want to know what was causing it.

Quentin continued his pacing inside the flat, apparently not yet ready to talk. James decided to head to the bathroom for a piss and to rustle up some aspirin.

He came out a few minutes later wondering if he could put Quentin off until the aspirin took effect. The spook was doing a fine job wearing out a path in the floor. James felt himself growing proper nervous. He'd been with Quentin in some dire situations and had never seen him like this.

"I take it from your pacing and general angst you didn't come over to just crack open a beer and tell me about your wild night?"

Quentin finally stopped moving. "Where's Anya?"

"Sleeping. Or at least that's probably what she was doing before you decided to bang on the door at this ungodly hour."

Before Quentin could say anything else, the bedroom door opened and Anya slipped out. She was wearing slacks and had a cardigan wrapped tightly around her torso.

"What is going on?" she asked. "Is there a problem?"

Quentin looked from one to the other, clearly not knowing what to say.

"Mate, spit it out."

"I was here earlier, talking with Anya. You hadn't come back from work yet when I left."

It was slightly unnerving to think of Quentin and Anya collaborating in his flat while he wasn't there, but he supposed it made sense. She had to stay out of sight, and they couldn't be seen together. Still, it was his space, not some damn safehouse.

"I was out with a bloke from work. Well, we don't work together exactly, him being a diplomat. But we've known each other a while."

"How long? Did you meet on some operation or something?" Quentin asked.

"Twenty or so years. And no, we both played rugby in uni. Different teams, but we met up often enough."

Quentin sat down abruptly. Leaning his head back on the sofa, he began to rub his temples.

James concluded he wasn't about to get back to bed anytime soon. So he went into the kitchen to brew a pot of tea. He wasn't sure if Quentin drank tea, but at this time in the morning he didn't bloody well care. As he waited for the water to boil, he reflected that he was used to the spook's roundabout way of asking questions, but also that they were never idle. Quentin wasn't the kind of bloke who engaged in a lot of meaningless chitchat. It left James with a churn in his stomach that had nothing to do with the whisky from the night before. The question about Edward wasn't about Quentin being polite.

He wanted to know about Edward for some reason. Given Quentin's line of work, that reason couldn't be good.

James carried three cups of tea into the living room. He set them down on the table. Anya had curled up into the sofa looking alert but confused. James sat down beside her and sipped his tea in the silence, letting Quentin decide when to break it.

"You know what I do here," Quentin said.

"Vaguely," James replied.

"Yeah, but you understand the basics. I collect and share information. And sometimes I act on that information."

"Aye, although I've never heard it put that way before."

"People like to make things more complicated than they are. Intelligence work is ultimately about information. You can't take action unless you have good information. Usually I get that information from intermediaries who have access to places and people I'm curious about."

It was a bit surreal, this line of chat. He'd known from the beginning what Quentin was, but their odd friendship seemed always to be based on Quentin wanting or needing a connection that had nothing to do with his job. So they didn't much talk about it.

"Those'd be your agents or assets then?"

"Right. Like Anya here. We trade, usually information for money, but sometimes the currency changes."

The silence descended again as Quentin seemed to weigh something in his mind. James sipped at his tea, proper nervous now. What in the Christ it could be, he couldn't imagine. But it couldn't be good. All the times they had spoken about the trouble Jillian managed to find, or Quentin's concerns about James's journalist girlfriend Jasminka, the room had never been as full of tension as it was now.

James stared, not able to imagine where this was going.

"A month ago, Anya was given a new contact by the Stasi. Because it was information that might support further activities, she told me about him. A British man who wanted to continue passing information to the East Germans. The same man who you were having dinner with earlier."

James almost dropped his tea into his lap. "What?"

Anya gasped, looking unnerved.

"You heard me."

"You're saying you think Edward is a double agent or something? Committing treason?"

"You tell me."

James narrowed his eyes. "Even if he is, which I don't believe for a second, why in the Christ do you think I'd know anything about it?"

"Why don't you believe it?"

James felt his eyebrows climb up to his hairline. "He's, well, just your average, entitled posh Englishman."

"So helping the Communists is a way to kill the boredom of his upper-crust life."

"No, that's not what I said," James sputtered.

"He wouldn't be the first," Quentin said.

"I bloody well know that." James could feel himself getting angry. "But you're wrong. You have to be. Edward is a good guy. His father is Lord Ashton, Earl of Fenwick, and the Secretary of Defence."

"Double agents don't need to be assholes. As for his father, all that means is he probably has access to top quality stuff," Quentin said.

"You must have it wrong."

"I don't make mistakes like that."

James turned to Anya. "What is this? Are you setting him up? Setting me up?"

Her jaw dropped. "No. Me? I set nothing up." She turned to Quentin, "This is true? My last client is connected to here?"

"Yes," Quentin said, "but for what it's worth, I think it's an unlucky coincidence."

Anya turned back to James, "Are we safe?" She stood up as if she was going to grab her daughter and rush out the door right now.

"Aye. At least I think so. He doesn't know where I live. He's never been here. And tonight was nothing about any of this. Or anything really. Oh, Christ."

James sprang up, beginning to pace himself. His downstairs neighbors were probably wondering what in the hell was going on.

"Twenty years I've known him. Not once has he expressed sympathy for the Communists."

But that wasn't quite true. Thinking back, even on the conversation tonight, there might not have been any pro-Soviet statements, but there were, and always had been, anti-British sentiments. Sure, it had been cloaked in wry humor and self-depreciation, but James knew Edward didn't think much of the British nobility and the whole upper echelon into which he'd been born. He wasn't supportive of the policies regarding India or Ireland and had often expressed disdain at the colonial activities from Canada to Kenya. James had always assumed it was more about fighting his father, the earl who seemed to have such an iron grip on Edward's life. But it was possible that Edward's feelings ran much deeper.

How deep? Enough to sell state secrets? James was forced to admit that he really didn't know.

James was about to ask Quentin what in the hell he was supposed to do with this speculation when he realized there was a great chasm full of shite opening up in front of him. There was no way forward without stepping right in it.

This was the kind of information that one could never unknow. It couldn't be ignored or forgotten, or dismissed as a crackpot story told in the wee hours of a particularly bad morning.

"I don't suppose we can rewind time to where I don't bother answering the door and you just go away?"

"I'm sorry," Quentin said. James could tell he meant it. "I can't ignore it either. And even though I'm breaking all kinds of rules telling you all this, I thought, well, you shouldn't be blindsided. In addition to any worries you might have about the bigger implications to your country, suspicion is going to fall on whoever he's spent time with here."

James sat his arse back on the sofa and sighed. He could feel his headache gaining intensity. "Suspicion from who? What do you do now? What am I supposed to do now?"

Quentin ran his hand over his jaw. "I don't know."

"Ye have no plan?"

Quentin laughed in a sort of desperate, disbelieving way. James knew exactly how he felt.

"No, I don't have a damn plan. Suspected treason by an ally is not something I deal with every day."

"I take it then there's no established protocol?"

"What about you? Ever get any briefings on this scenario?"

James shook his head. "Not for someone who isn't in uniform."

Quentin sighed. "No one likes dealing with these situations. And this one crosses country lines. I pass this on, and at some point it gets passed over, then who's doing the investigating? We'll open a file for sure, but we can't avoid someone if they have the confidence of your country. And then it just sits like a virus, infecting the people around it."

"We Brits don't exactly inspire confidence on that front, do we?" James reflected. "There's a pretty persistent rumor the powers that be let Philby escape to Moscow because they didn't want him in open court. Too many well-connected people would have had to admit they'd dismissed concerns about him for years."

"Including ours."

James shook his head. He could see the problems piling up in his path. "It's going to be the same with Edward. Son of an earl. Some of the bluest blood possible. That lot aren't going to want to see suspicions fall on one of their own. They'll let him run off to Dresden and quietly remove him from Debrett's."

"In the meantime, how many operations get exposed? How many people die while no one wants to deal with it?"

"It's a no-win situation, isn't it? It's going to be shite no matter what."

Anya had been following the conversation between the two men. James was sure she was bursting with questions, but it had to be obvious there weren't many answers to be had.

"Why did you tell me this way?" Anya asked Quentin. "When you recognized the connection, why did you not keep it a secret?"

"What good would that do? I'm going to need your help."

Anya's brows raised. "My help?"

"You're the connection. We have to find out more about what he's doing over here. Now it's more personal. So yeah, you're going to keep looking for information about him."

James looked out the window and saw the beginnings of the sunrise. "I need to sleep on this. I don't suppose he's going anywhere in the next twenty-four hours. And, well, as much as I trust you, I'm going to need more than your word that you recognized him from somewhere else."

"Yeah," Quentin said, "we're both going to need that. That's what Anya here is going to provide in exchange for staying in your apartment."

James noticed a flash of anger on Anya's face, but at least she wasn't looking scared anymore. "I am already asking about him. But these are not contacts I planned to need after I left."

"Do what you can," Quentin said. "He must be somewhat worried that his new courier disappeared."

"They would not tell him I escaped. They wouldn't want him to run or to not have faith in them anymore."

"Still," Quentin said, "he must be nervous. Maybe you can capitalize on that."

"I am busy, you know," Anya said, "with a task that will get you far more information than scraps about this one man."

"Yes, but this man is the one who's causing the biggest problem right now. So help."

Her eyes flashed, but her expression didn't change. "Fine. I will make a special effort to find out more about this Edward."

James turned to Anya. "I know it's upsetting. I'm not exactly thrilled that an old school mate might be committing treason. But I want you to know, because it seems like this is turning into a proper clusterfuck, that I'm not going to do anything that would hurt your daughter. So don't be treating me like the enemy."

Anya didn't say anything, but the tightness around her mouth relaxed a fraction.

James looked at Quentin.

"I was thinking," James said, "any chance he's a triple agent? You know, giving stuff to the GDR at the request of the crown?"

"That's not exactly what a triple agent is, but yes, he could be doing that. Or he could be working for the French or the Austrians. Or he could be being blackmailed by any of the aforementioned parties."

"Christ Jesus, I don't know how you keep any of this straight. Or really, why you'd want to at all."

Quentin took a long drink from his mug. The tension in the room started to diffuse, as everyone seemed to settle in to the new task before them. "These days, I'm not sure myself. Since I've been back from Nicaragua, it's starting to feel, I don't know, repetitive. When I started—I think when anyone starts in this business—you imagine you're working toward some goal. One day you will win. Communism will disappear. World peace will ensue. That all this shit you're doing, you'll be able to see it making a difference. Then the years pass and nothing gets better, and there stops being a difference between you and the guys you're fighting except the country that pays your salary."

It sounded depressing as hell to James, but then it always did. Not once in all his interactions with defense intelligence did he ever want to try it out. He much preferred the overt persuasion. He tried to get people to want what he wanted. Tried to convince them to tear down the Wall with their own hands. That's how Communism was going to end—when so many people pushed for it that their governments wouldn't be able to silence them.

"How easy is it for you to quit?"

"Since I'm American and not Russian, painful but not impossible. They prefer you to wait until retirement, but there's no sense having people out in the field who don't want to be there. It puts the whole system at risk."

"You'd be lazier and more careless, I reckon."

"And more bribable."

James felt a little ping go off in his brain. It wasn't much, just the very basic seed of an idea, but maybe the key to figuring out Edward was to learn how much of his life was his choice. Like Quentin said, frustrated people were vulnerable to manipulation.

"Not that I don't support your career change, but could you hold off until after you get this woman out of my apartment?" James said, gesturing to Anya.

Quentin laughed. "Yeah. I'm not quitting this month, don't worry. I have to get a few things sorted out."

Anya didn't look pleased at his attempt at a joke. Black humor was obviously not a refuge for her.

"Do you plan to see your friend again?" she asked him.

James wished for something to ease the tension out of his shoulders. "I'm meant to. Tonight, he asked me if I would take a book over to East Berlin."

Quentin's head snapped up. "What?"

"This is not safe," said Anya. "You should not see him again. And you should not carry anything for him."

"I didn't know that earlier," James said, "but I quite clearly know that now. But if I back out and avoid him like the bloody plague, won't I just tip him off?"

Anya sighed. "What if you tip him off by accident? Because you are transparent, and I don't think you know how to pretend enough to keep everything the same?"

James wanted to bristle at the lack of confidence but knew that she was right.

"And what would you have me do?" He pointed a finger at Quentin. "You could have kept quiet and let me go on my merry way. I don't know a damn thing about what Edward's doing, so even if he gets caught, they would have let go of me eventually."

"I thought of that," said Quentin, running his hand through his hair. "I'm still not sure I made the right choice. But I didn't want Edward using you. I didn't think it was fair to let you be exposed like that."

Anya looked at both men. "I am not used to these kinds of relationships. But I see it is everyone's interest if more is found out about your friend. I need to be safe here, you need to stay out of trouble," she said, pointing to James, "and you," directing this last at Quentin, "need to justify meeting my demands. I know the Stasi structure for handling people like him. Foreign agents are handled carefully by only a few people. So I will work with you, and we will figure this out."

James thought it sounded like a self-interested offer if there ever was one, but he didn't have much choice.

"We will talk about this again soon," Anya said, standing up. "Now, I go back to bed before Lena gets up and needs breakfast."

James waited until Anya had closed the bedroom door behind her.

"It's a big flaming deal to accuse a friend of treason. Especially a friend so well connected. Do you think we can trust her?"

"In general? No," Quentin said. "My impression is that Anya will throw anyone under the bus to get to where she's going."

"That doesn't make me feel better."

"The thing is, she has to give me something. We're not in her way. She's got some big plans to execute before she goes—plans she might still need some help with. And she needs to stay here; it's the perfect place to hide. So we can trust her for now because all our interests align."

Why didn't that make him feel better?

"You're a pain in the arse, you know that?"

Quentin stood up. "Sweet dreams. I'll be back tomorrow."

James just scowled as Quentin walked out the door. Of all the situations he thought he might ever have to deal with, an old friend being a double agent wasn't one of them. He'd been inside enemy territory hundreds of times in his almost twenty-year military career. He'd been shot at. Once seen colleagues get blown up. Navigated night drops and handled interrogations. It never stopped him from trusting people. Never shook his belief there were more good people in the world than bad and that small actions could make a powerful difference.

He showed up every day trying to do the best for his country. No, the United Kingdom wasn't perfect. Far from it. But the politics and entitled upper crust aside, there were some good people in the country. Lots of them, who worked hard and had been sending their sons to war for almost a century nonstop.

James knew in his heart he wouldn't ignore what Quentin and Anya had told him about Edward. As sad as it was, James wouldn't be able to live with himself imagining even one British bloke ending up in the Siberian torture chambers because he'd been sold out by one of his own.

He didn't really need to sleep on it. He just had to work up the courage to find out the truth.

CHAPTER FIFTEEN

Jillian knew it was a test.

Sebastian had invited her out, ostensibly to further their friendship. He wanted to know more, he said, about her knowledge of all things electrical so he might take advantage of her skills in a future art show.

When she got to the bar, he'd introduced her to his friend Peter. The two men were roughly the same age, but whereas Sebastian was of medium height and looked like he could hold his own on a hockey rink, Peter was tall and lanky. He had looked at her with skeptical brown eyes, and Jillian felt she had just been placed under a microscope.

They settled into a table with a round of beers, and the questions began.

On the surface it all seemed friendly. Who she was, what she did at the science institute. They asked her about Canada and her family and what they did there. They asked her about where she'd traveled to. They asked her about her impressions of Berlin, and where else she'd been in the country, and if she'd ever been east. They asked her so many questions she wondered what they were trying to figure out.

Jillian wanted to put their minds at ease, because she was really no threat to whatever they were doing.

Both she and Veronica were convinced Sebastian was up to something related to the Wall, and Jillian was dying to know what it was. So she didn't mind answering their questions as honestly as she could. If it would help them take her into their confidence, she'd tell them every birthday present she'd ever received.

"Do you work at the telecommunications company too?" Jillian asked Peter as Sebastian got up to get them another round of drinks.

"No," he replied, "I am studying to become a lawyer."

"Oh, cool. What kind?"

"I wish to work in international law. To help make the treaties, especially for human rights."

"Wow," Jillian said. "It sounds so meaningful. Is there a particular reason you're interested in human rights?"

He gestured around him. "How can I not be, living in this city. I have only to look at the Wall to see menschenrechte being violated."

Fair point. "Well, I wish you success."

Peter smiled and finished off his pint. "Sebastian told me you know much about electricity. He said you are an engineer."

"I am," Jillian agreed. "Do you work on the art shows with him? He seems to think I might be able to help with his next show."

"No," Peter said. "Sebastian's art shows are…well, let's just say I am not creative enough to help. To me art is still something you hang on a wall. I do not easily understand the immersive experiences his group designs. But I go to them."

"Oh, were you at the one last week? With the goo falling from the ceiling?"

"Yes. I thought it one of their best because they remembered to have fans. The audience is not always so lucky to be able to clean up afterward."

Jillian laughed. She'd remember that when she was getting dressed for the next one.

Sebastian returned to the table carefully carrying three pints in a triangle. He set them down gently before sliding back onto his chair.

"You were talking about me, yes?" said Sebatian with a grin.

"Of course, you conceited ass," Peter said, returning the smile.

It was obvious that the two were very good friends. "How did you two meet?" Jillian asked.

"It was the first day of grade two," Sebastian said. "He was new to the class so didn't know anyone to eat with. He did, however, have quite the lunch. Me, I had only an apple I found at the bottom of my bag. My parents are very good at noticing grades and achievements, not so much when the cupboards are empty. I sat beside him and watched him eat, and he took pity and gave me half his sandwich."

"I heard his stomach rumbling. And my mother, she always packed too much trying to fatten me up."

"It's never worked," Sebastian said. "She still tries to feed him all the time. His refrigerator is filled with containers of food. I hardly have to buy any groceries."

Jillian smiled. "That's a pretty convenient friendship. Does his mother know she's still feeding the both of you?"

"She feels sorry for him," Peter said, "so she doesn't mind. He came over for dinner on the same day he shared my sandwich. We never really got rid of him."

Jillian thought it was charming, that beginning to their shared history. As much as they might be on different paths now, they had those memories to keep them together.

"Jillian," Sebastian said, "I am curious about your work. I always thought engineers designed bridges and buildings."

"That's civil engineering," Jillian said. "There's actually lots of different types—chemical, mechanical. Like I told you before, I'm an electrical engineer. There's some overlap, but not much. There's so much to know, it's hard not to become specialized."

"Mechanical I understand. Machines, yes? But what does a chemical engineer do?"

"These days, mostly make new kinds of plastic."

Sebastian's eyes widened. "I did not even think of this. But yes, it is a form of engineering."

"And electrical engineers," Peter jumped in, "what do you do?"

"Circuits, signals, power, transmission. These days there's electrical in almost everything—satellites, microwaves, radios, hydro grids, batteries. Anything that requires power has been touched at some point by an electrical engineer."

"So you are never going to be out of a job," Sebastian said. "My parents would like this."

"It's true," Jillian smiled, "there's a lot going on. And I really like it, so when I'm done with one project, it's pretty easy for me to think of a dozen other things to work on."

"I'm normally great at puzzles, and even I can't figure this one out," Jillian said, pouring her and Veronica each a Fanta. They had decided it was safe to get together at Jillian's apartment, since Veronica didn't seem to be doing any espionage at the moment.

"You know, unknowns are part of the business. Right? You just accept that you're never going to know it all, that you can't. But this, I have to admit, it's getting under my skin," Veronica said.

"I get it. I'm equally intrigued. Nothing's changed as far as you can tell?"

Veronica shook her head. "Not much. Sebastian's not going quite as often, but he's still heading out to Spandau at least four nights a week. With the information you were able to get on his friend Peter, I've been able to do some more digging there too. He's even less quirky than Sebastian. He's almost done a law degree. His parents live in Reinickendorf. He lives one floor below Sebastian. He drinks a lot of coffee and takes his bike everywhere. The two of them, their history checks out. Nothing even remotely suggesting there's any sympathies toward the Soviets or the GDR. Two cute, easygoing German guys."

"So maybe they're just good people, super curious about how the power grid works."

"No," Veronica said. "It doesn't play. Sebastian at least works for a utility, but the other one, in law school. No way does he have any legit reason to be playing around in that house."

"You think it's important to find out what's going on," Jillian said. "What did Frank say?"

"I imagine the same thing he said to you."

Jillian had spoken to Frank earlier that day. This time it had been easy. For the first time in forever, they weren't speaking about anything classified. Sure, they'd both been careful not to divulge location details, but she'd been able to call him from her apartment.

"Veronica wants to stay," Frank had said, "until she solves the mystery of that house. What do you think?"

Jillian hesitated, mostly because she was unprepared for Frank to ask her opinion. "There's something, and they're doing a really good job hiding it. Given Sebastian's small but critical role in my life, I agree with Veronica. We need to find out. Because, well, if he gets into trouble, I could get into trouble."

Jillian could hear Frank exhaling. He must be smoking. "Yeah, it's always the same vulnerability, isn't it? But I agree with you. Better to know, so then you're not blindsided later."

"You're going to let her stay?"

"I'm not that kind of boss anymore," Frank laughed. "We're forging new territory here. Plus, I need to be home for a while, and Veronica's got a lot to learn. Might as well learn it in Berlin. I won't have a new assignment for us for a couple of months."

Fine by Jillian. "That's good for me."

"You're getting along, I take it?"

"Yeah. She's, well, I like working with her. It's great to have someone to talk to."

"Where's James?" Frank asked.

"He's here. I still see him. He's been busy lately, I think."

"Good. You need more than one person. Anyway, anything you need, send it through Veronica, but she's pretty much tapped it dry on this. We've got nothing so far, and I don't expect that to change. It looks to me like you're dealing with some regular people who have a quirk of some sort. Maybe they're painting each other nude or growing marijuana in the basement."

Jillian smiled. Frank was right. It could be one of a hundred random things, none of which would be relevant to her and the mission in West Berlin.

Refocusing on Veronica, Jillian told her about the end of the conversation. "He's right, as in the Wall could be a giant red herring."

"I don't think there's any more I can do in terms of reconnaissance or investigation," Veronica said. "The best bet is for you to keep developing the friendship and get him to invite you over."

Jillian had been thinking along the same lines. "It's going to require finesse, because I can't just say, 'Hey, I know you spend time at this house in Spandau, could you take me there?'"

"I know his route. You could run into him on his way back, ask him what he was doing. See what he says."

"Have you ever seen anyone else there?"

"No. No other friends. No one goes with them. Just Sebastian and Peter."

"So whatever they're doing, they're not including their larger social circles. It must be something they want to keep secret."

Veronica started to rub at her eyes. "We can speculate all we want. We're not going to guess sitting here. We need more information. Either I need to break into the house, or you need to get invited for a tour."

"Okay, point taken. But it's also not something we need to know this week. Frank said you're staying for a while, so let me keep working on the friendship. I get the feeling Sebastian is building up to something. I had a good time the other night, but it came across like a friendly interrogation. He and Peter were looking for something. I don't know if I gave it to them, but he's already called me about getting together again, so I didn't scare them away."

"That's good. After talking to Frank myself, I'm pretty sure whatever they're doing in that house, it's not going to change anything for us. I mean, even if they're digging under the Wall, they aren't going to get very far."

"I guess the only concern is if Sebastian is doing something that could get him into trouble if he gets caught, because what he does for us is leverage. I've been in this situation before, and it sucked. I don't want to be someone's leverage."

"Point taken. That's why we're pursuing it. Because once we know, we can prepare."

Hopefully that's true.

CHAPTER SIXTEEN

Jillian was so deep in her signal analysis she almost didn't hear the knock on her office door.

"Have you eaten?" Quentin asked, stepping inside and closing the door behind him.

Whatever was in the bag he carried, it smelled fantastic. Lunch had been a while ago, and Jillian's stomach started to gurgle in anticipation.

She stood up, twisting her neck to get a kink out. She watched as Quentin cleared a space on her desk to put the bag down. When she was sure he wasn't going to drop it, she leaned up to kiss him.

It felt good. Really good. They let it go on for a while. As she pulled back, Jillian wished they could do that more often and not in her cramped workspace. "You taste like a fruit of some kind. Like a berry, but not quite."

Quentin pulled a small tin out of his jacket pocket. "Blackcurrant."

Jillian took the tin and opened it. Inside were small, purple hard candies covered in a dusting of powdered sugar. "Mmm. They smell good."

"They taste good too. I'll give you one after we eat."

"You could just leave me the tin."

He took it away from her, smiling. "Get your own."

Jillian turned to dig into the bag of dinner. "I guess we should get into this before it gets cold."

She pulled out two containers while Quentin grabbed napkins and cutlery. They settled into what was revealed as schnitzel from a small restaurant close to campus. She'd never gone in and now realized she'd wasted two years eating lunch in the cafeteria.

"This is amazing," she said.

"It is good. But, sadly, not the best I've ever had."

"Oh, and where was this best-ever schnitzel? Will you take me there one day?" Jillian asked.

"Not any day soon," Quentin replied. "As it's a local hole-in-the-wall in Chicago."

Jillian narrowed her gaze. "Really? Here we are in West Berlin, Germany, and you're telling me the best schnitzel you've ever had was in Chicago. Are you sure there's not a little nostalgia going on?"

Quentin laughed. "What, like it was a simpler time?"

"Yeah," Jillian said, smiling, "something like that."

"Well, how about this? One day I'll take you there, and you can compare and let me know."

"It's not going to work," Jillian said. "I'll be thinking about how romantic it was when we had to meet clandestinely and share quick dinners in my undercover office. If we ever get to Chicago together, it won't be nearly so dangerous."

"All the romance will be gone."

"Yep. We'll both be boring."

"The trick is, we have to become boring at exactly the same time," Quentin said. "Then it's not such a big deal."

"Noted."

They ate in silence for a bit. The schnitzel was really very good. Crispy and moist at the same time. She could definitely eat this again.

"So, how did your thing work out? With that woman's daughter?" She assumed it was generally okay, because Quentin looked normal enough. If he'd blown some operation with a kid, she imagined he would look a lot worse.

"Fine. I got the kid out."

"But?"

"But it wasn't over like I thought it would be," Quentin said. "So let's just put them in the category of loose ends that I'm hoping to tie up very soon."

"I wish you luck," Jillian said.

Quentin suddenly looked uncomfortable. "Thanks."

"Have you seen James lately?" Jillian asked, thinking a change of subject was in order. Unfortunately, it increased the tension in Quentin's posture.

"No. Why?"

"No reason," she said. "I'm just making conversation. I haven't seen him in a couple of weeks, which is unusual. The last time we talked, he was moping about Jasminka, and I think

I should probably go and visit soon. To make sure he's not still feeling sorry for himself."

"I get the impression he's really busy."

Jillian was confused. "How would you get that impression if you haven't seen him? You don't exactly work together."

"Can I ask you to leave it alone, Jillian?"

Her heart started to pound. "Leave what alone?"

"James. I know you care about him, but don't go over right now."

Jillian was instantly scared. She couldn't help it. James and Quentin had become friends over the last year, but she was the original connector. There was nothing that Quentin did that James should be involved in.

"Is he doing something for you?"

"No. Can you please trust me and just give him some space for a bit?"

"Is it something with Jasminka?"

Quentin hesitated. "Look, Jillian, I don't want to lie to you. So no, it's not Jasminka, but please don't ask me any more."

"Is he in danger?"

Quentin's eyes flashed. "That would be my fault?"

"He's a radio broadcaster. Any risks he's taken in the last little while have been on account of me or you. Is it so crazy that I'm worried?"

"You were the one who suggested I have him drive that kid out of East Berlin."

His words slammed into her. "I...I," she sputtered. Then she shut up. Because she had done that. When it was an intellectual exercise, she had evaluated the options impartially.

She was so angry with herself. If there was anything she should have learned by now, it was never just an intellectual exercise. Not when people she cared about were involved.

"Did he do it? Did he drive the daughter over?"

"No," said Quentin, stabbing his fork into the schnitzel box. "I did."

Jillian gave him a moment. "That was a big risk. Your cover as a journalist doesn't give you a free pass."

"Well, I wasn't going to trust anyone else to do it. I don't need the death of an eight-year-old on my conscience."

"You already have a lot on your conscience," Jillian said. "You can't save everyone."

"I'm not trying to," he snapped at her.

"I think you are," she said, not backing down. "I think you're trying to make up for losing Isabella in Nicaragua all those years ago and leaving her son without a mother."

"That has nothing to do with it."

"Does the CIA regularly drive kids across the Berlin Wall?"

He glared at her. "If we need to. What's your point?"

"I think you take more risks than you should trying to atone for something you can't change."

"Don't tell me how to do my job."

"I wouldn't dream of it," Jillian said. "You don't share anything anyway."

"Then why bring any of this up?"

"Because I care about you, you idiot. You look out for me all the time, and I can't do the same for you?"

Quentin raised his fingers to her cheek, taking a deep breath as the tension left his face. "You're right," he said. "And

I hear you, I do. But moving the daughter out got the mom onside, and intelligence wise, it's a good deal."

"And James?" Jillian asked. "Where does he fit in? Because James is really important to me. He's one of the most important people in my life, and as much as he blusters, you and I both know that he's more like me than you."

Quentin stood up and took her hand, pulling her up beside him. He put his other arm around her waist and stepped in close. "I know. And I promise, Jillian, that I'm looking out for him. But something came up, something I never expected, and to not involve him would have put him in an even worse position. Trust me, he's just in the wrong place at the wrong time. So I'm trying to get him out. It's just…fuck. It's just complicated."

She wound her arms around him and held him tight. "I trust you. With my life I do. So I'll back off. But please, if you need help. Anything. I owe him more than I can ever repay."

They just stood there for a while, Quentin stroking her back. "For what it's worth," he said, "I don't think the situation is dangerous. It may impact his career, and he might get tied up in bureaucratic paper shuffling for a decade, but I don't see any risk to his life."

Jillian sighed against his chest. She knew Quentin wouldn't tell her if there was a risk that serious. He'd be too afraid she'd insert herself in the middle and end up taking risks herself. And then he'd have to look out for both of them.

She knew she had to let it go for now. She had enough to worry about.

Jillian broke the contact and eased the conversation to a different subject. Now wasn't the time to tell Quentin about her own brewing mystery.

CHAPTER SEVENTEEN

Anya stood in the back room of the tobacco shop. She had left Lena in the apartment with zimtschnecken, her favorite bakery confection, coloring pencils, and permission to watch as much television as she wanted. Anya hated leaving her. The worry was persistent, a small sleeping pit viper curled in her stomach. Lena alone was Lena vulnerable, and Anya wanted always to be where she could see her daughter. The apartment was safe enough— safe as they were ever going to be in this city. But she knew the reach of her ex-husband was long, and most worrisome, Lena would open the door to him with joy. She did not yet understand who her father was and what he was capable of.

But she could not do her business from the apartment, and if she was going to leave Berlin free, then it was business that had to get done.

David looked up as he finished counting her money. "Two West German passports?"

"Yes," Anya confirmed. "I know I am paying you well. Part of that is for your discretion."

She had worked with David on occasion for many years. He could be trusted as much as anyone for sale could be trusted. For the right amount, he would forget that she'd paid him for his silence.

He was not a Stasi contact. A devout Catholic, he was no fan of atheistic socialism. She had worked hard to find sources like him, knowing that one day she would need her own independent network.

"It will take me a week," he said. "You brought pictures?"

"A week is fine." She reached into her bag to pull out the pictures of her and Lena. Her hand shook a little. She did not want the picture of Lena to be in this man's hands. In anyone's hands. It would be able to circulate and could end up in front of the wrong eyes. Anya knew, however, that it was necessary. They needed passports if they were going to live free of the tentacles of the GDR.

David took the pictures, giving them a quick glance. "A kid?"

"My daughter."

David met her eyes for a moment but didn't say anything more.

"I need to ask you also," Anya said, "have you seen Lucinda recently?"

"Did you try the bar?" David asked.

"Yes. She has not responded to my message."

"You know Lucinda, always off on some fight."

"If she comes in, can you please tell her I'm looking for her."

David leaned back in his chair and lit a cigarette. "Sure. But I wouldn't rely on her. She could be in Austria or Switzerland or Swaziland. Her list of injustices to correct is long."

Anya bit back her retort. It would do no good to offend David. She needed him—at least until he was done with the passports.

"Yes, I am familiar with Lucinda's passions. I have some information she might find quite useful for one of her quests."

She turned to leave.

"By the way," she heard David's voice behind her, "Anya suits you. Much better than Valentina."

"Yes, well, I'm sure you understand why I had to take that precaution."

David's laugh cascaded over her, leaving her feeling as if she was covered in dirt. "Of course, Anya. Of course."

She left the room, walking through the tobacco shop, grateful that there were no customers and the clerk appeared busy putting out a new shipment of rolling papers. She had two more stops to make before she could go back to Lena.

Anya pulled the collar of her coat up. It was a cold day. The weather had changed abruptly, and the wind had a bitter edge that hinted at winter. She was done with gray Berlin winters. Maybe she and Lena should settle in Portugal, in the Algarve, close to the coast, where they could enjoy some sun even in February.

She made her way to a warehouse that she'd been to many times. The front was a furniture store, a cavernous space filled with chairs and tables and whatever else could be made of wood. The proprietor was an older man who was hard of hearing and didn't notice what his daughter was up to in the staining shed around back.

Anya knocked on the back door out of habit but knew that it couldn't be heard above the blaring metal music that was exploding through the material of the walls. She pushed the door open, finding the music obnoxious. How anyone could work through the noise, she didn't understand.

She closed the door and flipped the lock. Anya preferred to not be disturbed, and she wouldn't be able to hear anyone come in amidst the deafening screech filling the space.

Walking further in, she found Rose busy at work, staining what looked like a baby's cradle.

Anya had to get right up in Rose's face before she noticed her. My goodness, anyone could just come in. She shook her head at Rose's vulnerability but knew there was no point in saying anything. Rose lived in the present, never worrying about security or her future.

Rose's face lit up in a smile as she registered Anya. "The music," she yelled, reaching behind her for a knob.

Anya waited until the sound was reduced to background noise. "Rose, hello. You seem busy."

Rose looked around as if noticing all the furniture for the first time. "Yes. We have many new orders. There must be a baby boom happening in West Berlin, because I've been working on new cribs for weeks."

Anya stamped down the surge of desire that jumped through her. Just another thing her ex-husband had robbed her of, a sibling for Lena.

"I am happy for you, to be so busy doing something you love."

Rose smiled at her. "But this isn't just a social call."

"No," Anya agreed, shaking her head. "It's time."

"Are you sure, Anya?" Rose chewed at her bottom lip. "I know we've talked about it, but if you do this and it doesn't work, he'll never leave you alone."

"He will not leave me alone unless I give him something else to focus on." Yes, she wanted to pay back the exact amount of pain her ex-husband had caused her. But she also wanted him so plagued with problems that he wouldn't have the resources to find her.

"If you're sure," Rose said.

Anya had never been more sure of anything in her life. Michael Polenz, chief Stasi interrogator and the largest hypocrite in the GDR. For years she watched him bury people in the prison system for committing lesser offenses than he did on a daily basis. She had planned how to break his control, how to reveal him as a fool so that no one in the East would take him seriously ever again.

"I know you have built it," Anya said, pulling out a piece of paper from her purse. "Is there anything else you need to prepare?"

Rose waived the paper away. "A few details. I have everything I need here. Have you talked to Lucinda?"

"No. I haven't found her yet. She was in Austria I know, but she was supposed to be back."

"You'll find her. She knows how important this is." Rose let out a deep breath. "Once we do this, it's going to attract attention."

"That is the point. Lucinda loves attention. So it will all work out."

"I hope so," Rose said. "No one deserves it more than Michael. But I'm worried. A lot could go wrong."

"We've always known that. But you also know how carefully I've planned, how carefully we've all planned. This is our only opportunity."

"I know. And I know we have to take it, and how much there is at stake."

"It's okay that you're nervous," Anya said. "You should be. So am I. You just have to remember the good we're doing. The lives we will save, like your grandfather's."

Rose nodded and gave her a hug.

Anya knew that her plan was far from foolproof. There were some dependencies she couldn't get away from. But she had to try. For herself, and for Lena, she couldn't just walk away from what she knew to spend the rest of her life jumping at every shadow that appeared in her path. If she exposed him, her ex-husband would lose the resources to pursue her.

"I will come back in two days with Lucinda. Then she can get started learning what she has to do."

Her final stop was the graveyard she and Quentin had met in many times back when they were still Rob and Valentina.

She saw him standing beside a crumbling stone, the moss and mold slowly erasing the identity of the person it had been erected to remember. Graveyards were a wonderful reminder of why it was important to live. Everything was forgotten eventually.

"Anya," Quentin said as she arrived next to him.

"You would like something," she said.

"Yeah, some sign of good faith. A reason for not turning you in to the agency. Something to convince me to ask James to keep taking the risk of sheltering you and Lena."

"What would suffice for today?"

"More information on James's friend Edward."

Anya paused. "I have found out that he has not met up with his new courier. He didn't like the double change."

Quentin looked thoughtful. "It must have made him nervous. The book thing must be his own initiative."

Anya was silent for a moment. "It is a business to be nervous in. But because he is not active, I cannot find out what he means to share. I never got to that stage with him. I can confirm that he is the same man who is friends with Jamie. You will tell him, so he knows to protect himself."

"I don't suppose you'll tell me how you managed that?"

"I am not the only one who wishes to be free of the life the Stasi has imposed on them. I have many friends. No one I trust completely, because of the sacrifices people often have to make for freedom, but trust enough that I don't believe they would lie to me about something like this."

"Is James in danger?" Quentin asked.

"That I do not know. But I don't think so. Edward is passing information willingly, not under duress. The Stasi do not require immediate leverage over him."

"I don't know if that makes it better or worse."

"In the GDR it is enough to accuse someone, but in the West you need more than this."

"Yeah, we require proof. Something that can't be dismissed."

"Or buried."

"That too," Quentin sighed.

Anya knew it was time to open up more to Quentin, to share with him all that was at stake. She needed him to be on board with her plan and invested in its success. "My ex-husband, he is responsible for all the double agents in service to East Germany. He is the one who vets them, who collects information about them, who knows how they can be manipulated and compromised. He is the one who directs them, who tells them the information needed to provide value to the GDR. You know him as the chief interrogator, but he has an army of people to do his bidding. He saves his interrogations for those he suspects of betrayal, especially the foreigners. They are constantly tested, always being asked to prove their loyalty. One slip and they get caught in his web.

"He keeps meticulous records. He has a very good memory, but no one is perfect. Being responsible for the foreign agents gives him an incredible amount of power. He is well connected and able to spread misinformation far and wide."

"What are you saying, Anya?"

Anya took a deep breath. "If you can wait, I can give you much more than information about this one man. I can give you files on every foreign agent passing information to the GDR. Enough information that people cannot hide, and you can, what is expression, stop the bleeding?"

"Holy shit," Quentin said, staring at her.

She had surprised him. Shocked him so much that his usual mask had disappeared.

Quentin started walking slowly through the gravestones. Anya followed, staying close enough that to any observer they would be two friends out to pay their respects.

"How long do you want me to wait?" Quentin asked.

"Not long. I have been planning for years, and I know I do not have much time. I have everything in place. But you know there are always obstacles. One can't plan for everything. Nothing to worry about. I am only waiting for a few pieces."

"What's your plan B if you fail?"

Anya hardened. "I will not fail."

Quentin seemed to take a moment to process her resolve. He must have seen what he needed to because he nodded once before walking off.

She would not fail him, Anya knew, because she would not fail herself.

CHAPTER EIGHTEEN

James was avoiding Edward. He was trying his best to make it appear natural. He pleaded work, as if it was just about a blip in the schedule. He was still in for the book delivery, but had moved it by a week and had put in for permission to do a crossing. He knew he was supposed to carry on as usual, not raise any suspicions and all that, but James had felt he just couldn't do it. He couldn't be with Edward wondering if he was committing treason.

Walking briskly in the rapidly cooling evening, James reflected that at some point he was going to have to get over it. He was going to have to figure out a way to talk to Edward. Every time he imagined it, though, he wasn't sure how to start.

Part of him resented being put in this position, but he didn't know where to direct that resentment. At Edward for seeking him out in Berlin? At Quentin for revealing what he learned about Edward? At Anya for being in the right place to connect the two? It was a tricky situation, and James would have preferred to remain ignorant. He could have just had his occasional beers with Edward and let Quentin sort out the treason part. It would have been so much easier that way.

Right on the heels of that line of thinking, shame started to creep in. Why was he so quick to want to push this all back on Quentin? Why should there always be someone else to sort out the hard stuff? James was in uniform. Regardless of the ease of playing rock music, he was still out there trying to fight for his country. This thing with Edward, it was just another fight.

He supposed that in many ways he'd become complacent. It was easy to play rock music. He liked it anyway. And yes, he spent time pulling from the lyrics to try to speak directly to the citizens of East Berlin, but he'd been doing it for years, and it wasn't all that hard. The fact was, he hadn't been challenged professionally in ages. Not interested in promotion, he'd settled into his role. James performed it well, but mastery might actually be a ditch lined with stale actions.

Taking a deep breath, James realized he needed to hold himself accountable. Here he was, feeling sorry for himself at the news that an old school chum was likely selling out British secrets to the enemy. Navel-gazing at its best.

He needed to be better. For his country, yes, but also for himself.

James slowed his pace so he could walk and strategize at the same time. Lord knows he didn't want to go over it at home with Anya and her daughter hanging around.

Using the same approach as he did to craft psyops messaging, James decided to start at the end and work backward.

If he was successful at whatever it was he was going to do, then what would that look like?

He imagined the first success scenario would be Edward exonerated. James would help uncover information demonstrating mistaken identity at best or evidence of coercion at worst. Something that could put his mind at ease that he wasn't friends with a traitor.

But let's say Edward was guilty, that he was passing British secrets to the GDR. What would success look like in that situation? James knew for sure that without compelling evidence, he would get dragged into the inevitable quagmire of suspicion as well.

The first problem was that his initial suspicions were based on unverifiable sources. He couldn't just point to Quentin and Anya and say "Hey, they told me." Anya would be long gone, and he couldn't imagine her getting officially involved anyway. If she wouldn't talk to the CIA, she wasn't going to talk to MI6. Plus, James would be under suspicion for even having that contact. The reality was too improbable. Quentin also needed to be careful. James was sure Quentin would be in trouble for revealing any part of this to a man far outside the intelligence community.

James's position was thus a problem. There was no good reason why a British officer working in radio broadcasting would know any of this. When he was debriefed, if not interrogated, they were inevitably going to wonder how he became involved.

If James couldn't give them Quentin or Anya, then he better have some damn good evidence to take himself out of it.

It occurred to him then that the best course of action would be to gather what information he could then find a way to get it in front of the right people anonymously. Maybe Quentin could tip off someone in MI6. Or James could leave it on the desk of defense intelligence at the base.

Liking that idea, he moved on to what said evidence needed to look like. It would have to be concrete. If it was mostly supposition, then James would be shooting himself in the foot. First, the powers that be might not take it seriously. Second, if they did decide it worth looking into, then the net would be cast wide. The more verifiable details, the more it would likely stay away from James and everyone associated with him. It also increased the chances that Edward wouldn't be able to slip through and run away to the East Germans—or worse, be allowed to continue doing whatever it was he was trying to accomplish.

James couldn't help but wonder why Edward would be pursuing a life like this at all. His family was both wealthy and well connected. Edward could probably do anything he wanted. Become a philanthropist and give some money away. Run off to Canada and build a house in the mountains. Sponsor the arts. Save whales. There was no end of options for someone of his background.

He realized then that knowing what Edward was doing was not going to be enough. It was important to James to also know why.

He arrived at his flat to find Quentin sitting in the living room with Anya. Lena, presumably, was tucked away in the bedroom.

It unsettled him at first, like the space had ceased to be his. But really, he reflected, it was better to have them speaking. Hopefully it meant that his problems would be sorted out sooner.

He shrugged out of his jacket and hung it up before crossing to the fridge and grabbing a beer. He went for the Radegast tonight. Thank Christ Jasminka wasn't around. With her being a journalist, this situation would have been even more complicated.

"Am I interrupting anything?"

"No," said Quentin. "Anya and I were just discussing the new identities for her and Lena."

"Are they easy to get?" James asked. He was curious, having never known anyone who needed that service.

"For the average citizen, no. For me, not too hard. If I can run it through the station here, which I can't always do. So Anya here is just sharing a couple of contacts with me."

"I see," said Anya, "you tell each other many things."

"Normally he doesn't say anything interesting when he comes over," James said, gesturing to Quentin. "It's all about baseball and how tired he is."

He didn't miss Quentin's eye roll.

"It's necessary, Anya," Quentin said. "If you're going to stay here, James needs to know enough to protect himself."

Anya looked at both of them, lips slightly pursed. "Okay. I am not used to this type of sharing, but I understand that it is important to not be surprised. So," she said, turning to James, "I am getting new passports, yes. I have also found information about your friend Edward. I have connected the two—your friend and the man I was told has been passing information to the Stasi for years. I am sorry to say they are the same man."

James could feel his blood pressure start to rise. Hearing this East German woman talk about the situation made it concrete. There was something to know about Edward. If he were playing by the rules, Anya would have no reason to know anything about him.

"Can you tell me how you first met him? As I'm sure you've guessed, I don't have much of an idea of how these things work."

"He was told to contact me. Given a pass phrase and a location. He came to my store and introduced himself. Not with names, of course, but I know because of what he says that he is to give me information. We talk briefly then set up a meeting schedule. But I am not his original Berlin courier. This is the first time I meet him, just before I leave. So I do not know yet what type of information he provides."

"Why would someone switch couriers?" James asked.

"There could be many reasons," Anya shrugged. "Most likely his old courier was unavailable. Moved. Dead. In prison. Or maybe they wanted a different level of security. I was…trusted."

"How long has he been giving the GDR information? Do you know?"

"No, I do not. But I am sure it has been for a while. When I was given the contact, I was told he was an old friend. He had already proven himself in some way, and the relationship was important. That is partly why it was given to me."

James sat back, thinking. "Do you think you'll be able to find out any more about him?"

"The one thing you want to know is, I assume, what information he is giving, yes? The secrets he is sharing. Then he can be stopped, and you can figure out the damage he has done."

"Aye, that is important."

Anya tipped her head to one side. "You would like to know something else?"

"Yes, I bloody well do. I want to know why he's selling out his country."

"Ah," said Anya, "this I may not be able to tell you."

"Don't you ask? I mean, before you accept someone's state secrets, don't you check their reasoning?" James could feel his agitation building. How could anyone be so cool and calm in the face of all this? He knew, of course he did, that for Anya and Quentin it was business as usual. But knowing that it happened every day just made it all that much harder to understand.

"Yes," Anya said, "we ask. For many reasons. To make sure they are not plants sent to give us misinformation. To know how far they can be pushed. To get leverage in case they change their minds. But the true reason, that is personal, and sometimes it never comes out. I am working on something else, something I have to do before I leave. It might be that I will be able to give you everything you ask for. But I can promise you won't be satisfied. No matter what reason you see, will it ever be good enough?"

She had a point. A very good one. What reason could Edward possibly have that would make his actions acceptable?

"If you want to know the why, one day you will have to ask him yourself," Anya said.

"Just so we're clear," Quentin said, "that day is not anytime soon."

"Right, I'm not a bloody fool. I know my biggest challenge is to not tip him off. It's why I've been avoiding him the last few days."

"Not enough to make him suspicious, I hope," Quentin said.

"No. We're not those kinds of friends. I've gone years without seeing him. It's just convenience. I'm here and he's working out of the base."

"He is?" Quentin asked. "That's interesting. I thought you said he's a diplomat."

"As far as I know. But like you often point out, diplomat can be a cover for all sorts of shite."

"Can you find out more about what he's doing on the base?"

"Surreptitiously, I suppose," James said.

"It would help," Quentin said, "because we'd be able to better figure out what damage he might have done."

"What if it has nothing to do with his official job? What if he's in West Berlin to promote cultural exchange or something? Arrange a special exhibit at the British museum or whatever?" James asked.

"Maybe I do not understand," Anya said, "but the Stasi would only be interested in his information if it related to something useful. Technology research. Political challenges. They are not so interested in people who work in culture."

James noticed the mixture of distaste and disbelief that crept on her face as she said the last word. This woman was all business. If ever anyone needed to be emotionally torn apart by a night at the opera, it was Anya.

"James?" Quentin said.

"Right," he sighed. "Well, I was just thinking it could be related to Edward's dad. He's a very powerful man. He's got the ear of the queen, the prime minister, a boatload of money, and wide-ranging interests. To be honest, Edward could have the secret to Coca-Cola and still not be anywhere near as interesting as his father."

"I see," Anya said. She didn't offer anything else. Christ almighty James hoped it was okay to trust her. It was the daughter, he realized. It was each of their roles in protecting Lena that made it possible for them to trust each other like this.

"You've got to set up that book delivery," Quentin said. "It will tell us a lot, like what he wants to share and who he wants to share it with."

"I've put in the request for going over. I'm on the pre-cleared list. The East German government doesn't like it when I go over, but the border guards don't give me any hassle, as they all listen to my show. It's not going to be hard to bring a book over as long as it's a regular book."

"There's a good chance it will be," said Quentin. "My guess is that with Anya here gone, there's some confusion over who to trust. It's likely that Edward is reaching out to someone that he has no concerns with. Someone he's known for a while."

"That's what he said. Someone who stayed with him in England in the fifties."

"A resident of the GDR?" Anya asked, looking thoughtful.

"I have no idea." James said. "Was it an old family friend? Someone who was visiting? Living in England? Could be anyone."

"Well, when you get a name, we can start doing some digging. There might be records."

"You'll have to be careful," James said, feeling a pool of dread expanding in his stomach. "Looking into Edward means looking into his father. And I don't think anyone is going to be too happy about a stain on the Secretary of Defence. If there was anyone in a position to make things go away, it's that man."

"It always is the most powerful people who do the most awful things," said Anya.

Aye, and wasn't that the truth.

"I've got to get going," Quentin said, standing up. "I'll be back as soon as I can. Hopefully at that point, one of us will have more information and we can start to put this thing to bed."

James watched him go. *High treason. What an uncomfortable bed that was going to be—for a lot of people.*

CHAPTER NINETEEN

Jillian waited for Sebastian outside the S-Bahn station. The day was bright and crisp. The perfect autumn sky made her think of apple picking and leaves the color of fire. It was Jillian's favorite season at home, and she had never seen it as beautiful anywhere else.

She was a long way from Ottawa today, but the excitement of West Berlin in 1976 compensated for the more mundane scenery.

Feeling a tap on her shoulder, Jillian turned around to see Sebastian.

"I'm sorry I'm late," he said, clearly out of breath. "I didn't notice the time passing, and when I looked at my watch, I had to run here."

Here being the station in Spandau that was becoming familiar. "Did you come in on an earlier train?" she asked.

"Yes, the first one I could get. We, Peter and I, just wanted to make sure everything was ready. As much as it can be."

He looked nervous. Usually calm and easygoing, Jillian could tell that whatever he was going to show her today, it was causing stress. She presumed they were going to the house by the Wall, but of course she hadn't let on that she had any knowledge of it. When Sebastian had said the other day that he had something to show her, she knew this was it.

She wished she could ease his nerves, but that would mean sharing more than was wise. She hoped that whatever it was, she wouldn't be put in a conflict.

He started to walk, and Jillian fell into step beside him. They talked of his art, of Canada, and of their favorite books. As they turned up the street, the Wall looming at the end, Sebastian stopped.

"What I'm going to show you," Sebastian said, "you cannot tell anyone. Peter and I have trusted no one with what we've found. We are sharing with you because we need help, and I think you can help us. I don't want to make a threat, because I don't believe in them, but I think we can trust you because you trust me to do something important for you. You will see, I hope, why this must all be quiet, for now."

Sebastian turned and kept walking, obviously not expecting an answer at this point. Jillian was so intrigued, the curiosity having built for months, that she hoped it was something spectacular. She knew it was better if the secret was mundane. It would be disappointing, but safer. But she couldn't help wanting to be completely blown away in the next half an hour.

They were just a few meters from the house. She'd find out soon enough.

Sebastian led them through the side gate and locked it behind him. Another lock, and they were through the back door.

She could instantly hear the whirr of electricity. The power made her skin tingle.

She was in the substation, part of the municipal electrical grid. Looking around, she saw that the setup was similar to substations at home: big equipment, neatly organized and labeled, conducting electricity into homes in the neighborhood.

"You know what this place is?" Sebastian asked.

"Yes," said Jillian, "I know exactly what it is. I have to say, I'm curious as hell about what two guys with no technical backgrounds could be doing in here."

Sebastian grinned at her. "Come, I will show you."

He led her to the far wall where there was a metal ladder leading down into a basement. There was a light on, and she saw Peter at the bottom. Jillian made her way down, Sebastian following behind her.

Down here it was a mass of cables and boxes and other equipment, all bound, organized, and feeding into the machinery above.

Peter led her along the wall underneath what corresponded to the back of the house. Halfway down there was a steel door. They led her through it and arrived in a concrete tunnel with even more cables snaking along the ceiling in both directions. This had to belong to the city, these tunnels being the foundation of the grid that provided power to West Berlin.

"Power lines and communication lines are in this tunnel," Sebastain said, "but that isn't what we want to you to see."

He walked about twenty feet down the tunnel and came to a large piece of painted plywood.

Whatever it was they wanted to show her, it was behind that wooden barrier.

Sebastian and Peter moved the plywood aside. All Jillian could see was a black hole. She had no sense of how deep it was.

The men shone their flashlights into the void, and Jillian saw, perhaps a few feet ahead, the light glint of metal. What was this?

"Come," Sebastian said, taking the lead. "It is much better if we show you."

Following him, Jillian saw that the dirt walls stopped after about four feet. The air was still cool, but less damp as they moved into a metal tunnel. Jillian felt the wonder creeping up on her. In the light of the flashlights, she could see they were in a completely reinforced passageway. There was some rust where sheets of metal were bolted together, but most of it looked to be in excellent shape.

"What is this place?" Jillian asked.

"It is a tunnel system built by the Nazis during the war."

Holy shit. Jillian ran her hand along the wall. "Really? What was it for?"

Sebastian shrugged. "This we do not know. But the Nazis built many tunnels."

"They did?" Not that she was an historian, but her war knowledge was pretty good, and she had never heard of tunnels like this.

"Yes. All over this part of Germany. And in Poland. And maybe other places. Some are just dirt passages with four-foot ceilings, but there are some like this one."

"It's incredible," Jillian said, almost unable to fully take in what she was experiencing. "How big is it?"

"There are over two kilometers in the system we are in," said Peter. "We believe we have mapped it all, but there are many dead ends, and some parts have crumbled, so we don't know if there are broken passages."

"Where does it connect to?" Jillian asked. "Like, where would one have originally entered?"

"This we are not sure of either," Sebastian said. "There are three doors that go out into the forest on the other side of the Wall, in GDR territory, and one that is blocked. We have tried to map the area above that one, and we think it goes to a building that the East Germans still use for something."

Jillian was fascinated. "Is there anything else down here? I mean, why would the Nazis have built this?"

"They were crazy," said Sebastian. "Living in a world that didn't exist, planning for a future that wasn't possible. Who knows why they built all the tunnels. To smuggle goods? People? But where were they going to go? Perhaps they wanted to escape to another time and place."

"Another planet is more likely," said Peter.

"We have found much, but nothing valuable, except as history. There are uniforms, rations, piles of papers, and empty crates. It's almost a junkyard. But it is hard to see with just our flashlights. This is why we decided to share with you, Jillian. We are hoping you can help with all these wires. Come." Jillian looked up to where he was pointing and saw the ceiling was lined down the middle with cables of various sizes. One was definitely for lighting, as Jillian could make out a light bulb in a metal cage above, and she assumed there would be more every twenty feet or so.

They started walking, moving slowly as Sebastian frequently consulted the map in his hands. After about ten minutes, they came to a sort of antechamber. Maybe eight feet square, it had a large metal box on one wall, a broken pipe in a smaller square piece on the ceiling, and the ubiquitous wires overhead. There were piles in the corners, but Jillian couldn't make out what they were. Sebastian crossed to the box and pulled out a screwdriver from his jacket pocket. After a few moments he removed the metal box, which was a cover for an electrical panel underneath.

"You want me to look at this?" she said, gesturing to the panel.

"Yes," said Sebastian. "We are hoping you can at least make the lights come on."

"Could I borrow your flashlight?" she asked.

Sebastian handed it over, and Jillian walked up to the panel for a closer inspection. Following the cables from where they left the panel, most connected to the ones that were attached to the ceiling and fanned out through the entire tunnel system. But two went straight up and disappeared into the metal, presumably going through to another room, or box, above.

"What is on top of us, do you know?"

Peter pointed to the small metal pipe coming out of the ceiling. "This is the fourth door," he said. "There must have been a wheel or some other cranking device at one time, but it's gone now. The old writing is still visible, warning users to be careful of opening the door as there might be people above. We think there is a building directly overhead. You can see it from one of the platforms two streets up from the house. It's hard to know exactly, but the distance seems to match."

"Hmm," said Jillian, "so maybe that was the original access point. That way it would be hidden. You don't know what is in the building?"

"We don't know either the official or unofficial use. It's an old brick building that was built before the war, maybe as a school, but the Nazis could have turned it into anything. And the East Germans, well they probably use it to spy on West Berlin."

It was a reasonable guess, given the proximity.

Jillian examined the panel again. "It's a pretty standard setup. Like in a house, all the connections are isolated from one another, meaning you can turn one on or off without affecting the others. But I'm pretty sure there are capabilities for power here. Is this tunnel connected to the substation?"

"I don't know," said Sebastian. "The substation was built after the tunnel. After the Wall went up, there was a scramble to reroute things so that East and West were separated. But I have looked at schematics, and I don't think anyone knew about this Nazi tunnel in 1961. Where else could power come from?"

"I'm not sure," Jillian said. "It depends on the order of how things were built and what the Nazis originally connected to. If they wanted to keep this tunnel a secret, it's likely that you can turn on the power down here without impacting anything else. So, like, if they had to retreat down here, and the above building was occupied by the enemy, they would still be functional as long as no one shut off the main power to the whole system. If someone were in the building above, of course you'd want power, and it would never occur to you that you were also powering a subterranean tunnel system. But the power might not come from there. It could be connected to the grid at some other point."

"So can you make it turn on?"

Jillian smiled. "Maybe. But not right now. I'm going to need a few things, plus it's all dependent on how well the system was built and if it's survived aging. A few hungry mice, and the cables might not connect everywhere." From what Jillian could see in the edges of the flashlight's beam, Sebastian looked disappointed. "I'm sorry that I can't be of more help today."

"It is okay," he said. "I knew it was too much to expect for you to find one switch and make it all come on."

"What are you hoping for if I can get the electricity to work?" Jillian asked.

"Understanding," said Peter. "The Nazis must have built this tunnel for a specific reason. More light will help us do a better job of mapping. Some of the pathways just end. It all looks like an octopus right now. And we can more easily go through the stuff they left behind."

Jillian studied the panel again. "Well, I can tell you that there's power here for more than just lights. See these four cables?" She pointed to two clusters of two that were mid-panel. "They're marked differently. I'm not sure what they are."

"Can you find out?"

"I'll try. It's about determining what is being transmitted across those wires."

"Like what?" Peter asked.

"Think of all the things that require electrical connections. It's not just plugs for lights and toasters. Telephones and televisions are the two obvious ones. Sound and images are ultimately just electric impulses that are passed along cables as well."

"That makes sense," Sebastian said, shining his flashlight around. "They would want to light these tunnels but also communicate from one end to the other."

"I can check that," said Jillian. "And we can see if we can get anything running again. But I have to ask, what's your plan here? Do you have any ideas about what you're going to do? I'm sure a museum would be interested."

"Our problem is that it is all mostly under East German territory. If it were all under West Berlin, the situation would be different," Peter said. "If the East Germans find out, they will dig it up and seal it off. They care nothing about preserving Nazi history, and they would be terrified it would become another escape route."

It was a valid point. Not only were the tunnels themselves unnerving and surreal, but the idea that they were walking around under the GDR was challenging. For Jillian to be caught on this side would be a disaster.

They left the antechamber to head back to the entrance in the house basement. She had to admit that she was creeped out by the idea that she was walking under the Berlin Wall.

Of all the things Jillian had imagined about what Sebastian was up to, she was blown away by the reality. Yes, she had wondered if they were tunneling under the Wall. Never would she have dreamed that they uncovered a prebuilt reinforced tunnel system going back to the war.

She had never heard about the Nazis building tunnels like this, but she wasn't surprised. It was well known that as the war went on, Hitler spent more and more time in his underground bunker, and many of his trusted advisors like Goebbels even moved their families in. Jillian could see how that kind of thinking would have pervaded further, causing Hitler to demand the building of an entire secret network. It could be that it was part of an escape plan.

There was no question, however, that Hitler was paranoid long before the need to escape became more and more likely. So, what else would these tunnels have been built for?

The air was musty and damp. There was obviously little air circulation down here, but there must be a venting system to allow for some fresh air. The oxygen wouldn't last forever with people using the tunnels.

"How far does this go into West Berlin?" Jillian asked.

"It doesn't, not really," Sebastian answered. "Just the western edge of Spandau."

"How did you find it originally?"

"I was inspecting the Telekom lines. It's the kind of job you don't need to know much for, just look at the condition of the cables and the tunnels. One day I stopped to eat lunch, and across from me was this peeling plaster over brick. It was out of place, because those tunnels are concrete. I wondered what it was hiding, and, being an inspector, I thought it my duty to figure it out.

"I pulled the brick away—the connecting mortar had crumbled anyway—and it opened up into this system."

It's extraordinary, the kind of serendipitous event that ends up completely changing one's life.

"How did you end up using the house?" Jillian asked.

"It's the closest access to the main Telekom tunnel."

"Neither of you work for the electrical company. How do you manage it?"

"I have access so I can get to the Telekom cables at various points," Sebastian said. "Of course, I should only be using this access point once or twice a year. But if I get caught, I don't care for my job anyway."

It made strangely perfect sense to Jillian. Many cities had tunnels to hide the infrastructure that kept the city running, and they were often multipurpose, as it was far cheaper to share. The problem here was likely a result of changes that had been made when the city was divided. It would be useful to know if the Nazi tunnel was part of the larger system before the division, but she admitted it was unlikely. The Nazis must have built around whatever was in place at the time, using existing tunnels to connect to power only.

"We think it is an important find," Peter said. "We are not hurting anyone by using a utility house. Better than digging from someone's basement. But we still don't know what to do with it."

As they continued walking back to the basement entrance, Jillian reflected that no ideas immediately sprang to mind for her either. The whole tunnel system should rightly belong to a museum or cultural preservation organization, but the situation was complicated by the division of the country. To share its existence would be to compromise its existence.

But what a spectacular discovery.

They were nearing their destination as Sebastian had started to slow down. Before he pushed through the wooden barrier, he turned to Jillian. "I hope you can help us. Once we understand what all the wires are for, and if we can get the lights on, it will be better. But if you can't, I hope that you will not tell anyone about what is here. You must see how special it is. It would be a shame to lose it because of political differences."

"I know how to keep a secret," Jillian said. "And I agree with you. What you've uncovered here is remarkable. I will do what I can to help you."

"Thank you."

CHAPTER TWENTY

"It's a what?"

Two days later, Jillian was sitting with Veronica in the Tiergarten. The weather was definitely getting cooler, but it was still warm enough in the afternoon to relax on a bench. Jillian had bought them both hot chocolate, and Veronica had shown up with more Ritter squares.

Jillian had just finished telling Veronica about Sebastian and Peter's tunnel discovery.

"It's incredible. Really. I'd love for you to be able to see it. It's completely surreal. You can just imagine Hitler having a panic attack sometime in 1944 and ordering it to be built. I bet at one point it connected to his bunker."

"Do you think so? That it was built as an escape tunnel?"

Jillian thought for a moment. "Maybe. I guess I'm being fanciful. I think it's more likely it had multiple purposes that changed over the years. A lot of work went into it, so it's possible it was built earlier, but why I have no idea. Then as the war went on, sections were added and the focus changed."

"Do you think you'll be able to figure out the electrical?"

Jillian shrugged. "I hope so. Wires and connections degrade over time in any circumstances. Here you have a system that likely hasn't even been turned on in thirty years. But I'm going to try, mostly because it's cool and I love puzzles. But also, I'm curious. With the power on, we might be able to figure out the full scope of what it was built to do."

They sat there for a while, sipping their hot chocolate and munching on the Ritter.

"What do you think that will do?" Veronica asked.

"What?"

"Finding out more about the tunnel."

"Truthfully? Nothing. It's just about fulfilling my curiosity at this point. Even if I find out that it was built to protect Hitler from aliens, what can I do? What can Sebastian and Peter do? Their point that almost the whole system runs under East German territory is the game changer. Can't go to a museum, or a university, or the government. The East Germans would think nothing of filling in a Nazi relic in order to prevent people from leaving the GDR. Even if they only cut off the part that goes under the Wall, it means the people of West Berlin wouldn't have any access. So, it's all a big circle that confirms there's no point in telling anyone anything. Until that potentially-never-going-to-happen time when Germany gets reunited."

"Do you think," Veronica began, "that it would be useful for people who want to go in?"

"Where? To East Germany?"

"Yeah," said Veronica. "People like me. People who want to go in unofficially."

Jillian thought for a while. "I don't know. Say you were going over; if you didn't go in undercover, you'd be what while you were there? Invisible? A ghost?"

"Something like that. I was just thinking, it's an opportunity."

"I get it. I think, theoretically, you're right. But, like, how much paperwork did you have to complete to come over here? To get approval to go in as a ghost, well, HQ would want to know how you're going to do it. And us Canadians, we don't have that many people that we want to send over to spy in the GDR. So let's say we tell the CIA, because I'm sure they have a dozen IOs here they don't know what to do with. How many people are going to have to know? I mean, every time I'm in a meeting with NSA, there's like forty of them and three of us."

"Good point. This kind of infrastructure, everyone's going to have a different opinion about how to use it."

"Yeah, and with Sebastian and Peter being West Germans, I doubt I'd be able to convince them to tell the Americans but not their own government."

"Ah, well," said Veronica. "I don't know why, but it just seems like a waste to me to find something like that and not be able to do anything with it."

"I get it. I feel the same way. I think that's why I'm willing to help them learn more about what's down there. Part of me is hoping that in all that effort, something will come to me."

"In the meantime, you're doing something interesting."

"Yeah," Jillian smiled, "another story to add to my memoirs."

"Better than having no stories at all," said Veronica.

"Absolutely."

———

Jillian had gone shopping and collected some tools and parts she thought might be useful down in the tunnel. Her first priority was to see if there was a way to connect to a power source. After that she would see if she could make anything work.

This time down in the tunnel it was just her and Sebastian. He explained that he and Peter had both come out to Spandau a lot in the lead-up to telling Jillian, and it was wreaking havoc on their social lives. "Peter, he is interested in this girl who works in a restaurant and is studying to be an architect. The food is terrible there, but he goes two or three times a week just to stare at her."

"What's it going to take for him to ask her out?"

Sebastian smiled. "Peter, he has a formula."

"Really?"

"Yes. Me, I would just ask and get it over with. If she says no, well at least I'd never have to eat their soggy pizza again. But Peter, he says once she makes eye contact for four seconds, then he'll ask. So far they have only made it to three."

Jillian laughed. "It makes sense to me. Life is much easier when there's a formula."

"There is never a formula," Sebastian said. "Not for the things that really matter."

"I know. But for people like me and Peter, it's okay to pretend. That structure simplifies what we do. Like, if he jumps the gun and asks her now and she says no, he'll think that he didn't give her enough of a chance to be interested. Plus, it puts off the moment when he actually has to ask her out, with all the stress involved."

"What if he waits and she still says no?"

"He'll update his formula. Next girl, it'll be five seconds."

Sebastian grinned. "One day he'll say they have to stare at each other for half an hour, and he will never go out with anyone."

"He'll be okay," Jillian said. "He's pretty cute. I don't think he'll have to go more than six or seven seconds before his formula pays off."

They arrived at the house. Sebastian took out a key and let them in. Jillian felt comforted by the familiar whirr of electricity.

"Aren't you worried the neighbors are going to get suspicious of you coming in here all the time?" she asked.

"No," said Sebastian. "I have introduced myself to everyone on the street. I showed them my Telekom badge and said we were cleaning up the connections for this area. It's a six-month project. No one seemed to care."

They went down into the basement, and Jillian began to systematically evaluate the equipment. "Do you want to know what I'm doing?"

"Sure," he said, then shook his head. "But it won't mean anything, and I won't remember it."

"This might be a little boring then. I'm looking for a spare conduit. Most municipal substations have them to allow for growth in the area. Once I find that, I'm going to try to connect our tunnel to it. I don't know where the Nazis originally drew their power, but it doesn't really matter. We have power here, so we might as well use it."

"I came prepared," Sebastian said, pulling out a sketchpad from his bag. "If you don't need me for anything right now, I'm going to continue sketching the tunnels and making note of all the locations and signs, and trying to catalogue all the junk. I want to have a record of everything we find. If one day the East Germans discover this tunnel, I don't want them to pretend it never existed or distort it in some way."

"Makes sense," Jillian nodded. "I don't need you right now. Maybe check in once in a while. I might need to go farther into the tunnel to test how far the power goes, and I don't really know where I'm going. I could get lost."

Sebastian pulled a folded piece of paper from his backpack. "Here. A map. I will come back, but you never know. I made copies for us—all of us. To manage some of the risk. In the tunnel, we are mostly under East German territory."

Jillian took the paper, surprised and grateful for the thoughtfulness. It was true, she thought, as she watched Sebastian exit the room. It was risky being down here on so many levels. Not just because the East Germans were above, but because this tunnel could have other entrances. There could be more people who knew about it. It could also be structurally compromised given its age and neglect. But it was far too fascinating a find for Jillian to ignore it.

Twenty minutes later, Jillian had her spare conduit. She went into the Nazi tunnel and located the wires that led to lights. As close to the exit as she could, she cut and spliced so she could have a connection to the substation. She made her way down the concrete tunnel, hiding her connection behind the existing wires.

She got back to the substation basement and stood in front of the service panel. Now for the risky part. She was going to connect to the line side of a circuit that, as best she could tell, wasn't metered. This way, no one would notice the power being used. But there was a danger to doing it live.

Jillian put on protective goggles and gloves. She started attaching her tunnel wires.

Immediately the electricity started sparking and arcing, putting on a show. She did her best not to get distracted given that she didn't want to electrocute herself.

Jillian finished the connection and stood back. It was solid. She'd dirtied up the jackets of the wires so they wouldn't stand out as new during a cursory examination. Everything was connected, and she hadn't shut down the power to the western edge of Spandau. A win.

She removed her googles and stepped through the door. Now was the real test. *Let's see if the tunnel will light up*. Moving the plywood, she was instantly greeted with an orange glow.

Success.

"You have lights," Sebastian exclaimed, coming down the left passage.

"Yes," Jillian smiled. "I'm assuming it's a complete, closed circuit. So the lights should work everywhere. Next time I come, I'll start trying to isolate the other wires to figure out where they connect and what they do."

"What are the possibilities?" Sebastian asked.

"Well, like I said, communications cables are the most likely. In that antechamber you showed me, some connections were running aboveground. Now that we can see, we can find out if there are other places where it's the same." She set down her tools and gear at the tunnel's entrance. "We should spend some time now trying to see where to turn the lights on and off. No one should notice the draw on power, but still, we don't know the condition of the wiring. I don't think we should leave it on all the time."

"Yes," Sebastian nodded. "That makes sense. We are lucky to have found you, Jillian. As smart as Peter is, he knows nothing about electronics. And me, well, I've never stopped to wonder where the power comes from when I turn on my lights."

Jillian smiled, trying to ignore the frisson of unease that tickled the back of her neck. "Of all the bars in all the world," she said.

"Oh, not that part," said Sebastian. "I do work at the communications company, after all. We figured someone there would know what to do with electrical connections. No, the lucky part is that you seem to have bigger secrets to keep than we do. Although, given the size of this tunnel, your secrets must be very big indeed."

A fragile trust they had, but trust it was. "I don't know, Sebastian," Jillian said, looking around. "This might be my biggest secret yet."

CHAPTER TWENTY-ONE

Anya walked slowly along the path, smiling as she watched Lena run after the pigeons. They had brought more than enough seed to feed all the pigeons in West Berlin. The poor creatures, they didn't know what to do with the little girl running through them. She was moderately terrifying, but bird seed was flying out of her pockets, too tempting to justify flying away.

They were in Litzenseepark on the far west side of the city. It was a place Anya never had occasion to come to, far as it was from the center and the part of the Wall she had to pass through frequently.

It seemed a different place out here. Quieter, less of the bustle of a city. It was a hard time for parks, when the softness of autumn had faded, the ground hardened, the colors dulled as everything prepared for winter. Soon the frozen lake would be full of sledders, but now there wasn't much to do other than walk.

They had passed a few people, and Anya nodded in greeting while Lena flung her bird seed everywhere. No one paid them much attention, which to Anya felt wonderfully soothing. Rounding a corner, she let herself fantasize about the time when she could spend every day in complete obscurity.

Catching sight of a woman jogging across the field, Anya forced her focus back to the present. The job to do today would bring about the future she desired.

Lucinda caught up and fell into step beside her, only slightly out of breath. Lucinda was always running somewhere, and Anya knew her to be in excellent shape.

"Anya," Lucinda said, pulling her into a giant hug. "That creep David said it was okay to call you Anya now. Of course, he didn't know you before, so it's new to him, but you know what I mean."

Anya smiled slightly. It was funny to hear Lucinda call David a creep. He most certainly was, but what Anya enjoyed about her was that Lucinda saw no need for discretion about her opinions of people or their failings. She was blunt, but somehow also so charming that no one seemed to mind.

"Lucinda," Anya said, returning the hug quickly before pulling back. "It is wonderful to see you. I am always worried you will go off without telling anyone and I'll never know if you're rotting in a jail somewhere."

"I was only in Austria collecting money," Lucinda laughed, as if the idea of her ever being on the wrong side of the law was farfetched. "Don't worry. I promised you I wouldn't leave until after I helped you. I will go to South America because there is so much to do there, but only after we are done."

Lucinda wasn't that much younger than Anya, but still Anya worried about her like a daughter. Beautiful Lucinda who broke hearts and captivated minds wherever she went. Who had more courage in one finger than most men had in their whole souls. Who was determined to save the oppressed everywhere on the planet. Anya knew it was no exaggeration to fear that one day Lucinda's charm would fail her and she'd be locked up—or worse—for her role in some revolutionary activity.

Lucinda thrived on the risk. Anya couldn't change that. And she needed her. To compensate she kept no secrets from Lucinda regarding what she was asking her to do. Lucinda could have said no. The truth, however, had been compelling, and Lucinda saw an opportunity to fight injustice. It was thus a win-win for both women.

"I can only ask that you stay careful until we have finished and you are safe to leave. Remain out of sight as much as possible. We do not want him to notice you."

"I must be far down on his list by now. So many other people to torture."

Anya didn't comment because it wasn't necessary. Her ex-husband was a monster. She hated him. It was something, one detail of many, that she and Lucinda had in common. Anya knew it was no good to dwell on that hate, to let it rise up like bile in her throat, because then she would make poor decisions. Yes, Michael Polenz was a hypocrite and a murderer. Yes, he deserved to have every piece of skin slowly peeled from his body until he died in the most excruciating pain. But Anya knew there was no karma. No guarantee that Michael Polenz would ever feel a fraction of the pain of his victims. Any German had learned that life did not work that way.

Anya knew he would never atone. Never believe that anything he did was wrong. That was really what made him such an asshole.

Her only desire was freedom for herself and Lena. If someone else used the momentary vulnerability she created to further exploit her ex-husband, she would raise a toast to them when she was settled in Portugal.

In the meantime, she had work to do.

"Are you ready to practice on the safe?" she asked Lucinda.

"You've confirmed Rose will have the plans and all the parts?"

"Yes. Everything is built."

"Quiet Rose, who spends her days staining wooden furniture and listening to Black Sabbath. Who would ever guess she builds master safes in her spare time."

Anya pursed her lips. "Anyone who knows who her grandfather was, which, lucky for us, is almost no one."

Lucinda laughed, a jovial sound that seemed to ricochet around the expanse of the park. Anya didn't admonish her. Lucinda was careful, slow to trust, and incredibly brilliant. But she wasn't paranoid like Anya. She hadn't grown up in the East German system, in the web of deception and despair that made people afraid to have thoughts that didn't follow the party line, as if the Stasi could invade the sanctity of the skull and arrest you for an errant idea.

"I like Rose. She finds happiness in the most unusual pieces of life."

Anya sighed, and that was why she loved Lucinda. She was so alive in a way that Anya struggled to understand. Rose too. Grounded and courageous. They had listened to her and accepted her. Anya was desperate for her freedom, such a powerful motivator, but ultimately so selfish. But Rose and Lucinda, they were willing to take risks for others. For her. There were some other motivators, but nothing that meant life or death in the world of either woman. She didn't fully understand them and could admit to herself that she was not sure she would do the same. But Anya would never betray either of them. So she worked to prepare as best she could so there were no surprises.

"From now on we will meet at Rose's shop in the evenings, after it has closed, but not too late to arouse suspicion. She often works odd hours given that she rarely is in the front, dealing with customers. Where will you be staying?"

"Right now I'm catching up with Phillipa," Lucinda smiled. "Once you gave me the go ahead to get in touch, I was going to ask Rose if I could sleep on her sofa. It seems ideal for what we have to do."

"Yes, that is a good idea." That way Lucinda was less likely to get distracted and so put more hours on practicing the safe.

Anya opened her mouth to ask if Lucinda needed money when Lena came running up to them.

"Mama," she said, "I am all out of food for the birds."

Anya was surprised it had lasted as long as it did. "Well, we will just have to come back and feed them another day. Here, say hi to my friend Lucinda."

Lena looked up and smiled, eyes widening in awe as she took in the pink streaks in Lucinda's hair and the shocking glitter of her scarf. Anya sighed. Now she would be bombarded with requests for streaks of hair color.

"Oh my, you look just like your mother," Lucinda knelt down and smiled at Lena, "which means you are probably just as smart as she is. Tell me, what do you love to study most?"

"Art," said Lena without hesitation, "but I am also very good at math."

"I bet you are. It's no surprise to me that you're multitalented. Shall we go get some hot chocolate at the end of the park and get to know one another better? I've wanted to meet you for a long time, and I'm dying to know some of your mother's secrets. Something she does when she thinks no one's watching."

Lena smiled at Lucinda and offered her hand. "I would love some hot chocolate. Thank you. But I don't know any secrets to tell you."

Lucinda laughed in her usual captivating boom. "Tell me, does she at least sing in the shower?"

Lena looked back at her mother, as if struggling to imagine it. "No. But I have heard her singing to a song on the radio. 'Dreamboat Annie' by these ladies named Heart. Our friend Jamie plays it for her on the radio, he says, so now she sings to it."

Lucinda raised her brows at Anya. "You've got someone playing music on the radio for you? Well, you do collect the most fascinating people."

Anya tried not to let the trepidation take over. This was new territory for her, a world where the important people in her life knew of each other. For years she had kept Lena isolated to protect them both. Two weeks ago, Lena and Lucinda meeting would have been a disaster. But now they were in West Berlin, where no one cared.

She had grown up in East Germany, had been part of the grand experiment since the moment it began. She was only two when the war ended and so had never known anything else.

The time she had spent in West Berlin in the last few years was always as an interloper, someone who did not really belong. It was only through Lucinda and Rose that Anya had any appreciation of how life worked over here. But old tendencies take time to dissipate. It would be years, or maybe never, for her to let go of the caution that had ruled her life for so long.

"He is providing us a safe place to stay." Anya paused, feeling like she should say more. "It is safe because he is on the radio. He has a…different life. Not the kind of person I would have interacted with before."

"How did you meet him?" Anya knew Lucinda's question came from a place of concern. She knew how vulnerable Anya was, how long the reach of her ex-husband.

"The man who drove Lena over. They trust each other. It was enough for me, and better to have someone unknown. Not connected to anyone that came before."

"That's good," Lucinda said, putting her arm around Anya, "because we're in the home stretch. I so want to be able to completely fucking humiliate that prick you used to be married to. So this Jamie better keep you safe."

Anya smiled. "He is not really that kind of man. Not that I've seen anyway. He's kind enough but doesn't seem to want to get involved at all."

"Well," said Lucinda, "that makes him perfect."

They reached the door of the café where Lena had been promised hot chocolate. Before opening the door, Anya said, "Let's work out our schedule. David said the passports will be ready soon, and looking for me should be providing Michael with a distraction. The sooner we can do what we want, I think the better the chances of our success."

<hr>

Anya balanced the bags of groceries as she turned her key to enter James's apartment with Lena. She hesitated momentarily as she heard shouting through the door. It stopped as quickly as it had started, and there was no response, so Anya pushed the door open gently, keeping Lena behind her.

As she went in, she turned toward the living room. She saw the flickering of the TV, the screen filled with green, and Jamie leaning forward, tightly gripping a beer. Ah, he must be yelling at some sports game.

Anya stood back to let Lena in, then locked the door behind them. Jamie turned to see her taking off her coat after she'd set the groceries on the floor.

"I can't quite get used to someone coming in on their own," he said, standing up. "Been living alone way too long."

"Yes, I can imagine. I have brought some food. I was going to make chicken soup and dumplings. Would you like to join us?"

"That sounds right lovely," he said.

Anya got Lena set up with her art then moved to the kitchen and began chopping vegetables and sautéing the chicken. She loved soup and dumplings. It was a comfort food to her, taking her back to her grandmother's kitchen and the rare time in her life when things were simple.

Jamie continued to watch the game, yelling occasionally but omitting the swearing. It was a sweet gesture, although Anya knew that Lena wouldn't understand the English obscenities anyway.

The stock began to take shape, the aroma filling the kitchen and spilling into the rest of the apartment. Jamie's game must have ended, because he turned off the television and carried his empty beer bottle into the kitchen.

"Smells wonderful," he said, coming up to lift a lid on the pot. "I don't remember the last time I had a homemade dumpling."

"They do not have these in Scotland?" she asked.

"Oh, we've got our own version of a cooked bread ball, like the pastie, but they're not in soup. It's more that I don't get home very often, and my culinary skills don't include anything that fancy."

Anya raised a brow. "They are very simple to make. If you like the dinner, I could show you. A gift."

He looked on the verge of declining until her last two words. "Right then, I suppose I should be looking to expand my kitchen repertoire. No sense in eating the same five things the rest of my life."

It was clear to Anya that Jamie enjoyed the dinner. He had so many dumplings that Lena's eyes had rounded in amazement.

She read to Lena while he did the washing up. It was something about him that she admired. If she cooked, he did the cleaning, no questions asked. It was something her ex-husband never would have done, seeing as he lived a life where he imagined everyone existed to do his bidding.

Later, after Lena was in bed, Anya returned to the living area and sat down across from Jamie. He was flipping through some magazine, but he'd made her a cup of tea and had set it on the table between them.

"Jamie," she said, a little sorry to interrupt him.

"Hmm?"

"I have a favor to ask of you."

He raised a brow at her but didn't say anything.

"I know you have already given so much. Staying here, helping Lena feel safe. I know too that you will not be sorry when we're gone. Me, as well, I am anxious to leave this place. In order to give Lena the best possible chance at a good life, we have to leave Berlin with more freedom than we have now."

"I have wondered, you know," Jamie said, "what you had to give up in order to get this far."

Anya shook her head. "You could say that I paid for Lena's crossing in advance. So, I am not in debt. Except maybe yours, a little. It is instead about what we are leaving behind."

She paused for a moment, taking a breath. She had to think carefully about what to tell him. Enough to secure the help, but not so much that it could impact her plans. And too, she liked him. She did not want to see him come to harm on account of her.

"My ex-husband is a horrible man who has a lot of power. He will not let us go easily, not because he loves us, not even Lena, but because he does not want to let go of anyone that he can control. I have a plan I have been working on for a long time. With Lena safe, now is the time to execute."

"You're telling me all this because you have to," Jamie said. "What do you want from me, Anya?"

It was funny. All the years she took what she had to without caring about anything other than her goal, and it was this moment that made her feel guilty.

"I will have to go out in the evenings. I, of course, will not leave West Berlin. But there are things I need to do. Could you watch over Lena when I am gone? I promise it will not be at the times when you need to go to work."

Jamie was silent for a long moment. "Aye," he said. "That I can do."

Anya's hands shook with the rush of gratitude. "I promise, too, that I will give you information about your friend. I know it isn't easy, but knowing something will be better than imagining everything."

Jamie shook his head. "I wish I could say that I'll not be needing that, but I suppose I do. I can bury me head in the sand about a lot, but even I can't ignore suspected treason. But Anya, so you know, I'll look out for Lena because every child should have people looking out for them. If you don't find anything about Edward, so be it. I'll sort something out."

"Thank you," Anya said.

"After all, I've got Quentin, who owes me a favor or ten. Putting up with him has got to be good for something."

CHAPTER TWENTY-TWO

James was surprised Edward wanted to meet in the mess. He'd always imagined that double agents conducted their affairs in shadowy alleys or in the middle of a forest. The mess hall seemed too public, but he wondered if that was the point.

He had just brought his pint to his lips when Edward slid into the seat across from him. He looked tired and a little spooked, but maybe James was projecting. He thought committing treason must be hard on one's quality of sleep.

Edward put a package on the table—about the size of a good hardcover, but thinner, and wrapped in brown paper. James assumed this was the special delivery request.

"You don't mind if I get a gin before we get into it, do you, old chap? End of the day and all that, might as well do it all civilized."

James just nodded. Edward jumped up and crossed to the bar. James noticed that his fingers instantly began a staccato tempo on the polished wood.

James knew he was meant to make all this seem normal. Be the naive and ignorant bloke Edward obviously assumed he was. The trick was going to be to ask enough questions. James just wanted to grab the package and get out, but clearly that would raise a fair bit of suspicion.

And, of course, too many questions and it was going to come over like an interrogation.

So to find the sweet spot. Thank Christ he didn't do this for a living.

Edward came back to the table, gin in hand. "I haven't seen you around much lately," Edward said before raising his glass in a toast.

James clinked his glass and took a healthy swallow. "Ah, you know, at my age I end my shift excited about a pint on the sofa in front of the telly. Plus, I had a bit of a cold for a few days. That time of year."

"Yes, I guess it's different for you here. Almost like a regular nine to five."

"Aye. The uniforms do like a consistent schedule. You been busy, then?"

Edward shrugged. "No more than the usual. The never-ending parade of meetings to discuss one issue or another."

"I've got to say, you don't come across as a ringing endorsement for a career in diplomacy."

Edward mustered up a smile, but his sincerity was lacking. "It's not so bad, really. Parties and alcohol and underlings everywhere to do the research and prepare the notes. It never feels like we're doing much. The Wall's still up. The world's still a mess, pumping out nuclear weapons like we can afford to use them. If humanity is so bloody stupid, it might be better to just get drunk and get it over with."

"Why do you keep doing it, then?" James asked, wrapping his hands around his pint like it was an anchor in this sea of confusion. "Surely with all the money sitting in the family coffers, you could chuck it all in and spend your days like Hemingway: a permanent fixture in some bar in a hot third world country, steeped in gin and ranting at the tourists."

"Ah, Jamie, you don't know how often I'm tempted. Unfortunately, my life is not my own. When one is an eldest son in a family with a title, you aren't your own person. Have to carry on the family line and make sure the entail isn't squandered away. More than one family has lost their prestige on account of a male family member spending too much time at the gaming tables."

"So you stay on the straight and narrow to make sure Britain continues to have her fill of little bluebloods? How devoted of you."

"For Queen and Country," Edward said, raising his glass to the portrait of Queen Elizabeth II that graced every mess hall in every outpost of the British realm.

"When are you going to get on with producing the heir and the spare then?"

A look of despondency passed over Edward's face. "I'm thinking of following in the footsteps of the more famous Edward and stepping aside in favor of my brother. Then I really could get away."

James wanted to press. He was curious. Edward didn't seem happy, not by anyone's definition. If abdicating, or whatever the hell it was called in the lesser ranks, was an option, then why hadn't Edward already taken it?

"Just have to sign some paperwork?"

Edward grimaced and stared at his drink. "It's not that bloody easy. There is the formidable obstacle of my father. I daresay he quite despairs on choosing between his sons. At least I have some semblance of responsibility to the family name. My brother's turned into quite the entitled dilettante. Sleeps all day and lives his life as if there can never be any consequences for someone like him."

Which, James reflected, there obviously weren't. Rich people had a way of cleaning up after their children so no natural consequences could possibly impact their behavior.

"It's hard to feel sorry for you, mate. But I get it. Parental expectations have a way of ruining the potential of their children's lives."

"Right-o," Edward replied. "Don't worry, I'm not yet ready to whinge to the *Daily Mail* about the problems of being a future earl. No need to play into the popular opinion on the worth of the British nobility."

"Showing that stiff upper lip?" James smiled.

"Just carrying on tradition," Edward replied.

"Right then, tell me about this mysterious book you want delivered."

Edward waved his hand over the package as if dismissive of its contents, but James could see the tension ratchet up around his mouth.

"Oh, just an old tome that's been sitting in the library in the family seat for decades. It's some ancient Greek volume that one of the previous earls probably bought to impress his intelligence on his visitors."

James took a drink of his beer, trying to think of what a natural level of curious would be in this situation.

"It's not something you're repatriating, then?"

"Lord no. Since our monarchs stopped being German on account of World War I, it's been decidedly unfashionable. No, our library is stocked only with those English essentials—Chaucer, Locke, Hume. Nothing German, and god forbid, nothing French."

James felt like he was shadowboxing. Edward was playing up the old English stereotypes. Why? To impress his Britishness on James. To make him think that a self-depreciating, reluctant noble would never have the brains, let alone the motivation, to undermine his country.

"Who's it for again?"

"An old school chum from my Cambridge days, believe it or not. I know we're going on twenty years now, but Dieter was the reason I scraped through my classics lectures. I haven't seen him in years. Not surprising, with the Wall up and all, but I was in a meeting the other week, and his name came up. It reminded me how lucky I was that he had the room next to mine in our freshman year."

It was an interesting story. It also had the ring of truth. As soon as James had a name, it was a verifiable story.

"Of course, we've only been able to exchange the odd letter over the years. The bloody East Germans make travel near impossible, and the couple times they've let him out, it's been all official business surrounded by minders. That's the Communists for you. If you're afraid everyone's going to leave, what does that tell you about your system?"

It was the right thing to say. It made sense. It's exactly how James felt about the East Germans.

He was suddenly struck by how hard it must be when one was a spy. How would you know the difference between a lie and a truth? Listening to Edward, his position was consistent with most of the Western world. There were millions of people who thought the same way. Obviously they weren't all double agents. It was like playing to the law of averages. Spies hid in plain sight by trying to be top of the bell curve on everything. There was nothing about what Edward was saying that was grossly atypical. If it hadn't been for Anya's assurance that he was one of her contacts, James would never have suspected him at all.

"Must be someone halfway important then, if they let him out at all."

"Not important so much as useful. He's a mechanical engineer. He came to England originally because of the work Turing had started on computing machines. Wanted to study at the source and all that. I imagine they have him working on whatever they're doing on trying to keep up with the rest of us. Not that I know anything about computers. Managed to completely avoid them so far."

"What does a book in ancient Greek have to do with computers?" James asked.

"As far as I know, nothing. Like most geniuses, Dieter's interests were wide ranging. I remember he got quite excited by it, and my father isn't going to bloody miss it. The man only reads the same two books by Clausewitz and Sun Tzu."

"That's nice of you to remember that he liked it and to bring it all the way here."

"I guess it's too many years trying to make peace. Catch more flies with honey, don't they say. You never know who you're going to need to work with one day."

James forced himself to lean back and relax. Forced himself to toss a mouthful of beer down his throat. "That's why I'm on the radio playing rock music, mate. Like a giant spill of honey flowing over the Wall."

"Let's hope you catch a lot of flies," Edward said.

James felt his pulse begin to thud in his neck. Time to get out of this conversation. "Where am I meant to take this book?"

"I've got an address. I don't imagine you can just drop it in the post when you're on the other side?"

"If it doesn't get confiscated on the way over."

"Right. There's a high probability of that. I wouldn't mind so much, as it's just a book, but I'd hate for it to sit on some bureaucrat's desk because they're worried the ancient Greek was in code or something."

James waited a few beats, as if he was thinking. In truth, he'd already worked through how to proceed in as many scenarios as he could with Quentin. "We have a military bag. Both sides do. The Soviets get them too. The border guards are allowed to inspect them, but they aren't allowed to keep anything. They respect the protocol because we extend the other side the same courtesy. It's only for military, and it's effectively like a briefcase. We don't put anything sensitive in it. I use mine for my research notes, things like that."

"Ideal. Will you be able to drop it off directly?"

James shrugged. "Should be able to if it's in East Berlin. I've got to stay within city limits. And, you should know, I'll definitely be followed there. They don't even bother to hide. The militaries escort each other. I'm only telling you in case there would be trouble for your friend, having me show up on his doorstep."

"I can't imagine it'll be a problem. I've only got the work address anyway, and it's just a book."

The reality of the situation shot like a weight into his gut. Now he knew. It was on this point that James felt Anya's claims were confirmed. Because had the whole plan been innocent, it absolutely would have caused a great bloody problem for this bloke Dieter. Edward, immersed in the diplomatic nuances that he was, would know that. His dismissal of the threat was the most suspicious part of the conversation.

"Right then. I'll do my best. I'm meant to go over Thursday right after my shift in the booth. If I can't get it to him directly, are you okay with me leaving it with a receptionist or something?"

Edward thought for a moment. "At the lab or whatever it is? Sure. But not with anyone in border control. Just bring it back if that's the case. I'm sure someone else I know will be going over eventually."

James nodded, and they finished their drinks. It was easy enough talking about sport and the latest royal family drama. James felt the occasion should be marked somehow, but he supposed that was what made it all the more dangerous. It was wrapped up tightly in the commonplace.

James was itching to open the packaging and look at the book, as if it would be able to tell him something definitive, confirm or absolve his fears about Edward.

He waited until he was home and Anya had left for the evening. Lena was tucked up in bed, and Quentin was sitting across from him on the sofa.

He gently unwrapped the brown paper, peeling the tape carefully so he could put it back together the same way. Inside lay, as promised, an old, leatherbound book with Greek lettering on the cover. He flipped it open, careful not to stretch the binding on the spine. It creaked and cracked in his hands, and James was sure the thing had never been read in its entirety.

He looked over the cover page, the table of contents. He turned to random pages. Checked the index at the back.

"I can't see anything useful at all," he said to Quentin, handing over the book.

"What were you expecting? Detailed notes in the margins? A letter tucked into the front cover?"

"Hoping mate, hoping."

"If he's good enough, and important enough, to get assigned to Anya, figuring out what he's communicating with this book is going to be more difficult than that."

"That's why I have you," James said. "Something to drink while you solve the mystery?"

"A Coke if you have one."

"Aye." James crossed into the kitchen and got a Coke for Quentin and a Tennent's for himself.

"What do you reckon then? Some secret code? Ten letters underlined in the whole book?" Both of which would take all ruddy night to figure out. "Because you know, I need me beauty sleep."

"All the sleep in the world isn't going to fix that face," Quentin said.

James laughed. "Ach, hard on a man's confidence, aren't you?"

"Somehow I doubt that," Quentin said. "Do you have a ruler?" he asked.

James got up and began to rummage around in the kitchen drawer where he threw all the random bits that ended up in his apartment. "You're in luck. Normally I wouldn't, having never had a great use for one, but the girl, she insisted she needed one the other day. To design her buildings and whatnot."

"So you went out and bought her one?"

"Her mother did. But then Lena decided it was a hindrance more than anything, so it ended up in the odds and ends drawer."

Quentin took the ruler and began slowly moving it down a page.

"You're not going to go through the whole bloody book like that, are you?"

"Aren't you in psyops?" Quentin asked. "Where's your patience?"

"Christ Jesus. It seems like a task for Jillian."

"Yeah, she'd be about a hundred times better at this. But we are not involving her."

"What if you don't find anything?" James asked.

"We are not involving her."

"Right."

"So, how's it going with the roommates?" Quentin asked. "Making you yearn for domestic bliss?"

"Anya is not a woman to inspire that." James chuckled. "Wound up tight as a clock, that one. Legitimate, of course. But sure doesn't make me want to give up bachelorhood. Lena though, she's fun. Devoted to her art and intense like her mother, but still a kid. Reminds me of my nieces and nephews, and how I don't get to see them as often as I'd like."

"Has Anya told you anything more about what she's doing here?"

"Probably not as much as she's told you, but she did happen to mention she's got some vendetta to settle with her ex-husband before she can kiss Berlin good-bye."

"Did she tell you who he is?"

James paused for a moment. "No. Would I know him?"

"Probably not," Quentin shrugged. "Not in your line of work. He's well known to us and sits on some pretty important information."

"Ah, so that's how it's a win-win for the two of you. She takes her pound of flesh, and you get an intelligence windfall."

"Something like that. Although, to be honest, I'm not sure how she's going to pull it off. Most people, they just name names. Maybe a few photos. It's hard to carry out a ton of concrete proof. But Anya says she can get that. When she hands it over, she can just ride off into the sunset."

"What are the chances of it all going off as simple as that?"

Quentin looked up from the book. "Close to zero."

"What then?"

Quentin put down the ruler and leaned back into the sofa with his Coke in hand. "I don't know why you always act as if I've got some working crystal ball."

There was a faint smile on his lips, but he was betrayed by his stillness. Quentin was nervous.

"This isn't something I deal with regularly, you know," he continued. "Defectors. It doesn't fit my cover, and I don't have the resources to help them. Anya didn't need help, apart from a place to stay, but even having her here is such a risk."

James knew it was a risk for himself, given the shite that would rain down on him if his superiors ever found out what he was up to. But he'd not much considered the risk to Quentin. "More than the usual?" he asked.

Quentin took a long drink from his Coke. "You aren't supposed to know that I'm CIA. I get how it happened, but technically, once you knew, I should have pulled back and spent some effort trying to distance myself."

"You can't be the first person to break that protocol."

"I'm probably not. You're from an allied country, and I could make the legitimate argument that you might be a useful contact. But not for what I've asked you to do with Anya. I just couldn't see another way forward. She didn't want to go in and would have run if I pushed it. The information she's offering, it's big. Tip-the-scales-in-the-Cold-War big."

"So you're hoping, whatever happens, the intentions are factored into the results," James said.

"Something like that."

"Well, if it's any consolation mate, I was probably going to get involved anyway. The unfortunate connection with Edward was bound to tangle everything up. At least this way we're not going to blindside each other, and working together, as it were, might stop it from being a total cock up."

Quentin smiled into his Coke. "Well, if you put it that way."

James gestured to the book lying on the coffee table. "Any ideas about that then? Or should I just deliver it and be done?"

"Having the guy's name is good. It could be a cover, but that's easy enough to figure out. And it could just be the book itself is the message, like, hey, I need help. Send someone." Quentin was silent for a while.

"But?" James asked at last.

"But I don't think so. Edward already has a new contact. Anya confirmed someone replaced her." Quentin gestured to the wrapping with the name and address for the book delivery. "He wants to communicate with this Dieter Venmar for some other reason. We don't even know if Anya was the trigger. Maybe he's unhappy with the current demands, and he thinks this guy has the power to do something about it.

"But if it was a regular contact, he wouldn't be going about the communication like this, especially the part about involving you. No, this is something he wants to keep away from his usual Stasi minders. There's something in this book, but I can't tell what it is."

"Jillian and I are overdue for a dinner."

Quentin let out a long sigh. "Fine. You're right. Bring it to her. Tell her your suspicions, but nothing about Anya. If she gets nosy, remind her of all the times you were polite enough not to ask any questions."

"I'm sure that will go over well."

Quentin opened his mouth as if to respond, but James held up a hand. "Aye, I understand. She's normally up to her eyeballs in enough shite that I don't need to be adding to it. I'll go see her tomorrow. Edward isn't expecting me to take this over until Thursday, so I'll still be on schedule."

Quentin looked resigned. No doubt he felt that this situation was fast getting out of control, forcing all his compartments to spill over into one another. But, better to do it right than have regrets and pay the price later.

James watched as Jillian examined the book. She was carefully going through the pages, periodically holding one up to the light, and running her fingers along the text. He'd brought his own book to read, well prepared for the amount of time it could take her.

He'd told her the outline of the story. An old acquaintance currently employed as a diplomat for the British government had turned up on base and had, among other things, asked him to carry this book over to an old school chum in East Germany. He was suspicious but didn't want to cause trouble without proof.

It was the truth, just not all of it. James tried to ignore the churning in his gut. He didn't much like lying, especially to

Jillian, so he sat there trying to convince himself she wouldn't want to know anyway.

"There could be a coded message. There's no pattern to the smudges."

James narrowly missed choking on his tea. "You figured that out right quick then, didn't you?"

"What, kicking yourself over the hours you've already wasted when you should have just brought it to me in the first place?" She smiled sweetly at him.

"Fine then, and how do you know there's a message?"

"I don't, not for sure. But it's an old book, printed before anyone wanted to use it to encode something."

"Back up. What in the bleeding hell are you talking about?"

"The ink is smudged every once in a while," Jillian explained. "At first glance, you'd assume it was introduced by the printing process. Except this book is old enough to have been done by a press with movable type. Meaning, each symbol would be carved on a separate plate, and the printer would put together all the plates needed for each page, one or a few at a time. So, if the omega produced a small smudge on page one, it should produce the same smudge on page five, because it would be on account of a defect in the original metal plate. But that's not the case here."

James looked at the book skeptically. "So you're saying it might have been smudged on purpose."

Jillian shrugged. "It's a guess. The smudges might be from the oils on the hands of the people who've handled it over the years, but the book doesn't look like it's actually been read much. The smudges occur closer to the spine, where hands are less likely to touch."

"You're not helping."

"I would start with the smudges," Jillian said, "but I'm saying that they could also be a red herring. Maybe the guy receiving this already has the key and knows what letters to pick out. In that case, you'll never get anything from this without more context, like knowing the encryption method or something."

"You're saying it's a fool's errand then?"

"I'm just saying, that's the point of encryption—to keep communications a secret. Not many people use a straight substitution cipher anymore. The smudges are interesting, just don't get your hopes up."

"Let's say you're right. The smudges mean something. Then what?" James asked.

"Well, you'd have to copy them all out to start. They'd form the message that you have to decrypt."

"A task that requires some skill."

"Yeah. I could help you, but I'm no expert myself. I take it, though, there's a time sensitivity here?" Jillian asked.

Yes, as he was supposed to do the delivery tomorrow.

James let the silence fall as he contemplated what to do. "My friend doesn't even know if I'm going to be able to deliver it. Which means that any message is not likely to be hot-off-the-press details."

"True," said Jillian. "He could be setting up a code for the future. Or communicating something that may be important, but isn't urgent."

James looked down at the book. A message that Edward would have prepped in case of emergency, and he clearly felt he was in one now.

That meant that the connection was likely more interesting than the message itself.

"All I really wanted was to see if my suspicions were correct," James said, "and you've done that. I'm not sure what I'm going to do about it, but I'll think on it."

Jillian was chewing on her lip, clearly contemplating a course of action. "I do have a way of creating microfilm at my lab. I use it for, well, that's not important. I use it to ship stuff home because obviously it's easier to hide than a magnetic tape. We could take pictures of all the pages and load them onto the film. I mean, it won't get you answers tomorrow, but at least you'd have a record."

James felt a rush of gratitude. "A fine idea, that. Do you have all the equipment?"

"I do," Jillian said, "but it would be great if we could both work on it. A book is a lot of paper to photograph."

"What time can we go to your lab?"

Jillian thought for a moment. "They're used to scientists keeping weird hours, so I say we could go anytime. I think between two and five a.m. we might have to leave, just so it won't be suspicious."

James looked at his watch. It was eight p.m. He'd promised to be back at the apartment to watch Lena. Anya wasn't usually gone too long, but he didn't think it fair to Jillian to drag her out of bed near midnight. "Could you start now? Go at it for a few hours? I can be there right at five a.m. tomorrow and hope to get the rest done before my shift starts."

"Of course," Jillian smiled. "It means I owe you one less favor."

"There's still about nine hundred on my side of the ledger."

"I know, but one at a time. I'll even it out eventually."

CHAPTER TWENTY-THREE

Anya picked up her pace. She didn't know whether it was the darkness of the night or her own unsettled thoughts, but she felt trepidation snake around her as she made her way to Rose's.

The streets looked the same. She had verified multiple times that no one was following her. Lena was tucked up tight with James keeping watch. She imagined it was her own panicked desire that was causing the nerves. Her plans, begun many years ago and painstakingly constructed, were finally coming to fruition. She was almost free in time, but not in deed. Within weeks it would all be over, but what had to happen between now and then was monumental.

She carefully checked Rose's street, waiting patiently in a dark doorway to observe who else might be out and about. Anya was nothing if not patient. She would not blow it all now because she was too anxious to get going.

Looking up at the windows to Rose's apartment, Anya's heartbeat stilled for a moment. Fear began to squeeze her lungs.

Something was wrong.

A sixth sense suggested something was off about this night. Anya pulled herself back into the doorway as far as she could and waited.

She and Rose had developed a code. There were two windows in Rose's apartment that were visible from the street. If the lamp was on in the left one, all was safe to come up. If the lamp was on in the right one, something had happened and Anya should stay away.

Part of her was tempted to just keep walking. Be a stranger passing by and get out of there as quickly as she could, hoping that all would be fixed for the next time. But this was the second night that the warning lamp was on.

Whatever was going on hadn't resolved itself. Rose was still nervous. Two nights in a row. Anya didn't have enough time to wait indefinitely.

She tried to ignore the rising anxiety. She had been so careful, but she knew nothing ever went according to plan—in life, but also in this city. Too many people had to be involved, and allegiances were constantly shifting. It was impossible to hold it all together and be guaranteed of the outcome. There were more variables than the weather.

She had to get in touch with Rose, had to connect somehow to find out what was going on.

The next step of the contingency plan was to meet at a bar about six blocks away, toward the university. It was always lively and easy to get lost in the crowd. Anya checked her watch. James was with Lena and didn't have to leave until morning. The bar would close well before then. She pulled her hat lower and hunched in her jacket as if cold. She didn't see anyone on the street, but knew there was a risk of Rose's apartment being watched. Stepping from the doorway, she headed to the bar, hoping that whatever was going on, Rose would be able to meet her there.

As expected, the bar was busy, mostly with students. The people flowed around, drinking and laughing. There were some tables around the edges, but most people congregated five deep at the bar, yelling and flirting. Anya liked meeting in these types of places, where the groupings seemed to ebb and flow as people caught up with others they recognized. It made it easy to move around.

She bought a beer to blend in and eased her way over to the edge of the bar top. There were enough graduate students so that she did not seem out of place. Maybe she should have been wearing more makeup, or a less conservative blouse, but she hadn't anticipated ending up here tonight.

Anya carefully studied the patrons while avoiding eye contact. She didn't want to get hit on. She glanced toward the door frequently, hoping to signal that she was waiting for someone. She would give Rose one hour. Rose knew her schedule, knew when she was able to leave Lena. Their plans had her being at Rose's apartment every other night for an hour between eight and eleven. Some variation in the schedule was important, but they were too close for Anya to stay away for too long. Since they hadn't met last night, Anya was hoping Rose had adjusted.

If not, she'd come back to the bar tomorrow.

Forty-five minutes later Anya put down her beer as she saw Rose rush into the bar. She waved unobtrusively, one friend calling out to another. As Rose got closer, Anya saw in the dim light that her eyes were puffy and red. Anya trampled down the worry and gave Rose a hug.

"Where have you been?"

"Oh, Anya," Rose said, burrowing into Anya's neck as fresh tears began to fall.

Anya looked around. They had to get out of here. Rose was clearly in distress, and it was going to attract attention.

As gently as she could, she pulled Rose around the corner in the direction of the toilets. Having familiarized herself with the layout when she'd chosen this as a meeting spot, Anya knew there was a door at the end of the hallway that led to a back alley.

She got them both outside without incident. Propping Rose against the brick wall, Anya shrugged into her jacket and took a look around the alley. It was lit well enough for her to see they were alone, but she didn't want to stay there. It felt too conspicuous.

She linked her arm through Rose's and began to slowly walk to the street.

Rose gripped her hard but got her tears under control.

"It's Lucinda," she whispered, voice breaking. "She was attacked two nights ago outside Philippa's. She's in the hospital now. They don't know if she's going to make it."

Anya couldn't stop the tremble that coursed through her. "Have you heard any details of what happened?"

"No," Rose said. "The police are involved. I've only been to see her once. Her mother is meant to be flying in from Marseilles, and so far they are restricting visitors. They let Philippa in once as well, both of us to confirm her identity."

"How did she look? How bad is it?"

"It's awful." Rose's voice cracked, but she took a steadying breath and carried on. "She was beaten badly, and strangled too. I could see the bruising around her neck. Blood had matted in her hair, and her face was so swollen. I only recognized her because of those earrings she always wears, those ruby studs she got from her grandmother. After a few minutes I could see Lucinda under all the damage, but it was so hard."

"Do the police have a suspect?"

"No one. She still had her wallet on her, not that there was much money in it, but still, they've concluded it can't be a robbery. They asked me if Lucinda had any enemies, anyone who would want to hurt her. I could only think of one person, but of course I didn't tell them. The West Berlin police would be able to do nothing if he is behind it."

He. Him. Her ex-husband, Michael Polenz. Chief asshole in an organization of many.

Anya struggled to organize her thoughts.

First, was he really behind the attack on Lucinda? It was definitely possible, but she knew better than to jump to conclusions. Overlooking another threat would be disastrous.

Second, what was the goal? If he'd wanted to stop Lucinda, killing her would have been more appropriate. Attacking her, beating her into near oblivion, seemed more like a message. To whom? Lucinda herself? Anya? The two of them?

Third, how had he found her? How long had he been trailing her? And therefore, how much did he know?

"Was she still staying at Philippa's then?" Anya asked.

Rose nodded. "The safe is done. But the mechanism, the one to open it, is jammed. I have my grandfather's notes, but so much was in his mind. I'd hoped to have it fixed within a couple of days, because I know we're running out of time. Lucinda said she'd move in when it was ready. When she could practice. In the meantime, she said there were a few things to help Philippa with."

Anya tried not to let frustration cloud her judgment. Philippa was an agitator, constantly trying to stick it to the bourgeoisie, the capitalists, the people in power. Whoever happened to be pissing her off that day. She floated in and out of the Red Army Faction and organized protests across the country.

Anya had always stayed away from Philippa because she was too public. She'd never known anything of intelligence value and would have broadcasted it anyway. Lucinda had been attracted to some of Philippa's causes when the values lined up.

But Anya had repeatedly warned her that being associated with Philippa might put her in the spotlight. For someone with Lucinda's past, that wasn't a good idea.

She allowed herself a moment of despair that Lucinda hadn't followed her advice. She should have gone to Rose's right away and kept her head down. But she didn't. Anya could only deal with where they were now.

"You cannot go back to visit her," Anya said. "If Michael is behind this, he's doing it to flush me out. He obviously felt having her followed was getting him nowhere, and he's looking to see who she's connected to. He doesn't know you, but if you're at the hospital, he'll have you followed. We can't take the risk of him tracing you to the furniture shop. He remembers your grandfather, and it won't take him long to make the connection."

"What about Lucinda?" Rose asked.

"There is nothing we can do directly. She is in good care at the hospital, and her mother has the resources to get any help Lucinda might need. The best thing we can do for Lucinda is to carry on and expose Michael for the hypocritical scum that he is. That way, he won't be a danger to her, or any of us, anymore."

Anya could feel Rose take a shaky breath. She hoped she was getting through. She needed Rose, needed her knowledge and her support. Anya could not bring down Michael without Rose.

"Are you afraid?" she asked.

There was a long silence as they continued to walk arm in arm. The city seemed quiet tonight. There were few other pedestrians, and even fewer cars passing. Sound spilled out of the bars and clubs as they walked by, but it was quickly muffled by the heaviness of the cold night. Anya's world seemed to be shrinking in on itself, and she felt as though she was grasping in a dark passage, trying to find a way forward.

"I am," said Rose. "I am afraid, but I always have been. I'm afraid of the world that creates such monsters. But I will still help you, because if I don't—and if Michael did this to

Lucinda—he won't stop. He will kill her and then kill you and who knows how many others."

"Yes," said Anya. "He will not stop on his own. His methods have brought him success for too long."

"What do we do now?" Rose asked.

"We have to assume that he gave the order to attack Lucinda. He must have been following her, for how long I don't know. He has been obsessed with her for years, referring to her always as his one failure. But still, he is not a god. It would have taken him time to know she was back in the city. I met with her last week and there was no one following us." Anya thought the situation was telling. Like all obsessions, Michael's fixation had clouded his judgment. It was because of his desire to always have control that Lucinda had been able to escape him when she was caught in Leipzig.

"Perhaps it was a mistake," Anya said, "to have asked her to carry out my plan. I should have known that he wouldn't have let her go. He has to assume she'd come to me. Her being in West Berlin so soon after my escape with Lena, he must have known it couldn't be coincidence."

"Lucinda did not give you a choice. She wanted to help you destroy him."

"Yes, but it was an oversight on my part. What happened with him and Lucinda was so long ago, I didn't realize he was still waiting for the chance to correct his failure. I should know better. After all, it is the reason I'm doing all of this, because I know there are some things he can't let go of."

"What now?" asked Rose.

"Lucinda never would have been able to go over. I see that now. I need someone unknown."

"How are you going to find anyone this late? You've been planning for years."

"Lucinda was not the only person Michael angered. There are many people yearning for revenge." However, the truth was she had no one in mind. No one she'd vetted. No one she trusted.

"You will keep me informed?"

"Yes," Anya said. "Finish the safe. I will find someone who wants to do the job. There is much I can offer in return for taking such a risk."

That, at least, was true, because Michael Polenz had one major weakness: He didn't trust anyone. That meant he insisted all of his most important papers never be copied, and he kept them locked up tight in the same place. In his study, in a safe, an exact replica of the one Rose was building.

"I must talk with you," Anya said as she picked through the apples. The secret, she thought, was to never pretend. She selected four of the best and placed them in a bag.

"There's a church two blocks south. On the west side is a gated entrance to a public courtyard. Meet me there in fifteen minutes."

Anya gave a small nod to show she understood but did not watch Quentin walk off. She had passed the church on her way here.

She purchased her apples and wound her scarf tightly around her neck as she left the store. Snow was in the air. The days were getting shorter so that it was always dusk by the time she left the apartment. She was like a creature of the night, living her life to nocturnal rhythms. But going out in the darkness was safer, and it meant Lena wasn't home alone, so Anya didn't mind.

She found the church gate with the aid of a streetlight. It was kept unlocked to offer sanctuary to whomever needed it, so the gate glided smoothly on its hinges, obviously well cared for.

Before she was three steps in, Quentin stepped out of the shadows and steered her to a dark corner. Out of the wind, with the city sounds muffled to a murmur, it was almost peaceful.

"Are we alone?" she asked him.

"Yes, I did a circuit. There's no one else in here right now."

"Good." Because she had a lot to tell him.

"What's up, Anya?"

"I have a problem," she said, "and I need your help."

She had never expected to ask this much of him.

He stayed silent in the shadows next to her as she told him about Lucinda, her suspicions that her ex-husband was involved, and what it meant for her plan. "There is a part I cannot do myself. It is over in East Germany. I need to know if you have someone you trust who would be willing to go over."

Anya could feel Quentin's eyes on her. The questions loomed in his continued silence, and Anya was suddenly terrified she had overstepped.

"You're going to have to tell me a lot more," he finally responded, "before I agree to approach anyone. What they have to do, but most importantly, why are they doing it. What's the end result? What are you going after?"

Anya sighed, but she knew he was right. If the situation were reversed, she would feel exactly the same. She only hoped that what she could offer was enough. "My ex-husband, he trusts no one, you understand. That is where his life has led him, a shell who lives only to exercise power. He collects information outside the regular channels. He has for years. And he keeps it in a safe. It's personal. It's not at work. There are many interesting things in this safe: documents, evidence against people. It's how he controls them.

"But I know you would not be interested in all of it. Truthfully, most of it should be burned. They are petty mistakes and indiscretions that he has made people pay for, for years. Too long. Myself included.

"What you would find valuable, however, and what I also want, are his records on the foreign agents. He has been responsible for running the foreign agents for a long time. Other members of the Stasi, they know about some agents, but Michael, when he started, quickly saw an opportunity to expand and exploit his power. He has, many times, used existing foreign agents to recruit new ones. These new ones, are, how do you say it? Off the books? They exist only in the files in his safe. Not even Erich Mielke himself knows all of the foreign agents under Michael's control."

Quentin was silent again for a moment. "I'm assuming there are Americans in these files?"

"Americans, British, French, West German. Everyone. It is not only their names. It's a record of their activities. The kinds of information they have shared. How much they charge, what they ask in return, or what Michael holds over their heads so he can keep manipulating them."

"Why do you want this information, Anya? I get why it's valuable to me, but you said you wanted it as well. Why?"

Anya steeled herself to tell the rest of it. "Whatever you may think of East Germany and the people who run it, there is a certain nobleness to the original ideas that brought them together. A world where everyone helps each other, works together, shares what they have so no one is hungry or desperate. East German socialism was supposed to do that. It was supposed to eliminate poverty as well as excess wealth and create a society where everyone had the opportunity for a good life."

She held up her hand to ward off an interruption. "I am aware that it has failed. I do not understand enough to know if it could have worked if we didn't have to give everything we had to the Soviets, if we had been allowed to develop without their insidious influence. But I do know one reason it failed is because those in power don't follow the same rules they force on everyone else.

"My ex-husband uses his foreign agents to obtain riches that are not available to the East German people. He extorts money and goods and lives a life of luxury while condemning people to years of torture and prison for not being good enough socialists. East Germany does not have a chance with people like him in charge. He needs to be exposed for who he really is and thrown into those same prisons he has been filling for years."

The words were like black tar coming out of her mouth. A purge of all the anger she had been storing for years.

"You have a plan? A good one?" Quentin asked.

"Yes. It is very good. Very precise. My ex-husband is ultimately weak, and his weaknesses are the kind that can be easily exploited."

Quentin was silent again.

"Oh, and it must be a woman. The way I have to get into his house, the cover will only work for a female."

"What attributes does she need to have?"

"Not much," Anya shrugged. "Not too old. She must speak some German, of course. But it would be better if she didn't stand out in any way."

"I'll rent a room at the Hotel Kir on Friday and leave the number with the desk for Valentina. Meet me there at nine. I'll try to have someone for you."

Anya nodded and turned to go.

"But Anya," Quentin said, holding her arm so she had to face him, "I can't make any promises, because I can't order anyone to do this. You don't want to officially go to the CIA, which means you've cut me off from my resources. So all I can do is ask. You'll have to sell it to her, and if she says no, you respect that. Don't lie, and don't underplay the potential consequences."

Anya nodded again, and this time Quentin didn't stop her from leaving.

It was so easy to be morally good when one's life wasn't at stake. She didn't consider herself evil, not like her ex-husband. She didn't use people, sucking what she could out of their lives before she threw them away. But the pressure of survival sometimes justified nuanced choices.

She wasn't going to be responsible for another Lucinda. The value of the information, however, was worth a great deal of risk.

CHAPTER TWENTY-FOUR

James sat in the passenger seat of the truck as it rumbled up to Checkpoint Charlie. He was driving with Cedric, a sergeant in the comms unit. They'd made this crossing many times together, having served their previous tours here at the same time as well.

Cedric was a broadcasting technician. His job was to keep the radio shows transmitting as far and wide as possible. His purpose for crossing was to take what he called "signal samples." They would drive around East Berlin and confirm that they could pick up the British public radio signals. If the signal was weak, which happened often, or jammed, Cedric would test for interference in the area and make notes on how to adjust the output when he was back on base.

Since, for James, these were research trips, the two purposes complemented each other. James rarely had particular destinations in mind. Sometimes he'd want to look at the restoration efforts on certain historical buildings, but mostly he just wanted to soak up the atmosphere.

It was impossible to be inconspicuous, as they were in uniform. Going into a café to buy a coffee made him feel like a panda at the zoo. He did it anyway, but it was more the driving around that gave him ideas.

They couldn't leave the city, but they did push right up to its edges.

It was never boring for James over here. As much as he wanted the Wall to come down, he couldn't deny his fascination with the social experiment that it had created.

Severing the city, closing off one side completely from the other, meant that West and East Berlin had evolved differently. Of course, the Wall was relatively new in the grand scheme of it all, and so hundreds of years of shared history meant Berliners on both sides were more similar than different. It was really in the little things. The length of the skirts, the type of cookies on the shelf in the store, the way one side had advertising everywhere while the other saw no real need to advertise at all.

It felt different. West Berlin was pulsing, the people and ideas pushing out in all directions, reaching for the new. It was vibrant and exciting.

East Berlin was sedate. Orderly. Prams were pushed and goods purchased with no expectation that today would be any different from the day before.

One thing both sides had in common was the volume of bicycles that raced around the streets.

Years of working in psyops had taught James there was a difference between talking and communication. Anyone could talk. To communicate meant to seek to be understood. And to have understanding, you had to talk to people in their language, to meet them where they were. Not just their technical language, the words that came out of their mouth when they spoke, but their emotional language. Those words reflected how they perceived their reality.

You couldn't learn that language from a book. It had to be acquired through experience.

So that's what James did on his research trips: learn the language of East Berlin so he could talk to the people and convince them to tear down the Wall.

The door opened, and Cedric jumped up into the driver's seat of the truck. "They make it so bloody hard. We only do this all the damn time. Every day, someone in uniform going back and forth, but you hand over your documents and you'd think it's the first time they'd ever bloody seen them."

James had let Cedric deal with the book as part of the stack of papers and notebooks and tools and parts that he'd disclosed to the border guards. He figured it was less suspicious that way, mostly because he was worried he'd make an ass of himself trying to pretend it was no big deal.

Cedric rubbed his hands together, blowing on them before shifting into gear and driving through the rest of the crossing. "Forgot me gloves. Ran out of the apartment so fast. The kids were in a mutiny over the football, and my wife looked like she was about to start throwing things. So I got out of there as fast as I could."

James laughed. He'd met Cedric's wife. No doubt she could do some damage if she decided to start launching the knickknacks.

The truck finished weaving its way through the multilayered barriers the East Germans had erected to stop people taking a run at the border with their cars. James had made a study of history's walls, seeking to understand this one better, and the Berlin Wall was a historical anomaly. Most of them had been constructed to keep threats out.

Cedric started to drive south. For some reason, he preferred a counterclockwise path along the border to do his work. After crossing, they'd head south in Treptow, following the border north through Marzahn-Hellersdorf up into Pankow, then cruise back down along the Wall into Mitte.

"If you don't mind, mate, I've got a specific stop to make tonight," James said. He held up the brown paper package. "I'm meant to drop this book off at the Academy of Sciences of the GDR. You know, that big stone monolith not far from the checkpoint. We can head there just before we cross back."

"No problem," Cedric said, "as long as you don't mind our friends knowing."

James glanced in the mirror. "I wouldn't have expected anything less."

"Nosy little buggers, aren't they. I wonder if they actually learn anything from all the time they spend following us."

"Most of it must be a proper waste, because people's lives are filled with a lot of mundane, repetitive activities. Going to the grocery store, visiting family, taking the kids to the doctor. None of it tells you anything except the baseline. So they're waiting for that one moment out of the ordinary that might never happen."

"Wouldn't be a job for me, sir."

"Nor me."

They carried on in silence for a while, James content to look out the window and watch the people go about their evening. Lots of people carrying groceries, on their way home to make dinner. Occasionally some children playing in the streets, making the most out of the fading light before the darkness made the ball too hard to see. It always seemed to him that everything and everyone in East Berlin had their proper place, and no one wanted to stand out by not fitting into it.

He made some notes on turns of phrase as they passed signs, getting out once in a while to peer in shop windows, checking out the type and variety of goods that were on sale. It was all fodder for his radio program. Finding ways to connect.

They finished their circuit and had begun to drive along the Wall, heading south out of Pankow. The science building wasn't far. James hoped the drop off would be easy. They were a little later than he would have liked, but surely someone was manning the door at this hour.

Cedric pulled up in front, leaving the engine running.

"I'll just be a minute, then," James said.

Shutting the door behind him, he looked both ways up and down the sidewalk. The street was near empty—the evening quiet of East Berlin, despite not being far from the Brandenburg Gate. He assumed the border surveillance had pulled over somewhere, preferring to watch what he was doing. Based on his experience, they'd just make note of the stop rather than intervene in any way.

The academy itself was in a large stone four-story building that took up a whole city block. The size of it implied it had always been an official building of some sort.

He walked up the steps to the entrance and pulled on the heavy wood door. Inside, the light had that particular greenish tone that seemed to be found in all institutional buildings. The floors were gray linoleum, the wall some nondescript shade made worse by the lighting. There was a metal desk to his right. Behind it sat a receptionist or a guard, James wasn't sure.

He saw the man's eyes go wide, and he imagined it was the uniform. Probably didn't get too many from the British military dropping in.

"Hi, I'm looking for Professor Dieter Venmar. Cybernetics and Information Processing department. I've got a delivery for him," James said. If possible, the man's eyes got even wider at the sound of his perfect German.

The man pointed up and to the right. Receptionist, then. A guard would have some procedure to follow in this unlikely scenario.

"Which floor?"

"Second. Down the hallway on the right. About halfway."

James knew that as soon as he started walking the man would be on the phone finding someone to report this to. He wasn't worried about getting detained, but he'd rather be gone before the Stasi showed up or the border surveillance team following them got curious about the unusual stop.

He climbed up the stairs and made the turn at the top. Walking down the hallway, he peered at the names on the doors. Many of them were slightly open, lights shining through.

About halfway down as promised, he found the office of Dr. Dieter Venmar. He knocked on the way in. A man was sitting behind a desk covered with stacks of papers and books. A blackboard on wheels filled most of the room, tilted at an odd angle that seemed to lock the professor in place.

"I was asked to drop this off," James said, putting the package down on the desk. "It's from Edward Ashton. I take it you're old friends."

Dr. Venmar was staring at James in complete shock. So he wasn't expected. Interesting, but something to ponder later.

"I can't stay," James continued, "as I'm sure you can appreciate. But I was coming over to do some work, and Edward asked me to give this to you. I think he'd have rather put it in the post, but he wasn't sure if it would reach you."

Venmar's hand shook a little as he reached for the package. Picking up some scissors, he cut through the seal and pulled back the paper. As soon as he saw the cover of the book, his face relaxed. A smile hovered around his mouth for a moment.

"Thank you," he said. "I know what trouble it is to make a delivery of this sort. If you turn left when you leave my office, there is a stairway through the last door on the right. Behind the landing is a door to the outside. If you are in a rush, it might be better to go that way."

James considered the man for a moment before offering a brief nod and turning to follow his directions.

He hadn't expected that reaction, but it was genuine.

He found the exit, motioning to Cedric to pull up away from the front doors. Cedric didn't waste any time, and James was back in the truck before anyone had caught up with them.

They finished their rounds in East Berlin and crossed the border without incident. James wondered if the Stasi hadn't yet put two and two together, that he was the one visiting Venmar. It was quite possible that he and Cedric weren't the only uniforms who'd crossed over that night. Or maybe the pressure was on Venmar himself. After all, they could hardly pull James in for an interrogation.

He had no doubt his contact with Venmar would be in a logbook somewhere. Someone was going to have to explain it. James realized the reaction to the night's activities would tell him a lot about Edward and the relationship he had with the East Germans.

They waved to the Americans posted at Checkpoint Charlie but didn't stop. There was no need, as going in this direction, no one considered it a border.

Cedric turned to drop James off at his apartment before returning the truck to base.

"Another quiet evening, Guv," said Cedric, pulling up in front of James's building.

"When you're on the other side, the best kind."

"Isn't that the truth? Have a good one."

"You too, Sergeant Ames. Hopefully you still have some furniture when you get home."

"Oh, my wife has well learned that throwing pillows saves us a lot of blunt."

James smiled. "Smart."

He stood on the sidewalk, watching as Cedric drove off. Given that his apartment was no longer his alone, he needed a minute to collect his thoughts of the evening before going up.

Just after the truck turned at the next block, Quentin materialized beside him.

"Up for a walk?" he asked James.

"Aye." James tucked his hands into the pocket of his coat as he and Quentin began to move down the street.

"How did it go?" Quentin asked.

"To be honest, I didn't know what to expect, so maybe it went fine. I don't have much of a baseline to compare it to."

"Well, you didn't get detained or cause an international incident, so we can probably judge it a success."

"That's a low bar, but I hear you. Around here there's always the potential for much worse."

"So, the man that you delivered the book to, any thoughts?"

James was silent for a moment, going over his impressions of the evening. "You know, I think he's exactly who he was supposed to be. I didn't get the feeling there was any subterfuge. The name on the package matched the name on the door. When I got there, it was clear he wasn't expecting me. There was no setup. His office looked well used, not staged. He didn't react much when I mentioned Edward's name, but when he saw the book he visibly relaxed. It struck me at the time, like he was worried that he was being set up. But the book confirmed that I was on the up-and-up as well."

"Any idea about his relationship to Edward?"

"Honestly, I'm thinking it's exactly as he told me: someone he went to school with, someone he'd be friends with, except for the Iron Curtain makes it hard to stay in touch. In the end, I'm not even sure there was a message in the damn book. It could have just been a present."

"Not exactly a smoking gun," Quentin said.

"Not at all. And that leaves me feeling a bit buggered."

"In my experience, things have to give up their shape before you can hope to tease out any underlying structure. I get that you feel the intentions were good all around, but you need to remember why you're even in this situation in the first place."

"You see suspicious activity everywhere," James said, "but occasionally you must be wrong."

Quentin laughed. "James, I'm wrong most of the time. That's the reality in a job that deals with rumors and innuendo more than facts. Connecting the dots is almost always best guesses, but they're still guesses."

"Ah then, I suppose I should cut you a little slack."

"Look," Quentin said, "I know you don't want Edward to be guilty of anything. You want there to be a benign reason for all the secrecy, that he really just wants to share old books with a friend. But until you can explain how he ended up with Anya as a courier, you've got to assume that it's all smoke and mirrors."

"What would you do? If someone you trusted told you an old school chum was committing treason, what would you do?"

"Exactly what we're doing now. Try to collect some corroborating or exonerating information so I didn't sink a good man's career based on a rumor, but still did the right thing for my country. The problem with double agents is that they often leave an ocean of destruction in their wake. A lot of people lose their livelihoods, and some people lose their lives. That's why it's important to ferret them out, and that's what you have to keep in mind."

"What do you suggest next?" James asked.

"Anya has promised to deliver the information you need to put this to bed one way or the other. There are a few obstacles there, but she's got more skin in the game than anyone. I don't know if she can do it, but if she's successful, Edward won't be your problem anymore."

"And if she isn't?"

"I don't know what to tell you," Quentin said. "You're going to have to figure out the course of action you can best live with. In the meantime, you could try to find out more about the history of Dieter Venmar in England. There would be records of his time at Cambridge. It might help when it comes time to make a decision."

CHAPTER TWENTY-FIVE

Jillian arrived at the café late. She hated being late. It made her anxious, so she always aimed to be everywhere ten minutes early. She'd rather have extra time with her thoughts while waiting for someone else than move under the pressure of wasting someone else's time.

Today, however, she failed.

It was her fault, as in, nothing prevented her from being on time. But she was exhausted from processing the microfilm for James, and she'd slept right through her alarm.

She found Veronica at a table in the back, two drinks and food already on the table.

"Do you know the difference between a strudel and a streusel?" Veronica asked as Jillian sat down and shrugged out of her coat.

"Yes," Jillian said, "although it took me a while to pay attention. It's only when I kept getting cake that I figured it out."

"I ordered both," Veronica said, gesturing to the table. "I didn't understand they were something different. I just nodded to everything."

Jillian picked up a small cupcake topped with streusel. "Well, it won't go to waste here."

"No one ever talks about German food. Not like they do Italian or French. But this stuff, I could happily eat this every day."

Jillian smiled. "How much longer are you in Berlin?"

"I'm not sure. My training assignment is scheduled to go for another month. As you know, outside the military we don't have much going on here, so I've been collecting info for Frank. He's using it to make the case that we can be more conscientious about our various collections without breaking the bank. Small ops at strategic locations."

"Where do you think you'll go next?"

"South America. Probably Chile. There's a lot going on there, and the latest intelligence assessments were pretty weak."

"I've never been there. I've actually not been many places," Jillian said.

"Neither have I. So at this point, honestly, as long as I'm not in Ottawa I don't much care where I go."

"Not a fan of the city?"

"Not a fan of most of the people I work with," Veronica replied. "There's nothing for me at headquarters right now. Back there I'd just be going numb compiling media reports. Another year of that, and I'd probably explode. I love being in the field. It's what I dreamed about when I signed up. Any field is fine."

Jillian understood what Veronica was talking about. It was hard, as a woman, to get the overseas assignments. People had a natural bias toward promoting people like themselves, and since their agencies were run by men, that's where the promotions often went.

"Anyway," said Veronica, "I needed to meet with you for a reason."

Jillian had assumed Veronica just wanted an update on the tunnel. "Something's come up?"

"You could say that. It doesn't have anything to do with your current extracurricular activity. Quentin found me yesterday."

Jillian raised her brows. "Really?"

"So it's news to you. I wonder how he knew where to find me."

"Don't take this the wrong way, but it's from when you first came over. I told him Frank was sending you to me. I think, well, he just wanted to check that everything was above board."

"Why wouldn't it be?" Veronica asked.

"Because sometimes it hasn't been. A woman that he worked with, she was shot last year by the Soviets while her boss stood by and did nothing."

Veronica expelled a breath. "Wow. The women around him don't have much luck, do they?"

Jillian shook her head. "That one actually had nothing to do with him. I know you're referring to Isabella dying in Nicaragua on his watch, but the one I'm talking about, Claire, she was out of the embassy. They were connected only insofar as they were from the same country. I guess what I meant is that people who should have your back don't always."

Veronica seemed to consider this as she ate her strudel. "I'm not sure I really trust him, you know. Not that I think he'd sell me out to the Soviets. It's more that…I think he makes questionable choices."

"Don't we all at some point? All I can say is I think he tries to do what's right. But you and I know, no two people have the same definition of what that is. What does it matter anyway? You don't work with him."

"He's asked me to help him out with something."

Jillian didn't bother trying to hide her surprise. "What?"

"He didn't tell you?"

"Not a thing."

"Just in case I said no," Veronica said.

"Maybe," Jillian replied. She wasn't angry. She knew what he did, and she knew it was often none of her business. Just like she didn't tell him one detail of the satellite collection. Rather, her pulse was hammering at the idea of worlds colliding. "Can I ask why you're telling me?"

"Because if something happens to me, I want you to know where I am in case I need help. I learned that from Frank."

Jillian's hand stilled on her glass. "What has he asked you to do?"

"There's a woman, recently of East Germany, who somehow has access to every file the Stasi has on Western double agents. The only problem is, she can't get it herself. The job has to be done by a woman apparently, and the one she had lined up is currently fighting for her life in the hospital. Quentin thought of me as a replacement."

"Why doesn't he just get someone from his own agency?"

"Two reasons. One, they don't have a female IO over here right now. And two, this defector is insisting the CIA can't be involved. She doesn't want to be sucked into a lifetime of debriefs and surveillance."

Jillian ate some more of her second cupcake. She didn't have a ton of knowledge of how human intelligence operations worked. In her business, SIGINT, it was almost impossible to make unilateral decisions because no one had much autonomy. SIGINT was a large system of connections and cables and data, and no one person had the ability, let alone the knowledge, to interact with every part of it. If Jillian decided to make some change at a collection point, there would be impacts downstream that she would have no visibility on and no ability to manage. If she wanted her change to be effective, she had to work with the teams who, say, processed or decrypted the data.

From her two years in Berlin, she knew that HUMINT was different. The nature of the work meant it was easier to make spontaneous decisions, to pursue leads without disclosing them, to go after sources on a hunch. After all, not everything worked out and led to useful intelligence.

Thus, Veronica had a lot of leeway to decide whether pursuing this collaboration was the right choice for her, given her mandate and responsibilities.

"Have you talked to Frank?"

"He's out on a vacation. Not back until tomorrow. I thought I'd collect as much background as I could before I presented it to him."

"Do you want me to talk you out of it or into it?"

Veronica smiled. "I'm not sure."

"What are your thoughts?"

"That I spent the first seven years after I joined collecting dust in a basement in Ottawa. That in order to get recognition and respect, I'm going to have to do the job ten times better than any of the guys. That this may be an opportunity that could make my career. Can you imagine the intelligence value of what's on offer?"

Jillian could. Every Westerner secretly working for the Stasi? They'd make movies about it one day.

"What's holding you back?" Jillian asked.

Veronica bit at her lower lip. "Do you think Quentin could be lying to me? It seems…unbelievable that this just fell into his lap."

"No," Jillian said. "He's not lying to you. Not about something like this. He would never manipulate you into taking that kind of risk."

She believed that, she really did. Every interaction with Quentin, everything he'd done for her, she had to believe he'd have done it for anyone. Veronica, however, still looked worried.

"Do you think he'd cut me out?"

"You mean, take the information and give you nothing?" Jillian asked.

"Something like that."

Jillian wanted to say no, but she couldn't let her beliefs about Quentin's character influence her. She didn't want to convince Veronica that everything would be great. That wasn't her role.

"I don't think so," Jillian said. "Meaning that, all things equal, I don't think he would because he's too smart to have to rely on that kind of betrayal. The people, the relationships, matter to Quentin, and I know that's gotten him into a lot of trouble in the past."

"I sense a 'but'," said Veronica.

"But there's no guarantee that all things will be equal. We don't know anything about this woman and who else might be involved. Maybe she's playing him. Or maybe the CIA is going to have to get involved, and it'll all be out of Quentin's hands. When you're dealing with partial information and a lot of variables, it's hard to know. Maybe the better question is, how can you protect yourself?"

Silence fell between them as Veronica took time to think.

Jillian looked around the café, taking in the people laughing and talking. She almost wished she were one of them—more carefree. Able to leave the job at the end of the day and go out and have fun and not worry that some word or action was going to cause an international incident.

Jillian turned her attention back to Veronica.

"I'm meeting with Quentin and this woman tonight," Veronica started to speak, "and so I will shelve all my feelings until I have more information. I know this job is supposed to be hard. As Frank says, if we could get it easily, it wouldn't be intelligence."

"That's true," Jillian agreed. "But, well, you're supposed to live to fight another day."

"Right. But how do I distinguish between being apprehensive because I'm scared and being apprehensive because the plan isn't good enough?"

"Is there a plan that would make you feel no apprehension at all?"

"No," said Veronica.

"Then I think you just have to trust yourself."

Anya arrived at the hotel and picked up the key from reception as instructed. She had come from Rose's, the problem with the safe now fixed. The next part of her plan was almost ready to put into action. She just needed someone to replace Lucinda.

She performed the appropriate sequence of knocks. The door swung open, and Quentin stepped back to let her in. He closed and locked the door, then stopped in front of her.

Anya pushed her hope aside and turned her chin up to look at Quentin. "Is she here?"

"Yes," he said. "She's far from committed, but the payoff is intriguing. So ask her what you need to, and answer her questions. And Anya, don't fuck with either of us."

"We have the same goals," she said. "It doesn't help me if she gets caught. I get one chance at this." She wanted to remind him that she still held the power. If she wasn't impressed, it wouldn't go forward. Doing it well was more important than proceeding quickly. It was a constant balance—how long she could risk staying in Berlin versus finishing what she needed to do. Anya knew that she was only ever going to get one chance to bring Michael to his knees.

She followed Quentin into a standard, nondescript hotel room. There was a bed covered in a dark-green patterned spread, an armchair in the corner, a small television on a worn dresser. The brown curtains were closed, but all the lamps had been turned on.

Anya sat in the squat brown armchair, taking her seat as she evaluated the woman seated on the bed.

She'd long ago stopped having expectations about what people would look like. It was never accurate, and time was wasted working through the surprise. The woman seemed to be around the same age as her, possibly a little younger, but not much. Taller than average, but it was harder to tell with someone sitting. Average build, black hair pulled into an average-length ponytail. The only features that stood out were the slight golden color of her skin and the upward tilt of her eyes. It was different. Anya couldn't place it.

"Thank you for meeting with me," Anya said. "I know that both of us are being interviewed here. I have to be confident in you, and you likewise need to be the same in me. So I will ask my questions. When I am done, it will be your turn."

The woman nodded. Time for the interrogation to begin.

"Your name?" Anya asked.

"Veronica."

"You are American?"

"No. Canadian."

Anya paused. As much as she had kept her mind open for this meeting, she had assumed Quentin would bring her another American. Canadian, or any other nationality, had never occurred to her.

She looked at Quentin. "You will tell me how this situation has come about. Why are you not working with someone from your country?"

"Veronica and I do not work together. We have, though, in the past. She is in town for unrelated reasons. You need someone, and I don't know anyone else. We're a little short on trained female intelligence officers in West Berlin right now."

Anya pursed her lips. It was an interesting development. She wondered how tight their relationship was if their loyalties could not be the same.

"How is your German?"

Veronica winced. "Not great," she replied in German, and yes, her accent was rough. "I could never pass for a native German speaker," Veronica continued in English.

Anya considered the situation. Perfect German was not required, but if improvisation was needed, a lack of German would be a problem.

"Do you speak any other languages?" she asked.

"Yes, French, Spanish, and Russian."

Anya relaxed. "Russian is good. It invites less questions."

She let her mind churn through the scenarios with this new information. What would she have to change? The entry process would be the same, but the backstory modified. Heddy wouldn't care. Soviet and East German were both the same. Cleaning needed to get done. No one much notices who is doing it.

"Is your hearing good?"

Veronica started a little at the question. "As far as I know."

"I will need you starting tomorrow. You must prepare. What do you do in West Berlin?"

"I'm on assignment with the Canadian signal corps on the British base. Civilian training."

"Can you take some time off?" Anya asked.

"I can't disappear for a week, but I have some flexibility in my schedule."

"Could you stay with a friend of mine for a short time? Would anyone notice if you were gone at night?"

"No," Veronica shook her head. "No one here would miss me. I keep a pretty low profile."

"Good," Anya said. "Now, what are your questions for me?"

"Well, what would I have to do?"

Anya took a deep breath. This was the plan she had been working on for years. Days and months and seasons of careful planning. Of holding many balls in the air, being a mother, working for the Stasi, cultivating the relationship with Quentin, making the connections she needed until every moment was accounted for. She choked on the words. She hadn't realized how hard it would be to speak it all out loud.

"Many years ago, I was married. Not long after I had my daughter, I realized I was married to a monster. The worst kind of man. One who persecutes people for the same crimes he commits himself. I also knew that if I ever wanted to get away from him, I mean truly away, then I would have to take the source of his power. The information he controls.

"He keeps all of his important papers at his residence in Wandlitz. My first task was to figure out how I might get the papers one day. I discovered that his safe was made for him personally by a man from Berlin. That man is very old now, but I found that he has a granddaughter who possesses the same skills.

"I contacted the granddaughter and persuaded her to help. I developed a plan for how someone would get into the residence and have time to open the safe, as well as get away and cross back to West Berlin. There are very few people who know any details of my plan. The woman who makes the safe, the woman who enters the house, and the woman who steals the papers. It is this last one who is in the hospital because my ex-husband cannot imagine that he isn't in control. She is the one I need you to replace."

Anya took a deep breath, counting slowly and forcing her shoulders to relax. She would not justify what she was trying to do. The horrors in her memories were hers alone. "So you must cross into East Berlin, meet your contact who leads a cleaning team, go with her to my ex-husband's residence in Wandlitz, open the safe, steal the files, come back to East Berlin, cross over the Wall, and bring everything to me."

"So, a regular day at the office?" Anya saw Veronica's smile and guessed it was a joke of sorts.

"The woman who runs the cleaning crew, how did you recruit her?" Veronica asked.

"When you get into the safe, there are two types of files. Black ones and gray ones." Anya could see that Veronica thought she was evading the question. She pressed on. "The black are those you are interested in. They contain all of the Western contacts he has. Everyone who gives him anything from outside the Iron Curtain—information, money, goods.

"There are more, many more, gray files. These are all files on East Germans. They essentially are a record of everything he knows that he can use to blackmail and control people. Heddy, the woman who runs the cleaning crew, her brother has a file. The woman who was supposed to go over, she has a file. So do I. When you are there, you must burn all the gray files. Heddy will supply the lighter fluid."

"This is all about you seeking vengeance?" Veronica asked.

Anya shrugged. "Vengeance, justice. You can call it whatever you want. I don't care. Would you rather it be for political gain? Or because I want money? There are no noble reasons. You have not lived in a country where the main purpose of the government is to recruit citizens to spy on each other. They govern by eroding trust and community, so you aren't even sure who you are. You have also, I presume, not lived under the thumb of a man who further exploits people's weaknesses until freedom becomes something that is found as often as a unicorn. You can do the job or you cannot. The rewards for you are significant. You do not need to understand my motivations."

"It all seems pretty clear," said Veronica. "If I say yes, what's next?"

"I will introduce you to the woman who made the safe. She will train you on how to open it. This part you have to get very good at, because there won't be anyone able to help you in Wandlitz."

"You're sure that the files are still there? He hasn't moved them?"

Anya shook her head. "He might have. I cannot promise that he didn't. But it is unlikely. He had that safe made for him personally. Anywhere he could move those files would be less secure. Plus, Michael cannot imagine anyone is smarter than he is. It makes him vulnerable. I am confident that he has no idea those files are what I'm after. Part of my planning has been to direct his attention elsewhere when it comes to me."

"How can I contact you?"

Anya looked at Quentin. "As always, this is the most difficult part. It would be best if you could communicate through Quentin for now."

"How much time do you need?" Quentin asked Veronica.

"A few hours," she replied.

"Okay. I'll meet you at the same place as yesterday. Six o'clock."

Veronica nodded before turning back to Anya. "I get that this is personal for you. That scares me a little, because I find it often leads to poor decision-making. However, Quentin gave me some of your background. You've been able to survive, and plan, and get this far, which leads me to believe you know how to put the anger aside. I'm not going to lie to you. My motivations are selfish. I want those files. If they contain even a fraction of what you say they do, it will be the biggest take by a Western agency ever. If I can make that happen, it will make my career. In the long run, it will also help my country. Although I get the feeling there's going to be a lot of pain before that happens. It doesn't really matter to me why you're doing this, as long as I can be confident we have the same goals."

"I understand," said Anya. She appreciated Veronica's candor, "and I thank you. Trust is hard always, because the circumstances are never good. Quentin has vouched for you, and I believe our interests are well enough aligned that success looks the same for everyone. I will give Quentin the information you need to proceed, should you choose to do so."

Veronica stood up. "You will have your answer tonight."

"Thank you."

"I have to say, it helps that your ex-husband sounds like an asshole."

Anya smiled a little. "Yes, it is good to have a bad guy. But please, take my warning seriously, he is not a man to be underestimated in any way. You must follow my directions, but you also must be flexible. I have done my best to come up with the safest plan. I've been working on it for years. As you must know, there is no perfect plan. My ex-husband is dangerous, and he is looking for me. He has put my friend in the hospital. The only advantage we have is that he is focused on finding me. He does not yet seem to wonder if I am planning anything other than escape."

"Well," said Veronica, "let's hope it stays that way."

Anya watched Veronica leave, examining the residue of the meeting. It was hard for her to trust anyone, even people she had known for years, who had lived in her building, had brought her asparagus soup, and had watched Lena. Even those people couldn't be trusted with a whisper of conflicting emotion or curiosity about the rest of the world. With so little practice in trust, Anya didn't often rely on it.

Instead she took stock of the incentives. As she often reflected, it was easiest to work with people when everyone's incentives were aligned.

"You are confident she can handle the job?" Anya asked Quentin.

"I know she doesn't panic when shit hits the fan," he said. "We met on an op in Nicaragua. We were both interested in the same guy. I made a mistake and got captured. She stayed calm, figured it out, and with almost no resources got me out of there. I don't have to tell you there was no requirement for her to do that. I wasn't even technically on the job. As long as you've set up everything properly, I think she can handle whatever comes up."

"How you work, it is so different," Anya said. "I have never been able to trust those that I work with. In East Germany you must always be on your guard, because you are always under suspicion, and in the Stasi, we are all trained to monitor each other."

"What about these three women you're working with to get the files?"

"Lucinda and Rose are from the West. It took me a while to understand them, but since I wanted to live here anyway, there were many reasons to try. They are good people. Honest. Heddy is the only one from East Germany. It took me longer to develop a relationship with her. It's like a little dance. But what Michael has done to her family, it is like they are in a prison. We found that we could trust each other's hatred of my ex-husband."

"How long were you married before you realized what he was like?" Quentin asked.

"Not long. We dated for a long time before we married. He was ambitious. We only got married when he decided a wife was necessary for further advancement, especially a wife who was already well respected by the party," Anya said. "Of course, I did not see any of this then. I thought we were well matched and that we would serve our country together. It didn't take long before I saw the results of his corruption. I knew immediately that I could never let him see what I really thought. He has no idea how much I know."

Anya knew she sounded cold. Calculated. What woman would not fight for her marriage? Instead she had played the game by encasing her true self in a deeply buried box that would remain closed until she was sure she would never have to pretend again.

"What do you think his next move is?"

"You mean after putting my friend in the hospital?"

Quentin nodded.

"I have learned that it is never good to become confident in what you imagine other people to be thinking. My leaving and Lena escaping is an embarrassment. I believe his focus is on getting us back so he can save face. Even for a man as powerful as he is, to have close relatives escape is a stain on the reputation. There will be a question of his loyalty to the party. It is how the Stasi operate. I think he is now more focused on finding out where I am than discovering what I might be trying to do."

"Which is why time is of the essence," Quentin said.

"Yes. So I hope Veronica agrees to help. Then we will all have what we want."

Quentin pushed up from his position leaning against the wall. "I hope so too. What do you want me to give Veronica if she says yes later tonight?"

Anya handed Quentin a small piece of paper and a lapel pin in the shape of a small tiger. "This is Rose's address. If Veronica agrees to do the job, she must go to Rose and stay with her to learn how to open the safe. Veronica must give this pin to Rose. It is how Rose will know that I sent her. At the end of three nights, I will need a report. If we are to go ahead, I will then contact Heddy.

"I must ask you to courier between me and Veronica for the next few days. I need to stay away from Rose's until it is necessary. Michael would not hesitate to put her in the hospital as well, but more importantly he might discover the link to the safe he had made all those years ago."

"I can do that. I'll leave messages at James's when I need to."

Anya nodded. "Yes, it is better if we meet as little as possible. You see, on my way over here I discovered I was being followed. I lost them, of course, but it seems my ex-husband has found me."

Quentin's hand clenched briefly around the paper. "And he's not taking you off the street because?"

"Because of Lena. No amount of torture would ever make me reveal where she is. Plus, I imagine he wants to learn more about who might be helping me, who I've confided in. He will be going through all my contacts. It is good that there are so many that he cannot easily get to."

"You've got a lot of balls in the air, Anya," Quentin said. "What happens to Lena if something happens to you?"

She studied him for a moment. "I appreciate your concern, but it is better if we focus on where our mutual interests lie. Lena will be taken care of. So we are clear, I do not intend to fail."

"No one ever does. You, however, I believe. Well, good night. I hope next time we meet I've got good news."

Anya stood up, buttoning her coat and putting on a hat and scarf. Now that Michael had found her, it would be a longer walk back to the apartment. It was a relief in its way. She had been living like this for so long that there was some comfort being back in the normal pattern. She exited the hotel, taking in everyone on the street, and felt an immense satisfaction. She was good. Better than Michael had ever given her credit for. It was always easier to control the situation when you were being underestimated.

CHAPTER TWENTY-SIX

Jillian sat among a pile of parts, not remembering when she'd had so much fun. Trying to figure out the cables and wires in the tunnel was like that worm game she'd played as a kid, where you had to manipulate the worms in a specific order to be able to untangle them.

She came to the tunnel as often as she could. It was something to do, given that everyone else in her very small circle of friends seemed to be busy at the moment. Also, it was fascinating. From what she explored and discussed with Sebastian, she'd confirmed the system was at least three kilometers when they added up all the offshoots. There was a main corridor that ran fairly straight on an east-west axis. Then there were smaller spurs that took off in all directions.

From Sebastian's map it wasn't obvious what the intention of the original designer had been. Some spurs curved to meet up with others. Some spurs were short and dead-ended. Some, of course, had either caved in or never been finished. And some led to antechambers like the one she was currently sitting in.

There were only three of these, all seeming to have some connection aboveground. It was hard to map where those connections led. Jillian had been to the public records office to try to put it together, but of course no utility maps showed the Nazi tunnel.

Because she didn't know the original purpose—or purposes—of the tunnel, she didn't have a starting place for mapping the cable system. Turning on the lights was great, but basic, and it didn't give them any clue into what other capabilities the tunnel had.

One thing she had figured out was that whatever the tunnel was supposed to do, this vision was never realized.

She'd reached this conclusion after mapping the cables in the antechamber. Or rather, attempted to map. They were a mess. Most were not properly connected, being haphazardly tucked up with metal brackets on the ceiling. It seemed that the final installation was never completed, which was making it hard to figure out what any of the cables were capable of doing.

She was using different paint colors to trace connections and clearly show distinctions between cables when she heard Sebastian and Peter's voices echoing down the chamber. They seemed to be far away, and therefore yelling at each other.

Jillian kept at her goal, though she wondered what was going on. The raised voices were a first. Usually they all defaulted to almost whispering, as if any East Germans on the ground above could hear them.

Their voices got louder and louder until they both stomped into the antechamber. Sebastian looked mutinous, Peter angry. She wondered if she should try to play peacemaker.

Before she could say anything, Peter gestured to her while still glaring at Sebastian. "Ask her what she thinks of your plan."

"It isn't a plan yet. It's an idea."

Peter rolled his eyes. "Your idea then. Before you run around selling tickets, let's get an outside opinion."

Sebastian's eyes narrowed and his jaw clenched. Jillian thought it was good that Peter was ten feet away, by the doorway. Any closer and he might now be sporting a black eye.

"Fine." Sebastian took a deep breath and turned to Jillian. "I had an idea—an idea, Peter," he said, shooting his friend another look, "—that we could bring people to the tunnel if they were blindfolded along the way. We keep it a word-of-mouth experience but have a meeting place. Then once or twice a week we take a small group, blindfold them, and drive them to the house. We lead them down here and take them around and share what we've found."

Sebastian's eyes had taken on the sheen of excitement people get when some new magical path occurs to them but before they've put any thought into the implementation.

"Um, sounds interesting," Jillian said. "Just curious though, what's the purpose? Like, why do you want to bring people down here?"

Sebastian raised his arms, gesturing around. "Because it's incredible. It's amazing. It's part of our crazy German heritage, and people should know about it."

"Not to mention the money we could make," Peter said, still scowling.

"Blödsinn," Sebastian said. "You know I have never cared about money. Yes, I think people will pay to see this place, but it is not about that. If we don't share it, it dies. We can see that already it is falling apart. Bit by bit the earth is reclaiming the space. Berlin is built on a swamp. We cannot maintain this underground network. It will be forgotten as if it was never here."

"Telling one person is telling everyone, and then we will lose it. The East Germans will take it back, and the result will be the same."

Jillian sympathized with both points. She felt the same way: it should be shared. This tunnel was an incredible historical monument that needed to get on the record somehow. But she had as much faith in the East Germans as Peter did. It was unlikely they would pay to upkeep a Nazi relic and even less likely that they would let any West Germans enjoy it.

They were both looking at her, as if waiting for her to settle the argument. "I don't know what to say. I think you both have a point. I get how this shouldn't stay hidden forever, but I don't know how to make that happen in the current political climate of this exact geographical location."

"There is nothing we can do. Not right now," Peter said.

"We have to do something," Sebastian countered. "The tunnel is already over thirty years old. It won't last forever."

"I'm not talking about forever. I'm talking about right now."

The faces of both men were getting redder and redder, their lips compressed into smaller and smaller lines.

"You aren't going to solve anything fighting like this," Jillian said, standing between them. "Go for a walk. In separate directions. Give me half an hour, and I might have something to show you. Knowing more about the tunnel might help you decide how best to deal with it."

Peter looked at her and nodded, turning on his heel and striding away to the left.

"I thought, when we found this place," said Sebastian, "that it was the find of the century, that it would be this great gift to Germany and even beyond. When I realized it mostly went west, I deflated like a balloon, but I couldn't stop coming. Who could?"

"I know," said Jillian. "It is a remarkable piece of history. I'm sure one day soon you and Peter will figure something out."

"There might be nothing to figure out."

Jillian didn't know what to say, because there was a possibility he was right.

He gave a last sad look around the antechamber before shoving his hands deep in his pockets and exiting though the open door. He gave a quick glance left before turning and wandering away to the right.

Jillian went back to her cables. She was almost done with the identification. If she could just sort out the function of even one of these, it might help Peter and Sebastian chart a course of action and save the tunnel.

Twenty-five minutes later, her nerves started to hum. Two of the cables on the ceiling had one end exiting through the door of antechamber and the other end affixed in the panel behind her. She thought they continued up aboveground.

Jillian's best guess was that they connected to some building infrastructure. She peered into the panel trying to map out where they went. Catching sight of a ridge on the side, she found something that she'd missed earlier: the main panel had a door on the inside. She grabbed a screwdriver and carefully twisted the thirty-year-old screws, rusty from the pervasive dampness of the tunnel. Lifting the panel off, she found a speaker system.

She felt the excitement snake along her skin. A speaker system in the wall meant that there was at least one matching system somewhere. There were call and receive buttons, and a dial for adjusting the channel, similar to a walkie-talkie. Jillian pressed the receive button and had to use her thumb to apply enough pressure to get the button to move.

There was a crackle as the reception came to life.

She slowly turned the channel button, pausing at each click to see if the intensity of the sound changed.

Turning the dial to channel four, Jillian's knees almost buckled as a German voice came through loud and clear: "Did you bring me a coffee?"

"Can they hear us?" Sebastian mouthed, his voice barely disturbing the air.

"No," said Jillian. Even though she knew there was no way for their voices to carry along the cables, she too found it hard to get her voice above a whisper. There was something about hearing a conversation that made your brain automatically process the people as being in the same physical space.

The three of them listened for another minute.

Jillian's German wasn't good enough to translate everything in real time. "What are they saying? It's about their breakfast or something?"

"Yes, one man is saying his wife makes oatmeal every day, and he hates oatmeal now. Just once he would like toast, or an egg, and he'd make it himself, but she won't let him. Insists that breakfast is her responsibility but then just keeps making the oatmeal."

Jillian smiled. So much of intelligence working was wading through all the mundane details to find that one gem of useful information. Sitting here listening to two East Germans talking about their breakfasts and their marital issues, she felt right at home.

Sebastian and Peter seemed entranced, so they listened for a while longer. Eventually the conversation stopped. Other than the sound of movement or an occasional cough, there was nothing coming through.

Jillian turned off the receive button.

"That was pretty cool," she said.

"Incredible," said Peter, "that the tunnel is connected to something, that it still works. I wonder what's up there."

"It must be an old building," Sebastian said. "The East Germans just took it over, like everywhere else, because they don't have the money to build anything new."

"You know," Jillian said, "if we listen long enough, we could figure out what they're doing, which might help you identify why they're right above us. It might be something innocuous, like an accounting firm or something, but with the proximity to the Wall, I'd be surprised."

"Yes," Peter agreed, "they would never let any regular business happen that close. It has to be a government office for something."

"Something they want to keep out of the public eye," Sebastian added, "because I've looked over the Wall all along here, and it's mostly countryside. Their part of the city is in the other direction."

Jillian was intrigued. What could the East Germans be doing just above their heads? And did it have any value beyond being a curiosity?

"I would like to find out," she said.

"So would I," said Sebastian.

Peter looked a little worried. "Whatever we find out, it might make it even harder to figure out what to do."

"Or it could provide the right incentive for someone in the West to take care of it," Jillian countered.

"You mean using it to spy on the East Germans?" Sebastian asked.

"Maybe. I don't know. I was just thinking that it might increase its value."

Both men looked thoughtful. "Yes, I see that," Peter said.

"Look," Jillian said, "we can't evaluate the situation until we have more information. We need to listen to more conversations to know what is happening up there."

"We can keep coming every day," Sebastian offered, "and take turns listening."

"Or," Jillian said, "I can set up a recorder. It wouldn't be hard, because voice is easy and doesn't take up too much space. We can buy some tape reels and record a few days. Then we can listen to it at your apartment or something. It'll at least be warmer and more comfortable. We can fast forward through the silent parts."

"You can do this?" asked Sebastian.

"I'm an electrical engineer. This is like a first-year homework project. Voice recordings are really, really simple."

"This is great," he smiled.

"Yes," said Peter. "It will be much easier. If we find something interesting, we can share it without bringing someone down here. It will help us keep control until we figure out the best thing to do."

"Great," Jillian said as she began to tidy up the small pile of gear she left down here. "I'll go tomorrow to get the parts for the receiver, as well as the tapes. I should have it up and running by the end of the weekend. We'll probably get more valuable information during the workweek anyway." *And if I make myself a copy, just in case, well, it's always better to be prepared.*

CHAPTER TWENTY-SEVEN

Anya knew she was taking a risk, but she believed it was a necessary one. The game of cat and mouse she was playing in the city was in full swing, and it would be more sensible to continue trying to create confusion. But she had to know if Veronica had mastered the safe.

For the past three days, she had slipped out of the apartment at odd times, making her way to random locations all over the city.

She still didn't know how Michael had found her, but she had confirmed that he didn't know where she was staying. She had yet to pick up a tail from the apartment and hadn't seen anyone stationed doing surveillance at the building.

Once she went to her favorite café, bought a coffee and sat inside. She had picked up a tail then, and let them follow her for a while before losing them in the Pergamon museum. It was clear that her ex-husband had people stationed at what he knew of her familiar haunts. It was a good strategy, but one she had anticipated.

Each time she left the apartment, though, as careful as she was, Anya knew it was possible that she would miss someone. She didn't let her confidence distort her thinking. She reminded herself always that she was the mouse, and to remember to look up as well as around, never forgetting that cats can sit on high, surveying their prey below.

This evening, she was going to Rose's. She settled Lena in with a movie while Jamie read on the sofa then left the apartment earlier than usual. The faster she did her job, the faster she would be out of Jamie's life, so she didn't feel bad about leaving him with Lena. Nonetheless, she was grateful for his kindness and patience with her daughter and hoped that one day she could assuage the guilt eating away at her soul.

She went south into Stieglitz and got on and off the S-Bahn twice walking between stations. No direct routes, alternating between busy and quiet streets, and staying far away from any of the places Michael might look for her.

When she was satisfied no one was following, she reversed course and headed back to Charlottenburg.

Arriving at the furniture store, Anya checked the light in the window. Seeing the all-clear illuminated, she made her way around back and waited, almost disappearing in the shadows. There was no one in the alley. The part of the street she could see had few pedestrians, and no one had doubled back to walk by twice.

Finally satisfied that she hadn't been followed here, she knocked on the door.

It burst open. Rose ushered her inside and quickly locked up behind them. "Since Lucinda, you know, I make sure it's locked all the time."

Anya was grateful that Rose was finally taking security seriously, if only because of what had happened to their friend. It was one less thing to worry about during the long nights.

"How is she doing?" Anya asked, unbuttoning her coat and nodding to the back room.

"Oh, she is good," Rose said, "and very nice. I like her."

It was a point in Veronica's favor that she had connected with Rose, who preferred the company of her music and her dog to most humans.

"This is great news," Anya said, feeling one of the thousand knots in her stomach unwind.

"Oh yes, you must come see for yourself."

Rose led Anya into a side room behind the piles of furniture waiting to be stained. It was the tool shop where Rose kept all the various implements she needed to perform her craft. One wall had a large peg board covered with hooks hanging with tools. Anya knew one side of the peg board could swing away from the wall to reveal a door.

The board was now pulled back, and the door it normally obscured was propped open. It was in this backroom that Rose had constructed the replica safe and where Veronica was currently practicing.

Anya watched as Veronica slowly turned the dial. Her eyes were closed, the stethoscope connecting her ears to the tumbling of the mechanism inside.

She didn't know exactly how it worked, but Rose had explained to her previously that the pins inside the locking mechanism made a certain sound when they were aligned at the correct number. Presumably Veronica was listening for the precise sound that would tell her when that number was reached.

Anya waited patiently with Rose beside her, not wanting to interrupt the process. This is what she had come to see: Veronica in action. Anya only wanted to send her over if she was confident Veronica could open the safe.

Anya breathed into the silence, her eyes following every subtle twist of the dial.

The minutes flew by in the intensity of her focus. She wouldn't even be able to say how long she'd been here. She was aware only of the gentle clicks as Veronica twisted the dial of the safe around and around.

Finally, Veronica must have heard the final sound she needed, because she sat up and pulled the bar that was anchored across the door. The safe swung open, and for a moment Anya thought she might cry.

Veronica turned, smiling. "Wow, it's such a great feeling. I don't know what that says about me, but I think it's totally cool that I can now crack a safe."

"Just this one," Rose said, but her face split into a grin as well. "There are many kinds now on the market that use different mechanisms. But anything with a series of tumbling pins, you would have a shot."

"I want to say I'm not sure it's a skill I'll ever need again," Veronica said, standing up and stretching her arms, "but you never know now that I've got it in my repertoire."

"I am so happy," Anya said. "Happy and relieved. You have done this now a couple of times?"

"This was my third."

"And fastest," Rose added. "It gets easier when you know what you're listening for."

"Good," nodded Anya. "You will not be under too much time pressure. Heddy goes in the house to clean for three hours every Wednesday, so you will have all that time. You cannot leave early because everything must stay on schedule. The faster you open it, the better, because then you will have flexibility."

"And time to burn all those files."

"Yes," Anya smiled. "That too."

Rose motioned them back into the tool room, closing the door behind them and pulling the peg board back into place. They followed her through the furniture to the staircase that led up to her apartment. Rose's taste led to bright-red furniture and old war propaganda posters. Anya took a seat on the beautifully restored eighteenth-century scarlet divan beneath a poster that reminded her that the enemy saw her light.

"You are ready to go?" Anya asked Veronica, who had settled into the armchair opposite.

"Walk me through the logistics again," Veronica said.

"You will need to apply for a tourist visa for the GDR. These are not hard to get, but they are for one day only, so you must be back before the last train leaves Friedrichstrasse. When you arrive and clear customs, head to the Spach café, one block north. Heddy will meet you there and escort you to her van. She does not speak Russian, so your German will have to do, but everything is orchestrated anyway. She will have a uniform for you to change into. Then you will proceed to her van and pick up the other cleaners. There are two, and neither of them are involved."

"Won't they wonder what I'm doing when I spend my time at the safe instead of cleaning?" Veronica said.

"There is a greater risk to include them. It is almost impossible to trust in the GDR. Heddy knows what we are doing and will do her best to pick people who will ignore what is happening. That is a large group as well—those who don't want any trouble. She will assign the two others to different areas of the house and do her best to keep them away from you."

"On Wednesday?"

"Yes, two days from now. I will send a message here through Quentin, but be prepared to leave first thing on Wednesday morning. Now, let us run through the details one more time."

"Things have changed."

Heddy's voice came through the receiver, and Anya felt a gnawing pit open in her stomach.

"What do you mean?"

"We are more closely watched at the house."

Anya knew Heddy had to stay vague. She was no doubt using the phone in the basement of her brother's bar and so had to assume it was being monitored at all times.

"Is it business as usual otherwise?"

"Yes."

Anya's thoughts whirled as she tried to figure out the details. Heddy was still cleaning Michael's house in Wandlitz every Wednesday, but instead of her crew going in on their own, they were now supervised.

"The supervisor, is it the owner?"

"No."

Anya let out a little breath of relief. So not Michael himself then.

"Is it someone who works for him, maybe in the same office?"

"Hmm," Heddy said. "I think so. It is no one I recognize from the village."

So Michael was likely sending one of his underlings to monitor the work of the cleaning crew. This was a new development, obviously caused by her and Lena's departure. Anya refused to let despair take over. This situation was like a chess game. There were always moves being made. She had anticipated some changes but not others. She knew that to be successful she would always have to keep playing her pieces.

"Do you think, if there was an emergency somewhere else, your new supervisor might be distracted or needed?"

There was a pause while Heddy thought. "It would have to be a big emergency, but yes. I do not think we would always be the highest priority."

"Okay. Change nothing. Call me again at this time in three days, and I will let you know if anything can be arranged."

Heddy hung up, and Anya leaned against the side of the phone booth. She would not give up. Her plan was good, the needed connections already in place. She didn't have the years required to start fresh. Heddy's new situation necessitated an adjustment, that's all.

Anya arrived back at Jamie's apartment after doing her customary loops to make sure she wasn't being followed.

She walked in and hung up her coat. Lena was busy at the dining table cutting out dresses for her paper dolls. Jamie was reading in his armchair. Anya felt a momentary twist of sadness at how far she was from providing a stable home for her daughter.

Going over to Lena, she bent down and kissed her daughter's head. "These new dresses are beautiful."

"I especially love the blue one," Lena said, holding up a classic 1930s bias-cut gown. "I want to have a dress like this one someday."

"You will need to be a little taller and a little older, but I am sure you will be able to wear such a dress."

Lena continued taking her mom through her new collection. Anya was only half listening. Now that she was in the safety of the apartment, her thoughts turned toward solving Heddy's problem. How could she arrange for Michael and his underlings to have their attention diverted on the day Veronica went to Wandlitz?

Anya let her thoughts churn while making dinner, then while eating the meal. If Jamie noticed she was distracted, he didn't comment. She came and sat in the living room after putting Lena to bed, and still no solution had presented itself.

It seemed she needed to ask for help.

Anya waited until Quentin came over later, when the city was coated in a thick blackness. Even the streetlights outside the apartment seeming subdued.

She updated him on Veronica's progress, confirming that all was set. "But I have a small…what is the expression in English, hiccup?"

"We could all speak in German," Jamie offered.

"No, please," said Anya. "It is good for me to practice. And I do not wish Lena to overhear. It is better protection for her if she does not know what is going on."

"What's the problem?" asked Quentin.

"The woman who will take Veronica to Wandlitz, she works as a cleaner. She has cleaned Michael's house for years. This is a good way for her to get in. Hiding in plain sight, as you say. I knew he would make some changes when I left, when I got Lena out. But, of course, I could not anticipate every one. It seems he has Heddy and her crew supervised now, at his residence, by someone from his office in the city."

"That's not a hiccup, Anya. I'd say that's a big problem. How is Veronica supposed to get into the safe if some junior overachiever is watching over the house?"

Anya tried to keep her frustration off her features. "You must have dealt with setbacks before. Almost always there is a need for some improvisation."

"Having Veronica go in is already a big deviation from your original plan. Sometimes the plan isn't working because it needs to be changed," Quentin said.

"It is a good plan," Anya said, defensiveness edging her words. "There are very few options for getting in the house.

Joining the cleaning crew is one of the easiest ones. The contacts are already in place. Heddy and I haven't spoken to each other publicly in years, so Michael has no reason to suspect a connection."

"Then why has he got someone there now?" Jamie asked.

"Because I've gone." Anya felt her jaw clench and deliberately relaxed it as she counted to three. "He now must be suspicious of everyone until he has me back. I think you are misunderstanding the situation at Wandlitz. He has put one person there. One. Which means he does not think it is vulnerable. Meanwhile he has at least six men over here looking for me. Six that I've identified and managed to lose as they keep trying to discover where I am hiding."

"Jesus Christ, Anya, what if they follow you here? What about Lena?"

"They have not followed me here," she snapped. "I only let one of them see me briefly each day, so Michael's focus stays on West Berlin."

"You can't stay lucky forever," Quentin said.

Anya turned away, looking out the window as if there were answers falling from the sky. "I know," she said, turning back to both men. "I know better than you. If something goes wrong in my plan, you will both have a life to continue living. I will not. As you can see, the circle is already tightening, and I know I cannot stay one step ahead of him forever. So the job must be done soon. We will delay by one week, but next Wednesday everything must be ready. Sometime in the next week, we must think of a distraction that will keep Michael and the men he controls focused on East Berlin."

"What kind of a distraction?" Quentin said.

"Help me figure out how to use myself as bait. When he's running after me, Veronica can slip through."

"That's a rubbish idea," said Jamie. "You'd be better off getting on a plane to Paris then heading to parts unknown. There are still places you can hide."

"I don't want to hide," Anya said. "I can't expect others to take a risk if I am not willing to myself. There must be something I can do that will achieve success."

"I need some time to think," said Quentin. "I'll be back tomorrow. Same time. We'll see if we've got any bright ideas then."

CHAPTER TWENTY-EIGHT

"Captain, get in here now."

James stopped midstride and did an about-face as his commanding officer bellowed out of his office.

"Sir?"

"Come in and close the door."

James was confused but did as he was told.

"Murphy, what in the Christ have you gotten yourself into?"

"Sir?" James repeated.

"One more 'sir' and I'm going to assign you recruit training. Tell me why I've just had my arse chewed out—by the base commander, no less—on account of the arse chewing that started all the way at the top."

James was mystified. He had no idea what his boss was talking about. The major was looking at him expectantly, and James was racking his brain trying to figure out what he'd done wrong.

"Ah, is this about the unscheduled stop in East Berlin on last week's recon visit?"

"No Murphy, it's not about that. But since that's news to me, we can deal with it after we sort out the other issue."

"Perhaps sir, if you tell me the origin point, the first arse chewing as it were, I might be able to shed some light on the issue."

James saw the major's lips twitch, but he did a remarkable job holding in the smile. "Our top boss, Murphy. The man who sits on top of the pyramid. Lord Ashton, Secretary of Defence and Earl of Fenwick. He set it in motion, and it rolled all the way from London down into my lap. Now I'm tossing it into yours and asking you to tell me what in the hell is going on."

The pieces immediately fell into place. But understanding didn't come with an easing of the tension.

"I'm friends with his son, Edward, who happens to be working out if this very base at the minute."

"I know that Murphy. I didn't know that yesterday, seeing as it had nothing to do with my job running the psyops unit, but it came up in the aforementioned arse chewing."

James spread his hands out. "I'm at a loss, sir. Edward and I have known each other over fifteen years. Not close, mind you, but it's never resulted in a problem before."

"Maybe it's because you haven't made inquiries into his old school chums before. Or am I mistaken about that?"

Partial understanding shimmered to the surface, but unfortunately it raised more questions than it answered.

"You aren't mistaken, sir. I also didn't realize I was asking after sensitive information. That unscheduled stop in East Berlin was for Edward, who wanted me to hand off a package to the old school chum in question. Naturally, I did my due diligence to make sure I wasn't out of line by agreeing to the request."

The major looked thoughtful. "And what did you find out about this old school chum?"

"Nothing, sir. I was only able to identify that he did in fact exist, and that he was at Cambridge the same time as Edward. As I'm sure you know, I've telephoned a few more inquiries, but I'm now understanding they won't be answered."

"Sit, Murphy."

James complied, having been in this chair many times. Major MacTeague might currently be his superior officer, but the two men went way back. As often as not there was a bottle of Scotch out after hours accompanying an informal discussion.

"I have to say," the major continued, "this morning's arse chewing was a tepid affair. I could tell the colonel wasn't into it, given that it all seemed to have no bearing on our mission down here. It was, all in all, perfunctory."

"Understandable," James said, "as it comes across like a right temper tantrum."

"You had no official reason for asking about Lord Ashton's son."

"Aye, but I didn't need one. The old school chum of any other bloke and we wouldn't be sitting here."

"Ah, Murphy," the major said, "therein lies the problem. The son of Lord Ashton isn't just any bloke."

"Yes, it always seems to slip my mind, the entitlement of the titled. Different rules than the rest of us."

"There are some things you're going to change in this lifetime, Murphy, and some you are not. The wealthy and powerful protect their own and have done since the dawn of time."

"You're right," said James. "I guess what I'm wondering is why Lord Ashton, Earl of Fenwick, felt the need to jump in at all. What is it about this old school chum that Edward needs protecting about?"

"That is a rather excellent question," the major said. "Unfortunately, we are not detectives, Murphy. So as I promised the colonel, you have to let it alone. No more requests for information from Captain James Murphy on this subject."

James knew his boss didn't really have much choice. Not when the cease and desist came from the top.

"However," the major continued, "you are not owned by the British army. I have no control over what you do in your spare time or who you might enlist to help track down information."

James smiled. "That you don't, sir."

"I don't know what you've gotten yourself into, Murphy, and we'll leave it like that for now. But you did have a good reason for making those inquiries, and given the players involved I would understand if you felt compelled to make sure everything was on the up-and-up."

"I appreciate that, sir."

"Just watch yourself. A couple calls out to Cambridge on a former student shouldn't have raised any flags, let alone resulted in the turmoil that it has. Even if you stumbled on a secret, the smart move would've been to delay the response with bureaucratic platitudes and wait until it went away. The top boss is afraid of something, Murphy, and he's got more power in his little finger than you and I will attain in a lifetime. Whatever you do, make sure it's worth risking your career over."

"Aye, sir."

James left the major's office and headed back to the broadcast booth. He wasn't on air for another hour, but he felt it was a fine place to have a think without interruptions.

He nodded at the lieutenant currently broadcasting and settled into a chair in the corner.

He didn't hear the news updates or the music selection. James tuned it all out to focus on what he'd just learned so he could come up with some plan on what to do about it.

The truth was, he hadn't expected anything to come of his calls to Cambridge. He'd contacted the registrar's office and the faculty of engineering and assumed all he'd get back was a stock response. Yes, this person attended the university. No, we can't tell you anything more about him. The most he'd been hoping for was some idea of what Venmar had worked on while at the school.

But the earl getting involved, now that was an unexpected development. James had assumed that whatever Edward was doing, whatever information he might be passing to the East Germans, it was without his father's knowledge. Lord Ashton had never given the appearance of being anything other than dedicated to queen and country.

James cast around for other explanations, but still he kept coming back to the obvious. Why would the earl feel the need to protect his son if he didn't know what Edward was doing?

But if he did know what Edward was doing, then why react so strongly and draw attention to the situation?

The major was right about one thing. He wasn't a damn detective. He couldn't go around poking into the family history of the Earl of Fenwick without finding himself suddenly posted to Northern Ireland or some such shite location. He took stock of the resources he had available and what he actually needed in order to make this all someone else's problem.

A few minutes later and the conclusion was inescapable. He'd have to tell Jillian the whole story, but it would be well worth it for her help. Because the most obvious asset he had was a copy of that book.

"So let me get this straight," Jillian said. "You think a friend might be in trouble, or causing trouble, and you've elected to help until you have the information you need to make a good decision for yourself."

James looked at her. He didn't like her tone or the smirk creeping onto her face.

"That's about the sum of it, yes," he said.

"Why aren't you just telling your commander and washing your hands of the whole thing? Putting yourself first and not risking anything?"

"I see where you're going with this," he scowled.

"Do you?" she asked, all innocence.

James wasn't fooled. "You seem to be drawing a right parallel to when you were finding out what happened to your friend Lisa, and I was after you to let it all alone."

"And?"

"You're a pain in the arse, as I've told you many times. But fine, I will say it so we can put it all behind us: you were right. Sometimes you have to fight a little before you can know the proper way to go. I'm not blind, seeing that you're a woman and the expectations seem to be different for you. I've got my major giving me his blessing and warning me to watch my back, while you got every man in your professional life telling you to stay at home and be a good little girl."

Jillian smiled at him. "Thank you."

"Right, it's probably me who should be thanking you. Now that I'm enlightened, I'm sure I'll have an easier time of it with me mum and sisters."

"Not to mention Jasminka."

"Don't, then."

"She'll come back to you, James," Jillian said.

"Since neither of us can see the future, let it alone. I didn't ask to meet you here just for the chat."

Jillian looked around the busy café. Normally she and James were having dinner at one of their apartments or out for a beer. They'd never had coffee in the morning close to campus.

"I need your help," James continued. "I don't have any other way of getting information that isn't going to get me demoted down to lieutenant second class and stationed in Belfast for the rest of my career. I can't cast suspicion on an innocent man, but I can't ignore suspected treason. This contact of Quentin's might come through, but best I can figure, there's a lot of moving parts in that one that might come to nothing. In the meantime, I've got the images we made of the book. I reckon it's going to be tedious as hell, but I've got to give it a try."

"It may not be as bad as you think. When it's not your language, the differences stand out better. Your brain doesn't get sidetracked into the story. And it's a short book."

"It's still hundreds of pages of ancient Greek."

"In dialogue format," she said. "Lots of spaces. It's the play *Antigone*."

"My classics are a little rusty."

Jillian smiled. "It could be worse."

"Aye, lass. It could always be worse."

"Do you have time now to come to my office?"

James finished up his coffee. "Aye, that why I suggested we meet here. I can't be taking a decade to figure out what to do. Now that I'm on the radar of the Secretary of Defence, I better get something concrete before I come under suspicion myself."

Jillian's features tightened with worry. "Do you really think that's going to happen?"

He told her about the phone calls to Cambridge and the result with this boss. "From that reaction, I've got to assume I'm being checked out. I want to make sure I'm not also being set up."

"Yeah," said Jillian, biting at her lower lip. "There's definitely something going on."

"Aye. So before it gets any worse, let's see what I can find out from that book."

They left the café and headed to Jillian's office on campus. James had never been here before and was surprised by how much equipment was packed into the small space.

"You know how to use all this stuff?" he asked, gesturing to the machines that were whirring around them.

"Yes," she laughed. "These machines are my tools. It's what I do every day." She held out her hand for his jacket.

Handing it over, he took a proper look at her face. There were purple circles under her eyes. It occurred to James that he'd been so busy with figuring out Edward and watching over Lena that he'd not paid much attention to Jillian lately. "Everything the same with you?" he asked.

She looked up at him, startled. "What kind of a question is that?"

James narrowed his eyes. "And that's a suspicious answer. You do seem to get involved in adventure with some regularity, and we've not seen each other much in the last few weeks. Nothing life-threatening going on, I hope."

"Fine, yes. Things are basically the same. I'm not involved with any Cuban spies or German vigilantes. I'm not being hassled by anyone in the CIA, nor have I stumbled upon any cover-ups by old Canadian spies."

"You must be proper bored, then," James grinned. "Still, you look like you need a bit more sleep."

She rolled her eyes at him and hung up their coats. "Have you ever used microfilm before?"

"No."

"It's pretty easy, the reading of it anyway. It's essentially just little pictures. You feed them into a reader, and then you can click from image to image at your own pace. I would just make a note of every symbol with a smudge and see how many you get in an hour. Some of them may be superfluous. I think the thing you should really pay attention to is if there is any obvious way to group them."

"Like what?" James asked, feeling so far out of his element that it felt like the first day on his first job ever.

"I don't know. Another mark on the page? A symbol that appears frequently after a grouping?"

James shuddered. He had a feeling the next few hours were going to result in a lot of pain.

"Right, then, I guess you should set me up and hope I don't die of boredom in your office."

CHAPTER TWENTY-NINE

Jillian was back in the antechamber of the tunnel. It was cold, damp, and dark, and she couldn't remember when she'd last been this alert. Finally, she was making progress on figuring out the communications of the tunnel system.

It had started two days earlier, when she was listening to the recording of the comings and goings in the room above. It was usually just the same two men sitting there all day. A lot of silence. A lot of idle, social chitchat. But once in a while someone, presumably their boss, came in. Based on those interactions, Jillian figured something out. They were in the same business she was.

Once she started to listen to them through that lens, it became obvious. They were in signals, processing and listening to intercept they were getting from somewhere.

Of course, they could just have a bunch of directional receivers pointed at West Berlin, but Jillian didn't think so. Those would be pretty obvious to anyone looking over the Wall.

It stood to reason that they were intercepting cable signals, and thus those signals were traveling across the same cables that wound through the tunnel.

When she'd thought about it, it didn't seem much of a leap. The East Germans were likely in an old Nazi building connected to the tunnel. It was unlikely the Nazis had connected the tunnel to only that building. There must be others. Even if the tunnel pathway had caved in or never been fully finished, the cables themselves could just be buried and connected to other buildings—some of which had to be over in West Berlin.

Sebastian and Peter had done a good job of mapping the tunnel, but it was clear it wasn't a completed structure. They hadn't bothered mapping all the cables, but it didn't matter. There were more cables than tunnel. There had to be.

Since she wouldn't be able to follow each communication cable to its destination, Jillian had decided the simplest course of action was to put a tap on as many as she could. She would start with the ones connected to the antechamber, and thus the building above, and going out from there if necessary.

Taps were smaller, cheaper, and easy to put together. Recording equipment was also simple, but bigger and more expensive. So as to not raise too many suspicions by purchasing an abundance of electronic products and carting them all out to the house at the edge of Spandau, Jillian was connecting each tap to the recording device. She'd then install a timer, so the recorder progressed through each tap, maybe collecting an hour at a time from each one.

There was no buffer, so it couldn't run that long, but she didn't need it to.

She only needed a basic understanding of what was flowing along each cable. Given the age of the system and the fact that the people using it had no idea of the full extent of what they'd stumbled upon, some of the cables were likely not transmitting anything.

But at least one of them was. She'd bet her career on it.

"What are you doing?"

Jillian started, her heart pounding. "Augh, you scared the crap out of me," she said.

"I am sorry," Peter said, coming into the antechamber. "I thought you must have heard me. I sing when I think I'm down here by myself. I didn't know you were coming here this morning."

"I didn't know either," Jillian said, "but I had an epiphany yesterday."

She had thought carefully about what to tell Sebastian and Peter. Ultimately, she wouldn't hide anything from them—not that she'd be able to in the long run. But she needed to confirm her suspicions first, because if she was right, she might have to break part of her cover. That would be no easy decision, so she had to be certain about what were, at the moment, only suspicions.

"I just assumed, at the beginning, that the tunnel was a closed system. The Nazis built it for whatever purpose, but that purpose was no longer being filled. For obvious reasons."

"I don't understand," said Peter.

"The electrical infrastructure," said Jillian, "I thought it was only here for the tunnel. Lights, communications, whatever, I thought it was all confined to the tunnel, except for the connection to whatever power source they used. But when I discovered that transmission, that the tunnel was connected to the building above, on purpose, and that the system was designed for above and below ground to communicate with each other, it got me thinking."

"What if there are other buildings?"

Jillian smiled. Smart guy. "Exactly."

"Yes," Peter nodded, "I wondered the same thing. How can you find them? The tunnel, it just stops in many places."

"But the cables don't. I think they're buried underground, and some of them still connect to the other buildings the Nazis wanted attached to this infrastructure. I'm going to tap them and see if anything is flowing."

"Such as?" asked Peter.

"Communications," said Jillian. "Direct lines between other buildings and the one above our heads."

"So it may not be a closed system?"

"I don't know," Jillian answered truthfully. "It's possible that it is still. Just a giant base or bunker with no connection to the outside world, and that the building above was an isolated part of the original infrastructure. It's also possible that some of these wires are connected to other buildings, possibly even the larger communications structure. That's what would make it so interesting to the East Germans. See, I think the guys above us, they just stumbled onto some interesting connections. I think there are communications flowing through this infrastructure that the East Germans are picking up on."

"Like what?" Peter asked.

"I really don't know. The telecoms companies will have mapped all the infrastructure they're using. However, when you build a comms network, you always include spare terminal blocks in the rack to account for growth. If the original drawings were lost, then someone above us in the GDR might have just been looking for an unused line and found one that was being used but not accounted for. The infrastructure around here is actually a little messed up because of the separation. The East Germans cut everything, but they still had to lay parallel lines in some areas. And the West Germans had to reroute the severed connections. If this tunnel was ever part of the larger infrastructure, it could have some original routes that have been reconnected."

Peter sat back, apparently thinking it all over. "It is probably a connection to something that had a purpose back in the war but now is just vestigial. Like an appendix."

Jillian laughed. "Yeah, exactly like that. I don't think these East Germans have the keys to every phone call in West Berlin, but I do think they've found something moderately useful on account of the way the cables in here were connected to points outside."

"We are going to have to tell someone about this, aren't we?"

"I think you always knew that," Jillian said. "For all the reasons you've already outlined."

"Sebastian, he wants to find the magic, but this discovery, it's too big for us."

"I'm sorry, Peter, I really am. I wish the whole thing was under Spandau and you could sell tickets and be local celebrities. But the location always made it impossible."

"I know," he sighed. "I hope you find something interesting. I hope that it gives someone in West Germany a reason to keep the tunnel from falling apart."

"I believe, you know, that one day that stupid Wall is going to come down. Then it won't matter where the tunnel is, and maybe you'll be able to share it then."

He smiled at her but didn't say anything.

"If you want to prepare for that day, I'd document everything you can and put it in a safety deposit box. So there's no question of what is down here."

"You and me, we think alike. I have eighty photos already."

"I'll give you all these recordings too. To throw in your box."

Peter paused for a moment and looked around the room. "Can I help with anything?"

"Yeah, can you hold these two pieces together while I screw them in?"

Peter smiled at her, "Yes."

CHAPTER THIRTY

Anya screamed with frustration. She held a pillow up to her face and let it all out: all the pain, the fear, the desperation. Every nervous moment, every unshed tear. She screamed and screamed until her throat ached with rawness.

She was so close. So close to vanquishing her husband and having a life with her daughter. So close to freedom.

But she might as well have been miles. Like being in an apartment on Elsenstrasse and being able to see over the Wall into West Berlin. Close geographically, but miles and miles away. So far that the distance could not be overcome.

She could not think of a diversion—she, Anya, who had patiently developed contacts and gathered information for years, who had identified her ex-husband's vulnerabilities and convinced good people to help her bring him down. All that time living a double, even a triple, life. Anya the Stasi courier, Valentina the double agent, and Mama to the most beautiful little girl in the world. All that work of remembering the lies and the betrayals. Never mixing it up. Never falling apart. Never making a mistake. Yet here she was, walking beside freedom but so far from attaining it.

Anya had anticipated that Michael would react to her leaving. Of course he would. She had counted on it and prepared accordingly. She had thought his focus would be on offense, not defense. Trying to find her in West Berlin, making sure she couldn't just fly out of the city, coming after her, that was his style.

Why was he also protecting his residence at Wandlitz? It was minimal, but it was still there. Even if he wanted to find the people who had helped her and Lena escape, he couldn't suspect anyone in the village. It was too far. Heddy herself had nothing to do with it. Anya made sure that Heddy hadn't changed her routine in years.

Anya put the pillow down on the sofa, the screaming having done its job and run its course.

Taking a deep breath, she started to put her thoughts in order. It didn't matter why Michael had someone at Wandlitz. Not really. It only mattered that it was true. He was covering all his bases, no matter how peripheral to the situation.

There had to be something she could do. Something that would draw his attention and force him to concentrate his resources.

So far, she hadn't been able to think of anything big enough. There was, as always, no margin for error. It had to work on the right day at the right time, or the plan would fail. She'd tip her hand and spend the rest of her life looking over her shoulder.

Even stretching her imagination and using herself as bait, it was all too small. She was just one woman. As desperate as he must be to have her under his control again, he couldn't descend dozens of Stasi officers onto the streets of West Berlin.

Therein lay her problem.

She was somewhat protected over here. Even to take her by force, he would still have to be subtle.

That was exactly what she didn't need. She didn't need shadows and back alleys. She needed something large and visible. Something to cause panic—true panic, the kind the Stasi machine would swing into full gear for, that took time. Which she didn't have. So it was out of the question.

She turned her attention to the kitchen as Rose came in carrying a coffee tray. Veronica was right behind her with the pot. Here she was, risking again the connections of the plan, but Anya thought it only fair to tell both women in person that she was stalled, that it was all about to go up in the smoke of failure.

"Veronica is ready," Rose said, putting out cups and Leibniz cookies. "She is fast. Almost as fast as I am."

Anya looked at Rose's face. She thought of Lucinda, still clinging to life in the hospital. Of Heddy, whose brother was rotting away in hard labor. And of Rose herself, who had seen her grandfather get punished in order to guarantee his silence. The agony twisted around in her chest. It was more than her and Lena. It was all the people she was failing by not seeing that Michael's blackmail files were burned to ashes.

"I have hit an obstacle," Anya said. Better to get it out quickly. "Michael has someone stationed at the house in Wandlitz to keep an eye out. For me. For something. I'm not sure. Heddy cannot get Veronica in. Working on the safe is out of the question. I have tried to think of a way to distract him, to focus his attention in such a way that he would need to pull his resource away from the house, but I have not been able to solve this problem. There is only such a short time, and, well, that is it."

"Oh, Anya, we can think of something," Rose said. "You've worked so hard on this. We've worked so hard. Michael, he's not going to give up. I don't want you to hide for the rest of your life. I don't want any of us to hide."

It was sorrow that seemed to be bubbling up, squeezing her chest and clogging her throat. Anya realized she hurt everywhere. If it were possible, if Lena didn't need her, she would curl up in a ball and never open her eyes again.

"It can't be helped," she said to Rose. "We cannot try if I know it's not going to work. Maybe at some point, I will be able to think of something, and we can try again."

Anya said the words because they were expected, but she knew it was false hope. It would take years of being in proximity to Michael, and those days were behind her. The best she could try for was to run far and hope to earn the forgiveness of everyone she let down.

"Do you think he suspects you are going after the files?" Veronica asked.

Anya shook her head. "No. If he was really worried about those files, he would be watching from the bushes, hoping to catch me or have twenty men stationed there. I believe it is an automatic precaution."

"You're thinking to distract him, so that sentry, he doesn't go up to the house next Wednesday?"

"I was thinking that in an emergency, Wandlitz wouldn't be a priority. If he thought he could catch me, then he would focus his efforts on that. But if I make myself visible and vulnerable, I can't be sure he would pull in the Wandlitz man. Even Michael Polenz can't just send dozens of armed Stasi officers into West Berlin."

"What other kind of problem would he get involved in?"

Anya contemplated Veronica's question. "How do you mean?"

"In general. Like, if there were a large fire in East Berlin, would he be involved?"

Anya shook her head. "No. I do not think so. It would have to be a direct threat. An attack, for sure. A high-profile capture. Something like that."

"What about something unexpected? Around the city, maybe, where it wasn't obvious what it was."

Anya thought for a moment. "Yes, possibly. Anything large and unknown would be perceived as a threat. Until the government was certain, especially if it was happening around East Berlin, then, maybe, probably, Michael would be involved." Anya felt her heart fluttering strangely and realized it was hope. "Do you have an idea?" she asked Veronica.

"Maybe. I mean, I've got an idea. I'm not exactly sure what to do, or even how to do it. But there is a possibility that I might be able to arrange a pretty unusual distraction. Best part is, it's nothing that would hurt anyone, and no one's life would be at risk."

Anya was almost afraid to ask more. "I don't understand exactly. How do you know you can arrange this…distraction, without knowing what it is?"

"I can't tell you. Not right now. It involves a secret that isn't mine to share. Before you cancel anything, or run, give me two days to see if I can figure something out."

Anya began to tap her foot, an old habit she hadn't given in to for years. She was afraid to believe Veronica, afraid to give up control of any part of her plan, but she couldn't deny the hum of excitement. Before walking through Rose's door today, she had accepted defeat. Was devastated by it, yes, but had accepted there were no solutions to be found.

She hadn't expected this of Veronica—to go beyond her role, to try to keep the plan alive with an idea that was very clearly outside of Anya's capabilities.

Anya knew, however, to not let the hope blind her. Holding fast to the disappointment that had been her companion for so long, keeping space for it beside her so it wouldn't be too hard to access should Veronica not come through, she opened her mouth.

"Yes," Anya said, "I can wait two days. You will tell me though, when you confirm, what your idea is. It is my call if I think it has a chance to work and if we all take the risk."

"No problem," agreed Veronica. "You'll know better than the rest of us, anyway, how big the distraction has to be."

CHAPTER THIRTY-ONE

"Thank God it's nice out today, because I need to talk to you, and it's a conversation that's better outside. Way better." Jillian turned to lead Veronica deeper into the Tiergarten, staying in the sun as much as she could. Being November, it was cool, but the heat of the midday sun warmed her skin.

"Oh no. I have to talk to you as well. I hope it's not about the same thing."

Jillian regarded Veronica. "You first."

"Well, I wanted to ask how things are going with the tunnel."

"Funny you should bring that up, because that's exactly what I've got to talk to you about. I've discovered something."

"Something good?" asked Veronica.

"That depends on whose side you're on."

"We're on the same side, aren't we?"

"Yes," emphasized Jillian, "which is why I'm talking to you. You're the only other person in Berlin right now whose interests are aligned with mine exactly."

Veronica was quiet for a moment. "Would you be upset if I said that maybe we aren't precisely aligned at the moment? Close, probably. Like, parallel for sure."

"What's going on?" asked Jillian.

"You know that favor Quentin wanted me to do?"

"The one that seems to have dragged James in as well?"

Veronica started. "I don't know anything about that. Should I?"

"I don't think it matters. But those files you're going over to East Germany to get, one of them has to do with a friend of James. He's caught up right now in trying to figure out what the best move is for his country."

"Damn," said Veronica. "We're talking treason, aren't we?"

"Maybe. I guess James is hoping not, but until you have the files."

"If I can get them," Veronica said.

"Is there a problem?"

"Isn't there always?"

"What does the tunnel have to do with it?" Jillian asked.

"James must have told you about this woman, Quentin's contact, who set up this plan to get all these files from East Germany."

"Not East Berlin?"

"No," said Veronica, "a private residence in Wandlitz. This woman, she's got a way to get me in there on a cleaning crew, and she's covered all the details of what I'll need. It's simple, clever, and she's been working on it for a while."

"And the problem?"

"Her being in West Berlin has prompted a reaction. The cleaning crew is now being watched. Based on her sources, the oversight is minimal, the kind you assign to a week-old rookie, but it's still oversight. That means I can't get the files unless the person providing this oversight has more important things to do that day."

Jillian tried to put the pieces together, but nothing was clicking. "What does this have to do with the tunnel?"

"I'm not sure," Veronica sighed. "But, well, if we can't think of some way to get that guard out of the way, I'm not going to get the files. I think we're both in agreement that the files of every Western agent passing info to the Stasi are about as high importance as you can get in the intelligence business. So, I was thinking, wondering, hoping, that there was some way to use that tunnel to cause a great big distraction in that part of East Germany on the day I'm supposed to go get them."

"I wasn't expecting that," Jillian said, not sure whether to laugh or gasp.

"Of course you weren't. Who would?"

"They're going to think you're crazy," Jillian said.

"Who is?"

"Everyone. The woman you're helping. Peter and Sebastian."

Veronica scrunched up her nose. "I know. I think I'm half-crazy myself. But, as I'm sure you can appreciate, we don't have a lot of time to pull this off, no other good ideas have presented themselves, and I'd be truly crazy not to explore whatever options I have to secure those files."

Jillian thought about what Veronica was asking for. It was daring, even without any details filled in.

"There's been another interesting development in the tunnel," Jillian said. "I'm not sure how it affects things, but I've discovered that there's a cable carrying British communications that the East Germans are monitoring."

Veronica's eyes rounded. "What?"

"I don't quite understand exactly how the infrastructure is laid out, but basically the Nazis connected this tunnel to various buildings in the west end of the city. Now those buildings are on both sides of the Wall. Part of the tunnel was designed to facilitate direct communications between buildings, like a bunker system or something, somewhere to hide during an attack, I don't know. So the comms cables in the tunnel, they run through it but connect to various points outside. It's old, mostly unused, definitely not finished, and confusing, but it would seem that some of the cables are still used in active transmission. Obviously neither side seems to know about the tunnel. There's no reason for them to think that the communications infrastructure is anything but standard. But I tapped all the lines I could and found something unbelievable— British military transmissions. It seems the British took over some old buildings that happen to be connected to the comms cables running through the tunnel, and the East Germans have taken over at least one building that is linked to the same infrastructure. They must have been looking for unused lines when they moved in and picked up on this British voice transmission."

"Holy shit," Veronica said.

"I know. I mean, it could be thirty years they've been listening to this channel. The good news is, it doesn't seem to contain a lot of secret stuff. So far, it's been boring logistics, like pillow requisitions and uniform replacements. But still, over time, you could put together a pretty detailed picture of British military resource capabilities if you know how many pillows they need."

"When I was working with Frank in Nicaragua, he talked about this all this time, how getting good signals was often a matter of lucky location. We have the Ministry of Agriculture's phone lines running over our embassy there. No one would have planned that."

"It's so true," Jillian nodded. "When you're on defense, it's easier, because you usually have access to a detailed description of the infrastructure. But collecting enemy signals—outside the obvious, like on the undersea cables—is often just that: lucky location. Like what we have here. The East Germans took over a building that is connected to a part of a network that happens to contain British miliary communications. So they copy them, because there's no risk. They don't even have to go out and get them."

"Have you told Peter and Sebastian yet?"

"No. For a whole host of reasons, the most obvious being that they're probably going to wonder how I figured this all out."

"That and how suspicious it's going to look when you advise them on what to do."

Jillian rubbed her hand over her face. "I know. Really, the best course of action is for us to collaborate with the British and use that line to start passing misinformation about allied military activity in the whole country. But Sebastian and Peter, they're West German. I can't very well expect them to not tell their own country. To say nothing of the fact that this is all happening via a tunnel that mostly runs under East German territory."

"Could you tell people the what without disclosing the where?"

Jillian sighed. "I thought of that. The only way would be to do it anonymously, and there are so many problems with that. First, if I suggest to Sebastian and Peter they just drop some tapes off with the British, the result is most likely to be a ceasing of communications and the ripping up of phone lines. That means BND is going to get involved anyway. If they go anonymously to BND, I can't guarantee BND would then tell the British army, and then I wouldn't be doing my job. Plus, neither solves the problem of what to do about the tunnel. Peter and Sebastian rightly believe it's an important historical artifact."

Veronica looked thoughtful. "So, it's about how best to preserve that artifact?"

"Well, and I've got to make sure I address that intercept somehow. I can't knowingly let the British army comms keep getting compromised. They're allies, and we have a few Canadians seconded here. Our national interest is a factor as well."

They continued to walk along the path, letting the silence fall as the thoughts churned.

Jillian knew there was no real option with the tunnel. Once she'd discovered the intercepted communications, it had become of matter of national security—for a few nations. She would have to persuade Sebastain and Peter to notify BND, both of the tunnel and the intercept. Meanwhile, she'd have to arrange for the British army to be notified, a task she thought was best suited for Veronica via Frank, and all those official channels that linked the two countries.

But before she initiated that series of actions, there was Veronica's problem to address: a massive intelligence scoop way more valuable than what was going on in the tunnel.

"You know," Jillian said, "solving your problem might help solve my problem."

"In what way?" Veronica asked.

"Sebastian, he's the one who wants the tunnel to mean something, to have their discovery not go to waste. I wonder if I could convince him to make this grand gesture as a final good-bye to his discovery. To go out with a bang, as it were."

"He does like crazy art shows," Veronica said.

"And to bring beauty into the world," Jillian added.

Both of them thought for a moment. "It might work," said Veronica. "Some ridiculously over-the-top artistic gesture."

"Right beside the Wall. The East Germans wouldn't know what to make of it."

"It would distract them, because they wouldn't understand it at all."

"And if Sebastian could make it beautiful, he would love that."

Veronica stopped and turned to Jillian. "It has to happen next Wednesday. If he agrees, what he concocts needs to light up the countryside on Wednesday morning."

"I guess I better go sell it to him. Art to end Communism."

"That's about as big a gesture as you can get," Veronica smiled.

CHAPTER THIRTY-TWO

"A tunnel?"

Jillian could tell that she'd surprised him. Quentin, who had seen so much and wasn't fazed by any of it, was staring at her in disbelief.

"How big is this tunnel?"

"Kilometers," said Jillian, "mostly under East Germany. It's more of a tunnel system. I'm not sure why the Nazis built it originally. To hide? To transport goods or people? We don't know for sure, but it was clearly important to them. What's been built has steel walls snaking all over the place. Once I got the power working, most of it lights up now. It's pretty remarkable."

Quentin clearly didn't know what to say. "These two guys found it by accident?"

"Yes. How else would anyone find something like this?"

"Old Nazi maps," Quentin shrugged.

"I suppose. But no, one of them, Sebastian, found it while eating lunch during a routine inspection of the main telecoms cabling tunnels."

"They haven't told anyone about it?" Quentin asked. "Just you?"

"They couldn't figure out how to make the electrical infrastructure work, and Sebastian and I have a dedicated interest in keeping each other's secrets given that he's my contact at Telekom Berlin."

"What's it like? The tunnel."

"Cold. Damp. But fascinating. You should see it. It's almost like something out of a sci-fi novel. Like being on a spaceship, but not a fancy one. Not like *Star Trek*. It's like a really big fallout shelter."

"That can't be why the Nazis built it though," he said.

"No, of course not. I'm just trying to give you a sense of it. It's not just a means of getting from one place to another. You could spend time down there. It's full of old Nazi stuff that has to be valuable for posterity."

"Incredible," Quentin said, shaking his head. "How are you planning to use it to help Veronica?"

Once Veronica had told Quentin of her idea to help Anya, he had demanded to be involved. Jillian knew that to have two disconnected parts of his life colliding like this would be unsettling for him. Everyone who worked in intelligence compartmentalized everything in their lives. To have the barrier between two of those compartments dissolve was always a source of unease.

"The problem with the tunnel is its location. I think Sebastian and Peter would prefer to see it in the hands of a museum, open to the public, a glimpse of a unique part of German history. But almost the entire part that's in good condition is under East Germany. Once word gets out, it's going to be impossible to hide it from the East Germans, who will likely fill it in because they'll probably just see it as an escape route. That's the same reason to not try to use it for that purpose."

Jillian reached for her coffee and took a sip. "It was all at a standstill until I found out the tunnel is connected to buildings aboveground. To make a long story short, the East Germans are in one of those buildings intercepting British army communications that flow between other buildings connected to the infrastructure."

"No one knows it's all flowing through this underground tunnel?"

"Why would they?" Jillian shrugged. "Comms cable are out of sight, out of mind. Most of them are buried. No one would think to question they might be buried in something other than the ground."

"Did you tell your two new friends all this?"

"Some of it. I tapped a few lines and shared the results. I told them they had to take it to BND, and that maybe, with the intelligence value, BND would work to keep the tunnel intact and a secret."

"Did they agree?" Quentin asked.

"Yeah. Peter, I think was relieved. The stress of the secrecy was getting to him. Finding the intercept forces their hand, and

I think he's okay with it. It's a best-case scenario, because now there's a chance the tunnel might be preserved."

"Until the Wall comes down."

"That's the idea," Jillian smiled. "I mean, no wall in the history of the world has worked indefinitely. The less porous any wall is, the more likely it'll crumble due to pressure."

"So the Great Wall of China is over-hyped?" Quentin asked.

"It was symbolic more than anything. It never functioned well as a military installation. They couldn't maintain or even provision the outposts. Hadrian's Wall was probably one of the more successful ones, but that's because the Romans realized that allowing limited flow between the two sides actually stabilized the region. It's like the laws of thermodynamics."

"I bet they don't teach that in the physics one-oh-one course," Quentin smiled at her, "why thermodynamics prevents border walls from working."

"Analogy, my dear Watson, is the engine of science."

"I presume, then, the plan for Veronica is before all of this disclosure happens?"

"What's one week? The feed isn't earth shattering, but I think what she's going over there to steal is."

"Point of clarification," Quentin said. "Human intelligence officers, we don't steal, we collect."

Jillian laughed. "Fine. While Veronica is over there liberating those files, we'll be using the tunnel to create a spectacular diversion. But Quentin, I have to ask you, is there anything you're not telling me?"

He leaned in and kissed her softly on the lips. "There's a lot I'm not telling you. What specifically are you worried about?"

Jillian refused to let herself be distracted. "This multinational effort that doesn't seem to be on any official radar."

Quentin leaned back in his chair and sighed. "Part of it is circumstance, and part of it is choice. Is it the right call? We're not going to know until it's all over. But I do know that those files, they're incendiary. If she gets them out, they're going to cause problems that are going to ripple around our agencies for years. Some people are going to be grateful for the cleanup, for the long-term advantage it's going to give us. But, as I'm sure you can appreciate, careers are going to be ruined, right up to the top. This isn't a one-off like Philby. The heads of our nations are not going to be able to look the other way while someone slips off to Moscow."

"So it's better just to show up with the goods. A fait accompli."

"Exactly. It fell into my lap, and I don't know who else has it. Veronica can say the same thing. We're better protected that way."

"And James?" Jillian asked. "And that situation with his friend?"

"It's his call, Jillian," Quentin shrugged. "I'm not in his shoes, and I can't fix the world."

"Are you going to give him the files though?" she asked.

"Not all of them. Before you get on my case, you and I both know there's no way he'd want them. I'll make sure he gets the stuff about his friend if there's anything there. If he decides to share it, then he can suggest to his superiors there's more where it came from."

"Don't you think copies should go to every country affected?"

"Possibly, but we don't have these files yet. We don't know what they contain. Considering this guy has blackmail files, too, on a bunch of East Germans, what I'm saying is, we're not likely to be dealing with straight double agents in it for the money or the cause. Some people are likely being manipulated, and their secrets may have nothing to do with national security."

"And if the blackmailer is removed, there's a likelihood that those people won't continue."

"Exactly," said Quentin. "I'm just not sure who should be making that call."

"Are you and Veronica going to make sure you're aligned?"

"No. She makes her decisions, I make mine. Trying to control who sees the information, who deals with the fallout, I think, would put me in a position I don't want to be in."

Jillian sat back and cradled her coffee. She was thankful she wasn't a part of it. She was only peripheral. The hard decisions weren't hers to make. Intelligence was such an odd business. It dealt mostly with the gray. There were occasionally clear wrongs and rights, but most of it was a moral quagmire. She didn't envy Quentin or Veronica having their hands on information that was going to destroy people's lives, bring embarrassment to a lot of government agencies in a lot of nations, cause accusations and denials to fly around, and take the collective allied trust down to zero. It was going to be terrible, but the alternative was even worse. Continuing to bleed information to the Communist regimes behind the Iron Curtain was not a good idea. Jillian knew that the information passed wasn't always research and blueprints. Sometimes it was about military or undercover operations, and blowing those resulted in loss of life. Jillian wouldn't be able to live with herself if she turned a blind eye to information that could prevent tragedy, and she didn't think Quentin or Veronica could either.

A lot of people were about to deal with devastating consequences.

"So, are you going to tell me the grand idea?" Quentin asked, bringing her focus back into the moment.

"I love how you phrased that like a question." Jillian could see the tension in his shoulders, the pain of his past making him draw inward.

"Fine, but I don't need anyone else's death on my conscience."

"Fair enough," Jillian said, "but according to Veronica, it's the woman with the plan who's in charge. If you don't like it, but she does, you'll have to sort it out with her."

There was a slight tightening of the skin around his mouth as his jaw clenched briefly. "She's not completely objective right now. I would think that I'd be a better judge."

"You may very well be, but it's not my call. You, Veronica, and the mystery woman, it's your op. I'm only facilitating the diversion."

"Which is?"

"Possibly the largest outdoor art installation the world has ever seen."

The pause exploded, reverberating around the room. "What does that mean?"

"I'm not sure," said Jillian. "I only spoke to Peter and Sebastian last night, and most of that time was taken up with a very abridged version of what is going on with a lot of emphasis on how it's all in support of a mission that's good for West Germany too. This was right on the back of me explaining about the East German intercept of British military communications. So, although these are the two guys who've been mapping out a Nazi tunnel that extends past the Wall, you can appreciate it was a lot to take in. I told them to think about it. All of it: if they want to do it, if they have any questions, and if there is even anything to be done."

"When did the art installation come up?"

"It's really the only answer," Jillian shrugged. "Sebastian is an artist. It was how I got him on board. The tunnel has to become someone else's responsibility, they know that. But offering one final grand artistic gesture, I thought it would make the rest okay."

Quentin looked pained. "Jillian, I don't have any idea what you're talking about. What in the hell is an art installation in this situation? They can't go hanging paintings on the Berlin Wall."

Jillian smiled. "I don't know. You're asking the wrong girl. A couple months ago, I went to one of Sebastian's art shows. It was in an abandoned building near the Zitadelle in Spandau. Accompanied by music, and lit up with stage lights, these giant balloons popped over the crowd, raining colored goo on us. Then we were rinsed off as the music faded out in a decrescendo and dried off by giant fans outside in the sunshine."

"Christ. I don't even know what to say."

She leaned forward and rested her hand on his cheek. "I think you need to give it a chance. It may end up being totally crazy, but nothing diverts the East German sensibilities like something they don't understand. The bad guys, they prepare for what they can predict. I promise you, whatever Sebastian comes up with, it's nothing they're going to be ready for."

He leaned his forehead against hers. "One day soon, I'm going to chuck this all in. Move to an island, run the cantina at some middle-of-nowhere beachside motel, take pasty-white tourists out on diving tours, and accept excessive tips from hot middle-aged women."

"Can I come?" Jillian said, bringing her lips to his. "I could drive the boat, check in the guests, and wear brightly colored dresses covered in hundreds of flowers."

"As long as you don't mind all the flirting I'll have to do to earn enough to make ends meet," he murmured, pulling her closer.

"I think I can handle being entertained like that," she said just before the kiss deepened and there wasn't enough space for any more words.

CHAPTER THIRTY-THREE

James thought his eyes were going to end up permanently damaged. How was it possible that anyone did this for a living?

His eyes burned from too many hours staring into the microfilm reader. When he went to bed at night, ancient Greek symbols played like a slideshow on the back of his eyelids. Deltas and omegas danced in endless patterns from which there would be no escape until he finished his task.

Was he making progress? He had no bloody idea.

Considering what was on the line, he couldn't give up.

There was no information forthcoming from Cambridge. Ditto for the government departments who dealt in foreign students or any of their subsequent employment. James had to assume that all official channels had been shut down.

He hadn't seen Edward in a while. He had no idea if he was still in West Berlin, if he'd gone home, or if he was working somewhere else. Given the sensitivity of the situation, he didn't dare ask.

That left him with the book, a task he couldn't have been less suited for.

"How's it coming?" Jillian asked, shoving a cafeteria tea and muffin at him. He was grateful she'd made room for him in her lab, but it was a cramped space for two bodies trying to work at different machines.

"It is, quite possibly, the most painful thing I've ever done, and I once had to hand-drop leaflets from the bottom of a Hawker Siddeley Andover over Kenya."

"Are you looking for pity?"

"No," he scowled at her. "But ye could wave your magic wand and finish the job for me."

Jillian laughed. "I did a few pages yesterday evening. I know it's tedious, but the more you have, the better chance you have of figuring out the cipher."

"What do you mean?"

"Presumably the person receiving the book isn't going to do what you're doing, going through it page by page. They're going to have a key so they know exactly where to look to find the symbols that are part of their message."

"Like, fourth word, second sentence, third paragraph every tenth page?"

"Yeah," Jillian smiled, "something like that."

James looked at the book in front of him, renewed. He had been making note of the page numbers so he could find them again. Christ, he hoped it was going to be that easy.

When Jillian stood up at one point to stretch and take a break, he showed her the string he'd found so far. "I suppose I've got to translate these to English."

"Or German," she said.

"Aye, I'll start with those two languages and hope it's not done in Swahili. Do you reckon it's just a simple translation?"

Jillian thought for a moment. "I guess it depends partly on the message. This could be anything from a big state secret to a game among friends. It probably also depends on the skill of the people involved."

"You aren't giving me much hope."

"That's why people encrypt information to begin with. It's not supposed to be easy. Doing it the way you are, with only the encrypted text, could take years. Cryptanalysis is an entire field of study—patterns, frequencies, probabilities. It might seem tedious, but it often is the difference between winning and losing wars. The power results from mastering the micro details."

The horror must have registered on his face, because Jillian was looking at him with pity.

"I'm not trying to scare you," she said, "but what you're doing, it requires a lot of patience, time, and effort, and a little luck. You may not ever figure it out."

James took a deep breath and sat back in the chair. "I'm not sure this is worth all that effort, then. Even if I figured out the damn message, it's only my word that it's from the book I dropped off. None of this is going to add up to proof."

"It's always the problem," Jillian said. "Clues for a new direction but never a smoking gun."

"Listen," she continued, "I know it's sensitive material, but it's not officially classified. If you want, I can put it all on microdots and send it home to my father. He's more of a code maker than a code breaker, but he's going to be a lot better than you or me at figuring out if there's a coded message in that book."

James felt the relief burst in his chest. He knew the book was important. He'd bet a lifetime supply of Tennent's that the relationship between Edward and Dieter Venmar was the key to whatever Edward was doing with the East Germans. To have some help, to have a much better shot at getting some answers, lifted layers of worry and frustration.

"That, my dear Jillian, is the best offer I've had in a long time."

"Murphy, get in here," MacTeague shouted from his office.

Once more, James was at a loss. "Sir?" he said, coming round the door frame.

"The colonel wants to see you."

"Colonel Fornbridge?"

"Do you know of another colonel wandering around this base, Murphy?"

"No, sir. Any idea what it's about?" James asked.

"I was hoping you'd tell me. I'm not going to have to go visit you in the brig, am I?" The words might have been comedic in another situation, but the lines in MacTeague's forehead gave them a weight that could drown them in six inches of water.

"I hope not. Unless I'm being framed for something."

"And that last conversation we had Murphy, anything new there?"

James shook his head. "No, sir. I've been trying to figure out my next moves but haven't yet made any."

"Ah well, you better get over to his office, then. Find out what's going on and report back to me what you can."

James nodded before turning down the corridor. He'd never actually been to the base commander's office, but he knew where it was. He pushed open the door to the psyops building, blinking as the sun hit his eyes. The brightness was of the kind of intensity that made you ignore the sharp bite of the wind. There weren't too many sunny November days like this here in Berlin.

He crossed the main compound, avoiding the infantry drill practice in the hof. He almost ran into two corporals who were jogging and returned the salute of an old sergeant he'd worked with.

Reaching the building that housed the base commander and his staff, a lovely old house, he climbed the steps and entered.

"Captain James Murphy to see Colonel Fornbridge."

The secretary looked at him with naked interest. What in the hell was going on?

"Yes, sir," the secretary said, Kirkpatrick stenciled on his uniform. "The colonel said to bring you right in when you got here."

There was no way this visit was going to result in good news.

Kirkpatrick knocked on an open door. "Captain Murphy here to see you, sir," he announced.

"Come in," Colonel Fornbridge said.

James entered. His stomach was doing a proper job of tying itself into knots, but he kept his face calm as he saluted the colonel.

"Sit, Captain. That will be all, Lieutenant. Please close the door."

James took a seat on the other side of the desk from the colonel, who waited for the door to click shut before he spoke.

"I understand you're friends with Edward Ashton," the colonel said.

James's head began to pound. Surely to Christ Edward had more than one friend. They went back a fair number of years, fine, but they didn't see each other all that often. Edward was a sociable bloke. James imagined he could find someone to share a pint with in half the cities in the world.

"Of a manner, sir. We played rugby together in our uni days."

The colonel nodded. "Did you ever go up to visit him at Cambridge?"

"Almost twenty years ago? No, sir. We only met on the pitch. I was on the army team, and we played some matches against each other. We did a bit of training together when the schedule fit, have a pint after. That kind of thing."

Fornbridge sighed and looked out the window. "You know who his father is, Murphy."

James let out a sigh of his own. It wasn't a question.

"Why were you asking about Edward's friends at Cambridge?" This was a question.

If James had known such a bloody great can of worms was going to be opened as a result of those inquiries, he never would have made the damn calls. "Edward asked me to take a book to an old friend of his in East Berlin, someone he'd met at Cambridge. It seemed innocuous, as I've got a fairly easy time going over."

"But not completely innocent," the Colonel said.

"I didn't know. I still don't. He said it was harder for him to go over, that it would raise a few flags. I don't know if that's true, but then I'm also not the son of the Secretary of Defence."

"So you wanted to look up this friend. Why?"

"I suppose, sir, that I just wanted to make sure he existed. I wanted some assurance that I wasn't going to be party to anything…untoward."

"When was the last time you spoke with Edward?" Fornbridge asked.

James felt a shiver creep up his neck. "A couple weeks ago. We met at the mess, when he gave me the book. After I delivered it, he popped round to see if the delivery was successful, but I didn't have much time to chat that day. My shift on the radio was about to start."

"And was it successful? The delivery?"

"Aye. I dropped the book off at the science academy in East Berlin, to a proper bookish Dr. Dieter Venmar."

"What was the book?"

"A Greek copy of *Antigone*."

The colonel looked at him like he had made some confusing attempt at a joke.

"If I may ask, sir, what is all this about? Major MacTeague gave me the cease and desist on the Cambridge friends, and I've honored it."

"The thing is, Murphy, that book delivery you made has put me in hot water. Lord Ashton is asking what kind of base I'm running, what kind of officers I have, that they would deliver a package to East Berlin from anyone here without having its contents vetted by security."

James still didn't understand what was going on, but one thing was becoming increasingly clear: Edward's innocence was improbable, if not completely impossible. He was Anya's contact and was very likely sharing something with the East Germans. James would very soon have to come clean to his superiors about what he suspected.

"I know it's not official policy, sir, but we take items over all the time, things they can't get over there. Chocolate bars, music posters, band T-shirts."

Fornbridge waved his hand, dismissing the context. "I know. This isn't about you dropping off some book. This is about Lord Ashton keeping an eye on his son."

"I hope I'm not speaking out of turn, sir, but surely that isn't a job for the British army."

"That's the thing, Murphy. As much as I've more important tasks on my list, it would seem that Edward Ashton has gone missing, and his father thinks that you have something to do with it."

Shock dropped like a cannonball into his guts. "What?"

"Three days ago," said the colonel, "he didn't report in for some meeting. He was supposed to represent our government's position at a four-powers negotiation over city access. Never showed, and they had to postpone it. Next thing I know, I've got the Secretary of Defence himself yelling at me on the phone, threatening to tear my base apart, riddled as it was with incompetence."

James's head was spinning. "Not to point out the obvious, sir, but Edward works for the foreign office. Shouldn't they be the ones trying to figure it out?"

"They are. But for you Murphy, I don't think I'd be involved in this at all. But you wanted to know about Edward's Cambridge days, which are, for some reason, off limits. Then the man himself disappears, and his father is one breath away from accusing you of having him stashed somewhere and hauling you back to Blighty to be investigated for being a double agent."

James felt his head crack. How in the bleeding Christ had it come to this? "I suppose I'm meant to be taking it as a good sign that you're telling me all this instead of handing me a flight pass."

A faint smile edged briefly around the colonel's mouth. "If I didn't defend my men, then I wouldn't deserve to wear the uniform. MacTeague speaks highly of you, as does most everyone else. Furthermore, you're a radio broadcaster with an excellent record. I don't think you're a double agent, although you can bet someone in defense intelligence has been assigned to look into it. But I get the feeling there's something else going on here."

"Thank you, sir."

"Your story checks out. From what I can see it was the request to Cambridge that started this, and that's the one move that, in my mind, completely exonerates you. No double agent worth his salt is going to make a public request like that, especially in his own name. As far as I understand, the last thing a spy wants is attention. No, someone is trying to deflect scrutiny by questioning the reputation of this base, and I don't like that."

A rush of guilt hit him at the colonel's words. He had the support of his superior officer; meanwhile, he was sheltering an East German defector in his flat. Granted, it was all in the best interests of Britain in the long run, but if anyone found out it would shatter the faith that the chain of command had in him.

"What now, sir?"

"Keep on your business, but if you hear anything—and I mean anything, Captain Murphy—about Edward Ashton, you report it to me immediately."

As he walked back to the psyops building, James reflected that the crazy part was that he had no idea. He was the exact wrong person to be in the middle of all this. He knew nothing about espionage and had no ambitions to be anything more than he was. He hoped Edward was okay, but he also wished that his old rugby mate would fuck off out of his life.

After his shift, James arrived home to find a young man leaning against the wall of his building. More a *jung* really, in that awkward growth and acne phase.

"You are Jamie Murphy?" the kid asked.

"Aye," James nodded.

The kid handed him an envelope then took off. James tore it open and quickly scanned the contents. No one ever sent anything good via a messenger. The tension grabbed at his insides like a leech finding its next meal.

It was from Edward. He read over the note again. *Ah Christ, be careful what you wish for.*

James didn't bother going up to his flat. Instead, he turned and headed for the S-Bahn, to the address in the note. He was terrified at what he was going to find when he got there. The note didn't bother to explain. It was rather a summons: *Jamie, old friend. I'm in desperate need of your help. Please come. Immediately.*

CHAPTER THIRTY-FOUR

James arrived at the door to Edward's flat to find another man waiting there holding the same plain white envelope as James. They stared at each other for a moment, and James was sure he looked as unsettled as the face before him.

"Um. Hiya. You got a letter too, I suppose?"

James held up his envelope. "It didn't say anything about anyone else."

"Just that he needs help. We'll give it a few more minutes? Maybe there are others?"

James was fine with that. He couldn't imagine what was on the other side of that door, but no part of him wanted to find out.

"You a friend of Edward's?"

"Anthony," the man nodded and held out his hand. "We joined the diplomatic ranks the same year."

"Jamie. We played rugby together in uni however long ago. I'm stationed here with the army."

The conversation petered out as the threat of the immediate future loomed over them. James felt the seconds tick out in his heartbeat. He could hear the sounds of the street faintly through the window at the end of the hallway. The walls were a rich cream color and in excellent condition. Not a scuff mark to be found. The number three on the door was polished, almost glowing. No doubt Edward supplemented his government pay with a few coins from the family coffers.

A minute or ten later, James heard footsteps coming up the stairs. He looked at the new arrival, another well-put-together British bloke.

"Sorry I'm late," the man said before shakily running a hand through his hair. "Got caught up at work. Rodney."

It felt like a farce, but James couldn't laugh. He shook Rodney's hand as they completed the introductions. He knew they were all pretending that this wasn't unusual, that things weren't going to be dramatically different an hour from now. But James knew they weren't here for a dinner party.

"Well, should we go in then?" Anthony asked.

James nodded. Even if more people were meant to show up, he couldn't take any more waiting. He willed himself to touch the doorknob. No one else was making the move. The last lines of the letter flew up and made him hesitate: *I'm sorry for what I've done and what I'm asking you to do. There'll be further instructions when you get there. Know that I'm deeply grateful. To have friends in the end is one of life's great gifts.*

James turned the knob. The door was open. He led the way in. He wondered where they were supposed to go. He looked into the living room and knew he didn't have to go any further.

"Good God," he heard Anthoy murmur beside him.

Oh Christ. James stood frozen, eyes resting on the scene in front of him for a second at a time before turning away and staring at anything else. Most of the time we move through our lives in our own heads, only peripherally connected to the physical reality we're part of. When James boxed or shagged, those moments brought mind and body together. He loved those.

But now, now the physical world had pushed itself into his consciousness painfully, so that he was aware of the sensation of every molecule of oxygen making its way into his lungs.

He turned back to the scene in front of him. Dieter Venmar was slumped in an armchair covered in rich, green velvet. His head was tilted back, but it was impossible to maintain the illusion that he was resting. His face was pale and tinged blue, and there was a small amount of white foam settled on the right side of his mouth.

Even if he only looked at the pressed navy suit, the white shirt buttoned underneath, the faint stripes on the gray tie, James could see the death. There was no movement for breath, no natural tension keeping the muscles functioning. It was gone. Everything that animates a human had left Dieter Venmar.

"Who is that?" Rodney asked. "I mean, it's not what I expected. I'm not sure what I expected. But the letter." His voice trailed off.

James was having trouble pulling the sensations into something coherent. Incomplete thoughts sparked around his head as he stared at the dead body. "His name is Dieter Venmar. He's East German. Edward met him at Cambridge. And I don't have the first idea why he's sitting there, dead."

"Why?" Anthony shook his head. "Bloody hell, that sounds stupid. I realize there are many whys here. But the one I'm getting at is why us? Why are we here?"

James noticed an envelope sitting on the mahogany table to the left of the armchair. He crossed to it, suddenly terrified to be closer to the body. He averted his gaze, picked up the letter, and went back to his position by the door before opening it.

"It's addressed to the three of us."

No one jumped in, so James assumed he was okay to read what was inside.

James, Anthony, and Rodney,

Again, I apologize. I realize bringing you here is no small favor. You will never be able to unsee what I'm leaving you with. Death isn't pleasant for anyone.

You are my three most reliable friends in this city, and so that is why I've called on you today.

Why you are here, what I need from you, is to not let this death and my role in it be hushed up and hidden. I killed Dieter Venmar. I will not burden you with my reasons. They are mine, and understanding them won't change anything. Suffice to say that the burden of actions I am not proud of has finally become too much.

I ask you, my friends, please call the West German police, Der Spiegel, and Die Zeit. Please give them my name, my title, and my role in Our Majesty's government. You may also share a copy of this letter with whomever you see fit.

Again, I apologize, because I know the task is unpleasant and I will not be able to repay the favor. I am leaving you to deal with the wrath of my father, no easy task. Please don't think I'm avoiding the consequences of my actions. Rather, I must try to make some amends before turning myself in. It may not be in my power to do so, and I may come into the custody of the West German police before too long. It is, however, an effort I must make.

Thank you.

Edward Ashton, Viscount Amhurst

James's hand was shaking by the end as the physical reality caught up with him. The dead body of an East German was ten feet away, and he'd been asked to take on one of the most powerful men in Britain to make sure the whole world knew that his son was a murderer.

Fear and confusion started to rise, and James stomped them down along with the nausea that was threatening. He'd sort out his feelings later. Now the three of them had to figure out what to do.

"What are the other sheets of paper?" Anthony asked.

James had hardly noticed. He looked through what was in his hand. "Four copies," he said, "of the letter I just read."

That seemed to bring them all up short. There was no doubt Edward intended to make his role in Venmar's death as widely known as possible.

"Thoughts, gentlemen?" James asked.

"Bloody hell," Rodney said. "I don't know what to say."

James looked over at Anthony and found him staring in the direction of the body.

"Do you really think, if he'd gotten here first, that he would have covered this up?"

James knew Anthony was asking about the earl. James knew Edward's father would see this murder less as a crime and more as something that would reflect poorly on him and the legacy he was building for the future earls of Fenwick. He thought for another moment, the right words hard to find. "Yes," he said, finally, "I do. It's not just the murder, although he'd be ashamed enough of having that in the family. There's something else going on, some secret from those Cambridge years that the earl has been protecting. So yes, I do think he'd have someone cart the body out of here and make it disappear."

"He could too," said Rodney. "The East Germans can't investigate over here, and without a body the West Germans wouldn't have any reason to go looking."

"He doesn't want to lose his power," Anthony added. "That's the real problem. Having a murderer in the family, that's going to be a stain he'll never overcome."

"I reckon the question is, are we going to do it? As Edward asked: call the police and the papers, knowing that his father is going to absolutely explode? There's no doubt we're going to get caught up in it all. With Edward MIA, his father is going to cast suspicion on the easiest targets," Rodney said.

"Except Edward's the one with the history with Venmar. The earl can cast all the suspicion he wants. He's got to know that we'll fight him, and that means those secrets might come out," James said.

The three men fell into silence for a time. It could have been an hour. It could have been a minute. The enormity was filling up James's head. What choice did they really have? It was a dead body. The police would have to be called, and they all had a copy of a signed confession. It was, as they say in the crime dramas, open and shut.

"I will," said Rodney, apparently having enough time to think it through. "My parents run a grocery in Leeds. They saved for years to pay for my education after I got into the grammar school. When I got to Eton, Edward always looked out for me, not letting me get bullied for my middle-class background. When I went home with him at holidays, his father treated me like something he'd stepped in on the street. I always thought arseholes like him were the reason Britain was falling out of step with the rest of the world. Blood meaning more than merit. If he somehow manages to get me fired, I can always go back to the grocery and write a book."

James thought that was remarkably brave. He was also sure of his own position. He still didn't know the extent of Edward's treason, but covering up this death would only contribute to the mess. Edward asking them to shine a light on his killing of Venmar, maybe it was his way of shining a light on the events that led up to it.

"Lord Ashton is my boss, as he runs the war department," he said, offering up his position, "and I'm in uniform. But I've never had time for the nobility, and I'm about done with my service anyway. So I don't ruddy care if he sets himself as my enemy."

They both turned to look at Anthony, who was still transfixed on the body. "My maternal grandfather was a viscount," he said, turning his attention to them, "but with only having daughters, the title and entail went to an absolute fool in Australia instead of the woman who would carry the line with dedication. It worked out okay, as my mum fell in love with a rich American and ended up with more money than the viscount's ancestors ever had. It would seem Edward chose us well, because none of us seem to give two chuffs about his bloody father or the institution his title represents."

James noticed the calm settle over him. He knew that if there was too much time to think, he might worry about how crazy it was all about to get. Best to get on with it now.

"So, first phone call is to the police?"

Anthony nodded. "Seems about right."

James had to move closer to the body to pick up the phone that was tucked away on an escritoire along the back wall. After dialing in and reporting the murder, the emergency operator assured him the police would be there within minutes.

"The calm before the storm," Anthony said. "I feel like we should pour a whisky and toast to friendship, but I reckon we shouldn't muck about the scene too much."

"I also think," Rodney started, "we don't want to do too much that will allow Lord Ashton to turn it back on us."

"Good point, that," Anthony nodded.

James agreed. They were going to have to ride out enough wrath as it was.

"After we're done with the police, I'm going back to the base and reporting this in to my base commander. He's been told that Edward is missing. I think it's best to wrap that up before the search and accusations go any further. I will be showing him the letter."

"Yes, I'll inform everyone at our office as well," said Anthony.

"I don't have anyone to tell," Rodney said, "as my company is just working with the foreign office, and I'm here as a delegate. But, of course, if you need me to back you up in any way, I'll leave you my contact details."

Rodney found a pen and some writing paper in the escritoire. They swapped details, and James was sure they'd all be talking again, even if it was just to commiserate on the entire shite circumstance.

"I have to ask you two," James said, "seeing as you've been with Edward recently in a professional capacity, did anything he was working on involve the East Germans?"

"How do you mean?" Rodney asked.

"I don't know, exactly. I was just wondering if he had to work over there or anything." James didn't want to tell them about the book.

"We were working on a new agreement for city access," said Anthony. "The Soviets want more access to their monuments and don't feel they should have to be escorted every time. That didn't involve the East Germans. I mean, I know it does in reality, because they run East Berlin with the Soviets, but practically, they didn't have a seat at the table."

James had another idea. "Did you go to Cambridge with Edward?" he asked Rodney.

The head shook. "No, LSE."

"You?" James turned to Anthony.

Another shake. "Yale. Because of my father."

No further help regarding the mystery of Edward's Cambridge friends then.

James tuned in to the sound of boots in the hall. The police were here. The show was about to start.

James got back to his flat hours later, his limbs so leaden with fatigue he felt like a corpse himself. After talking to the police, he'd gone to the base and woken up Colonel Fornbridge. He told him about the murder and showed him the letter. The colonel's brows climbed as high as they could.

"It's not going to be pleasant," he had said, "but it doesn't have much to do with us now. Take a few days leave, Murphy. I'll notify MacTeague. Let the storm pass and move on to other parts."

"It wasn't just me there, sir. There were two others. All of us agreed to respect Edward's wishes."

The colonel was silent for a moment. "As you well should. But know, Murphy, that you will make an enemy, and for the rest of your career there's not going to be anything I, or any commanding officer, will be able to do about that."

"Aye, sir. I'll be out of the army soon enough. I've got to live with myself for much longer."

In his flat, he shrugged out of his coat and tossed it on a dining room chair. He went into the kitchen and pulled out his single malt. James thought there was nothing wrong with getting proper smashed tonight.

He sat down in the armchair with the bottle and a glass, belatedly noticing Anya curled up on the sofa.

"You're late tonight," she said.

"Can't sleep?" he asked.

"No. Too much going on in my head. Tomorrow morning, I will know if everything I've planned has a chance to work. If my daughter and I have a chance at a life."

James poured three fingers into the glass and swallowed it in one gulp. "I hope it works out for you, Anya. People, all people, deserve a chance at happiness."

"Something has happened to you tonight," she said, sitting up. "Something is wrong."

"It has nothing to do with you," James said. He paused, considering the whisky in the glass he'd refilled. "Or maybe it does. Edward killed his East German friend tonight and left me and two others a note to find the body in his flat. We reported it to the police, but given who his father is, the whole situation is far from over."

"I am sorry," she said. "I know it will not help, whatever I say. But it is hard for you, so I am sorry for that."

"You've seen it all before, have you?"

"Many times," she said, and James's breath got stuck as he took in the acceptance on her face. "Murder, suicide. There are so many different ways to die. What I do, or what I did, many people start only to find it's not as they dreamed. There is no glory, no resolution. Just an endless churn of secrets and manipulations that become like a python, squeezing the life out of its prey. I have seen many, too many, who lose the fight. They either cannot stay strong or separate themselves enough from their actions to remain untouched in their hearts, and they kill themselves. Or they lash out, thinking the pain of betrayal and emptiness will go away if they end the life of one who betrayed them. Of the two, I think suicide is the better choice. I have heard it said that suicide is only for cowards, but I disagree. Sometimes it is the only path to freedom."

James's hand shook a little as he lifted whisky to his lips. Was that something to wish for, then? There wasn't anything he could think of at the moment that would make this situation better except the liquid pouring into his mouth.

"I know he was your friend," Anya said, "but you were not close, no? What he was doing for the East Germans, it was not good for your country."

"That's the way of it," James said, staring into his glass. "I know this can't all be over. Yes, his treason stops. But if anyone starts digging, and I'm sure someone will, the secrets are going to release like a great Jesus volcano."

"You think his father will do that?"

"No," James shook his head. "No bloody way. He's the opposite sort, cover up all manner of shite behavior to protect the crown. What I mean is, I don't think it's going to end here. His father is too powerful. Questions are going to get asked—by him and of him."

"Yes," said Anya, looking thoughtful. "Questions like why did his son choose that path."

"God help me, I want to know too. Was it just the treason? Did he do it to piss off his old man? Who was Dieter Venmar? What did he do that led to Edward killing him?" James knocked back the rest of his whisky, comforted by the burn down his throat.

"You may never have answers to those questions. You cannot let this eat away at you. I'll tell you, because I have seen much more of people like this than you have, the answers are almost always the same: money, ideology, or boredom."

"What about you then? Why did you betray your country?"

"Ah," said Anya, smiling softly. "I am going the other way. For us, there is only one reason: freedom."

James looked at her for a long while. "If you get the file on Edward," he asked, "can I still have it?"

"Yes," said Anya. "The rest will be for Quentin and Veronica to share, but I will make sure that file is yours and yours alone."

"It's funny, Anya," James said, adding more whisky to his glass, although these fingers were for sipping, "but I feel like we understand each other. Maybe I'm just shite at this whole thing, but for some reason I think you care."

"I have lived in a world without choice for so long that I find myself almost overwhelmed by the choices I have here. But you, you have protected me and my daughter at great inconvenience, based on a friendship and a sense of duty. I do not care about Edward, but you have earned my loyalty and my regard. As long as it doesn't put Lena in danger, I will always help you if you ask."

James leaned back in his chair, "Well then, you can count me as a friend. I'm nowhere near as useful as you, but I always have whisky, rock and roll, and a spare bed."

"If I meet more people like you," she said, "I will be a very lucky woman."

CHAPTER THIRTY-FIVE

Anya emerged from the S-Bahn station in Spandau, wrapping her scarf one more time around her neck. It had started to snow since she got on the train, gentle flakes but coming in a torrent. The wetness had already covered her cheeks. Yes, she was definitely going to take Lena to Portugal where they could spend the winters walking around in sandals.

She crossed the street as instructed, walking north. After two blocks she cut west and saw Veronica waiting at the bus stop. They started walking together, the light of early morning softening and obscuring the features and details of the street.

"I have not been here before," Anya said.

"Yeah, not much action at the ass end of West Berlin. All the drama happens closer to the city Wall."

"It is peaceful."

"That's one word for it," Veronica said. "But I promise you, in about fifteen minutes, you're going to be amazed at what happens at the edge of Spandau."

"Where we are going, it is the distraction?"

"Yep. For your approval. I have to tell you, the approval is only about me going over. What you're about to see, these guys are going to do it anyway. You just have to decide if it's enough of a diversion."

Anya felt something so uncommon for her as to be almost unrecognizable. If she had to label it, she'd call it excitement. The idea that there may be a solution, that her plan might be executed—out here, in a place she never would have expected.

"When you asked to meet, to tell me the plan, I thought we would just meet in a café and you would present it. It would involve people I'd rather not know, and I would be scared about trusting more than I already have. But this trip to Spandau, in what looks like a very typical German kiez, I did not expect this."

Veronica smiled at her. "Just you wait, Anya, because I guarantee you every part of this morning is going to confound every expectation you have. Like I said, Jillian is a colleague of mine, but the other two, Sebastian and Peter, they're just regular guys who have access to an incredible opportunity. All they know is that doing their thing will help you do your thing, which might go a long way to reunification. So, they're in on that premise. You don't need to explain any more to them, because what they've got planned, well, like I said, they're invested now, and they're going to do it anyway."

Anya was almost bewildered, but she was grateful to see it all firsthand. Whatever it was.

She could see, even in the dawn, that the Wall was getting closer and closer. It amazed her that she was not afraid. The Wall was so powerful that she knew proximity didn't matter. It only mattered what side you were on.

Veronica led them down a small street that dead-ended at the Wall. Anya couldn't guess what was going on. They turned up the walkway of the third last house on the street. It seemed like an average house, but up close she could tell something was off.

The back door opened, and a young man ushered them inside. Anya looked around, confused. "What is this place?"

"An electrical substation. It delivers power to the houses in the neighborhood."

Anya's confusion only deepened. What could they be planning that would impact East Germany from here?

She followed Veronica down a metal ladder, carefully making her way around equipment to a door that led into a cement tunnel. The walls here were gray with cables bundled overhead and dim orange lights every few feet providing tepid illumination.

Heaped in the tunnel were limbs and heads and various other body parts. Haphazardly thrown together, she could make out a torso here and there, feet, hands. Hair poking through the mound at various points.

"Mannequins," she breathed, and in that instant knew Veronica was right. A thousand guesses and she never would have imagined this.

The young man in front turned around to speak. "It is easier to talk here. You are Jillian's friends. The ones who need help."

Anya and Veronica nodded.

"Yes," Veronica said.

"I am Peter," he said. "Welcome to our tunnel."

Tunnel?

"Can we see?" asked Veronica. "I…I'm just so curious."

"Yes," said Peter. "We need help anyway. Pick up as many body parts as you can, and I'll take you through to where we're going to go up."

Anya felt unsteady, as if on a boat churning through a storm, but she too was curious. She picked up three arms and a foot and followed Peter and Veronica through a hole about twenty feet down from where she'd entered.

As she walked through into this new space, made of steel and distinctly different, her eyes widened in disbelief. What was this place?

"The best we can figure is this is an old tunnel system built by the Nazis during the war," Peter said, evidently reading the expression on her face. "We found it by accident, but we have mapped the whole thing, the part that is still intact and safe to go in."

"Incredible," murmured Veronica.

Anya felt the same way. As they moved farther along the steel walls, deeper underground, she knew she was witnessing something remarkable.

They turned here and there, but the path was fairly straight, and Peter clearly knew where he was going.

"We are heading west," she said.

Peter turned and looked at her briefly. "Yes. Almost the whole thing that we can access is under East Germany."

Anya shivered. She never thought she'd cross that border again. Although she technically was in her country, the tunnel felt instead like a limbo space, a connector between the two that was neither here nor there.

Peter seemed disinclined to explain more, which Anya accepted. The reasons for them all coming together were varied and precarious. She didn't want to explain more than she had to, so she had no right to demand answers. She didn't need to be convinced of their loyalty or honesty. The tunnel was theirs. Whatever they were doing with it had nothing to do with her, not really. Parallel goals aligned for a moment, but Peter and his friends certainly weren't working for her.

They came eventually to a small room. It too was stacked with body parts and clothes. There was a pile of shoes in one corner. Limbs had been stacked along the wall outside the door, heading down the tunnel in the opposite direction from which they'd arrived.

Anya still didn't understand what the plan was, but an image was starting to take shape.

"This place is unbelievable," said Veronica to the other woman in the room. She must be the friend, Jillian.

"I know, right? Every time I'm down here, it never gets old."

Jillian turned and nodded at Anya. "The mystery woman. I would say it's nice to meet you, but I appreciate the circumstances are a bit bizarre."

"Where is Sebastian?" Peter asked.

"By the exit. He's starting to put full bodies together."

"I will go get him."

Anya watched Peter leave then turned her attention back to the parts stacked in the room.

"Did you bring all this in?" she asked.

"Yes," Jillian smiled. "The Nazis left a ton of junk down here, but not hundreds of mannequins. Sebastian worked with a friend to bring it all through different entrances to the main Telekom tunnel you were in, and we've been hauling it in here all night."

"What are you going to do with them?"

"I'm not entirely sure," said Jillian. "You're going to have to wait for Sebastian. He's the mastermind behind this plan. Me, I'm just labor. If you want to help, we need to keep separating the parts into piles. Sebastian will be here soon."

Anya started going through a dump of hands and feet. She supposed that it would be equally useful to separate the lefts from the rights, so she began to make four piles.

It wasn't too much longer before Peter came back with Sebastian. This new man, Anya noticed, was the same age as his friend. But whereas Peter looked calm but tired, Sebastian was crackling with energy.

"I think we will have over one hundred and fifty full bodies," he said, grinning. "Plus many more limbs. Not too many extra heads, but that is okay. There is so much to do, but we have time. Just enough. We have forty-eight hours, yes?"

Jillian and Veronica looked at her. "Yes," said Anya. "Whatever you are doing must be in place by Wednesday morning."

"We will put it all together at night anyway, so when the sun rises it will all be finished."

Anya looked around the room again. "I need to ask, what are you planning?"

"The most beautiful art show Germany has ever witnessed."

Anya swallowed, hiding her confusion. "I understand you are doing something to distract the East Germans in this area. I hope. I'm here because I need a distraction in order to get something from the East. I need the Stasi to have their eyes diverted and occupied on Wednesday morning."

"What are you getting?" asked Peter.

"Does it matter?" Anya replied.

"Will it hurt anyone?"

Anya felt inexplicably sad for this man who seemed so much younger than her. "No. I know you have no reason to believe me, but no. I am trying to stop many people from getting hurt, over and over, by one of the worst men you could imagine. What I get, it will stop him. Maybe not forever, but for long enough that many people might finally get to live without fear."

"That is good enough for us," the one named Sebastian said. "Jillian vouched for you, and I don't think she would do anything that will cause a tragedy."

Anya was grateful but also slightly amazed at the support. How easy it was for these Westerners to trust each other based on confidence in their connections. In East Germany, the trustworthiness of a friend did not necessarily extend to others in their circle.

"We will bring beauty to Germany, and you will have what you need."

Anya looked around the pile of body parts in the room. "I don't understand."

"You both are talking about the same thing. It's a distraction for you," Jillian said to Anya, "but for Sebastain it's art."

Jillian turned to Sebastian, "Can you explain it?"

"I have the idea, maybe a year ago, to use mannequins as a mirror," he said. "So I began collecting them. Wigs too, and old clothes. I have a friend who works at KaDeWe, and she says they throw out mannequins that are damaged because it cheapens the clothes. Every time they throw one out, she calls me. I hadn't yet decided the best way to use them. Then Jillian tells me her friends need help, they need some spectacular diversion to draw East German eyes. I realize that is what I have been waiting for. These mannequins, they represent exactly what East Germany is: empty, fake, hollow, everyone the same, shallow representations of humans. It is perfect. We will put them together, dress some of them, and put them out in the field above us. Hundreds of empty bodies reflecting the empty souls of the East German government. When the sun rises and shines on the field, it will be the most poignant moment of truth. The East Germans who witness it might, for one second, realize they are looking into a mirror."

Anya stared at Sebastian. The room fell silent around her. She looked and looked, for what she wasn't sure. All she knew was that in all her years, every plan, every intrigue she'd been a part of, the lives she'd ruined, the pain she witnessed, the lies and manipulations and justifications that had passed her lips, none of it had ever contained a moment like this.

She could imagine it. She, Anya, who tried never to imagine anything lest it break her heart with dreams of what could not be. She saw the sunrise over Berlin two days from now. Saw the field edging up to the East German side of the Wall filled with hundreds of mannequins. The sunlight hitting the frost and making them sparkle. These lovely, vacant, half-formed bodies, dressed up, ready to live. Wigs blowing in the breeze. Body parts that didn't fit scattered around, arms with bracelets, feet with shoes, as if they wanted to participate as well. Dresses rippling, jewelry shining. All these mannequins standing there, coming alive in the face of another grim East German day.

Suddenly Anya started to laugh—really laugh. The kind of laughter that had not passed her lips in years. The kind that was uninhibited and joyful and contained promise.

The laughter died off, but the joy remained. "Yes," said Anya, "I can see, it will be the most spectacular, beautiful moment in East German history. In even German history. It will be a day that is remembered forever."

Sebastian grinned. "It will do? Be the distraction you need?"

"Nothing like it has ever been done before. Just the kind of thing to block up the Stasi machine. They will wonder what is coming next."

"All the while not realizing that the moment is now," said Peter.

"If you can help," Sebastian said to her, "you should stay. The more we are, the more I can do."

Anya nodded. "Yes. I must go this morning to make some arrangements, but then I will come back and give you all the help I can."

"If you're okay with it," Jillian said to Sebastian, "I know two other guys who are great at keeping secrets and have nothing better to do in the next two days. Plus, they'd be pissed at me if I never found a way to show them this place."

"I know a good Italian restaurant," said Peter. "I can bring food here, so we don't have to go out."

"Sounds like it's going to be an interesting couple of days."

CHAPTER THIRTY-SIX

James was lost. Not physically. He had too good a sense of direction to get lost in this city. It was mental. A feeling of disorientation. Aimlessness. And the guilt that he should be doing something but not having the first bloody clue what it was supposed to be.

Dieter Venmar was dead. Edward was very likely a traitor and definitely a murderer. The only silver lining was that with Edward on the run, James didn't have to worry about being responsible for more British secrets making it through the Iron Curtain. Edward wouldn't be passing any more information.

James was unsettled. The whole business felt unsettled.

He didn't know whether to be angry, disappointed, or scared. Should he feel something for the dead man? Should he be afraid of Edward and what he might do?

The mystery had only become more complicated. What had driven Edward to treason appeared to be a combination of hatred for his father and contempt for his country. He had been at the top of the privilege pyramid. How could treason be the result? And what had driven Edward to murder? James suspected it was connected to the treason, but what was the trigger? Did he even want to know?

Lost in his thoughts, James didn't notice the limousine waiting outside his flat until the door opened and a voice called at him from the inside.

"James Murphy, a word."

A bit bloody Hollywood, but James had no doubt about who was waiting inside the vehicle. Figuring this confrontation had to happen sooner or later, James climbed inside and pulled the door shut behind him.

"Captain Murphy," the man across from him said. "You're a hard man to track down—harder than it should be, considering you wear a uniform. I take it you were recently gifted some extra leave."

However this conversation was going to go, James felt it prudent to make it clear he wasn't about to be bullied. "The colonel thought I needed a couple days after dealing with the dead body your son was responsible for."

The Earl of Fenwick pursed his lips. "I can see where your sympathies lie."

"I don't reckon you can."

"Edward's note has clearly left you with an impression, one that is not flattering to me. However, I would like to assure you that I have always protected my son and will continue to do so, even though he is on the run after confessing to a murder."

James felt like he was walking through a minefield, unexploded shells ready to go off at the first wrong step.

"Are you here to ask anything particular of me, sir?"

The earl was silent for a moment, seeming to regard James intently. "Are you and my son close?"

"No," said James, "we are not. I have known him for almost twenty years, and most of that time was spent on the rugby pitch. You often see a different side of a man in that context, and if you admire it, it builds a decent foundation for friendship."

"Ever see the side that could poison someone?"

Aggression on the pitch wasn't the same as aggression in life. James knew the glasses of hindsight would only lead to delusion. "No."

"Why were you hunting around for information about his friends at Cambridge?"

"Why does that scare you so much?"

"I would remind you, Captain Murphy," the Earl said, "that as Secretary of Defence, I have a significant amount of power over your career."

James sighed. "I think, sir, that our relationship is much more complicated. If you are here to pressure me to keep silent about Edward's treason, that doesn't respect the oath I took when I first stepped into the uniform. I'll not make unfounded accusations, but I won't cover it up if evidence comes to light. Even if it puts me in Belfast or gets me discharged."

On this point, James had found clarity in his long walk around the city. If Anya or Quentin brought anything to him that contained the seeds of evidence, James would turn it over to MI5. If it got covered up from there, so be it. But anyone that Edward had betrayed over the years, they deserved the truth.

"What are you talking about, Murphy?" The earl's voice had gone tight, and James saw the genuine surprise on his face.

James was taken aback. He'd assumed that Lord Ashton was here to clean up the residue of Edward's activities with the East Germans. Old friend or not, Edward clearly had a relationship with Venmar that was more recent than Cambridge.

He wasn't one to backpedal, but knew he had to tread carefully. "Edward gave me a book to pass to Dieter Venmar. That's why I made those inquiries that seemed to upset you so much. The book appeared to have a coded message."

Lord Ashton was still. James could all but see the thoughts racing in the man's mind. *Damn. Could this business get any more muddled?* Yes, he'd had a hard time believing the Earl of Fenwick had been complicit, even peripherally, in treason. But James figured he must have suspected, unless he'd had no knowledge of Edward's ongoing contact with Venmar. Still, with the man dead in Edward's flat, the earl must be connecting some of the dots.

"Do you have a copy of this book?"

"No." James's gut clenched at the lie, hoping it wouldn't come back to haunt him.

"How did you know there was a code?" Lord Ashton asked.

It was a fair question. How could he answer it without dragging Jillian into this?

"Edward said it was an old book that he'd taken from your personal library in England. I looked at it before I delivered it, to make sure it wasn't anything more than a book. It had been modified. The changes were subtle, but it made me suspect it was more than just a gift." James hoped to Christ the earl didn't dive too deep into how he would know that. To James, the deception had been effective. It was only Quentin and Jillian who had the experience to know the difference.

"So you assumed there was a code?"

"Yes, but I have no proof. After what happened when I asked about Cambridge, I didn't go looking for anything more. With Venmar's death, I figure that's the end of it, at least for me. I'll never know the truth of the mystery, and I'm fine with that. But, like I said, should anything ever come to light, I'll not be part of a coverup."

"Do you have reason to suspect there might be more out there?"

James was quiet. This man wasn't his ally, nor was he an adversary. "I got the impression from Edward that he was expecting an answer to his book. Maybe I'm wrong. But the sequence of events suggests that book was meant to achieve some purpose, and it's possible the murder is the result of that purpose being thwarted."

"What did Venmar do when you gave him the book?" Lord Ashton asked.

"He smiled. He looked…happy. Then he gave me directions on how to avoid the Stasi on my way out."

A rolling succession of disgust, anger, and despair washed over the earl's face as his hands clenched into fists. After a few breaths, the tension receded. Lord Ashton was left looking like a man who had just received notice a new front had opened in the war.

"Should you become privy to any information related to my son, I expect you to hand it over to me immediately. That is an order, Captain Murphy."

James simply nodded. They both knew that if James did come across anything further, the Secretary of Defence was going to have problems. Because if James had it, there was no telling who else did.

CHAPTER THIRTY-SEVEN

Anya watched James struggle to get a mannequin's arm into a dress sleeve. Beside him, the friend Jillian was laughing.

"Oh, I know it's right funny. But you see, I'm much better at taking the clothes off."

Jillian snorted. "I'm sure you are."

He winked at her and kept on with the dress.

Quentin was farther down the hallway, attaching heads to torsos. "Does it matter if they don't have hair?" he called out.

"No," Peter said, sorting through a tangled mess of plastic necklaces. "Sebastain will decide on the final details anyway. Wigs are final details. As many bodies as you can put together, that is all you have to do."

Anya was putting thigh-high single stockings on a pile of legs. There were socks for when she ran out of stockings. Lena was beside her, gently brushing out wigs. She thought it was great fun, a giant game of doll dress-up. Anya had been amazed when Lena, upon being introduced to Sebastian and being told what they were doing, had asked for a mannequin of her own to pick out clothes for. Sebastain had thought it was a charming request and had told her to even choose the wig and jewelry.

Quentin and James had arrived separately, but both had been shocked into silence when Jillian had brought them all into this dimly lit limbo world. They were walking through history, with signage from the Nazis contrasting with the surreal mannequin parts piled around, waiting for their moment in the sun.

Maybe it was because this wasn't a real place. Maybe it was because they all had so much riding on the outcome. Or maybe it was because the effort to get hundreds of mannequins dressed was daunting. Whatever it was, for the first time in her life Anya felt free.

It was obviously a new sensation for her, and not one she had expected to find here. She had thought when she held Lena for the first time in West Berlin that moment was freedom, but it was more relief after the pressure of trying to get out of East Germany.

Then came hope. Moving around the city, meeting with Rose, staying with James, she had begun to glimpse what her life might one day become.

But this—the openness, the interaction, the peace of working together—Anya thought this might be what freedom felt like.

Sebastian and Peter, the stewards of the tunnel, didn't seem bothered about knowing more about the people helping. Anya saw that Sebastian cared only about the art, about creating something that would make the world pause in awe, if only for a moment. Peter, she had learned, cared about preserving the tunnel and thought it belonged to all Germans. Both assumed reunification would happen sooner or later and this tunnel would be an important part of the shared history of the people.

They accepted that everyone else was here to help, not to spy, not with a covert agenda, not to manipulate or bribe or ruin the dream.

They did not know that Quentin was in the CIA. They did not know that she, Anya, was formerly of the Stasi. They did not know that Veronica was Canadian intelligence. They did not care that James was in uniform for the British. Although Anya did not know what Jillian did, with these friends it could not be something too different. They only thing they knew, the only thing that mattered, was that everyone was invested in keeping it a secret.

In her life, Anya had always been very careful to make incentives align. It was only then that she would trust people to do as they committed.

Here, although the goals of the mannequins were the same for everyone, Anya sensed that didn't matter as much. It was the reason they had ended up here, but it was not the only reason they stayed. They were here for each other, for curiosity, for the idea of the art. If she hadn't needed a planned distraction in East Germany, she thought they would be here anyway.

That, she thought, was freedom.

"Mama, I think this wig is the prettiest. The color is like honey, and the hair is so curly."

Anya turned and focused on her daughter. "Yes, that is a lovely one. If it is the one you want, put it aside. You can bring it to Sebastian later when he gives you your mannequin."

Lena grinned and walked to the corner, placing the wig gently against the wall. "This is so much fun, Mama. I did not know that there were places where you could dress up giant dolls."

Anya smiled. "Well, normally it doesn't happen in a place like this. Today is special because they're going to be used as art. But big stores, like the kind they have in West Berlin, they have people whose job it is to dress up the mannequins in different clothes every week."

Lena's eyes went wide. "That is what I want to do when I grow up."

"If that's what you want, you will be able to. In the meantime, we have to help as much as we can. Keep brushing gently so the dolls look pretty for their show."

Anya kept on her task as well, wrapping a ribbon around the tops of the legs when the stocking didn't look like it would stay up. She looked up when Quentin entered to talk to Jillian.

She watched the two of them, and it was clear there was something between them. She had known Quentin for over a year—most of that time knowing him as Rob—and their relationship was based on fragile trust constructed on the results of clandestine, five-minute meetings. It was interesting to see him outside of that life.

He and Jillian were not overt, but the body language was clear. Their affection for each other was evident. Anya was happy for him. The kind of life he led, there were few moments for unguarded happiness.

"I am going to pick up dinner," Peter announced, looking at his watch. "I have arranged for a friend to drop it off. I would like to bring it down here instead of all of us going up to the house. It will help us be more efficient with our time."

"I'll help you carry it down," Jillian said. The rest nodded. It did not matter to Anya where they ate, and for Lena it would all just be part of the adventure.

They left, and Quentin finished with his mannequin. He carried it out and turned down the tunnel passageway, presumably to deliver it to Sebastian, who was putting together final touches close to the trapdoor that would allow them to take everything to the field.

When Quentin came back, instead of starting a new body, he came up and sat beside her.

"What do you think?" he asked, gesturing around. "Is it going to work?"

Anya thought carefully. Many times in the last few hours, as the individual pieces started to take shape, she'd envisioned the scene as it would look on Wednesday morning.

"Someone will notice right away. This close to the border, and there are always people monitoring the ground. I worry that there will be a problem in the setup. I know they say it is a field, and the eyes on the Wall are directed east from here into the city, but still it is risky. Let's say they do, or at least they get enough to create something so different it will cause the sentries on the Wall to panic.

"The Stasi hate anything that is out of the ordinary. Dozens of mannequins in a field outside West Berlin, not to mention the body parts and shoes and whatever else he has planned, is not ordinary. It will have to be investigated to make sure it is not a precursor to some other more extraordinary event. Even more to our advantage, they will be desperate to know how it was accomplished. They will point fingers at everyone they can think of, except that no one will make sense, because I do not know who in East Germany could get their hands on so many mannequins. You've seen our stores.

"That confusion will happen almost immediately. Michael will definitely be involved. They will ask for his advice, and of course he will come here to see it because of the clues he will want to find. So yes, it might work. But it is so unprecedented, I can't be sure. If that's what you need, what Veronica needs, that I cannot say."

Quentin was quiet for a long time. "I don't control Veronica. I want you to tell her what you just told me so she can decide on her own. If she goes, I'm going over too. After your contact brings her back to Berlin, I'll meet her, and we'll cross back over together."

Anya narrowed her eyes. "She crosses at Friedrichstrasse. She must cross back that way. That was the plan."

"You made that plan for a different woman, a German woman who could talk her way past the guards carrying a suitcase full of files. Veronica's German isn't good enough, and there might be more files in that safe than you realize. It was always the weakest part. Even with a false bottom or whatever else you've got, it's too risky. Veronica and I can play boyfriend and girlfriend and cross back together. I met up with her after work, and we took in the evening sights together. It's non-negotiable, Anya."

She bit her lower lip, running through the scenario. "Okay, yes. You are right. It would be good if you were over there with her. Because, and I'm not sure, but it might be different at the border. I don't think they will close it, but there could be confusion. It's possible there will be instructions to pay close attention to everyone crossing because they will want to find the people responsible for the mannequins. They will look at their own, but they will also suspect everyone from the West."

"Exactly," Quentin nodded, "and with my journalist credentials and the fact that she's a Canadian attached to the military mission here, they'd have a harder time holding us for too long. I can put the files in the same compartment of the car I used for Lena."

"This is a very good idea," Anya said. She was troubled that she didn't think of it herself. Ever since she knew it was to be Veronica and not Lucinda who was going to Wandlitz, she should have evaluated every part of the plan to test the new scenario. But she hadn't.

"I am sorry," she said, meeting Quentin's eyes. "I did not consider that part well enough. I hope that you are not unsure about the rest of my plan."

"Anya," Quentin said, resting his hand on her arm, "you can't think of everything. I know you've had to for too long, but it's impossible to maintain forever. You've had to worry about Lena and throw off your followers every day. You've had to worry about your friend in the hospital and if Veronica could get trained up, not to mention this giant distraction that we've had to put together. It doesn't mean the rest of your plan isn't good. I've been through it, so has Veronica. We've debated it for hours. If what you've set up is in place, it will work."

"And if the sentry doesn't leave Wandlitz?" Anya whispered.

"Veronica can take him out," Quentin smiled. "The rest of the Stasi will be too busy with the mannequins to notice their junior officer hasn't reported in as usual. In terms of distraction, that's all we really need."

CHAPTER THIRTY-EIGHT

Jillian rubbed at her eyes. It had been a long two days assembling the parts of the mannequins, running up and down the tunnel with wigs and dresses and accessories mostly taken from the zu verschenken boxes around the city where people put unwanted stuff. Sebastian was like a drill sergeant. She thought artists got a bad rap for being lazy and unreliable. It was a lot of work to put on an art show of this magnitude.

It was just the four of them now: Sebastian and Peter, her and James. Plus the daughter, Lena. Jillian thought it was adorable how Lena was attached to James. She interacted with him like a friend or a much older brother, and Jillian was impressed that James responded in kind. "Years of practice," he'd said when she raised an eyebrow at his fashion knowledge, "with me sisters."

Veronica and Quentin were prepping for tomorrow's op, and Anya was staying available in West Berlin. Jillian thought Anya's role might be bigger, but she didn't ask, and no one had volunteered that information. She figured that since Lena had been entrusted to James, Anya might have more planned than sitting on her heels in an apartment.

The part of the tunnel leading to the escape hatch where Sebastian and Peter would carry out the mannequins was now filled with fully dressed bodies. They didn't all look like they'd come straight from the department store. Some were half-dressed, and other clothing combinations were challenging to the eye. Sebastain had added harsh makeup and positioned many of them in awkward, challenging poses.

He'd also procured dozens of plastic pig snouts, like for a costume at Halloween, and placed them on the heads of some of the mannequins.

When Jillian had asked about them, Sebastian had told her it was part of the message. The failure of East German socialism. Apparently, the country had a big pig problem.

Jillian imagined the final product would be gruesome versus beautiful. That was part of the statement.

She checked her watch. It was one in the morning. Lena had long ago curled up in a corner of the antechamber on a pallet of blankets Peter had found in one of the corridors. They were all getting tired, but it was almost time. They could sleep tomorrow.

Jillian and James were not going to go aboveground. It was just too risky. Jillian could never allow herself to be caught by the Stasi, and James said he needed to finish sorting out the situation with his friend and couldn't let a detainment get in the way. The two of them would pass the mannequins and individual parts up, ready to run like hell if Sebastian or Peter got caught in some spotlight.

Sebastian walked down the tunnel to examine the pieces of his installation, adjusting as he went. What he was looking for, she had no idea, but he clearly had a vision. She supposed it was all about making sure it would deliver the needed punch.

Finally, he announced he was ready. "We will go up. Jamie, you lift the mannequins to me or Peter. Jillian, you continually bring them up from the rear. The full bodies first, then the parts. We will keep working until everything is out or until we attract attention."

"Let's hope that doesn't happen," said James.

"It should not," Peter confirmed. "This entrance comes out in the trees. The field is about thirty meters to the east. I have gone up every day for the last week. There is nothing there. Some houses are to the north, but they are at least three hundred meters away. To the south is a large building—where we hear the communications, I believe. It is a government building and there are no lights there at night. The East Germans on the Wall, they don't bother looking this way, not anymore. No one could get over from here, and there are no crossings. It is not perfect, and it is not safe, but it makes possible what we want to do tonight. The sentries on the Wall will notice the mannequins eventually. We are lucky there is no moon tonight. If we work fast, we might make it. They will not find the trap door. It was never designed to be a major entrance, and I have created a cover of dirt and leaves."

Listening to Peter, Jillian couldn't help but smile. Peter and Sebastian were a good pair. Sebastain had focused on the details of the art, Peter on the logistics of the execution.

There were at least a half-dozen ways it could all go wrong. They could get unlucky with a patrol, or wind. They could get chased and not make it back to the tunnel. The East Germans could pursue them into the tunnel, and then they'd lose it. Sebastain and Peter didn't seem to be too worried about getting caught, but Jillian thought it was because they couldn't imagine the Stasi being interested in the perpetrators of such a stunt.

Then again, it might all go right. The East German guards would be greeted with a majestically crazy sight when dawn broke tomorrow morning.

"Before we start," Sebastian said, "I would like to take a moment." He pulled out a thermos and poured them each a small cup of coffee. "Tonight, we will create art. Part of the beauty will be its transience. There will be no record of our achievement, except in our hearts. It is true art because it does not desire to be preserved, only experienced. This vision has been in my mind for many months, and I have found the perfect canvas to express it. So I thank you for helping me bring it to life tonight."

Jillian was touched. Sebastian had adjusted to the circumstances, but he was still fully committed to his dream.

"Thank you, mate," James said. Jillian turned to him, surprised. "What you've put together, you're also helping a lot of people tonight. You were asked if you could create a great distraction, and you've sorted it beyond anyone's expectations. I don't think anyone else involved would have thought to put so many mannequins in East Germany beside the Wall that the

Stasi will be running around for weeks trying to figure what in the hell is going on."

Sebastain nodded. "A win-win, as you say." He drank the rest of his coffee. "Okay everyone, we are ready to go. Place all the bags at the end of the hall there, where it turns left. If we have to run, they will be easy to pick up on the way by."

James would pick up Lena, and the rest of them would grab the tools. Their personal items were back in the substation basement, and they would leave the mannequins.

They had prepared for all the bad luck they could think of.

Jillian packed up her coffee cup. Strangely, she wasn't nervous. In the last two years, she'd had to evaluate and manage so many risks that tonight's endeavor felt manageable. She wasn't going aboveground, and if she saw anyone other that Sebastain or Peter come down the ladder, she figured she could run back to the house a lot faster than whoever it might be could.

Suddenly, that was it. Everything was ready.

Sebastian opened the trap door and climbed out, Peter following with the great big burlap sack they'd fashioned to carry a half-dozen mannequins at a time. James followed with the first one, a saucy redhead in a paisley muumuu. It had begun.

Jillian carried mannequins up the tunnel for hours. She was too tired to think. One foot in front of the other. The minutes ticked on, and the execution kept going. So far, so good. No one had noticed them yet.

"I'm sleeping for two days after this," grumbled James, as he came down the ladder from hefting mannequin number one hundred and three up to the surface.

"This done. Quentin and Veronica back. No one arrested or detained. Then I can go back to my totally abnormal life."

"You better stay in your flat for the next six months. Do not talk to anyone. Do not try to make new friends or see new sights. Just stay home. That way I might get some proper rest."

"Hey, I'm not the one who decided to host a defector and her daughter in my apartment. We're here on account of your activities, not mine. When we get out of here, take your own advice."

"I damn well plan to. I reckon there is an endless string of nights in front of the telly in my future."

They kept working, with only a muttered phrase here and there. Slowly the tunnel began to empty, the mannequins placed in their new life.

Jillian helped James haul up the body parts and the extra shoes. They didn't want to dump them just outside the opening, as it would be a dead giveaway should someone come across their activities. Instead, they piled them at the bottom of the ladder and brought up a bunch at a time when Sebastain and Peter came back with the sack.

"We are almost done," Sebastian whispered.

Jillian took the risk and popped her head out of the small door in the forest floor. The night was overcast, but calm and cold. Cold enough to keep people inside and keep guards in their huts, fingers wrapped around mugs of sage tea in an attempt to keep warm.

It was quiet. The East German side of the Wall loomed in front, the no man's land invisible behind it and the lights of West Berlin illuminating the sky beyond. Over here in this part of East Germany, the night was a blanket that had tucked everyone in.

Jillian placed her fingers on the ground, a surreal feeling creeping over her. She was east. If she just looked at the ground, the dead leaves, and the dirt, or just listened to the breeze rustling through the trees, it was possible to believe for one moment that the place she was in wasn't all that different.

Sighing, she pulled her head back into the tunnel. It shouldn't be different. Germany should not be divided like this. Suddenly overwhelmed by the geopolitical maneuverings that never seemed to stop, she climbed down to sit at the base of the ladder.

"What is it, lass?"

Jillian leaned her head back against the wall of the tunnel. "It's possibly because I haven't slept in almost twenty-four hours, but sometimes I'm really not sure humanity is ever going to get its shit together."

James smiled and sat down beside her. "Aye, we're probably not. But, you know, the sun's going to burn out anyway. Nothing you can do but make the most of the time that you have."

"Yeah."

They sat there in silence waiting for the next run of body parts. There weren't many left.

They had done two more loads when suddenly Sebastian jumped down the ladder, followed quickly by Peter, who closed and locked the trapdoor behind him.

"We are done," Sebastian said. "Someone has noticed. The sky will start to lighten in about two hours. Until then, it will be too dark for them to see everything at once."

The euphoria of what they accomplished crashed into the exhaustion, keeping it at bay. "Are you satisfied?" Jillian asked him.

"I wish I could be on top of the Wall for one moment, just as dawn breaks. The East German side. I want to see our creation existing, the light hitting all the figures standing silently as witnesses. It will be beautiful. But I am satisfied with my memories of setting it up and walking through the final positions. I have been inside it, knowing where it was and the reactions it will cause. That is enough."

Jillian stood up and gave him a hug. "It's amazing, what you did. Who knows, it might make the news."

"In the meantime," James said, "it's time for me to get to a bed."

They walked out of the tunnel and emerged into the darkness of the early West Berlin morning. Looking up at this side of the Wall, Jillian sent a silent wish to the universe that their efforts would pay off.

Sebastian had borrowed a car from his parents and was driving them all back into the city center.

"It is going to be hard to say auf wiedersehen," he said.

"When are you going to contact the authorities?" Jillian asked. She instructed them that BND would be their best bet in terms of keeping the tunnel out of the hands of the East Germans.

"Monday," Peter said.

"Are you going to clean up the mannequin parts before?"

"Yes," said Sebastian. "This weekend."

"I'll come and help," Jillian said. "To say good-bye."

CHAPTER THIRTY-NINE

Anya had been out since nine o'clock in the morning, too wound up to sleep or stay in the apartment. Today was the day she'd been planning for years. Imagining what was happening—Veronica crossing to East Berlin, Heddy taking them up to Wandlitz, the blackmail files being burned to ash—Anya wished that dreams could make something real, that if she just visualized the success, it would happen.

She knew instead that she had to be patient. She had to assume the worst until she received news otherwise. She had left Jamie and Lena sleeping and went out into the cold Berlin morning to learn what she could.

Anya started at her favorite café. A coffee and franzbrötchen. She rarely ate them, but she needed something to settle her stomach.

There was no tail at the café. She squashed down the hope that arose. He couldn't have people everywhere.

Next was the hat shop. She loved browsing the colorful wares on display, everything from winter caps to wedding confections. Anya had a weakness for hats and was always amazed at the variety for sale in the West.

No tail there either.

Slowly over the course of the morning, Anya went to all her favorite places, everywhere in the city she visited with frequency, everywhere one of Michael's foot soldiers had picked her up before.

No one.

Anya's heartbeat started to accelerate. She kept walking, maintaining her focus, but as the morning wore on, she felt a lightness that she had not experienced in her adult life. It carried the nostalgia of youth, and she almost wept.

The distraction must have worked. Even now, dozens of Stasi must be swarming around the field in East Germany, staring at all the mannequins, desperate to know where they came from, and looking around for the hammer to fall. They would see something sinister because they would not understand the art. She imagined Michael standing beside Lena's mannequin, the one with the honey-colored hair and the blue velvet dress. All those dressed-up figures. He would feel like a fool. There was nothing he hated more.

By late afternoon she was back at Jamie's apartment and brushing Lena's hair while her daughter watched cartoons. She had only spotted one tail all day, a tall, impossibly young-looking man had tried to follow her around KaDeWe. He had clearly been a rookie and was no match for her skills. She had shaken him off easily.

Now, being with Lena, she allowed herself a sliver of hope. A thin one. No bigger than a shaving. It was a good sign that the usual had not come to pass. Things being different meant there was a possibility her plan was being successfully executed.

When Veronica called, she would know for sure.

That call should be coming in soon. The cleaners were done by four, back in the city by five. Quentin and Veronica had to try to cross before midnight. Within hours, Anya would know.

She must have fallen asleep, because she opened her eyes to windows cloaked in darkness. Lena was occupied with coloring on the coffee table, and James was up reading in the armchair across from her.

"What time is it?" she asked, glancing at the clock on the wall. Seven-thirty. Still early.

"No news yet," said James. "I imagine Quentin will contact you as soon as he gets back."

If he gets back. But she wouldn't voice those words. Not yet.

"My darling," Anya said, turning to Lena, "are you hungry?"

Lena shook her head. "No, I made Jamie and me ham sandwiches. They were very good."

"That they were." James nodded his head in agreement. "Then we washed them down with a nice cup of tea and some biscuits."

"I made one for you too, Mama. It's in the fridge."

Anya was hungry. "Thank you, darling. It sounds perfect."

She got up and went into the kitchen to get the sandwich out of the fridge. She ate leaning against the counter, settling in for the wait. Anya was good at waiting.

"Fancy a tea?" James asked, coming into the kitchen to stand beside her.

She didn't, not really, but she understood for the British it was something to do. To make the time pass easier.

"If it all works out," James said, "what will you do next?"

Anya took another bite of her sandwich to give herself the time to think. "I worry that I do not know how to be free," she said after finishing up the last of the wonderful crust. "For so many years, being away with Lena has been a fantasy. Like all fantasies, I put into it whatever I wanted: palm trees, lazy mornings staring at the ocean. Making the dream compelling is one of the things that keep you going, but I know it will have to be more than the snapshots I have in my mind. I have some money, but I will have to get a job. Lena will need a school. And we will have to figure out what it means to live without someone watching us all the time. I would like to start in Portugal. I've seen pictures, and it's those I used for my fantasies. But in many ways, I know I'm unprepared for this future I've chased."

It was a relief to admit it, to confess to not knowing. She, who had always had a plan, an ambition, was now on the verge of becoming adrift in the big world.

"It'll be pretty hard to make a mistake because there aren't too many wrong answers. Just loads of choices."

"That I am not used to."

"I'm sure you'll figure it out easier than you realize," James said.

"You are easy to talk to," Anya said, smiling. "I was very lucky that Quentin found refuge for me here. It has helped in so many ways."

"I can't say I'll be rushing into signing up for the next one, but I'm happy I was able to help you and your daughter."

Anya turned her gaze to the window as James began to prepare the tea. His idealism was staggering to her. She knew she would find it an anchor. Trying to make the world right for everyone in it would be an incomprehensible task, doomed to extinguishing all good feelings. He obviously found it an inspiration though, a reason to get up in the morning and a way through the obstacles. She admired it and was grateful there were people like him. But that kind of thinking wasn't for her.

She would save herself and her daughter. Maybe one or two others along the way. The rest would be sorted out by the vicissitudes of time.

Anya sipped at the tea Jamie handed to her. The promise of tomorrow didn't change her current reality. The coil of tension inside her was taught and would stay that way until she knew the results from Wandlitz.

Another hour passed. Anya held her daughter while the television flickered. It had to end at some point, but the slowness of the passing time was reinforced by each breath that seemed to get stuck in her throat.

Anya put Lena to bed and read her a story as if this was just another night. The words left her lips but didn't penetrate her brain, and she reached its end with surprise.

Back out in the living room, James was reading. Anya stared out the window, watching the city lights ebb and flow.

The ring of the telephone shattered the silence. The sound was almost deafening after the quiet of the wait.

"Aye," said James after picking up the receiver. He held it out to Anya. She crossed to it, feeling the air was suddenly viscous. This was it. The moment she had been planning for all these years.

"Yes?" she said.

"It's done," said Veronica. "Just as you wanted it. Almost. There were more files than we anticipated. Too many to fit in the fireplace in the time we had, so we had a small bonfire out in the yard. But they're all gone—every one that was in the safe, at least."

Pain zinged through her stomach as the tension began to release. "And you? You got what you wanted?" Because if Veronica and Quentin were happy, the last of the freedom pieces would be in place.

"Yes. We have to get to translating, but it looks like you delivered as promised. And Anya?"

"What?"

"You should get out of town. There's no hiding what we did. When it comes to you, your ex has nothing to lose now."

"I know. But…thank you."

"Same to you. Before you go, I want to ask—is Heddy going to be okay? She can't cross; what is this going to cost her?"

"She has a series of blackmail letters I wrote that threaten to arrange for her brother to be murdered in prison if she didn't help me. Michael and his men will squeeze her for a while, but I set up corroboration for her story, so she will be able to convince them she is a victim."

Anya could hear Veronica let out a breath. "Thank you. Good luck with your life."

"You too."

Anya hung up the receiver, surprised at the pain that racked her body. It was over. Done. Years of worry and fear released from her muscles, like a bleeding. She almost collapsed. It had been holding her together, and now it was gone.

James guided her to the sofa. "It's all right, then?"

She nodded. "Yes. It's all right."

"When are you leaving?"

"Tomorrow. I will take the first plane to anywhere."

CHAPTER FORTY

Anya stepped out of the hotel, holding Lena's hand and looking for a taxi.

She had just said good-bye to Lucinda. It had hurt to see her so battered, bruises still painting her face. It was also a relief to know that she was going to make it, that Michael hadn't inflicted lasting damage. Lucinda was being well taken care of by her mother and had smiled when Anya and Lena arrived.

She had broken into laughter when told about the mannequins and the bonfire at Wandlitz. Her file had gone up in smoke with the others. Anya had been so happy to give Lucinda that gift.

She looked at her watch. Their flight to Frankfurt was in one hour, a connection to Paris after that. They would stay in Paris for a few days. Live the dreams and give Anya a chance to plan for what would come after.

She turned, craning her neck to spot the familiar beige of a taxi, and stepped right into her ex-husband.

Her heartbeat kicked up a notch, but she wasn't scared. Not yet. Some part of her had known she was never going to make it out of Berlin without this confrontation.

"Michael," she said.

"Daddy," Lena squealed. Anya hadn't talked about Michael since they'd come West. No doubt Lena thought he was part of the going-away surprise.

Michael barely glanced at his daughter. His veneer of control had been cracked, and desperation oozed out the fissure. Lena had never meant much to him, and she would be of less importance now that his power was gone.

"I want my files back," he said.

The people coming and going to the hotel didn't pay them any attention. Michael's breakdown, although clear to her, wasn't so apparent to strangers.

"They are burned."

Pain froze his features. "You did not go there yourself. And you would not burn all of them. Some would be valuable, even to you."

"You're right. I didn't burn any of them. I instructed they should be lit until the flames reached the sky."

Lena was looking back and forth between her parents. Anya was grateful that her daughter seemed to sense the seriousness of the moment and wasn't interrupting.

Michael grabbed her arm. "You had to pay for someone to do that job. Someone who probably finds information more valuable than money."

Anya smiled. "Again, so smart. I paid for the burning of the gray files with the acquisition of the black ones."

The grip on her arm tightened, but Anya didn't care. She hadn't realized how much she wanted to see this: Michael falling apart before her eyes.

"I want them back."

"Why would I try to arrange that? They were my payment. I don't have them, and the people who do would not sell them back to me. They are gone. You will have to learn to live without them. Without all the perks you got with your blackmail. Live like a regular East German, without luxury. Under constant suspicion. After all you did in its name over the years, I'm sure it will not be a problem for you."

Anya didn't care that her tone was coated in viciousness, that each word was a little dagger driven into a wound. This was justice. A rare moment in the long history of those who abused their power.

She did not feel bad that she was enjoying it.

"You have crippled the German Democratic Republic, exposing our allies who are risking their lives. Handing them over to the enemy. For what? So you could travel with our daughter?"

Anya didn't even try to keep the disgust off her face. "I don't expect you to understand, but I want you to know that what I did has less to do with the GDR and more to do with you. I wanted to watch you suffer, see your panic as you become mortal like the rest of us."

"You ungrateful bitch. I gave you a great life, a life that you rejected. And still you want vengeance."

"You gave me nothing, Michael. Nothing except a life of lies. First it was the lie of your wealth, expecting me to live off the fruits of your blackmail. Then it was the lie of being a good citizen, while watching as you destroyed people for lesser crimes than you commit every day. The lies I had to tell my daughter, myself. You never loved the GDR. You never played by its rules. You are like a parasite, taking what you want with no concern for the host. The only thing you gave me was a reason to get up every morning. I survived because I wanted to make sure you didn't."

There was no missing the shock on her ex-husband's face. It seemed he had underestimated the depth of her hatred.

"Please," Michael said, his tone collapsing into a plea. "Without those files, I have nothing. My enemies will circle, and I will not be able to keep them away. They will put me in prison. Please, Anya, we have a daughter together."

Rage surged. She was sure it was coming right out of her eyes. "We have nothing together. Lena is mine. You deserve to experience prison like all the people you sent there over the years. I hope they keep you there for decades, until you have nothing left but madness."

Suddenly Michael shifted in closer. Anya felt without looking that he had a knife pressed to her stomach.

"I will not go that way. Tell me why I should let you live."

Anya clenched her jaw. She would not play this game. Would not beg him for anything.

"Killing me won't bring it all back. It will just change which jail you spend the rest of your life in. The life you had, it's gone forever."

Time stretched out around her and Michael. Anya could feel his breath on her face, could see fear in the clench of his jaw and the twitch in his eyelid. Anya felt the knife drop. She knew Lena must be terrified, but she would console her soon—after she finished with Michael.

"What am I supposed to do?" he asked her.

Never had her desire to hurt him been so strong. She wanted to rake her nails across his face. All the pain and suffering he'd caused, yet what had he really achieved? His power was a mirage, built on fear and lies. There would be no one rushing in to help him now.

"Go back and face the system you helped build."

She picked up the suitcase handle she'd dropped and grabbed Lena's hand. They had a flight to catch.

Anya left her ex-husband a broken puddle on the streets of West Berlin. She was finally done.

CHAPTER FORTY-ONE

James opened the door to his flat to let Quentin in.

"Tea or beer?" he asked.

Quentin held up a file. "You're probably going to want a beer. I'll take a Coke if you have one."

James glanced at the black folder. "Aye, you're probably right."

He went to the kitchen to get the drinks before heading to the living room. "I take it that's the file on Edward."

"Yes," Quentin said. "I haven't read it. Anya said it was for your eyes only, and I agree with her. Besides, I've got more than enough of my own to deal with."

"Delivering a shock wave to the entire allied spy network?"

"More like having the collateral to make some choices."

James raised a brow. "Looking for a different life, then?"

Quentin was quiet for a long while. He rotated the Coke around and around in his hands but didn't drink much. "The files Veronica got, they're un-fucking-believable. We haven't

415

translated them all, but I'm telling you, it makes me wonder what in the hell this is all for. So far, the majority aren't the Alger Hisses or the Kim Philbys. Those fuckers I would take down no problem. It's people who were in the right place at the wrong time. People who have access to information the East Germans or the Russians want, and were investigated until they could be blackmailed. Or, if that failed, they were compromised in a setup."

James felt the beer in his gut curdle. "No winners."

"Not many. Just a long sad story of desperation and manipulation. These people have to be stopped, but tried for treason? Shit. It's going to be rough."

"What does Veronica think?"

"I think she's disappointed. It's not revolutionary, it's sordid. But it has to be cleaned up."

"So that's what the two of you are going to do?" James asked.

Quentin shook his head. "I can't speak for her, but for me, hell no. I'm going to drop it at Langley and get the fuck out of dodge. Someone else can decide which heads are going to roll. One of those internal affairs types who's never been in the field and has the luxury of a binary morality."

James shuddered. It wasn't a responsibility he'd want either. "That's it for you, then? Your final farewell to the CIA?"

Quentin smiled. "I think it's a lot less dramatic than that. It's a job. Same for you. One day you're doing it, and then you're not. I felt like I had to atone for what I did in Nicaragua all those years ago. That's why I stayed."

"And Anya's files," James asked, "are your atonement?"

"That's the way I look at it. I've proved my loyalty and abilities. Now I can get out."

"To do what?"

"Live my life." Quentin paused. "I got recruited in college. I didn't know much about myself then, and the CIA? It sounded adventurous as hell. It's been over ten years now, and there are other things I want to do. I don't know if it's the same in the military, but have you ever seen old spies? Guys with failed marriages and distant families, no real friends. They don't know who to be outside of the job, and they've become addicted to knowing the secrets. They retire and they're cut off and they look around and they realize they've got nothing. I don't want to be one of those guys."

James could well appreciate the sentiment. Building your life and your identity around your career was fraught with peril. If the career ever went, the whole thing would fall down.

"You don't have to convince me, mate. I've enjoyed my time in uniform, but I also look forward to the day I get to give it back. I've got about a year to go, and there's no sadness in it."

"I meant to ask, did Anya and her daughter get off okay?"

James shrugged. "Truthfully, I've got no idea. She packed up and took a taxi to Tempelhof. She didn't come back, so I have to assume she got out of Berlin fine. There was a woman who wanted a new life, so I don't think we'll ever rightly know."

"I think I'm going to imagine she made it to wherever she wanted to go."

James thought that was a lovely sentiment. "Aye, and no reason to think she didn't. If there ever was a woman who could bend reality to her will, it was Anya."

The side of Quentin's mouth ticked up. "Getting out of East Berlin with her daughter. Planning the theft of her ex's files. All those years and all those details. Yeah, she'll be fine."

The sun had long ago faded from the sky in the early night of a Berlin December. As was custom for these two, they let the silence fall, drinking companionably and enjoying the break from having to do anything else.

The only thing James really had to do was look at the file on Edward, and he was in no rush.

Whatever it contained, the fact that it even existed meant nothing in it could be good. With Dieter dead and Edward's father focused on the publicity of the murder, James figured the file could wait a little longer.

"Did you see," said Quentin, "the mannequins made the news?"

James smiled. "I did see that. Don't know how the West Germans managed to get pictures, but with all the satellites orbiting the earth now, who knows?"

"They did a good job. It must have kept the Stasi running around for days, trying to figure out where they'd come from and if more were going to show up somewhere else."

"Aye. And what it all meant. They wouldn't see the humor in it, but I doubt they got the intended artist's message either."

Quentin smiled. "An invasion of mannequins, that's the headline I saw. Of course, given that no one over here knows anything either, it will remain one of life's great mysteries."

"One of those random historical tidbits that will resurface in an obscure book years from now," James chuckled. "In any case, the final result was pretty spectacular, from what little I could see from the woods. Through the trees I got a glimpse, and, well, I've never seen anything like it."

"And you never will again, my friend," Quentin said, standing up. "Thanks for the Coke. If you need help with what's in that file, let me know. I've got a few weeks yet before I hand in my notice."

James nodded, grateful to know that help was available. Just in case.

CHAPTER FORTY-TWO

James opened the door. Jillian stood there, paper in hand, looking at him like she had to tell him his dog died.

"Come to make my day worse?"

"As if I'd do that on purpose," Jillian said, coming in and taking off her coat. "I got something back from my father about the book. Given everything that's happened, it's heartbreaking."

James wasn't expecting that. He'd spent the night going over Anya's ex-husband's file on Edward. It was damning. He'd been passing secrets to the Stasi since the late fifties. He'd undermined efforts for peace and trade negotiations. He'd passed over classified research and development. A lot of it came from his role in the foreign office. More he got surreptitiously from his father.

He'd had many East German contacts over the years. He'd meet them in Berlin, or Vienna, or Geneva. According to the file, Edward had expressed a desire to see the final collapse of British influence and would do whatever he could to speed that along.

Upon first reading, James had felt his blood pressure rise, his heart set to explode. The initial anger made his insides churn about as if they were a boat caught in a hurricane. To think he'd felt sorry for Edward. Sorry for his relationship with his father. Sorry for his situation. It was a black-and-white case of arsehole.

Then, buried at the bottom of one of the pages in a foot note, James had come across the sentence that made the confusion roar back up.

He led Jillian into the living room and sorted through the papers he'd left on the table.

She sat down beside him, still holding her paper. "Aren't you going to ask me what the decrypted message said?"

"You'll tell me. And yes, I suppose I do want to know. But I have to be honest with ye, I don't right know what to make of this. Edward was a traitor. There's no excuse for that."

Jillian looked at him, eyes full of compassion. "There is a reason though, isn't there?"

"What did your dad find out from the book?"

Jillian gave him the piece of paper she'd been holding since she came it. "It was a love letter. I don't know who it was for, but it didn't contain any state secrets. Read it. It's just expressing devotion and longing, and it's sad because obviously it was either unrequited or unfulfilled."

James read through the letter. It did nothing to stop the anger or the guilt or the confusion. Surely to Christ it couldn't be as simple as Edward agreeing to spy for a lover because that relationship was more important than loyalty to family, nation, or values.

He set the paper down. "Edward was gay. Dieter Venmar was his lover whilst at Cambridge. The relationship all but ended when Venmar was sent back to the GDR. But obviously the feelings continued."

"You think that's it? The reason he did what he did?"

"I'm not sure," James shook his head. "It doesn't make it right, in any case. How is that enough?"

James knew the anger raging through him wasn't going to subside any time soon. But for the life of him, he didn't know what to do next.

"I think you should find Edward and talk to him," Jillian said.

James tightened his fists. He wanted to punch something, not look for a reasonable solution. "How am I supposed to do that? Even if I wanted to, he's probably long gone."

"I doubt it, unless he left right away, and from what you told me, there wasn't time. He's here, somewhere. Get his perspective, and then you can put it to rest."

"What I should do is just hand this file over to Edward's dad, let him cover it up, and be done with it."

"You'll never be satisfied if that's what you do. It will eat away at you for the rest of your life. But if you make it public as it is, it will be just as bad. You'll watch your friend get reduced to a punchline, and you'll know there was more to it than that."

"The subtlety isn't lost on me, you know," James said. "I'm well aware that we're more than a bit hypocritical about what we do in the name of protecting our values. But this kind of treason, lives get lost. It's that old adage: two wrongs don't make a right."

"I get it. But you're the one who taught me that one man's terrorist is another man's freedom fighter. Understanding what Edward did doesn't mean you condone it. If you find out his reasons, then maybe you can do your part in making sure it doesn't happen again."

James rubbed at his temples. "Aye. You're right. If only for my own future sanity. I'll read through the file again to see if there's any suggestion on where he would go."

James walked into the four-story building and climbed to the second level. He knocked on the door then put his hands in his pockets. Waiting. He wondered if Edward would open the door. James had no problem giving him time.

For all that he was an evil manipulator, Anya's ex-husband kept meticulous records. Short on reflection, but long on biographical detail. In the file Michael kept on Edward were the locations of two safe houses where Edward used to meet his Stasi handlers in West Berlin, presumably when the volume of information to be passed was more than could be handled discreetly on the street. Places where Edward could make copies of what he stole.

James had concluded that if Edward was still in the city, he was likely to be using one of these places.

After a wait that bothered James not at all, the door in front of him swung open.

"You're not going to go away, are you?" Edward said as James walked through the door. James turned to study Edward as he closed up behind them. He was impeccably turned out, as always, but the gray cast to his skin was an indication that Edward's recent actions had provided no relief.

"I suppose I should ask how you found me," said Edward. "Do we have less than ten minutes before the police show up?"

"That East German courier you had for a bit, the hairdresser, she's been staying in my flat for a while."

Edward started, eyes going round like he'd just been offered proof the Loch Ness monster was real.

"Jamie Murphy." He shook his head. "That's something I wouldn't have guessed if I had all the time in the world. I don't suppose you'll entertain me with that story instead of asking me for the one you came here to get."

James looked around the flat. It was sparse. A holding tank not meant to live in. "Are you planning on staying here until the noose tightens?"

Edward shrugged. "I don't have anywhere else I want to go."

"Why not just turn yourself in?"

"As I said, I don't have anywhere else I want to go." Edward motioned to the scarred coffee table and the worn paisley-patterned chairs beside it. "Shall we sit and have a drink? This will all be much more pleasant with a whisky in hand."

James acquiesced, taking a seat in the chair opposite Edward. He shifted a little to find a more comfortable position for the spring that was poking into his backside.

Edward poured them each a couple fingers and raised his glass as if making a toast.

"Where do you want to start?"

"I know the message you sent in the book," James said. "You loved him. Venmar."

Edward raised a brow. "You are a man of unexpected resources, Murphy."

"Is that why you sold out your country?" James continued. "Because he asked you to? For love?"

Edward sat back in his chair. "I've not told anyone this. Ever. I feel now the attraction of unburdening oneself at the end. You want to know the whole thing, do you? Fine. Should entertain you. The answer to your question is no. I approached him, many years ago. Not long after he left Cambridge actually."

"Because you wanted to prove something to him?"

"Tsk tsk, Captain Murphy," Edward said. "You've got all the answers; you can put them together better than that. Why don't you start by asking yourself why you didn't even know I was gay. We've known each other almost twenty years now, and yet, in all that time, it's never come up."

James swallowed. "You never told me."

"Why would I?"

James felt himself beginning to flounder. He'd never thought much about it. About any of it. "Right. I understand. We're not all that great with homosexuality in Britain, are we?"

Edward's face cracked into a smile. "An understatement. No, I don't think you understand anything. The East Germans, for all their failings, are quite accepting of homosexuality. They see it for what it is: one of the many natural ways human beings exist. There is a whole spectrum of possibility in all human qualities. When it comes to intelligence, or vocal range, we have no problem understanding that. But sexual preference has been given a tiny box that has no appreciation of biology. Truly, it is that box which is unnatural.

"We in Britian have chosen to revile homosexuality out of fear. Why on earth anyone is afraid of the sexual behavior of consenting adults is a mystery I have never been able to unravel. We wrap it up and call it deviant. In Scotland homosexuality is still considered a crime.

"So I do not think you understand, not at all, what it is like being told that who you are is a mistake. Shameful. Something to hide. What do you love, Murphy? What calls out to you with beauty and desire? Music? It's never occurred to you that you shouldn't love your music, that you should be ashamed of the way your heart beats faster when you hear a particularly lovely piece, that you should deny that uplift of your soul. Imagine if you were told from early on to deny that part of you that you can't change and isn't hurting anyone anyway. Can you? Can you glimpse for a moment what that might feel like?"

James looked at Edward and felt his words shatter a construct he didn't even know he'd created. It hit him then, quite forcefully, that he'd been blind to a very real struggle. He had never asked. Because, for everyone involved, it was better to pretend it didn't exist. He now realized it wasn't better for everyone. Not at all.

"You glimpse now, do you not? We are from a place that can barely acknowledge homosexuality, that has spent hundreds of years trying to legislate it out of existence. When I was first with Dieter, our country was still enforcing chemical castration on those proved to be gay. Look at what we did to Alan Turing.

The man won us the war, and we treated him like a monster, like something to be ashamed of."

"Why didn't you just move here, then? Cross over the Wall and spend your life with Dieter?" James asked.

"Do you think it fair that appeared to be my choice? Dieter in East Germany or my life in England?"

"No, but I also don't make the bloody rules."

"But those rules exist, so now we come to the truth of it. I hate everything Britain stands for. Everything my father stands for. The way it marginalizes everyone who isn't exactly like an Etonian, as if the straight, white, British man is the crowning achievement of evolution. How can a country that fought in World War II against the tyranny of Hitler practice that tyranny on countless others? Yes, I loved Dieter and was angry we couldn't be together. But it was much more than that. It was total disillusionment with the system that controls people and forces them into rigid conformity. I am a future earl, part of the establishment that has been bred to rule the country, only I'm not good enough because I prefer sex with men."

James was starting to appreciate the tragedy behind Edward's motivations. "Being here, with Dieter, wouldn't that have been better than the lifetime of stress and isolation in committing treason? And, if you loved Dieter so much, why was he found dead in your flat?"

Edward sighed. "I didn't choose the life I ended up in. Not right away. After he left, we met here a couple of times. I suggested I move. We planned it, a life in Leipzig, far away from England and my father. My application was denied. But the GDR appreciated my interest. Perhaps if I could share certain types of information with them, they would be willing to reconsider my application."

James felt as if at a carnival, jumping from one stomach-lurching ride to the next. "So they strung you along for over fifteen years, promising a life here that would never likely materialize, in exchange for information."

The anger of moments earlier ebbed out, and Edward's posture shrank in on itself. "Of all the things I've done, believing there was the possibility of a happy ending was perhaps the most foolish of them all."

"And Dieter?" James asked, now suddenly not sure he wanted to know.

"He found me. After you gave him the book. I confronted him, said I was tired of the life, and that I wanted to be with him." Edward closed his eyes briefly. "He. Well, he expressed surprise that I thought moving East was ever really a possibility. He had thought it a dream. He said that if I had come over, the Soviets would have taken me right to Moscow. I was safer where I was."

In all of James's assumptions about what confronting Edward might result in, the pain unfolding before him was deeper than any he could have imagined.

"He told me my expectations were rooted in memories that were almost twenty years old."

James knew where the story was headed and felt a genuine grief for Edward. "He didn't return your love."

"It's been a long time," Edward said, evidently remembering Venmar's words. "He had ... moved on. He told me that he would always value the memory of our time together, but he thought it would be cruel to commit to emotions he did not feel. It would suggest a promise of something that was never going to happen."

James sat there, brain reeling. What Edward had done, why he'd done it—it was a huge morass of ethical compromises and painful deception. He had reasons, but not justifications. Oh Christ, it was awful from every angle.

"He was sorry," Edward said. "It was then I realized what I'd done. Not betraying my country, as I might have done that anyway. But I had chased a fantasy. Loved a man who didn't really exist. For years, in the moments of the double life I led, it was my memory of Dieter that anchored me. Then I found out it had all been a mirage, that I was just another tool for the great GDR, and Dieter had gone along with it, exploited the memory of our time together for political gain. Well, as you now might understand, I realized there was nothing left. No utopia I could rest in when it was all over. I forced my cyanide pill into his mouth, watched him die, and wished I had another one."

James could hardly process his roiling thoughts and emotions. He had the story now. Edward had grown up in a country, a family, who told him he was wrong, deviant because of who he was. His days at Cambridge must have been one of his few glimpses of happiness. The love of his life gets ripped away, and a festering hatred grows at the discrimination and the judgment he must navigate. Britian suddenly becomes a jail—a hypocritical, oppressive jail.

James felt his bones ache with exhaustion. Damned if he knew what he was supposed to do about it all. "You can't undo what you've done."

"No. I can't. If I could go back, I would fight for myself. Laws change. Social sensibilities shift. I should have told my father to go to hell, lived like a mortal, and fought in the open. But it's too late now."

"I thought," James said, "coming over here, that I would leave just as angry as when I arrived. Even though I had found out you were gay and that it might be part of the story, I hadn't imagined that anything you would say would make me feel less angry about your treason."

"For what it's worth," said Edward, "I never did deal in military secrets, despite who my father is. Intellectual property, government strategy, and yes, livelihoods still get ruined. But I didn't knowingly send anyone to their deaths."

James matched Edward's posture. Sinking into the chair and ignoring the discomfort of the springs that seemed to poke everywhere, he cradled his whisky.

"It never is black and white, is it?" he said.

"I am sorry," Edward answered. "I know that isn't worth much, and it's because I'm sitting here with two shitty options before me, but I am. I should have seen it earlier. I didn't want to because I was too far in."

"I wish I could tell you that you could've asked for help, but I don't reckon that's true. Your father wouldn't have let that happen."

"Don't start feeling sorry for me, old friend. Having this drink with you, unburdening my soul as it were, it's kind. Too late to save me, but not too late to make a difference."

James didn't know what he wanted, but this as an ending certainly wasn't it.

"Maybe, if I could ask one thing: pay it forward," said Edward. "Next time someone's security clearance gets revoked because it's discovered what they do in the bedroom, speak up."

"Do my part so something like this doesn't happen again?"

"You could look at it that way."

"Or just speak up because for the last forty years we're meant to have been fighting for freedom."

Edward smiled. "That too."

James finished his whisky. "You should have made different choices. You know that. Selling out secrets was a fucking terrible idea. Especially because you gave them to people who are just as oppressive in their own way. But the way I figure it, you dying here, like this, lets both systems off the hook. I hope you mean it, when you say you'll fight in the open if given another chance."

Edward stared at him. "What in the bloody hell are you talking about?"

James pulled a piece of paper out of the inner pocket of his jacket. "Here's the contact information for a man in West Berlin who can get you a new identity. He's not connected to anyone you are, and he won't ask you any questions."

Edward picked up the paper, hands shaking. "Christ, Jamie, I. God. What can I say? Thank you."

James stood up. "I hope I'm making the right choice. If you can one day, let me know."

CHAPTER FORTY-THREE

James got off the elevator, looking for room 412. There was a man in a suit standing farther down the hallway. That had to be the one.

He was let inside without any question. The joys of being expected.

James went through the doorway to find he wasn't in a room, but a suite. In all his years in West Berlin, he'd never been in a suite in the Hotel Palace before. It was like stepping back in time, when walls were covered with velvet and furniture was accented in gold. The furniture was museum quality, with about as much history. It was beautiful, opulent, and completely appropriate for the Earl of Fenwick.

The man himself was sitting on the sofa, papers in hand, silver coffee service on the table in front of him.

"Ah, Captain Murphy. Please, take a seat." Lord Ashton gestured to the richly upholstered blue armchair across from him.

James did as instructed, trying not to let his discomfort with the luxury of his surroundings throw him off. He was proper nervous and not at all sure what he wanted the outcome of this meeting to be.

"You said in your message that you had something to share with me."

"Aye," James said, pulling out a copy of the file on Edward he'd received from Anya. "This fell into my lap. It's a Stasi file on the work Edward has been doing with them for the past twenty years."

Lord Ashton paled like he'd been punched in the gut. "Getting right to the point, I see."

"No sense in pretending I'm here for any other reason."

"How did you get this file?"

"Dieter Venmar." The lie rolled off his tongue easily. James felt no guilt at putting this in the dead man's lap.

Lord Ashton jerked so violently his coffee flew out of its cup. "That man has been the single worst thing that has happened to my family. I should have had him expelled from Cambridge after the first time Edward brought him home."

James didn't know what to say to that.

"Why did he give you that file?" Lord Ashton asked. "Why not make it public and have his final revenge?"

"Maybe your son killed him before that could happen." James held up a hand as Lord Ashton opened his mouth to protest. "I warn you, I'm not the only one who has it. When he gave it to me, Venmar told me there's been a breach in Stasi security. He was giving it to me at very little risk."

Lord Ashton dropped his head into his hands. James was sure it was a moment of weakness that few others had ever witnessed.

"So this is going to be coming at me from all sides?"

"I honestly don't know. I'm far out of my wheelhouse here. Venmar gave me the file because I gave him the book. He obviously didn't expect things to go the way they did with Edward. That's another mess I'm sure you're in the middle of. And I have no idea who is involved in the breach."

Lord Ashton sat up, regaining his posture if not his composure. "What does the file say?"

James hesitated. "Are you sure you want to know?"

"Of course I bloody well do," Lord Ashton said, eyes flashing. "I cannot prepare for an attack if I don't know where it's coming from."

James thought it an interesting choice of words. "This is a copy for you, then," he said, putting the folder he'd brought with him on the coffee table.

Ashton picked up the file and began skimming through it. The only visible sign of his distress was the tightening of his fingers around the edges of the papers. Getting to the end, he closed the folder and placed it beside him on the sofa.

"What are your intentions, Captain Murphy? I assume you've kept a copy of this file for yourself as protection."

James paused a moment then nodded. "Aye. I'm not after being anyone's scapegoat."

"Of course. But you must have some thoughts, some wishes. After all, you are in uniform. It appears my son has committed treason; that must mean something to you. Along with the murder, people will be digging around about him for years."

"It does," James said. "Although I understand his reasons, they don't excuse what he did. He hurt a lot of people when it seems the only one he wanted to hurt was you."

"Ah, so you think I'm the villain here. I should have just accepted my son's deviance, let the Fenwick line endure the shame, and loved him anyway."

"I think you might have had more happiness. It would have been a better storm to weather than the one you're about to face."

Ashton's jaw clenched. "I remember that summer when he came home with Dieter Venmar. I could tell. I had wondered for years, of course. There were never any girlfriends, never any stories of schoolboy debauchery. When I saw them together, I realized that Edward was a deviant, against the natural order of things."

"So you cast Venmar out, and what? Hoped that you could force it out of Edward?"

"Edward was not the only member of nobility to be afflicted with the condition," Ashton said, lip curling in distaste. "There was always the possibility of a wife. A woman who would understand to overlook the rare marital lapse."

"Edward didn't want that kind of life. There were limits as to what he would do for queen and country."

"You cannot put his treason on me. He had options."

James shook his head. Edward might have had options, but clearly none of them were very good. "Why didn't you just let him leave? Hand over the title to his brother and disappear to New Zealand or Canada or something?"

"Give him my blessing? Suggest that I condone that lifestyle?" The disgust slithered around the earl's features.

James felt himself becoming angry. "You backed him into a corner."

Ashton let out a long breath. "It would appear that I made some mistakes."

"Yes, I'd say you bloody well did. This all could have been avoided if you had seen the value your son had as a person instead of as a pawn to be manipulated."

"The continuation of the Fenwick line, our duty to the institution, is and has always been paramount. The eldest son does not have the luxury of personhood. His duty is to the name. Edward would not have been the only Fenwick to suppress his desires to keep the continuity of our lineage."

And that, James thought, was why the nobility made absolutely no sense. How could duty to the lineage matter more than the values they were supposed to uphold? Success at all costs was nothing but hypocrisy. It made him sick. All of it. The Earl of Fenwick and the empty image he was trying to protect.

"Well," James said, "I can't say it makes sense to me, protecting an institution that puts more shame on homosexuality than treason. That doesn't seem to be an institution that has any value to its country at all."

He stood up. "I'll leave you to it, then. I suppose you'll distance yourself from Edward's actions, claiming weakness of character in one area means weakness of character in all areas. You should know, Lord Ashton, that not many people will see it that way. I think you've been spending too much time with people just like you. You forget that there are a lot of us who are going to see right through that shite."

Leaving the room, James's only desire was to never see Lord Ashton again.

CHAPTER FORTY-FOUR

"Did Sebastian and Peter tell BND about the tunnel?" Quentin asked.

"Yes. On Monday. I helped them clean up all the mannequin residue. I don't know if BND is going to put that part together, but I'm sure it doesn't matter too much. I think they're sad about it, but also partly happy to be able to move on."

"So everything goes to its new normal."

Jillian smiled. "I imagine one day I'll be old, and I'll bring my grandkids over to Berlin. The Wall will be down and the tunnel will be a museum, and I'll tell them the story of what I got up to in there."

"Maybe I'll do that with you."

Jillian leaned her head on Quentin's shoulder, feeling for the first time in a while that they were together without urgency. They were in a hotel room, which was safest, and the hours stretched before them with neither needing to be anywhere.

"How's it going to be for you in the next little while, with those files Veronica got?" she asked.

Jillian felt his hand begin to twirl through her hair. "It's not going to affect me at all. We came up with a plan, and no, I'm not going to tell you what we did. Some of the information sharing is anonymous, and some of it is through her. After I read through the files, I realized I didn't want any part of it."

"Why not?"

"If I get involved, I think it's going to kill me. It's not pretty, Jillian. There are things in those files that I never wanted to know. There are a lot of assholes in there, but also a lot of sad cases. The accusations are going to fly around. Some of it is going to be covered up."

She understood how daunting the scope of it was. "And vengeance," she said.

"Right," he said. "I decided that I don't want any part of that."

They fell into silence for a while. Jillian began to trace her fingers on his stomach. "Veronica said those files were career making. Are you sure you're okay walking away from that?"

"My career there is over. I resigned this morning."

Jillian sat up, turning to look at him. "You what?"

"You heard me."

She looked into his eyes for a long moment, not sure what she was expecting to see. "How is that going to go?"

"It's ultimately a government job," he shrugged. "There'll be paperwork, and I'll have to go back to Langley for some deindoctrination. Someone will remind me I'm not ever allowed to talk about what I did at the agency. I'll probably have to let them know my general plans. No travel to the Soviet Union anytime soon. Stuff like that. But people leave all the time."

"That's not what I'm talking about. I meant, for you. How is that going to go for you? When you don't have that job facing you every morning."

"I'm hoping it'll be fucking fantastic," Quentin said.

"What are you going to do?"

He reached up and trailed a finger down her cheek. "Live my cover story. Be a journalist for the *Trib*. I'm actually pretty good at it, you know."

She smiled. "I do know. Is that what you want?"

"It's what I want for now. I can do the work and get paid and figure the rest out as I go."

"Sounds like life." Jillian paused. "I'm happy for you. I could tell that it all was wearing you down. I hope you find something that you enjoy more."

"I'm not going to be as useful to you once I leave," Quentin said, and Jillian thought he looked nervous. Not sure why, she leaned down to kiss him.

"You'll be useful enough."

"Christ, Jillian, every time I think you've hit maximum crazy over there, you surprise me."

Jillian was standing in a phone booth, talking to Frank. "I take it Veronica made it home okay?"

"That's a relative term, but yeah, she's home and scaring the shit out of her superiors at the moment. That information she brought back, it's like she walked in with grenades strapped to her chest. They don't know what to do with her."

"She'll be rewarded, right?" It was important to Jillian that Veronica was recognized for what she did.

"Unofficially, of course, but if she plays her cards right, she'll be able to call the shots on her career for a long time. Half of the organization is terrified of her, half are rushing to work with her. It's given our program a boost."

"Is she going to stay working with you?"

"I told her I'd be fine if she had a better opportunity somewhere else, but she thinks our unstructured unit is giving her all the opportunity she needs. I think they'll finally approve the paperwork, and we can go cause shit somewhere else soon."

Jillian smiled. "I might want to work for you when I get home."

"You can have my job. Retirement's starting to look pretty good. The dust will settle eventually, but it's going to be a rough ride for a while."

"Well, West Berlin is great at this time of year. Christmas markets, Gluhwein. If you need a vacation."

Frank barked out a laugh. "Yeah, I might just try to sell that to my wife. Anyway, keep your head down, but things should be pretty easy for you in the near future. The powers that be are going to be distracted and hanging on to any win they can find."

"Noted. And Frank, thanks for sending me Veronica. I don't think it would've worked out with someone else, someone who hadn't been forced to spend their whole career maneuvering around the edges."

"You two made a great team, one that you can call on in the future. Those types of relationships, you have them for life."

James sat on his sofa, enjoying his beer. It was nice to have the apartment back to himself.

He felt no satisfaction at the way things with Lord Ashton had ended, but he was happy it was over. James had accepted his decision about Edward and imagined it being a good one. Edward off somewhere, fighting for civil rights, tipping back the scales. Paying it forward.

It was snowing outside. Large flakes floated past his window. James loved the snow. Loved how it made everything quiet and soft. A muffling of reality that brought a momentary peace.

He looked at the postcard in his hand. It was from Faro. A collection of images. Palm trees. Bright neoclassical buildings. A beach.

A little figure had been drawn: a smiling girl in a blue dress.

He unfolded the letter that had come in a separate envelope. "It's very beautiful here. We have found an English tea shop where we go every week. The woman there tried to put sugar in mine, but I told her I was taught to take it only with milk. That it's proper tea that way. I have a new art book, and I've started school. Mama says that if your life ever gets as crazy as hers did, this is a wonderful place for a vacation."

It was, James thought, the best ending he could have imagined.

ABOUT THE AUTHOR

Rhiannon Beaubien is a writer of both fiction and nonfiction. *A Rumor of Spies* is the third title in her Cold War Berlin series, following *Alone Among Spies* and *The Wrong Kind of Spy*. Given her endless fascination with all things espionage and her experience working in Canada's signals intelligence agency, she will probably never get tired of writing spy novels.

She is also the co-author of the successful book series *The Great Mental Models*. Covering models from physics to systems to art, this series explains how you can use fundamental knowledge to improve your thinking and, ultimately, your outcomes. *The Great Mental Models Volume 1: General Thinking Concepts* was a *Wall Street Journal* bestseller.

Rhiannon lives and works in Ottawa and enjoys merengues, '80s music, and the absurd. You can find out more at rhiannonbeaubien.com

HISTORICAL NOTE

As always, truth can be stranger than fiction. When writing the tunnel scenes in this book, I drew inspiration from a book I came across called *Plunder* by Menachem Kaiser that described tunnels the Nazis built in Poland. For reasons that are far from clear, the Nazis seemed to have dug extensively, creating a range of tunnel sizes and types. From warrens with dirt walls you can barely stand in to sophisticated reinforced bunkers, they left traces of this aspect of their madness all over Eastern Europe.

Alan Turing is a major figure in the history of signals intelligence. A legendary mathematician, cryptanalyst, and computer scientist, his 1936 Turing machine helped lay the foundation for our modern computer age. During World War II, the Germans' Enigma codes were proving too robust for traditional code-breaking techniques. In response, Turing conceived of a revolutionary solution: the bombe, an electromechanical code-breaking machine that could crack the Enigma code, which changed the course of the war and saved countless lives. He was also a homosexual, a fact that seemed more important to the British government after the war than the enormous potential value of collaborating with him. He was convicted of gross indecency after admitting to a homosexual relationship, stripped of his security clearance and barred from working with the government, and chemically castrated in lieu of serving prison time. He died two years later. In 2009, the British government apologized for its treatment of Turing, and in 2014, his conviction was officially pardoned by royal decree. A few years after that, the British government expanded this type of pardon to other men convicted of offenses related to historically outlawed homosexual acts, and this law is now informally known as the "Alan Turing law."

To me, Turing's story is a clear demonstration of why discrimination is counterproductive and harmful on multiple levels. Suppressing genius and limiting contribution based on irrelevant factors hurts not only the individuals but also the societies that don't get to benefit from their contributions.

ACKNOWLEDGMENTS

Getting a book out into the world takes a village—don't let anyone tell you otherwise. Up front, a lot of smart people help me with the details, and it's not on them that I sometimes make mistakes—all of those are mine.

The first thanks goes to my early readers. They always send thoughtful feedback that makes the book better. Dave Langner, thank you for all the history tidbits, as well as encouraging some closure with a few of the characters. Rosie Leizrowice, thanks for steering me away from that trope to come up with something much more dynamic. Mariam Gabriel, thanks for the notes and the support. M.L., thanks for the wonderful comments. Phil Gurski, thanks for reading, sharing your stories, and your encouragement.

A big thank you to Darren Manneke for walking me through electrical grids, how they are constructed, all the small details of wiring, and how to make it all work.

Justin Beaubien, thanks for the feedback on the pitch.

Kristen Hall-Geisler, it's great to have an editor that supports the person while being tough on the project. It makes it so much easier to write knowing that you have my back.

Melissa Ousley and Sarah Currin, thank you for your careful proofreading and incredible attention to detail.

Yvonne Parks at Pear Creative makes beautiful books, and I will never work with another designer again.

To my mom and dad, thanks for being my in-house marketing team and for always supporting my writing. To Sylvain, maybe one day I'll write fantasy, so at least you can have a break from helping me work through espionage plots. Mylo, I love your engagement with my writing, and Zane, I love your questions. Both of you, your storytelling keeps me on my toes.

www.ingramcontent.com/pod-product-compliance
Lightning Source LLC
Chambersburg PA
CBHW061104310726
48974CB00002B/393